Enter at Your Own Risk:

Dreamscapes into Darkness

Edited by
Alex Scully

FIRBOLG PUBLISHING

Table of Contents

Enter at Your Own Risk

Introduction

Where are you *right now*, at this *very moment?* Standing in the aisle at a book store, perhaps? On a bus or a train? A passenger jet? A few of you, no doubt. A coffee shop? A sidewalk café? At home in your favorite chair? In bed? Are there others nearby? Pedestrians, fellow diners, passengers or patrons? They might have even made some harsh judgments about you regarding your choice of reading material—a subtle sniff of disapproval of the darkly lurid cover-art, the melodramatically cautionary title. *Enter at Your Own Risk* indeed! They are unaware that you and I are connected; that we are, *right now,* at this *very moment*, talking about them.

True, we may be separated by distance and time, but in fact I am writing these words specifically *for you*, and now, I am whispering in your ear, touching your mind, moving you, even perhaps piercing the veil between the living and the dead, for though my heart beats at this moment, that stout organ could hiccup and stop on a dime and render these words the murmurings of a phantom.

This book is more than a collection of stories; it is, in a way, a spirit cabinet. Some of the authors are long dead, and yet their words live, as vital and dynamic as they were the moment each was composed, arranged, and set down. Firbolg Publishing and your host, Dr. Alex Scully, have gone to heroic lengths, not only to collect new work from some of the finest storytellers of our generation, but stories by authors whose very names evoke a delicious thrill among horror aficionados: Shelley, Lovecraft, and Doyle; tales that have long languished out of print, buried alive in the curled, yellowing pages of defunct pulp magazines and newspapers.

Waiting, yes, for you.

Words, sentences, and paragraphs—such *glorious* paragraphs—each rendered with that rich precision of language that defines late nineteenth and early twentieth century prose. For instance, nestled in Fitz-James O'Brien's chilling tale,

What Was It?, a Hope Diamond of a paragraph—one of the finest and most evocative I think I've ever read: "*Things were in this state when an incident took place so awful and inexplicable in its character that my reason fairly reels at the bare memory of the occurrence. It was the tenth of July. After dinner was over I repaired, with my friend Dr. Hammond, to the garden to smoke my evening pipe. Independent of certain mental sympathies which existed between the doctor and myself, we were linked together by a vice. We both smoked opium. We knew each other's secret and respected it. We enjoyed together that wonderful expansion of thought, that marvelous intensifying of the perceptive faculties, that boundless feeling of existence when we seem to have points of contact with the whole universe—in short, that unimaginable spiritual bliss, which I would not surrender for a throne, and which I hope you, reader, will never, never taste.*"

You can discern the sonorous intonations of the narrator, feel the infectious dread skittering in the pit of his stomach, his reluctance to tell his tale trumped by his compulsion to cleanse his soul in its transmission. And despite the misconceptions of the dilettante, you and I know the true coin of the horror realm is not the flinch evoked by a cheap jump-scare, but the pit-of-the-gut shudder inspired by *dread* (Ahh, yes, Dear Reader, even now I can see the ghost of a smile tracing your lips. If you savor and cherish dread as I do—like an exquisitely dry sherry from a dusty cask—you will not be disappointed by this extraordinary collection.)

Firbolg Publishing has disinterred these worthy tales from literary tombs and placed them under the bright, pitiless lights of a coroner's laboratory. No extreme measures, surgery, or defibrillation were necessary to resurrect them, for they were never dead, evidenced by how seamlessly they twitch and shriek next to—occasionally artfully paired with—the work of contemporary masters like Faherty, Maberry, Newstein, Norris, and more.

There are gems in this treasure chest you now hold in your hands, a vessel that contains a king's ransom of thrills, chills, and shivers. And so, on behalf of Dr. Scully and the authors within, Dear Reader, I will leave you with the famous Roman epitaph attributed to Horace: *Eram quod es; eris quod sum* (I was what you are; you will be what I am). Plunder well this treasure; immerse yourself in the sibilant whispers of storytellers who, whether alive or long dead, have achieved a precious measure of immortality in the stirring of your imagination.

~ Daniel Knauf; Los Angeles, March 1, 2015

Incubus
by
Tanya Jarvik

This bed of nails in her stilted house
seems, if anything, to encourage him:
every night now he comes and crouches
on the great fat hams of her breasts,
glaring his quicksilver glare
and grinning his wicked red grin.

If he closed his eyes and shut his mouth
she couldn't tell him from the dark,
the cold prick of her own loneliness
sitting on her skin, a shirt of nettles,
the metallic bite of a bitter river
whose current drags her down to sleep.

Thus pinned, heart's rod and piston
laboring under unforgiving weight,
she finds strength enough to shake
her head from side to side,
just a little at first, then faster,
heat gathering in her hair
as if the sun were shining.

Her pillow ignites; her sheets are aflame;
an ecstasy of rage and pleasure burns
right through the back of her skull
and she's breathing fire, now, speaking
infernal tongues, all of them licking at once,
until she has consumed him for tonight.

Bad Things Happen
by
Nathaniel Lee

We interviewed the Vandal King. It was kind of a coup for us. Our little blog site hadn't broken any real news yet, but we'd been rising steadily in visibility, gotten some nice links, a couple of second and third-place interviews with minor figures. The Vandal King hadn't ever spoken to anyone, though, which was unusual for metaphysicals. Generally, they love to talk about themselves; the more people know about them, the better, or at least that's how I understand it. Why he picked us, I don't know; none of us had ever so much as glimpsed his shadow.

He met us in the park. I wasn't quite sure what to prepare for, so I'd dressed for business casual: plain skirt, unpretentious blouse, dark colors. When War spoke to the BBC, he'd appeared as a ten-foot-tall behemoth in spiked armor, something out of a medieval painting. The Lover had been on Oprah the year before she went off the air, manifesting as a glorious, long-haired beauty of indeterminate gender. They liked to go big, and so I thought… I don't know what I thought. But the Vandal King was there before we even realized it, a short and almost completely human-looking figure, like a homeless man in a shabby brown trench coat. His face was covered in stubble and he smelled of sweat and smog. The only hints of his true nature were his eyes, which were a pupil-less black, and his hands, where the fingertips grew to hooked and vicious claws.

"Good morning," he said. "It's going to be a beautiful day."

We walked, at his insistence. He moved with a constant, restless energy, his eyes darting, his smile broad. We kept our camera on him and he walked ahead of us, facing us, walking backward without a hitch. We passed a water fountain and he pulled a wad of gum from his mouth and wedged it into the drainage hole. He dropped a stick in the path of an onrushing bicyclist. A mother and child passed by, the little one holding a red balloon tightly in one sticky fist. With a quick gesture, the Vandal King popped it and grinned at the flood of tears. No one looked at him save for us; metaphysicals are never seen unless they want to be.

"Why?" I asked. It wasn't the first question we'd planned on, but I couldn't help myself. "Why do you do this?"

War had gone on at length about how the clash of ideologies was a purifying process. Disease had insisted that his deadliest children were the spurs of evolution. Pain had asked plaintively how anyone would know to keep safe if nothing ever hurt. I thought the Vandal King would have a similarly self-aggrandizing philosophy, explaining why it was to the betterment of the world that bad things happened, even to good people.

"Why?" he asked, idly uprooting flowers as we walked. He met my gaze, eyes glittering like a slick of oil over a bottomless ocean. "Because I can. Because it's there. Because it's beautiful."

I glanced back the way we had come. Disarray and chaos, with a soundtrack of heartbroken sobs. "Where is the beauty in wrecking things? I don't see it."

"I do." He smiled at me. His teeth were crooked and dirty. I suppose I'd expected fangs.

I shook my head and tried to get back on track. "They say metaphysicals have many names…" I began, and his eyes became hooded as something in him retreated to a safe distance.

The interview was successful. It was safe yet titillating, hinting at danger without containing anything unexpected: just the thing for everyone to consume over a cup of coffee and share on their favorite social media. New readers flooded in, donations and subscriptions blossomed, and for the first time since our inception, we were solidly in the black for the month's expenses. We could stop relying on Casper's trust fund to keep us afloat. The Vandal King, the Gremlin, the Lord of Misfortune had brought us success and pleasure instead of his usual gifts.

It bothered me.

I sat at my desk in the loft apartment we used for a communal office and clicked idly through websites, ostensibly doing research. My eyes looked past the computer screen, the words glowing black on white, and into the space behind, where only patterns of light and color tricked my eyes into seeing shapes or movement, fooled me into seeing gray-green as black. Contrast. They said metaphysicals could not lie. Was that why they were so boisterous in interviews? Be what is expected and avoid the hard questions, the ones you might answer inadvertently by refusing to speak. That feeling, at least, was familiar to me. The false shadows of my desktop made me think of eyes like pools of tar.

"I'm going out," I said abruptly.

"Taking an early lunch?" asked Reggie. "Casper said he'd be buying us all a nice meal to celebrate. You'll miss out."

"I'm not that hungry."

I plucked up my purse and strode from the room. My legs trembled with the need to keep moving; I paced around the elevator, one and a half steps per side. Out on the sidewalk, I nearly bowled over a meter maid, writing methodical tickets for every car on the block. Every car?

I peered at the nearest parking meter. Faint scratches etched a line down the sides, where fingers would have drifted if someone tampered with the knob. I glanced up and caught a brown coat disappearing around the corner. I ran after the Vandal King, my heels clack-clack-clacking on the concrete, my purse thumping me in the side as it slipped from my shoulder to the crook of my elbow.

"Hey!" I called. "Hey, wait!" I didn't use any of the names he'd given me; they might be true, but they weren't what he called himself, I knew.

I nearly ran into him as I veered around the corner. I stumbled against the crumbling bricks, scraping my knuckles. There was a snap as one of my shoe heels broke. I stood there, panting stupidly, and he stared at me with his dead-shark eyes. Something glimmered inside them.

"You called for me to wait," he said.

"Since when," I asked, "have you done anything at a mortal's pleasure?"

He grinned. "I do everything for pleasure. It pleased me to stop here, at this time." He turned, his coat swirling like a cloak, and strode away. "You may walk with me, if it pleases you."

The Vandal King was always busy, but for now he walked with his hands in his pockets, his ragged hair hanging over his face. People moved out of his way and averted their eyes, though whether they were unconsciously sensing that he was a metaphysical or just avoiding a smelly homeless man, I couldn't have said. No one looked at me, either, as I limped along beside him.

"I wanted…" I stopped. I couldn't put into words what I wanted to say. "You spoke yesterday about… beauty."

"Before all the stupid questions started?" The Vandal King sneered. "Yes. Did you understand what I said?"

"No," I answered honestly.

"That is unfortunate." He ran a hand along a car as we passed, and the chrome fender grew spotted with rust. I knew it would fall off soon, would cost a few hundred dollars to repair. It was the first miracle I had ever witnessed.

I turned to watch it as we traveled on, deeper into the outskirts of the city, the wild places where people like me didn't dare to tread unironically.

"Can you explain to me what you meant? Why you would… break things, ruin things like this?"

"Do you know the fable of the frog and the scorpion?"

"No." I tugged my purse straps higher on my shoulder, tucked it under my arms. I, at least, was drawing more attention in these darker neighborhoods.

"The scorpion asks the frog to carry it across a stream. The frog refuses, fearing the scorpion's sting. The scorpion points out that he will drown as well if he stings the frog in the middle of the stream." The Vandal King did not look at me as he told the story, speaking rapidly and without inflection. "The frog agrees to carry the scorpion, and so they go."

"So, what, different sides can find a common ground or something?" I vaguely recalled that fables have moral lessons to them.

"Then," the Vandal King went on, as if I hadn't spoken, "in the middle of the stream, the scorpion stings the frog, and they both drown."

"Why?"

"Ah." The Vandal King looked at me then, tossing his hair out of his eyes. I could see now that they were not black, not true black, but something else, something fractured and unnamable. They only looked black against the uncomplicated shades of his semi-real flesh. "The frog asked the same question. The scorpion told the frog that he could not help being what he was, and that is the moral of the fable. But it is a frog's moral, in a story told by a frog for other frogs. The true answer is this."

The Vandal King turned toward me, his eyes enormous, and I pulled back in surprise. I realized I had leaned in close to him during his story, close enough to smell his fetid body odor and the odd scent that underlay it. It smelled like raspberries and burnt toast, like the darkness between the stars.

"He did it because he wanted to."

I blinked, struggling to find my voice. "He wanted to die?"

"If you like." The Vandal King shrugged. "Or he wanted the frog to die. Or both. Or neither. Or perhaps he simply liked the pattern they would make, their bodies together on the sandy floor of the stream. Because it was beautiful."

The world was very quiet around us. I realized I could no longer hear cars or buses, nor people walking and talking, nor the blasts of music and electronic noise that filled the city I knew. I looked around. It had grown dark, suddenly. The street stank of decay. Buildings teetered on the verge of collapse. Hulks of dead cars hunkered in uneven clumps by the side of the road. Poles and signs lay where they had fallen, and the ones that remained were illegible under repeated scrawls of paint. I felt a surge of pain from my ankle, where I'd strained it walking with only one heel.

"And this?" I asked, my voice small. "Is this beautiful?"

"Yes," he said, and smiled.

Oh, I thought. *There are the fangs.*

"This is my world," said the Vandal King. "I have made it as beautiful as I can. But it is not where I belong. My place is in the ugly spaces, up there, with you." He pointed, and I could not tell if his finger was aimed at the city from which we had come or at my forehead, beaded with sweat. "If you see something ugly, you can change it to make it beautiful. That is what we do, we who cannot change ourselves. We do it for you, to make the perfect world for you to live in."

I heard a rustling motion behind me. I hoped it was only rats. "Are you going to leave me here?"

The Vandal King cocked his head to the side. "Do you want me to?"

"When have you ever done anything at a mortal's pleasure?" I laughed despite myself, feeling quite dizzy.

He looked at me without speaking, his expression as strange and alien as I had ever seen. I couldn't tell if he was smiling. He held out a hand. "I will take you home."

"Your home or mine?"

His eyes flickered, then went flat and unyielding. He said nothing, his grimy hand extended.

I reached out and took it.

The noontime sun was shining down on me. I stood on the street outside the office, watching a meter maid work. My purse was on my shoulder, and I stood firmly balanced on my high-heeled shoes. I stared around me. I realized my jaw was hanging open, and I shut my mouth and hastily began to walk. The streets were clean and shiny and full of a laughing stream of people. They wore nice suits. They had perfect white teeth. They were just like me. They knew nothing.

I paused next to a newspaper vending machine and a trash can. The store window behind me displayed slick little electronic devices that, according to the ad copy, would do all my work for me and fix my love life, to boot. I breathed in deeply and couldn't even smell the garbage from the can beside me.

There was a tube of lipstick in my purse for emergency touch-ups. I pulled it out. Uncapped it. Twisted it until it was fully extended. With rapid motions, I scrawled "FUCK" on the store window in my habitual loopy cursive. My penmanship was shaky, but it wasn't bad for a first effort. I stepped back to consider it. Then I turned and pushed the garbage can into the street, where it made a hollow clanging sound as it rolled along. I put a foot through the front glass of the newspaper machine.

Limping once more, I turned and hobbled away as quickly as I could, laughing wildly. The world was ugly, but I could make it beautiful. Everyone could, whatever beauty meant to them, whatever it meant to me. I'd figure that out for myself as I went along. Perhaps I would change my mind, eventually. That was my privilege. I wondered where I could find a good, long trench coat.

It was going to be a beautiful day.

What Was It?
by
Fitz-James O'Brien*

originally published in *Harper's*, 1859

It is, I confess, with considerable diffidence that I approached the strange narrative which I am about to relate. The events which I purpose detailing are of so extraordinary a character that I am quite prepared to meet with an unusual amount of incredulity and scorn. I accept all such beforehand. I have, I trust, the literary courage to face unbelief. I have, after mature consideration, resolved to narrate, in as simple and straightforward a manner as I can compass, some facts that passed under my observation, in the month of July last, and which, in the annals of the mysteries of physical science, are wholly unparalleled.

I live at No.—— Twenty-sixth Street, in New York. The house is in some respects a curious one. It has enjoyed for the last two years the reputation of being haunted. The house is very spacious. A hall of noble size leads to a large spiral staircase winding through its center, while the various apartments are of imposing dimensions. It was built some fifteen or twenty years since by Mr. A——, the well-known New York merchant, who five years ago threw the commercial world into convulsions by a stupendous bank fraud. Mr. A——, as everyone knows, escaped to Europe, and died not long after, of a broken heart. Almost immediately after the news of his decease reached this country and was verified, the report spread in Twenty-sixth Street that No.—— was haunted. Legal measures had dispossessed the widow of its former owner, and it was inhabited merely by a caretaker and his wife, placed there by the house-agent into whose hands it had passed for purposes of renting or sale. These people declared that they were troubled with unnatural noises. Doors were opened without any visible agency. The remnants of furniture scattered through the various rooms were, during the night, piled one upon the other by unknown hands. Invisible feet passed up and down the stairs in broad daylight, accompanied by the rustle of unseen silk dresses, and the gliding of viewless hands along the massive balusters. The caretaker and his wife declared they would live there no longer. The house-agent laughed, dismissed them, and put others in their place. The noises and supernatural manifestations continued. The neighborhood caught up the story, and the house remained untenanted for three years. Several persons negotiated for it; but, somehow, always before the bargain was closed they heard the unpleasant rumors and declined to treat any further.

It was in this state of things that my landlady, who at that time kept a boarding house in Bleecker Street, and who wished to move farther up town, conceived the bold idea of renting No.—— Twenty-sixth Street. Happening to have in her house rather a plucky and philosophical set of boarders, she laid her scheme before us, stating candidly everything she had heard respecting the ghostly qualities of the establishment to which she wished to remove us. With the exception of two timid persons—a sea captain and a returned Californian, who immediately gave notice that they would leave—all of Mrs. Moffat's guests declared that they would accompany her in her incursion into the abode of spirits.

Our removal was effected in the month of May, and we were charmed with our new residence.

Of course we had no sooner established ourselves at No.—— than we began to expect the ghosts. We absolutely awaited their advent with eagerness. Our dinner conversation was supernatural. I found myself a person of immense importance, it having leaked out that I was tolerably well versed in the history of supernaturalism, and had once written a story the foundation of which was a ghost. If a table or wainscot panel happened to warp when we were assembled in the large drawing room, there was an instant silence, and everyone was prepared for an immediate clanking of chains and a spectral form.

After a month of psychological excitement, it was with the utmost dissatisfaction that we were forced to acknowledge that nothing in the remotest degree approaching the supernatural had manifested itself.

Things were in this state when an incident took place so awful and inexplicable in its character that my reason fairly reels at the bare memory of the occurrence. It was the tenth of July. After dinner was over I repaired, with my friend Dr. Hammond, to the garden to smoke my evening pipe. Independent of certain mental sympathies which existed between the doctor and myself, we were linked together by a vice. We both smoked opium. We knew each other's secret and respected it. We enjoyed together that wonderful expansion of thought, that marvelous intensifying of the perceptive faculties, that boundless feeling of existence when we seem to have points of contact with the whole universe—in short, that unimaginable spiritual bliss, which I would not surrender for a throne, and which I hope you, reader, will never, never taste.

On the evening in question, the tenth of July, the doctor and myself drifted into an unusually metaphysical mood. We lit our large meerschaums, filled with fine Turkish tobacco, in the core of which burned a little black nut of opium, that, like the nut in the fairy tale, held within its narrow limits wonders beyond the reach of kings; we paced to and fro, conversing. A strange perversity dominated the currents of our thoughts. They would not flow through the sun-lit channels into which we strove to divert them. For some unaccountable reason, they constantly diverged into dark and lonesome beds, where a continual gloom brooded. It was in vain that, after our old fashion, we flung ourselves on the shores of the East, and talked of its gay bazaars, of the splendors of the time of Haroun, of harems and golden palaces. Black afreets continually arose from the depths of our talk, and expanded, like the one the fisherman released from the copper vessel, until they blotted everything bright from our vision. Insensibly, we yielded to the occult force that swayed us, and indulged in gloomy speculation. We had talked some time upon the proneness of the human mind to mysticism, and the almost universal love of the terrible, when Hammond suddenly said to me, "What do you consider to be the greatest element of terror?"

The question puzzled me. That many things were terrible, I knew. But it now struck me, for the first time, that there must be one great and ruling embodiment of fear—a King of Terrors, to which all others must succumb. What might it be? To what train of circumstances would it owe its existence?

"I confess, Hammond," I replied to my friend, "I never considered the subject before. That there must be one Something more terrible than any other thing, I feel. I cannot attempt, however, even the most vague definition."

"I am somewhat like you, Harry," he answered. "I feel my capacity to experience a terror greater than anything yet conceived by the human mind—something combining in fearful and unnatural amalgamation hitherto supposed incompatible elements. The calling of the voices in Brockden Brown's novel of *Wieland* is awful; so is the picture of the Dweller on the Threshold, in Bulwer's *Zanoni*; but," he added, shaking his head gloomily, "there is something more horrible still than these."

"Look here, Hammond," I rejoined, "let us drop this kind of talk, for Heaven's sake! We shall suffer for it, depend on it."

"I don't know what's the matter with me tonight," he replied, "but my brain is running upon all sorts of weird and awful thoughts. I feel as if I could write a story like Hoffman, tonight, if I were only master of a literary style."

"Well, if we are going to be Hoffmanesque in our talk, I'm off to bed. Opium and nightmares should never be brought together. How sultry it is! Good night, Hammond."

"Good night, Harry. Pleasant dreams to you."

"To you, gloomy wretch, afreets, ghouls, and enchanters."

We parted, and each sought his respective chamber. I undressed quickly and got into bed, taking with me, according to my usual custom, a book over which I generally read myself to sleep. I opened the volume as soon as I had laid my head upon the pillow, and instantly flung it to the other side of the room. It was Goudon's *History of Monsters*, a curious French work, which I had lately imported from Paris, but which, in the state of mind I had then reached, was anything but an agreeable companion. I resolved to go to sleep at once; so, turning down my gas until nothing but a little blue point of light glimmered on the top of the tube, I composed myself to rest.

The room was in total darkness. The atom of gas that still remained alight did not illuminate a distance of three inches round the burner. I desperately drew my arm across my eyes, as if to shut out even the darkness, and tried to think of nothing. It was in vain. The confounded themes touched on by Hammond in the garden kept obtruding themselves on my brain. I battled against them. I erected ramparts of would-be blankness of intellect to keep them out. They still crowded upon me. While I was lying still as a corpse, hoping that by a perfect physical inaction I should hasten mental repose, an awful incident occurred. A Something dropped, as it seemed, from the ceiling, plumb upon my chest, and the next instant I felt two bony hands encircling my throat, endeavoring to choke me.

I am no coward, and am possessed of considerable physical strength. The suddenness of the attack, instead of stunning me, strung every nerve to its highest tension. My body acted from instinct, before my brain had time to realize the terrors of my position. In an instant I wound two muscular arms around the creature, and squeezed it, with all the strength of despair, against my chest. In a few seconds the bony hands that had fastened on my throat loosened their hold, and I was free to breathe once more. Then commenced a struggle of awful intensity. Immersed in the most profound darkness, totally ignorant of the nature of the Thing by which I was so suddenly attacked, finding my grasp slipping every moment, by reason, it seemed to me, of the entire nakedness of my assailant, bitten with sharp teeth in the shoulder, neck, and chest, having every moment to protect my throat against a pair of sinewy, agile hands, which my utmost efforts could not confine—these were a combination of circumstances to combat which required all the strength, skill, and courage that I possessed.

At last, after a silent, deadly, exhausting struggle, I got my assailant under by a series of incredible efforts of strength. Once pinned, with my knee on what I made out to be its chest, I knew that I was victor. I rested for a moment to breathe. I heard the creature beneath me panting in the darkness, and felt the violent throbbing of a heart. It was apparently as exhausted as I was; that was one comfort. At this moment I remembered that I usually placed under my pillow, before going to bed, a large yellow silk pocket handkerchief. I felt for it instantly; it was there. In a few seconds more I had, after a fashion, pinioned the creature's arms.

I now felt tolerably secure. There was nothing more to be done but to turn on the gas, and, having first seen what my midnight assailant was like, arouse the household. I will confess to being actuated by a certain pride in not giving the alarm before; I wished to make the capture alone and unaided.

Never losing my hold for an instant, I slipped from the bed to the floor, dragging my captive with me. I had but a few steps to make to reach the gas burner; these I made with the greatest caution, holding the creature in a grip like a vice. At last I got within arm's length of the tiny speck of blue light which told me where the gas burner lay. Quick as lightning I released my grasp with one hand and let on the full flood of light. Then I turned to look at my captive.

I cannot even attempt to give any definition of my sensations the instant after I turned on the gas. I suppose I must have shrieked with terror, for in less than a minute afterward my room was crowded with the inmates of the house. I shudder now as I think of that awful moment. *I saw nothing!* Yes; I had one arm firmly clasped round a breathing, panting, corporeal shape, my other hand gripped with all its strength a throat as warm, and apparently fleshly, as my own; and yet, with this living substance in my grasp, with its body pressed against my own, and all in the bright glare of a large jet of gas, I absolutely beheld nothing! Not even an outline—a vapor!

I do not, even at this hour, realize the situation in which I found myself. I cannot recall the astounding incident thoroughly. Imagination in vain tries to compass the awful paradox.

It breathed. I felt its warm breath upon my cheek. It struggled fiercely. It had hands. They clutched me. Its skin was smooth, like my own. There it lay, pressed close up against me, solid as stone—and yet utterly invisible!

I wonder that I did not faint or go mad on the instant. Some wonderful instinct must have sustained me; for absolutely, in place of loosening my hold on the terrible Enigma, I seemed to gain an additional strength in my moment of horror, and tightened my grasp with such wonderful force that I felt the creature shivering with agony.

Just then Hammond entered my room at the head of the household. As soon as he beheld my face—which, I suppose, must have been an awful sight to look at—he hastened forward, crying, "Great Heaven, what has happened?"

"Hammond! Hammond!" I cried, "come here. Oh, this is awful! I have been attacked in bed by something or other, which I have hold of; but I can't see it—I can't see it!"

Hammond, doubtless struck by the unfeigned horror expressed in my countenance, made one or two steps forward with an anxious yet puzzled expression. A very audible titter burst from the remainder of my visitors. This suppressed laughter made me furious. To laugh at a human being in my position! It was the worst species of cruelty. *Now*, I can understand why the appearance of a man struggling violently, as it would seem, with an airy nothing, and calling for assistance against a vision, should have appeared ludicrous. *Then*, so great was my rage against the mocking crowd that had I the power I would have stricken them dead where they stood.

"Hammond! Hammond!" I cried again, despairingly, "for God's sake come to me. I can hold the—the thing but a short while longer. It is overpowering me. Help me! Help me!"

"Harry," whispered Hammond, approaching me, "you have been smoking too much opium."

"I swear to you, Hammond, that this is no vision," I answered, in the same low tone. "Don't you see how it shakes my whole frame with its struggles? If you don't believe me, convince yourself. Feel it—touch it."

Hammond advanced and laid his hand in the spot I indicated. A wild cry of horror burst from him. He had felt it!

In a moment he had discovered somewhere in my room a long piece of cord, and was the next instant winding it and knotting it about the body of the unseen being that I clasped in my arms.

"Harry," he said, in a hoarse, agitated voice, for, though he preserved his presence of mind, he was deeply moved. "Harry, it's all safe now. You may let go, old fellow, if you're tired. The Thing can't move."

I was utterly exhausted, and I gladly loosed my hold.

Hammond stood holding the ends of the cord, that bound the Invisible, twisted round his hand, while before him, self-supporting as it were, he beheld a rope laced and interlaced, and stretching tightly around a vacant space. I never saw a man look so thoroughly stricken with awe. Nevertheless his face expressed all the courage and determination which I knew him to possess. His lips, although white, were set firmly, and one could perceive at a glance that, although stricken with fear, he was not daunted.

The confusion that ensued among the guests of the house who were witnesses of this extraordinary scene between Hammond and myself—who beheld the pantomime of binding this struggling Something—who beheld me almost sinking from physical exhaustion when my task of jailer was over—the confusion and terror that took possession of the bystanders, when they saw all this, was beyond description. The weaker ones fled from the apartment. The few who remained clustered near the door and could not be induced to approach Hammond and his Charge. Still incredulity broke out through their terror. They had not the courage to satisfy themselves, and yet they doubted. It was in vain that I begged of some of the men to come near and convince themselves by touch of the existence in that room of a living being which was invisible. They were incredulous, but did not dare to undeceive themselves. How could a solid, living, breathing body be invisible, they asked. My reply was this. I gave a sign to Hammond, and both of us—conquering our fearful repugnance to touch the invisible creature—lifted it from the ground, manacled as it was, and took it to my bed. Its weight was about that of a boy of fourteen.

"Now, my friends," I said, as Hammond and myself held the creature suspended over the bed, "I can give you self-evident proof that here is a solid, ponderable body, which, nevertheless, you cannot see. Be good enough to watch the surface of the bed attentively."

I was astonished at my own courage in treating this strange event so calmly; but I had recovered from my first terror, and felt a sort of scientific pride in the affair, which dominated every other feeling.

The eyes of the bystanders were immediately fixed on my bed. At a given signal Hammond and I let the creature fall. There was the dull sound of a heavy body alighting on a soft mass. The timbers of the bed creaked. A deep impression marked itself distinctly on the pillow, and on the bed itself. The crowd who witnessed this gave a low cry, and rushed from the room. Hammond and I were left alone with our Mystery.

We remained silent for some time, listening to the low irregular breathing of the creature on the bed and watching the rustle of the bedclothes as it impotently struggled to free itself from confinement. Then Hammond spoke.

"Harry, this is awful."

"Ay, awful."

"But not unaccountable."

"Not unaccountable! What do you mean? Such a thing has never occurred since the birth of the world. I know not what to think, Hammond. God grant that I am not mad and that this is not an insane fantasy!"

"Let us reason a little, Harry. Here is a solid body which we touch but which we cannot see. The fact is so unusual that it strikes us with terror. Is there no parallel, though, for such a phenomenon? Take a piece of pure glass. It is tangible and transparent. A certain chemical coarseness is all that prevents its being so entirely transparent as to be totally invisible. It is not *theoretically impossible*, mind you, to make a glass which shall not reflect a single ray of light—a glass so pure and homogeneous in its atoms that the rays from the sun will pass through it as they do through the air, refracted but not reflected. We do not see the air, and yet we feel it."

"That's all very well, Hammond, but these are inanimate substances. Glass does not breathe, air does not breathe. This thing has a heart that palpitates, a will that moves it, lungs that play, and inspire and respire."

"You forget the phenomena of which we have so often heard of late," answered the doctor gravely. "At the meetings called 'spirit circles,' invisible hands have been thrust into the hands of those persons round the table—warm, fleshly hands that seemed to pulsate with mortal life."

"What? Do you think, then, that this thing is——"

"I don't know what it is," was the solemn reply; "but please the gods I will, with your assistance, thoroughly investigate it."

We watched together, smoking many pipes, all night long, by the bedside of the unearthly being that tossed and panted until it was apparently wearied out. Then we learned by the low, regular breathing that it slept.

The next morning the house was all astir. The boarders congregated on the landing outside my room, and Hammond and myself were lions. We had to answer a thousand questions as to the state of our extraordinary prisoner, for as yet not one person in the house except ourselves could be induced to set foot in the apartment.

The creature was awake. This was evidenced by the convulsive manner in which the bedclothes were moved in its efforts to escape. There was something truly terrible in beholding, as it were, those second-hand indications of the terrible writhings and agonized struggles for liberty which themselves were invisible.

Hammond and myself had racked our brains during the long night to discover some means by which we might realize the shape and general appearance of the Enigma. As well as we could make out by passing our hands over the creature's form, its outlines and lineaments were human. There was a mouth; a round, smooth head without hair; a nose, which, however, was little elevated above the cheeks; and its hands and feet felt like those of a boy. At first we thought of placing the being on a smooth surface and tracing its outlines with chalk, as shoemakers trace the outline of the foot. This plan was given up as being of no value. Such an outline would give not the slightest idea of its conformation.

A happy thought struck me. We would take a cast of it in plaster-of-Paris. This would give us the solid figure, and satisfy all our wishes. But how to do it. The movements of the creature would disturb the setting of the plastic covering, and distort the mold. Another thought. Why not give it chloroform? It had respiratory organs—that was evident by its breathing. Once reduced to a state of insensibility, we could do with it what we would. Doctor X—— was sent for; and after the worthy physician had recovered from the first shock of amazement, he proceeded to administer the chloroform. In three minutes afterward we were enabled to remove the fetters from the creature's body, and a modeler was busily engaged in covering the invisible form with the moist clay. In five minutes more we had a mold, and before evening a rough facsimile of the Mystery. It was shaped like a man—distorted, uncouth, and horrible, but still a man. It was small, not over four feet and some inches in height, and its limbs revealed a muscular development that was unparalleled. Its face surpassed in hideousness anything I had ever seen. Gustave Doré, or Callot, or Tony Johannot, never conceived anything so horrible. There is a face in one of the latter's illustrations to *Un Voyage où il vous plaira*, which somewhat approaches the countenance of this creature, but does not equal it. It was the physiognomy of what I should fancy a ghoul might be. It looked as if it was capable of feeding on human flesh.

Having satisfied our curiosity, and bound everyone in the house to secrecy, it became a question what was to be done with our Enigma? It was impossible that we should keep such a horror in our house; it was equally impossible that such an awful being should be let loose upon the world. I confess that I would have gladly voted for the creature's destruction. But who would shoulder the responsibility? Who would undertake the execution of this horrible semblance to a human being? Day after day this question was deliberated gravely. The boarders all left the house. Mrs. Moffat was in despair, and threatened Hammond and myself with all sorts of legal penalties if we did not remove the Horror. Our answer was, "We will go if you like, but we decline taking this creature with us. Remove it yourself if you please. It appeared in your house. On you the responsibility rests." To this there was, of course, no answer. Mrs. Moffat could not obtain for love or money a person who would even approach the Mystery.

At last it died. Hammond and I found it cold and stiff one morning in the bed. The heart had ceased to beat, the lungs to inspire. We hastened to bury it in the garden. It was a strange funeral, the dropping of that viewless corpse into the damp hole. The cast of its form I gave to Doctor X———, who keeps it in his museum in Tenth Street.

As I am on the eve of a long journey from which I may not return, I have drawn up this narrative of an event the most singular that has ever come to my knowledge.

*The first edition of this collection attributed the story to Sheridan Le Fanu. There are questions concerning the authorship of some of the early Gothic tales. Anonymous publications were common practice, and this has created doubt about the authors. Fitz James O'Brien's writing has also come under question in recent years, but the attribution for this story, at this time, belongs to O'Brien.

First Horse
by
Rob Smales

"Long ago, when things had no names as we know them, but everything was simply what it was, there was a Warrior, gifted beyond all others in his tribe. Warrior protected his tribe from many dangers: from the monsters of the mountains and of the plains to the other tribes of Man. Warrior was wise, and also humble, and so made offerings each day of food and drink and smoke and song, thanking the Spirits for their gifts. He thanked Dog of the mountains, and Horse of the plains, and Eagle of the air, all of the Spirits, Great and Small; in this way, he lived a life of balance, and his gifts of strength and speed did not fail him, and he did protect his tribe for many years.

"One day, when he was very old, a band of raiders came from the west, and his tribe needed him again. Without hesitation, Warrior picked up his spear and went to meet this new foe. He walked not with the stride of his youth, nor the same sharp eyes, but still he thanked the Spirits each day, and his gifts had not failed him.

"He fought through the day and night. Exhaustion filled his old limbs, his heart beating painfully, but still he fought for his tribe. Dawn drew near, and old Warrior had slain all but the leader of the raiders. Their fight ranged across the battlefield, and still old Warrior fought, and his enemy felt despair.

"But though his gifts had not forsaken him, and so Warrior was fast and strong, still he was very old. Just before the sun of morning touched the land, his old heart burst within his chest. The enemy saw the weakness and struck old Warrior's head with his war club. Warrior struck, too, slaying his enemy even as he died.

"At dawn the Spirits looked for Warrior, expecting his offerings of food and drink and smoke and song. They looked to the battlefield, but found only his spirit, wandering among his fallen enemies. Addled by the blow that killed him, old Warrior could not find his way to the Land Beyond the Sky.

"The Spirits watched him with great worry, for they knew it was wrong that Warrior should be forgotten, when he had been such a good man, and so attentive to the Spirits. There was much discussion as Warrior's spirit wandered, until finally Dog left the mountains and went to the battlefield. Dog greeted Warrior, welcomed him, and walked with him across the plains and the water, guiding him on his long journey over the sea and to the Land Beyond the Sky. And that is the story of the first Spirit Guide."

Jimmy stared at the old man.

"You really believe all this, Grandfather?"

"I do."

The hoarse whisper came from nowhere and everywhere, the face atop the withered body seated across from him so weathered by sun and time it was more wooden mask than face, thin, dry lips immobile in the shadows of the old cabin.

"As was told to me by my father, and his father before him, stretching back to Warrior himself, the first shaman of our tribe."

"And when you… I mean, when you… when your time is up and you… well, *go*, you believe…"

Amusement crinkled the corners of the ancient shaman's eyes.

"When my time in this world has run its course, Horse of the Plains will guide me to the Land Beyond the Sky."

"But it was Dog in the story."

The old man nodded. "We do not choose the Spirits, it is they who choose us. Horse of the Plains has walked beside me longer than the memory of the oldest members of our tribe."

Without any teeth, it took Jimmy a moment to recognize the old man's grin.

"Well, the oldest members besides *me*."

Jimmy sat for a full sixty seconds, images from the old man's story spinning through his head. The grinning shaman watched him.

"What is it you think of, James Tsosi?"

Jimmy started, somewhat guiltily. "I… I think…" He rose, stiff-legged from sitting so long on the floor. "I have to go. Uh, thank you for sharing your story, Grandfather." He staggered out of the smoky cabin, head whirling. Behind him he heard the old shaman chanting—or was he *laughing*?—even as his feet carried him, dazed, toward the corral.

Toward *her*.

Hair streaming behind, black as a raven's wing in flight; eyes, large and dark, beautiful even from a distance, shining with merriment; lips parted, revealing flashing teeth and releasing a rippling laugh, a laugh that set his brain on fire, turned his knees to butter, and left his own heart weeping for the sound of it, she rode toward the barn at the head of the small, thundering herd.

"You had a head start!" said Andrew Miller, sliding from his saddle with the other three boys she'd led in from the fields. A grumbling agreement rose from the group as they shuffled their feet.

"You were slow," corrected Alice Begay, still in the saddle and wearing a wide, white smile. "I said the first one back to the barn could take me to the Town Day dance. Looks like I'll be taking myself, then."

"Not fair," said Billy Yazzie, the first of the boys to actually get back to the barn. "You *did* have a head start." Smaller than Andrew, Billy was a better horseman—probably the best in the village, other than Alice herself—thus he usually garnered her favor.

But not today.

"You didn't impress me, Billy Yazzie." Her gaze took in the entire gathering, each holding the reins of their own blowing horses, her wide smile growing wider still. "Town Day is still a few days away. You still have time."

She laughed and wheeled her horse toward the fields, kicking back into a gallop before anyone could react. Billy Yazzie was back in his saddle in a flash, but you could tell by his face he had no hope of catching her.

The remaining three turned toward the barn, Andrew starting slightly in surprise.

"Oh, hi, Jimmy."

The bigger boy regarded Jimmy Tsosi curiously, wondering, Jimmy thought, what the Tsosi boy was doing down there at the barn. Jimmy did not own a horse, could not even ride very well, but Andrew simply shrugged and moved on, leading his horse toward its stall.

I'm surprised he noticed me at all, Jimmy thought bitterly. *None of the others did.*

He looked after Alice Begay and Billy Yazzie, and though they were long gone from sight, he smiled.

But they will.

Jimmy lay in bed, wide awake. Eyes closed, he saw Alice Begay, riding toward him across the fields, smiling, big and wide and friendly.

She was smiling at *him*. Behind her the other boys rode, eyes downcast, unable to keep up. Unable to make her smile, because she was smiling for *him*.

He opened his eyes and sighed, staring at the crack in the ceiling extending from the water stain in the corner. As he stared, it began to writhe, twisting like a worm. He knew it was just his eyes playing tricks, that if he closed his eyes the crack would return to normal, but...

He closed his eyes. Alice Begay smiled.

He opened his eyes. The crack waited to play its trick on him.

Closed. Alice.

Open.

Either way I'm not getting any sleep, he thought, *so I might as well...*

He closed his eyes, watching Alice Begay smile at him. Watching her *see* him.

*She'll see me when I win the Town Day race. They'll **all** see me then.*

Research, Jimmy thought, pouring himself another cup of coffee. *It all comes down to research.*

"How old is Grandfather Whitefeather?"

He took a sip of his bitter brew as his mother thought.

"I'm not sure. He's the oldest person in the village, I know that. But exactly *how* old? I don't know if even *he* knows anymore."

"Wow. Think he'll be around much longer?"

"Jimmy! What a thing to say!"

"Sorry. It just popped into my head is all."

He took another sip.

"Since when do you like coffee?"

Jimmy pulled his lips tight, simulating a smile as he forced himself not to choke on the nasty liquid sliding down his gullet.

"People change, Mom."

"I'll say. You never had any interest in our heritage before. Now, though, seems it's all you ever think about."

"Not quite."

In his mind's eye, Alice Begay laughed as they spun across the floor at the Town Day dance. The other kids, all the kids that barely even knew he was alive, looked on in envy. The boys were jealous of him for dancing with Alice, but Alice… Alice only had eyes for *him*.

"Well, I'm glad you're spending so much time with Grandfather Whitefeather. It's good for him, at his age, having a young person around, I think. Good for you, too, learning something of the old stories of our people."

"I'm just trying to get into the spirit," Jimmy said.

Then his own words struck him as funny, and he chuckled into his coffee.

His eyes burned. Everything felt… fuzzy.

Dreamy.

Well, he thought, slipping silently through the unlocked door, *I **was** looking for an altered state of consciousness.*

It was all in the research.

He hadn't had any experience with tribal lore until he'd started going to talk to old man Whitefeather, but he could read. And he could run computer searches. He was *quite* good at those. Google. Yahoo. Bing. Those were the tools of modern-day information gatherers. In the olden days his people might have cast the bones, looked at the stars, or consulted the spirits; today all he did was tap the keys.

Huh! I'm like a modern-day shaman!

He nearly giggled, crossing the silent room. It was hard to stop with his brain full of feathers, but he managed it. Barely.

He touched the door into the back room and froze, his stomach rumbling like thunder in the still of the night. He listened. Though his stomach gave a couple of lesser protests, no sound came from the room. His stomach growled on, and he clutched his middle, muffling the sound.

Many ceremonies of the Tribes had something in common: they might use days of fasting, hours of chanting, or even mind-altering drugs, but all those things were done with one goal in mind.

An altered state of consciousness.

After three days without sleep, consuming nothing but No-Doz and coffee, Jimmy certainly felt "altered." It was now or never, but he hadn't counted on all the extra noise his body was making.

That wasn't mentioned in the articles. Maybe the chanting covered it up.

Stifling another giggle, he pushed the door open and crept through.

The room was windowless and dark, and after he silently closed the door, stuffy. The air was thick with a concoction of scents, both bad and good: sweaty sheets, body odor, musty feet and sour breath, but also the clean scents of timothy grass and well-worn leather, freshly turned earth and the night sky.

Smells old, he thought. *Ancient. Maybe even*, he added, catching a faint whiff of decay beneath it all, *something dying. But not fast enough.*

He waited for his eyes to adjust to this new darkness, but realized quickly it wasn't going to happen: there had to be *some* kind of light for his eyes to be of any use, but this room held none.

The gloom of the grave. How fitting.

But Jimmy had been there before, and knew just how to fix *this* little problem. He fumbled beside the door.

The old man sure goes on about "the old ways" and stuff, but he wasn't old school enough to refuse the installation of—

With a soft *click*, brilliance flooded the room.

—*electric lights.*

A quick glance about told him he had been correct: this room in the back of the building had no windows to the outside world. With the door closed he need not fear nosy neighbors coming to investigate lights in the night. He crossed to the far wall just as the small figure lying there on the pallet began to stir. Black eyes fluttered open, squinting against the brightness. The ancient whisper drifted up.

"James Tsosi?"

"I'm sorry," Jimmy whispered as the pillow covered the old shaman's face.

He leaned into the pillow as slender, dry-stick arms lifted from the pallet to bat at him. He ignored them, leaning in harder; not so hard as to break the old man's hawkish nose, but enough to cut off the air from his gasping, lipless mouth.

"I need a horse. That's all they see. That's all they know. Horses and riding. But… but if I had a *special* horse, then it won't even matter that I can't ride worth a damn. They'll *all* see me! Alice will see me! She'll be *impressed* by me! *Me!*"

The thin hands became frantic, long, bony fingers scrabbling, scratching, but Jimmy had been ready for this. Research. Google. Bing. Jimmy had paused in the outer room long enough to don his big yellow rain slicker, and now the old man's hands could find no purchase; gouging nails slipped harmlessly over the slick surface.

"I know you're old. You're the oldest one in the village. You couldn't have lasted much longer."

Tears ran unnoticed down his cheeks as Jimmy felt Grandfather Whitefeather's defenses, already weak, weaken further. Hands patted rather than struck. Gouging claws became a gentle caress.

"But I can't wait, you see? You understand? I *can't*. Please understand! Town Day is the day after tomorrow, and they'll all be there, and I have to…"

Withered arms fell away, slid down his slippery sides to land with a twin muffled *thump* on the narrow bed. Jimmy had no more need of words. There was no one there to hear them.

Or is there? he thought. *This is why I'm here, after all.*

He tucked the pillow under the old, dead head, then sat on the edge of the bed to wait. A part of him—most of him, actually—watched all this happening as if it was someone else, in a movie perhaps, or on television. But another, smaller part *felt* it all happening and was revolted. Horrified. That part was thankful the pillow had pressed the old man's eyes shut, saving him from having to fold them closed: he didn't think he could have done that.

That part wept, tears still flowing. This was happening. It was real. But it all felt… it felt so…

You didn't stay awake starving yourself for three days for nothing, he thought. *You wanted an altered mental state, you got one.*

He sat there next to the man he'd just murdered and waited.

He did not wait long.

He thought… no.

No, it was nothing. But then…

…wait, yes, it was something. *Something,* at the very edge of hearing, like the memory of a sound. A sound he hadn't *heard* yet. He looked about but saw nothing. He went to the door to the front room, but it was no clearer out there, whatever it was—was *less* clear, in fact. Gone.

He'd imagined the whole thing.

Frustrated, he sat back down by the old man's body.

There it was again.

Maybe.

But maybe not. He huffed a sigh, closing his eyes in frustration.

Hoofbeats. One set. In the distance, drawing rapidly closer.

His eyes flew open. The hoofbeats faded instantly—the memory now of a sound he *had* heard.

He closed his eyes again.

Hoofbeats exploded into the room, pranced, slowed to a walk, the big animal nickering and blowing with exertion. He could almost **see** *the—*

He opened his eyes to bright light, the silence filling the room marred only by his own breathing. He looked to his companion, the cooling corpse of the old man who had thought to teach him.

His lids closed.

The ka-chuk ka-chuk of a walking horse stopped, the beast so close Jimmy smelled sweet equine sweat and the wind of the plains. He felt the heat of the thing, warm from its run—could **almost** *see Horse, standing next to the old man's bed, head lowering to sniff the body, or perhaps nose a friend. As Jimmy turned his head, eyes still closed, to try to* **see** *the visitor, something on the bed beside him moved. Not the body of the old shaman, but something* **inside** *it stirred, waking to answer the prodding of Horse of the Plains.*

"It's now or never," Jimmy thought. "I don't go now and this will all have been for nothing. Nothing."

Before his body could open its eyes again, Jimmy Tsosi imagined himself leaping, high and long, much higher than he could have managed had his body come along, and landed, legs spread, where he **knew** *Horse to be.*

He landed hard on the back of the invisible animal, fingers twining into the silky mane before him, and suddenly Horse was **there***, and* **real***, and the room was not. Horse was black and Horse was white, and Horse was roan and Horse was a hundred other colors, colors Jimmy had never seen on a living animal. It was Appaloosa and Paint and Pinto and a thousand other* *horses Jimmy had never heard of. It was every horse and it was one horse. It was First Horse, and it was strong and fine and beautiful and so, so* **real***.*

Jimmy had an instant to see the world around them, black-and-white and as real as a dream, or the memory of smoke from yesterday's fire. He saw the narrow bed, the old man lying atop it, and someone sitting beside the old man, eyes closed and still as the grave, and it was **him***, Jimmy Tsosi, sitting beside the man he'd killed. Jimmy astride Horse barely had time to register the look of guilt on his body's face before Horse bucked and spun and ran straight through the black-and-white wall.*

The sudden motion took Jimmy by surprise, only the clench of his terrified fingers, already entwined in the thick mane, kept him from being thrown to the ground. His heart stopped as they passed through the wall, then another, still real-looking but only solid as wisps of fog. They passed through the village— **through** *the village, gray houses no more substantial than the reflections of houses on a calm pond—Horse of the Plains bucking and leaping, spinning and twirling.*

Jimmy clung like desperate kudzu. Horse swelled beneath him, the barrel of its sides spreading his legs, and still Jimmy hung on, fists locked in the mane, legs squeezing for his life. He knew Horse should have thrown him, **would** *have thrown him had he still worn flesh, but he did not. He had* **seen** *his body sitting on that narrow cot and understood in a flash that he was no longer of the World, but of Spirit, and there would be no second chance, no getting back on Horse if he fell. He saw arms and legs, but knew he* **had** *no arms and legs, not really. He was Spirit, and he was Will, and he bent that Will, focused all that he now was on what he thought of as his hands, locking them in what he thought of as mane, and thought, (or maybe said, there seemed to be no difference in this Place),* "***I Will not fall***."*

He concentrated, and the World drew away: there was nothing but Horse beneath him and two hands in front of him, twisted into the mane with an unbreakable grip.

Horse, apparently sensing the implacableness of his foe, changed tactics. It hadn't grown tired—indeed, Jimmy had the impression it would **never** *tire,* **could** *never tire—but had possibly grown bored with bucking and dancing.*

It tried running.

Things flashed past—houses, trees, even people—colorless things that were mere impressions to Jimmy as Horse flew along the ground. Things went past them, they passed **through** *things, it all seemed as one to Jimmy, clinging like a limpet to the back of speed itself. He no longer knew whether his eyes were open or closed; it seemed to make no difference in this Place outside the World. A great Plain spreading out before them, behind them, in all directions, an unending flat pan, so perfect for running it might have been designed for it.*

Suddenly Horse shifted beneath him. With no visible cues from the flat, unending plain, the only hint Jimmy had that Horse had entered a long, sweeping curve was the play of the muscles under him, the brush of phantom wind across his face—and the pull of centrifugal force as his own inertia pushed him away from the back of Horse with ever increasing strength.

As if in response to his realization, First Horse ran still faster, hoofbeats filling the unending plain with the thunder of a stampede, the forces of speed and curve trying to tear the desperately clinging Jimmy loose. He gasped, tried to catch his breath—and realized he wasn't holding his breath, he was simply not breathing. Nor was his heart beating, he now noticed. It hadn't been since he leaped upon Horse.

"So how can this pull me?" he thought. "How can this force of curve and speed touch me? It's a physical law, and I'm not physical—I'm a Spirit! How can anything physical hurt me?"

At this thought the pull disappeared, vanished entirely, leaving Jimmy riding Horse unmolested across the vast, otherworldly Plain.

"Give up?" Jimmy said. Or thought. He still wasn't sure, in this Place.

In answer, Horse slowed to a trot, its whicker echoing throughout the flat space. Jimmy marveled at how fast Horse had capitulated: from all he had heard, he'd anticipated a much longer struggle. He maintained his grip on the mane, just in case.

"Then take me back. Take me back to where you found me."

Horse turned about (though, again, it was hard to tell in this featureless Place) and broke into a gallop. The universe blurred. They stood once more in the old man's narrow room, before the old man's narrow bed.

*The narrow, **empty** bed.*

"Where am I?" he said. "Where is Grandfather Whitefeather? What happened?"

Horse merely twitched an ear.

"Home…" Jimmy said, confused. "I… I think I have to go home."

Horse walked through the wall and into the bright sunshine of the village.

"Daylight? But it should still be the middle of the—"

"It's a shame about Grandfather."

Two of the village women walked by, shaking their heads.

"Oh, I know. Passing just before Town Day like that. He missed everything. It's a shame. And did you hear about the Tsosi boy?"

"Oh no!" Jimmy kicked Horse into a trot, then a canter. He'd thought his struggle with Horse had lasted mere minutes—less than a half hour—but a day and a half must have passed in that race across the endless Plain.

"I missed Town Day! They must have found us, found our bodies and thought I was dead! Was I dead? Am I? No, of course not! I have to find where they put me and get back in. Mom! God, Mom must think I'm—"

He was passing the town hall and heard the music. It was flat and soft, like the rest of the World now, but still he heard it.

"The dance. I missed everything, every chance… but maybe it's not too late. I have Horse, and if they could only see…"

Horse turned, stepped through the wall into the Town Hall, and into the midst of a party.

"Hey, did you *see* Jimmy today?"

"Yeah. *That* was cool!"

All done up in shades of gray, like everything else in Jimmy's new way of looking at the world, it took him a moment to recognize Billy Yazzie. He was talking with one of the other boys who had been at the corral chasing Alice Begay, though Jimmy could not recall his name.

"I know," said Billy. "I thought I was good, but I can't do *half* that stuff he did. I don't get it—Tsosi doesn't even *own* a horse."

Jimmy slipped from Horse's back in a daze.

"Hey, is it me? Are you guys talking about me?"

They didn't respond, didn't even look at him. They just stood side-by-side, staring toward the dance floor.

"What a lucky bastard," Billy said. Jimmy followed his gaze and saw…

…himself, dancing in the middle of the town hall with Alice Begay.

*"But… that's me! But it can't be me! **I'm** me!"*

*He leapt in front of Billy and his companion, blocking their view, but they simply stared at him—stared **through** him. He waved his arms.*

"Guys? Guys! I'm right here!"

They continued chatting, completely unaware of him.

Frustrated, Jimmy shoved Billy—and, expecting resistance but finding none, stumbled right through the boys. The two of them walked off, unaware he had even been there.

Jimmy shouted, panic rising. "What's going on? Somebody tell me what's going on! Anybody? Please?"

There was applause as the music stopped. Jimmy looked to the dance floor and saw himself break away from Alice Begay's embrace. She held his hand, making the touch linger as he walked away until the distance became too great, then she reluctantly released his fingers. As Jimmy watched, his body walked through the crowd toward the punchbowl at the back of the hall.

He hurried, passing through men and women, boys and girls, on his way to meet himself and find out what was going on, but slowed as he neared himself, the realization of what he was seeing pushing through the shock and panic.

He was in color. Everyone else in the hall was colorless and drab, the way he'd seen the world since landing on Horse's back. Even Alice Begay was colorless, almost lifeless, but he, Jimmy Tsosi, was full of color, and full of life, and so, so *real*.

Like Horse of the Plains.

Jimmy opened his mouth to speak as his body used a dipper to fill his cup with punch, but his body spoke first.

"Hello, James Tsosi."

The words, the voice, to his ears it sounded like his own voice, but in his head it was different. The words felt dry and precise and raspy and familiar. They felt like—

"Grandfather Whitefeather?"

His body nodded, smiling.

"What are you… how did you… I—"

"You killed me, James Tsosi," said the old man's voice in his head. *"Murdered me in my bed. That was a bad, bad thing, but I was an old man. My time was almost at hand. I was preparing to pass over, to take the Great Journey across the sea to the Land Beyond the Sky. Horse of the Plains had come to guide me, and I was ready to go."*

Grandfather Whitefeather turned to look at Jimmy Tsosi, using Jimmy's own head to do it, and the smile became hard.

"And then, James Tsosi, you stole Horse. Took my Guide and left me lost in the World of Men. But you left something behind, James Tsosi. Right next to my old body, with its burst lungs and shattered brain, you left your young, strong, healthy body. Left your body empty, without a spirit."

His body chuckled, an old man's chuckle, a dark, unpleasant sound.

"An even trade, I thought. You took my life and everything I had left. I took yours. You should have let Horse of the Plains take you to the Land Beyond the Sky, James Tsosi, for there is nothing left for you here."

"But I—" Jimmy began, turning to look for Horse.

"It is too late. You have stepped from the back of First Horse here in the World of Men, but first you frightened him. First you angered him. He has left you here, James Tsosi, as lost and alone as old Warrior in my story. But unlike Warrior, you have made no offerings. You have not honored the Spirits, but abused them. Horse will not return for you, nor will Dog come for you. Nor will any other Spirit, Great or small, come to help you as you wander this world."

Grandfather Whitefeather drained his cup.

*"I have to get back now, or they will miss me. I can see from the memories in this body that you believed the young people of the village to be concerned with horses above all other things. I can tell you that you were right—it is a good place for someone to grow up if they have great knowledge of horses, and trick riding is much easier if the horse **wants** you to succeed."*

Grandfather Whitefeather placed his cup in the barrel by the punch table.

"You have received your greatest wish, James Tsosi. The people here see you. The girl of your dreams likes you, and you fill the boys with envy."

Grandfather Whitefeather turned his back on Jimmy and began walking back toward his new friends.

*"It is a shame, is it not, James Tsosi, that you are no longer **you**?"*

*Jimmy stood by the punch table and watched himself walk away, watched the other kids close up about him, slapping him on the back or reaching to touch him in greeting, watched Alice Begay smile her beautiful smile, and it was for **him**.*

*And he wept, crying for someone, **anyone** to help him. To hear him. To see him. But they all walked past him—even **through** him—without ever noticing he was there.*

End of the Road
by
JG Faherty

Tyler Jones only turned his back to the convenience store windows for a moment, but that was long enough for him to miss his father walking in.

"Well, ain't this just my lucky night. You're making things easy for me, boy."

Tyler reacted instantly to his father's voice, dropping his soda and dashing for the door, but he was still too slow. Henry grabbed him by the jacket and spun him into a rack of potato chips and pretzels. Snack bags flew in all directions as Tyler fell to the floor, plastic and chips crackling and snapping beneath him.

"You made a fool outta me, sonny-boy. Now be a man and take what you got comin', and we'll go home and put this behind us," Henry said, clenching his hands into meaty fists.

Tyler wasn't surprised his father had come after him, although he hadn't expected to be found so soon. Henry Jones wasn't the kind of man to sit back and wait when he wanted something. Especially if that something was revenge for Tyler exposing him to the whole town as a wife beater and child abuser.

"I ain't goin' home," Tyler said, kicking out with both feet.

Henry grabbed him by the ankles and pulled him forward. Tyler kicked and pulled until his feet slid from Henry's grasp, leaving the older man holding two sneakers. Henry stumbled back, and Tyler used the opportunity to get up and run out the door.

Halfway across the parking lot, he heard his father yell, "Go ahead and run! I'm still gonna beat your ass when I find you!"

Tyler glanced back. Henry stood in the doorway, his craggy features twisted in anger. Willing his legs to move faster, Tyler sprinted across the road and into the line of trees bordering the street, his only thought to put as much distance between him and his father as he could.

The rough, pitted blacktop road meandered through the landscape like a hungry blacksnake, with scattered stars and a thin sliver of moon providing just enough light to see by.

Since escaping his father at the convenience store, Tyler had spent the past two hours cutting through yards and crossing neighborhoods. He'd followed Swamp Road for a ways, hiding behind trees whenever headlights appeared, and then taken Dark Hallow Road when he came to it, making his way slowly toward the only safe place he could think of: his Aunt Cindy's house. She lived past the Fountainville town line, however, a seven-mile trek that seemed more like a hundred miles in the lonely darkness.

The soft slap of Tyler's sock-clad feet made him aware of the curiously silent night. Whereas before there'd been a concert of chirps, screeches, and rasps from nocturnal insects and birds, now the wildlife seemed to have paused, while his own labored breathing followed like the panting of a great wolf pacing him just out of sight. The wisps of fog swirling across the ground added to the eeriness, and the occasional snap of branches as something dashed for safety in the woods didn't help, either.

A bright glow appeared up ahead, and Tyler descended into the gully bordering the road, even though it didn't look like his father's truck. Henry's '79 Chevy pickup had a distinctive look, with fog lights on the roof and across the front grill, but Tyler knew he couldn't take the chance that Henry might've sent some of his beer buddies out looking, too.

The car went past without slowing down. Deciding he needed to take a rest, Tyler found a spot where he could sit down out of sight. Closing his eyes, he leaned back and took several deep breaths, trying to relax. The damp soil soaked through his pants, adding to the chill of the spring night, but it felt good against his sore leg muscles. His feet, which had gone numb a long time ago, came back to life, screaming their agony at him. He didn't have to look to know his socks were torn to shreds and his feet covered in cuts and blisters.

A quick glance at his watch showed there were still several hours of darkness left. He figured it would take all night to reach Aunt Cindy's. That meant he couldn't waste time sitting on his butt. He sighed and slowly got to his feet, wincing as they made contact with the rough gravel.

"Are you okay, son?"

Tyler jumped at the voice, his body reacting even as he realized it wasn't his father. A short, thin man stood at the top of the embankment, looking down at him with a sad expression. He wore dark pants and a long, shapeless coat that seemed too warm for the night.

"Yeah, I'm fine." Tyler climbed back up to the road. "I'm Tyler. What's your name?"

The man, who looked about fifty or so, stared at him and then shook his head. "It doesn't matter anymore. Can I walk with you?"

"I guess. Where you goin'?"

They started down the road, the man's dark clothes blending with the night so well that at times he almost seemed nothing more than a disembodied head floating down the highway. Despite the oddity of coming across someone on an empty road, Tyler's relief at having company outweighed his natural suspicion of strangers. Besides, he had the old man by a couple of inches and twenty pounds, should the guy turn out to be a weirdo.

"Nowhere in particular. Just walking," the man said.

Ahead of them, the road rose up in a long, steep hill. Tyler's legs protested at the added work, and a small moan escaped him.

"Are you sure you're all right?" the man asked again.

"I told you, I'm fine. Just tired, that's all."

"What did he do to you?"

Tyler glanced over at the stranger. The man's head was down, but his voice carried the bitter sorrow of shared experience.

Maybe he's some kind of counselor or shrink.

"Nothin' he ain't done a hundred times before. I came home from school and found him hittin' my little sister. I tossed my basketball in his face and took off. Called the police. Now I'm headin' to my Aunt's, gonna stay there a while 'til things cool down."

The dark-haired man didn't say anything, just kept walking, his pale face still aimed at the ground.

"What's your deal?" Tyler asked. "You in trouble or something?"

The man nodded. "I did something wrong. Something bad. Since then I've been all alone."

Tyler opened his mouth to respond but had no words. The man's voice dripped with so much pain it made Tyler feel like crying. He tried to imagine what the man could have done that was so awful it cost him his family and friends. Did he cheat on his wife? Murder someone?

What if he's got a gun?

It came to Tyler that maybe walking with the man wasn't such a good idea after all. Keeping an eye on the man's hands, he moved toward the edge of the road as they reached the top of a long rise, putting several yards between him and the stranger. If the man noticed, he didn't say anything.

Tyler was trying to decide if he should duck into the woods when he heard something behind them, a low growl like a wild beast, only he recognized the sound as something much worse.

The sound of an idling engine.

Tyler turned around, then threw his arms over his face as bright headlights burst to life a hundred feet down the hill.

Oh, hell.

He started running, all thoughts of the stranger forgotten. He had no idea how long Henry had been following him, creeping closer, seeing how near he could get to his prey. A mechanical roar shattered the night as his father hit the gas, the 350-horse power engine propelling the truck forward.

Tyler veered to the left, thinking he could jump into the ditch, climb the other side, and head into the woods. However, somewhere along the way the gully had disappeared; now the edge of the road ended at a sharp drop-off that went down at least twenty feet to the jumbled rocks of a dry stream bed.

Henry's truck drew closer as the road flattened out, and Tyler knew he had only seconds to make a decision.

If I can get over to the other lane, maybe I can make it into the woods on that side before he turns the truck around.

Putting all he had into a last burst of speed, he cut across the road. Everything stood out in clear detail as the truck's headlights and roof lights turned the road bright as day.

With less than ten feet to go, and the sound of the Chevy louder than anything he'd ever heard, Tyler did something he hadn't done in years.

He prayed.

Please God, let me make this. Please—

Something heavy hit him in the side and the world exploded around him. The ground fell away from his feet and then rose up again to batter his chest and shoulder, dirt and gravel slicing him like a thousand tiny knives. He fought to regain his breath, dimly aware of the truck skidding to a stop nearby and then backing up, the twin high beams pinning him like spotlights.

Colored spots danced in his vision as he rose to his knees. The left side of his body felt numb and painful all at once, like the time he'd hit the water wrong after jumping from the high board.

Something moved toward him, a blurred image that resolved into his father's blocky form.

"Boy, you better hope you didn't dent my door." Henry laughed once, low and mean, and then snorted through his broken nose, a wet, nasty sound that ended with him spitting a bloody gob of snot and mucous onto the road next to Tyler. "That'd be another beatin' on top of the ones I'm already gonna give ya."

Tyler's gaze rose up from his father's heavy work boots, up and up. Henry seemed to have grown ten-feet-tall. In the harsh light of the headlamps, Henry's face resembled a primitive, angry stone god come to life.

Henry prodded at Tyler's leg with one foot. "Get yer ass moving, boy. 'Less you want me to kick you like a dog."

Tyler hauled himself up on shaky legs, prepared for the inevitable.

"Leave him alone," a quiet, serious voice said.

The man in the black clothes emerged from the darkness. In the stark glow of the truck's lights, his skin was the same pale white as a fish's belly.

"And just who the hell might you be?" Henry asked. Next to him, the stranger looked more like a child than Tyler did.

"You won't hurt him anymore," the man said, his voice barely audible over the rumbling motor of Henry's truck.

For a moment, Tyler thought the stranger had said *I won't hurt him anymore*, but that didn't make sense. Tyler rubbed his head, wondering if he'd hit it harder than he'd thought.

"Got yourself a friend, Tyler? Maybe I'll just teach the both of you a lesson." Henry took a mighty swing, grunting from the effort.

The stranger remained motionless while Henry's fist passed right though him.

"Jesus-H-Christ." Henry stepped back, his eyes wide.

That's when Tyler realized who the man was. Growing up, he'd heard the tales of the ghostly figure who roamed Dark Hallow Road, a teacher who'd abused his students a century ago and now haunted the area where the schoolhouse used to be, his spirit doomed to never move on until he atoned for his sins. Everyone knew someone who said they knew someone who'd seen the ghost walking the roads at night, and over the years more than one accident on Dark Hallow Road had been attributed to cars swerving to avoid the man with the haunted eyes.

The apparition took a step toward Henry, who backed up again in response.

"There's no escape," the man said. "Not for me, not for you."

"Get away." Henry retreated two more steps.

The ghost continued walking forward, forcing Henry into the center of the road and back toward the Chevy.

He was halfway there when the delivery truck came over the rise, a big one loaded with beer and soda and already accelerating into the flat. The driver had time to blow his horn once, and then the tortured screams of twisting steel, air brakes, and skidding tires filled the night with a prehistoric-sounding cacophony.

Tyler dove to the ground and covered his head with his arms as the truck plowed into the Chevy, sending tons of steel crashing into Henry. Glass and metal rained across the highway, stinging Tyler's exposed flesh like angry bees. Only when the noise of the crash disappeared, replaced by the tick of cooling metal and the hissing of escaping steam, did Tyler get to his feet and cautiously approach the smoking wreckage.

The two vehicles had ended up a hundred feet down the road. The driver of the delivery truck hung halfway out of his windshield, unmoving. The Chevy was a crumpled mess, its twisted body wedged in the truck's grill as if being consumed. One of Henry's denim-clad legs, still wearing its boot, lay by itself in the middle of the road; an arm peeked out from beneath the Chevy.

Something moved in the dim glow of the rig's one remaining headlight. The ghost stepped forward, passing through groaning steel as easy as wind through empty branches, the somber look still on his face.

"Thank you," Tyler said, no longer afraid.

The man raised his hand and then turned away. The wind picked up out of nowhere, peppering Tyler's face with dirt and flapping the ghost's coat as he walked toward the far side of the road. When he reached the gully, his body dissolved into a swirling gray mist that quickly turned into a ball of hazy blue light and floated away into the woods.

Tyler blinked sand, grit, and tears from his eyes. When he looked again, he stood alone.

A feeling of release washed over him, and he wondered if maybe he wasn't the only person who'd been set free.

He sat down and waited for help to arrive.

For the first time in years, Tyler Jones was looking forward to going home.

His Wife's Deceased Sister
by
Frank R. Stockton

originally published in *A Chosen Few Short Stories*, 1895

It is now five years since an event occurred which so colored my life, or rather so changed some of its original colors, that I have thought it well to write an account of it, deeming that its lessons may be of advantage to persons whose situations in life are similar to my own.

When I was quite a young man I adopted literature as a profession; and having passed through the necessary preparatory grades, I found myself, after a good many years of hard and often unremunerative work, in possession of what might be called a fair literary practice. My articles, grave, gay, practical, or fanciful, had come to be considered with a favor by the editors of the various periodicals for which I wrote, on which I found in time I could rely with a very comfortable certainty. My productions created no enthusiasm in the reading public; they gave me no great reputation or very valuable pecuniary return; but they were always accepted, and my receipts from them, at the time to which I have referred, were as regular and reliable as a salary, and quite sufficient to give me more than a comfortable support.

It was at this time I married. I had been engaged for more than a year, but had not been willing to assume the support of a wife until I felt that my pecuniary position was so assured that I could do so with full satisfaction to my own conscience. There was now no doubt in regard to this position, either in my mind or in that of my wife. I worked with great steadiness and regularity; I knew exactly where to place the productions of my pen, and could calculate, with a fair degree of accuracy, the sums I should receive for them. We were by no means rich; but we had enough, and were thoroughly satisfied and content.

Those of my readers who are married will have no difficulty in remembering the peculiar ecstasy of the first weeks of their wedded life. It is then that the flowers of this world bloom brightest; that its sun is the most genial; that its clouds are the scarcest; that its fruit is the most delicious; that the air is the most balmy; that its cigars are of the highest flavor; that the warmth and radiance of early matrimonial felicity so rarefies the intellectual atmosphere that the soul mounts higher, and enjoys a wider prospect, than ever before.

These experiences were mine. The plain claret of my mind was changed to sparkling champagne, and at the very height of its effervescence, I wrote a story. The happy thought that then struck me for a tale was of a very peculiar character; and it interested me so much that I went to work at it with great delight and enthusiasm, and finished it in a comparatively short time. The title of the story was "His Wife's Deceased Sister;" and when I read it to Hypatia she was delighted with it, and at times was so affected by its pathos that her uncontrollable emotion caused a sympathetic dimness in my eyes, which prevented my seeing the words I had written. When the reading was ended, and my wife had dried her eyes, she turned to me and said, "This story will make your fortune. There has been nothing so pathetic since Lamartine's 'History of a Servant girl.'"

As soon as possible the next day I sent my story to the editor of the periodical for which I wrote most frequently, and in which my best productions generally appeared. In a few days I had a letter from the editor, in which he praised my story as he had never before praised anything from my pen. It had interested and charmed, he said, not only himself, but all his associates in the office. Even old Gibson, who never cared to read anything until it was in proof, and who never praised anything which had not a joke in it, was induced by the example of the others to read this manuscript, and shed, as he asserted, the first tears that had come from his eyes since his final paternal castigation some forty years before. The story would appear, the editor assured me, as soon as he could possibly find room for it.

If anything could make our skies more genial, our flowers brighter, and the flavor of our fruit and cigars more delicious, it was a letter like this. And when, in a very short time, the story was published, we found that the reading public was inclined to receive it with as much sympathetic interest and favor as had been shown to it by the editors. My personal friends soon began to express enthusiastic opinions upon it. It was highly praised in many of the leading newspapers; and, altogether, it was a great literary success. I am not inclined to be vain of my writings, and, in general, my wife tells me, think too little of them; but I did feel a good deal of pride and satisfaction in the success of "His Wife's Deceased Sister." If it did not make my fortune, as my wife asserted that it would, it certainly would help me very much in my literary career.

In less than a month from the writing of this story, something very unusual and unexpected happened to me. A manuscript was returned by the editor of the periodical in which "His Wife's Deceased Sister" had appeared.

"It is a good story," he wrote, "but not equal to what you have just done. You have made a great hit; and it would not do to interfere with the reputation you have gained by publishing anything inferior to 'His Wife's Deceased Sister,' which has had such a deserved success."

I was so unaccustomed to having my work thrown back on my hands that I think I must have turned a little pale when I read the letter. I said nothing of the matter to my wife, for it would be foolish to drop such grains of sand as this into the smoothly oiled machinery of our domestic felicity; but I immediately sent the story to another editor. I am not able to express the astonishment I felt when, in the course of a week, it was sent back to me. The tone of the note accompanying it indicated a somewhat injured feeling on the part of the editor.

"I am reluctant," he said, "to decline a manuscript from you; but you know very well that if you sent me anything like 'His Wife's Deceased Sister' it would be most promptly accepted."

I now felt obliged to speak of the affair to my wife, who was quite as much surprised, though perhaps not quite as much shocked, as I had been.

"Let us read the story again," she said, "and see what is the matter with it."

When we had finished its perusal, Hypatia remarked, "It is quite as good as many of the stories you have had printed, and I think it very interesting; although, of course, it is not equal to 'His Wife's Deceased Sister.'"

"Of course not," said I; "that was an inspiration that I cannot expect every day. But there must be something wrong about this last story which we do not perceive. Perhaps my recent success may have made me a little careless in writing it."

"I don't believe that," said Hypatia.

"At any rate," I continued, "I will lay it aside, and will go to work on a new one."

In due course of time I had another manuscript finished, and I sent it to my favorite periodical. It was retained some weeks, and then came back to me. "It will never do," the editor wrote, quite warmly, "for you to go backward. The demand for the number containing 'His Wife's Deceased Sister' still continues, and we do not intend to let you disappoint that great body of readers who would be so eager to see another number containing one of your stories."

I sent this manuscript to four other periodicals, and from each of them was it returned with remarks to the effect that, although it was not a bad story in itself, it was not what they would expect from the author of "His Wife's Deceased Sister."

The editor of a Western magazine wrote to me for a story to be published in a special number which he would issue for the holidays. I wrote him one of the character and length he asked for, and sent it to him. By return mail it came back to me.

"I had hoped," the editor wrote, "when I asked for a story from your pen, to receive something like 'His Wife's Deceased Sister,' and I must own that I am very much disappointed."

I was so filled with anger when I read this note that I openly objurgated "His Wife's Deceased Sister."

"You must excuse me," I said to my astonished wife, "for expressing myself thus in your presence; but that confounded story will be the ruin of me yet. Until it is forgotten nobody will ever take anything I write."

"And you cannot expect it ever to be forgotten," said Hypatia, with tears in her eyes.

It is needless for me to detail my literary efforts in the course of the next few months. The ideas of the editors with whom my principal business had been done, in regard to my literary ability, had been so raised by my unfortunate story of "His Wife's Deceased Sister" that I found it was of no use to send them anything of lesser merit. And as to the other journals which I tried, they evidently considered it an insult for me to send them matter inferior to that by which my reputation had lately risen. The fact was that my successful story had ruined me. My income was at an end, and want actually stared me in the face; and I must admit that I did not like the expression of its countenance. It was of no use for me to try to write another story like "His Wife's Deceased Sister." I could not get married every time I began a new manuscript, and it was the exaltation of mind caused by my wedded felicity which produced that story.

"It's perfectly dreadful!" said my wife. "If I *had* had a sister, and she had died, I would have thought it was my fault."

"It could not be your fault," I answered, "and I do not think it was mine. I had no intention of deceiving anybody into the belief that I could do that sort of thing every time, and it ought not to be expected of me. Suppose Raphael's patrons had tried to keep him screwed up to the pitch of the Sistine Madonna, and had refused to buy anything which was not as good as that. In that case, I think he would have occupied a much earlier and narrower grave than that on which Mr. Morris Moore hangs his funeral decorations."

"But, my dear," said Hypatia, who was posted on such subjects, "the Sistine Madonna was one of his latest paintings."

"Very true," said I; "but if he had married, as I did, he would have painted it earlier."

I was walking homeward one afternoon about this time, when I met Barbel—a man I had known well in my early literary career. He was now about fifty years of age, but looked older. His hair and beard were quite gray; and his clothes, which were of the same general hue, gave me the idea that they, like his hair, had originally been black. Age is very hard on a man's external appointments. Barbel had an air of having been to let for a long time, and quite out of repair. But there was a kindly gleam in his eye, and he welcomed me cordially.

"Why, what is the matter, old fellow?" said he. "I never saw you look so woebegone."

I had no reason to conceal anything from Barbel. In my younger days he had been of great use to me, and he had a right to know the state of my affairs. I laid the whole case plainly before him.

"Look here," he said, when I had finished, "come with me to my room: I have something I would like to say to you there."

I followed Barbel to his room. It was at the top of a very dirty and well-worn house which stood in a narrow and lumpy street, into which few vehicles ever penetrated, except the ash and garbage carts, and the rickety wagons of the venders of stale vegetables.

"This is not exactly a fashionable promenade," said Barbel, as we approached the house; "but in some respects it reminds me of the streets in Italian towns, where the palaces lean over toward each other in such a friendly way."

Barbel's room was, to my mind, rather more doleful than the street. It was dark, it was dusty, and cobwebs hung from every corner. The few chairs upon the floor and the books upon a greasy table seemed to be afflicted with some dorsal epidemic, for their backs were either gone or broken. A little bedstead in the corner was covered with a spread made of New York *Heralds*, with their edges pasted together.

"There is nothing better," said Barbel, noticing my glance toward this novel counterpane, "for a bed covering than newspapers: they keep you as warm as a blanket, and are much lighter. I used to use *Tribunes*, but they rattled too much."

The only part of the room which was well lighted was at one end near the solitary window. Here, upon a table with a spliced leg, stood a little grindstone.

"At the other end of the room," said Barbel, "is my cook stove, which you can't see unless I light the candle in the bottle which stands by it; but if you don't care particularly to examine it, I won't go to the expense of lighting up. You might pick up a good many odd pieces of bric-à-brac around here, if you chose to strike a match and investigate; but I would not advise you to do so. It would pay better to throw the things out of the window than to carry them downstairs. The particular piece of indoor decoration to which I wish to call your attention is this."

And he led me to a little wooden frame which hung against the wall near the window. Behind a dusty piece of glass it held what appeared to be a leaf from a small magazine or journal.

"There," said he, "you see a page from the *Grasshopper*, a humorous paper which flourished in this city some half-dozen years ago. I used to write regularly for that paper, as you may remember."

"Oh yes, indeed!" I exclaimed. "And I shall never forget your 'Conundrum of the Anvil' which appeared in it. How often have I laughed at that most wonderful conceit, and how often have I put it to my friends!"

Barbel gazed at me silently for a moment, and then he pointed to the frame. "That printed page," he said, solemnly, "contains the 'Conundrum of the Anvil.' I hang it there so that I can see it while I work. That conundrum ruined me. It was the last thing I wrote for the *Grasshopper*. How I ever came to imagine it I cannot tell. It is one of those things which occur to a man but once in a lifetime. After the wild shout of delight with which the public greeted that conundrum, my subsequent efforts met with hoots of derision. The *Grasshopper* turned its hind legs upon me. I sank from bad to worse—much worse—until at last I found myself reduced to my present occupation, which is that of grinding points to pins. By this I procure my bread, coffee, and tobacco, and sometimes potatoes and meat. One day while I was hard at work an organ grinder came into the street below. He played the serenade from 'Trovatore;' and the familiar notes brought back visions of old days and old delights, when the successful writer wore good clothes and sat at operas, when he looked into sweet eyes and talked of Italian airs, when his future appeared all a succession of bright scenery and joyous acts, without any provision for a drop curtain. And as my ear listened, and my mind wandered in this happy retrospect, my every faculty seemed exalted, and, without any thought upon the matter, I ground points upon my pins so fine, so regular and smooth, that they would have pierced with ease the leather of a boot, or slipped among, without abrasion, the finest threads of rare old lace. When the organ stopped, and I fell back into my real world of cobwebs and mustiness, I gazed upon the pins I had just ground, and, without a moment's hesitation, I threw them into the street, and reported the lot as spoiled. This cost me a little money, but it saved me my livelihood."

After a few moments of silence, Barbel resumed. "I have no more to say to you, my young friend. All I want you to do is to look upon that framed conundrum, then upon this grindstone, and then to go home and reflect. As for me, I have a gross of pins to grind before the sun goes down."

I cannot say that my depression of mind was at all relieved by what I had seen and heard. I had lost sight of Barbel for some years, and I had supposed him still floating on the sun-sparkling stream of prosperity where I had last seen him. It was a great shock to me to find him in such a condition of poverty and squalor, and to see a man who had originated the "Conundrum of the Anvil" reduced to the soul-depressing occupation of grinding pin points. As I walked and thought, the dreadful picture of a totally eclipsed future arose before my mind. The moral of Barbel sank deep into my heart.

When I reached home I told my wife the story of my friend Barbel. She listened with a sad and eager interest.

"I am afraid," she said, "if our fortunes do not quickly mend, that we shall have to buy two little grindstones. You know I could help you at that sort of thing."

For a long time we sat together and talked, and devised many plans for the future. I did not think it necessary yet for me to look out for a pin-contract; but I must find some way of making money, or we should starve to death. Of course the first thing that suggested itself was the possibility of finding some other business;

but, apart from the difficulty of immediately obtaining remunerative work in occupations to which I had not been trained, I felt a great and natural reluctance to give up a profession for which I had carefully prepared myself, and which I had adopted as my life work. It would be very hard for me to lay down my pen forever, and to close the top of my inkstand upon all the bright and happy fancies which I had seen mirrored in its tranquil pool. We talked and pondered the rest of that day and a good deal of the night, but we came to no conclusion as to what it would be best for us to do.

The next day I determined to go and call upon the editor of the journal for which, in happier days, before the blight of "His Wife's Deceased Sister" rested upon me, I used most frequently to write, and, having frankly explained my condition to him, to ask his advice. The editor was a good man, and had always been my friend. He listened with great attention to what I told him, and evidently sympathized with me in my trouble.

"As we have written to you," he said, "the only reason why we did not accept the manuscripts you sent us was that they would have disappointed the high hopes that the public had formed in regard to you. We have had letter after letter asking when we were going to publish another story like 'His Wife's Deceased Sister.' We felt, and we still feel, that it would be wrong to allow you to destroy the fair fabric which yourself has raised. But," he added, with a kind smile, "I see very plainly that your well-deserved reputation will be of little advantage to you if you should starve at the moment that its genial beams are, so to speak, lighting you up."

"Its beams are not genial," I answered. "They have scorched and withered me."

"How would you like," said the editor, after a short reflection, "to allow us to publish the stories you have recently written under some other name than your own? That would satisfy us and the public, would put money in your pocket, and would not interfere with your reputation."

Joyfully I seized that noble fellow by the hand, and instantly accepted his proposition. "Of course," said I, "a reputation is a very good thing; but no reputation can take the place of food, clothes, and a house to live in; and I gladly agree to sink my over-illumined name into oblivion, and to appear before the public as a new and unknown writer."

"I hope that need not be for long," he said, "for I feel sure that you will yet write stories as good as 'His Wife's Deceased Sister.'"

All the manuscripts I had on hand I now sent to my good friend the editor, and in due and proper order they appeared in his journal under the name of John Darmstadt, which I had selected as a substitute for my own, permanently disabled. I made a similar arrangement with other editors, and John Darmstadt received the credit of everything that proceeded from my pen. Our circumstances now became very comfortable, and occasionally we even allowed ourselves to indulge in little dreams of prosperity.

Time passed on very pleasantly; one year, another, and then a little son was born to us. It is often difficult, I believe, for thoughtful persons to decide whether the beginning of their conjugal career, or the earliest weeks in the life of their first-born, be the happiest and proudest period of their existence. For myself I can only say that the same exaltation of mind, the same rarefication of idea and invention, which succeeded upon my wedding day came upon me now. As then, my ecstatic emotions crystallized themselves into a motive for a story, and without delay I set myself to work upon it. My boy was about six weeks old when the manuscript was finished; and one evening, as we sat before a comfortable fire in our sitting-room, with the curtains drawn, and the soft lamp lighted, and the baby sleeping soundly in the adjoining chamber, I read the story to my wife.

When I had finished, my wife arose and threw herself into my arms. "I was never so proud of you," she said, her glad eyes sparkling, "as I am at this moment. That is a wonderful story! It is—indeed I am sure it is—just as good as 'His Wife's Deceased Sister.'"

As she spoke these words a sudden and chilling sensation crept over us both. All her warmth and fervor, and the proud and happy glow engendered within me by this praise and appreciation from one I loved, vanished in an instant. We stepped apart, and gazed upon each other with pallid faces. In the same moment the terrible truth had flashed upon us both.

This story *was* as good as "His Wife's Deceased Sister!"

We stood silent. The exceptional lot of Barbel's super-pointed pins seemed to pierce our very souls. A dreadful vision rose before me of an impending fall and crash, in which our domestic happiness should vanish, and our prospects for our boy be wrecked, just as we had begun to build them up.

My wife approached me and took my hand in hers, which was as cold as ice. "Be strong and firm," she said. "A great danger threatens us, but you must brace yourself against it. Be strong and firm."

I pressed her hand, and we said no more that night.

The next day I took the manuscript I had just written, and carefully enfolded it in stout wrapping paper. Then I went to a neighboring grocery store and bought a small, strong tin box, originally intended for biscuits, with a cover that fitted tightly. In this I placed my manuscript; and then I took the box to a tinsmith and had the top fastened on with hard solder. When I went home I ascended into the garret, and brought down to my study a ship's cash box, which had once belonged to one of my family who was a sea captain. This box was very heavy, and firmly bound with iron, and was secured by two massive locks. Calling my wife, I told her of the contents of the tin case, which I then placed in the box, and, having shut down the heavy lid, I doubly locked it.

"This key," I said, putting it in my pocket, "I shall throw into the river when I go out this afternoon."

My wife watched me eagerly, with a pallid and firm, set countenance, but upon which I could see the faint glimmer of returning happiness.

"Wouldn't it be well," she said, "to secure it still further by sealing wax and pieces of tape?"

"No," I said. "I do not believe that any one will attempt to tamper with our prosperity. And now, my dear," I continued, in an impressive voice, "no one but you, and, in the course of time, our son, shall know that this manuscript exists. When I am dead, those who survive me may, if they see fit, cause this box to be split open and the story published. The reputation it may give my name cannot harm me then."

The Story of Alfred Maus
by
David G. Robertson

On the morning of his fifty-third birthday, Frances Maus gave her husband a sincere kiss and a subscription to the world's five oldest literary magazines, as was their custom. Alfred surprised her by beginning to sob quietly into his tea. Mediocre tears of timid desperation rolled down his face and sploshed onto the *Times* crossword.

"Alfred, what's wrong? This is not like you."

"I've left it too long," he said, sniffing loudly.

"What do you mean, Alfred?"

"My writing. It's too late. I'm never going to be able to write anything."

Mrs. Maus, having been in love with a Post Office Assistant for almost thirty years now and never with a writer at all, sighed and rubbed his quivering back. "You just have to start getting it down, Alfred. Get some practice in."

He peered up at her through steamed, circular lenses. "There's no point writing anything if it's not going to be good enough. There's so much dross out there already. So much vacuous verbiage, echoing emptily in the earhole of eternity." His voice was like wet gravel.

"Do you think that whoever it was that painted the Mona Lisa did it the first time they picked up a brush?" she asked. "Are any of your favorite books the first thing that the author ever wrote?"

"What do you know of literature, Frances?"

"Maybe nothing," his wife replied, and looked across the breakfast table, the spotless crockery, the tea and toast and marmalade made just the way he liked them. "But I know a damn site more than you do about life, and about getting things done."

Alfred went to work at the Post Office as always, and when he returned that evening, his supper was on the table waiting for him, as always. Afterwards, as his wife settled down with her knitting to watch soap operas, he retired as always to his tiny study, to sit tight-lipped with pen poised over the blank page of the notebook lying on his immaculate desk. He knew that if he didn't write something soon, anything, then he never would, and this additional pressure did not help the situation. In the past three months, he had managed to add not one sentence to his already slim canon. It has to be good, he thought, has to be worthy of print. His work must shine out like a beacon, an Eternal Flame to the stronger metaphor, the higher concept, the faster wit. Such an idea cannot be forced; it comes when you're ready. Clearly, he was not.

Some writers write because they have to; they are driven to get whatever was eating inside of them out onto the page; the Brontës, or Kerouac, maybe. Others, such as Swift, wrote to get across a point they had to make. Then there are those novels written primarily out of necessity, simply because by penning such tales you can earn the money you need for your family—a job, more or less. But Alfred saw that Golden Chain stretching back through history, its beginning lost now in the mist, and wanted to forge the next link and add his name to that exclusive, magical list. So much of his mental time and energy had been spent in planning some terminated tale or other, hanging plot-pieces from the barbs on a concept, only for it to be finally abandoned; comparatively few were the opening paragraphs which languished stillborn atop the long, blank pages of the notebooks in his study.

He found himself wound up too tight to sleep. He sat up drinking brandy and watching the cat trying to catch a bluebottle. The cat was poised on the russet tiles, one paw raised, her sleek keen head following the fly as it circled. She seemed caught in a loop; she just watched, ready to pounce, and never made her move. Maus watched until close to dawn before finally creeping up the back stairs to his bed.

Fate was to intervene as he slept that night. The Idea came to him in a dream.

In the morning, he trotted off groggily to work, to the job that was only ever intended to last the summer while he saved enough money to go and write his masterpiece. As he weighed and stamped all day, cashed giro and settled bills, his dream was being processed in the sorting office of his subconscious. Symbolism checked it over, and finding the structure sound, dispatched it. Logic, finding some problems, marked it Address Unknown and sent it on to Memory, who furnished a couple of characters and smoothed some of the edges. Finally, it was delivered into the inbox of Consciousness at second post, and Alfred suddenly remembered his dream as he sauntered home. It had vivid imagery and a remarkably strong narrative, and even a twist at the end.

Frances noticed the uplift in his spirits that very evening as she heaped mashed potatoes onto his plate. The story was slowly taking shape in his mind. But Alfred Maus being the man he was, it was a long time yet before he put pen to page.

Over days and weeks, Maus considered every detail with intense care. Structurally, he knew the timing was everything. The tension had to be built carefully so the release came as an utter shock. He pondered and re-pondered every single sentence, shuffled synonyms and similes, until he was absolutely certain.

Then he pondered them all again, removing any clichés which had slipped through the net.

One muggy evening in July, after letting his Shepherd's Pie go down, he sat himself at his walnut desk and finally began to write. His silver Parker biro, a Christmas gift from his daughter, reflected the greenish lamplight. He ran the first line, so precious, so often considered, through his mind a couple of times, and it poured out onto the crisp foolscap. It was followed by a second, then a third. He paused, gazing lovingly and breathlessly at the raw, fresh paragraph that lay there. Pure thought transcribed via structure.

Then the fear took him again, the fear that it would turn out to be dross in the cold light of day, and his hand froze. It wasn't as good an opening as "In the beginning was the Word," was it? It was not as good as "riverran, past Eve and Adam's…," nor even, "It was a bright, cold day in April, and the clocks were striking thirteen." It was just another extraneous piece of literary fluff in the navel of the corpus.

The whole idea faded as if his mind were cheap fax paper. He laid his pen down with a sigh and went to bed.

The next evening, he sat down at his desk again. He had rehearsed the moment in his mind all day, planning exactly what he must write next. He focused himself and began to write, slowly and decisively, the muscles in his arms and shoulders tense. Ten minutes later, there they were: two whole paragraphs. He relaxed as a proud joy flooded him.

Then, a wonderful thing: a new sentence, one which he hadn't planned, appeared fully-formed in his brain. In shock, he wrote it down. He read it with his head cocked: it wasn't bad. He smiled to himself, amazed, and continued with the plan. He retired after savoring for the first time the experience of turning the page and continuing to write.

Over the weeks that followed, the story slowly emerged like a butterfly from its pupa, slowly at first, then quickly and easily. As he worked through all the drafts, he thought of diaphanous, multicolored wings drying in the sun. After putting down the closing sentence, he turned back to the first page and wrote the title at the top in large letters: *Quod Scriptus Scriptus*. He carefully typed two copies onto good quality paper, as crisp and white as his wife's china, and slipped a paperclip onto the corner of both. He laid them dead center on his blotter and sighed. His labor was complete. It was perfect, as much as he was capable of.

Then the old doubts began to resurface. What he needed was some objective, impartial criticism.

In her armchair by the fire, with a mug of milky tea and the cat curled purring on her lap, Frances Maus considered the manuscript with care. Her favorite TV show was ceremoniously missed as she read. Twice, a smile burst across her ruddy face. After finishing, she sat for a minute in silent thought.

"It's good," she said. "I like it."

"Didn't you think that the ending was a bit... odd?" Alfred asked nervously.

She shook her head. "No. It makes a kind of sense. Like a dream. It works." She pointed to a sentence on the third page. "I liked this bit."

It would take a further ten days of almost sleepless nights before Alfred Maus summoned the courage to post the envelope, prepared and sealed five days previously, which contained one story, typed; one cover letter to the editor, hand-written; one SAE, folded; and one glinting paperclip. He dithered by the post box a full four minutes before successfully dropping it in.

Shortly after, Alfred and Frances were delighted by a visit from their only grandchild. Martin was eleven, bright and well-behaved. After supper, he asked if it would be okay to watch Top of the Pops on television, and Frances said of course.

To Alfred, the pulsating noise the androgynous musicians produced could hardly be described as music. "Is this the fashion nowadays? Is this what you listen to?"

"It's called House music, Grandad. You do it with samplers."

"What on earth's a sampler?"

The boy shrugged. "I dunno."

Frances appeared in the kitchen doorway, tea towel in hand. "Stop going on at him, Alfred. Why don't you tell us all about what you're doing at school, Martin?"

The boy's face brightened immediately. "We're doing all about inventors. Alexander Graham Bell invented the telephone, and John Yogi Bear invented the TV."

"Would you like to be an inventor when you grow up?" asked Frances, and the boy nodded. "What would you invent?"

"Spaceships. Or laser guns."

"But someone's already invented those, Martin," said Alfred, patiently. "If you want to be an inventor, you have to come up with an idea that no one else has ever thought of."

The boy's face fell. "But there's none left! Everything's been thought of already!"

Alfred laughed kindly. "It always seems like that, until someone thinks of something new. Like Isaac Newton. People weren't asking why apples never fall up before he thought of gravity, were they, eh?"

The boy shook his head. "There isn't any more ideas, Grandad, not any more. We used them all up, so we got to use the old ones again." He nodded sidelong toward the TV. "That's what House music's all about."

One crisp Saturday morning in October, a large manila envelope woke the Mauses by thumping rudely onto the doormat. Alfred, in slippers, pajamas, and robe, retrieved it groggily. Recognizing his own handwriting, he realized immediately what it must be. It had been five weeks.

His SAE was heavy with paper. He forced his hand to break the seal and open the flap. A small sheaf slid into his hand; a letter and his manuscript, its paperclip gone and a thumbprint on the first page. It had been read.

Dear Alfred,
     I read your story with great interest.
     Your writing is rich and economical, and the word-play was excellent. I especially liked that bit on the third page.
     However, I regret to inform you that I cannot accept it, as it bears a strong resemblance to a story we published in Vol. 12 No. 4. I can only assume that this was accidental, or coincidental, so I return your manuscript with thanks, and look forward to reading any future contributions.
                         Yours,
                         Dave Canon, Editor

Alfred rubbed the sleep from his eyes and read the whole thing again to make sure he'd taken it in properly. Plagiarism? Am I dreaming?

"What is it, love?" his wife called sleepily from their room.

"Nothing really, I…" The thumping in his chest seemed so loud, drowning his words. It couldn't be a joke, could it? But who? He had no enemies, he hadn't even mentioned it to the girls at the Post Office.

He shuffled urgently into his little study, where the curtains that were never opened glowed with a cold dawn pink, and switched on his desk lamp with a tug. No, it was clear what had happened; the clique of toffs at the *Favourable Review* had decided to make an example of him, and give themselves a good old laugh in the process. *Well*, thought Alfred, *I'm not just going to lie down and die.*

On the shelves above his desk were his magazines, going back decades in chronological rows. He found number four of volume twelve of the *Favourable Review* in seconds, for that was what his neat ordering was meant to facilitate, after all. His finger scanned down the contents page, and his heart fell as he found the listing: *Quad Scriptus Scriptus*, by M.L. Ruthven, page twenty-three.

And there it was: that same opening line (not as good as the Gospel of John or *1984*), the same economy of description, same joke on the third page, same twist ending. An exclamation mark in parentheses appeared in his mind. Alfred was… stunned. Flabbergasted? No, that wasn't the right word… dumbstruck? He closed the magazine in a daze.

"What have I done?" He stared at the cover that mocked him and began to shake. Shame, thy name is Volume four, Number twelve.

Except he saw now that he held Number eleven. He had been reading the wrong magazine, they must have been the wrong way round on the shelf. He laid it down slowly, found the right one, and leafed to the contents page. *Quad Scriptus Scriptus*, by Adam Kadmon, was on page forty-two.

It won't be the same story, he thought, it can't be. It'll just be a coincidence. He felt curiously calm.

But it was the same. Before him, inky and tantamount, lay again the words that he had written, each noun identical, every verb verbatim. This just could not be. He turned to the next piece.

Quad Scriptus Scriptus. It simply started over again, beneath a different name. He flipped eight pages forward, and there was that opening again, so long and carefully considered. He tried to call his wife, but his throat made no sound.

He was turning pages quickly now, four or five at a time, heart pounding in his chest. On every one, *Quad Scriptus Scriptus.* Six times, all told, in that issue. He pulled down another and again saw page after page of his words. If they were ever really his at all.

He began to pull books from his shelves, seeking now not confirmation, but contradiction. *1984* had shed its opening in preference for his. Every book fell open at his story, no matter how many he tried. The dictionary was no longer alphabetical, but ran in the order he had spent so long refining, cycling the words he had used again and again. He scanned down the contents of *Shakespeare's Complete Works*, but the Bard had written only this one story, two hundred and eighty-two times. The same old tall tale told once more. Nothing was ever new, and never would be. The room began to spin.

His wife found him lying unconscious, a Bible lying open on the floor beside him.

The Interlopers
by
Saki

originally published in *The Toys of Peace and Other Papers*, 1918

In a forest of mixed growth somewhere on the eastern spurs of the Carpathians, a man stood one winter night watching and listening, as though he waited for some beast of the woods to come within the range of his vision, and, later, of his rifle. But the game for whose presence he kept so keen an outlook was none that figured in the sportsman's calendar as lawful and proper for the chase; Ulrich von Gradwitz patrolled the dark forest in quest of a human enemy.

The forest lands of Gradwitz were of wide extent and well-stocked with game; the narrow strip of precipitous woodland that lay on its outskirt was not remarkable for the game it harbored or the shooting it afforded, but it was the most jealously guarded of all its owner's territorial possessions. A famous law suit, in the days of his grandfather, had wrested it from the illegal possession of a neighboring family of petty landowners; the dispossessed party had never acquiesced in the judgment of the Courts, and a long series of poaching affrays and similar scandals had embittered the relationships between the families for three generations. The neighbor feud had grown into a personal one since Ulrich had come to be head of his family; if there was a man in the world whom he detested and wished ill to it was Georg Znaeym, the inheritor of the quarrel and the tireless game-snatcher and raider of the disputed border forest. The feud might, perhaps, have died down or been compromised if the personal ill-will of the two men had not stood in the way; as boys they had thirsted for one another's blood, as men each prayed that misfortune might fall on the other, and this wind-scourged winter night Ulrich had banded together his foresters to watch the dark forest, not in quest of four-footed quarry, but to keep a look-out for the prowling thieves whom he suspected of being afoot from across the land boundary. The roebuck, which usually kept in the sheltered hollows during a storm-wind, were running like driven things tonight, and there was movement and unrest among the creatures that were wont to sleep through the dark hours. Assuredly there was a disturbing element in the forest, and Ulrich could guess the quarter from whence it came.

He strayed away by himself from the watchers whom he had placed in ambush on the crest of the hill, and wandered far down the steep slopes amid the wild tangle of undergrowth, peering through the tree trunks and listening through the whistling and skirling of the wind and the restless beating of the branches for sight and sound of the marauders. If only on this wild night, in this dark, lone spot, he might come across Georg Znaeym, man to man, with none to witness—that was the wish that was uppermost in his thoughts. And as he stepped round the trunk of a huge beech he came face to face with the man he sought.

The two enemies stood glaring at one another for a long silent moment. Each had a rifle in his hand, each had hate in his heart and murder uppermost in his mind. The chance had come to give full play to the passions of a lifetime. But a man who has been brought up under the code of a restraining civilization cannot easily nerve himself to shoot down his neighbor in cold blood and without word spoken, except for an offence against his hearth and honor. And before the moment of hesitation had given way to action a deed of Nature's own violence overwhelmed them both. A fierce shriek of the storm had been answered by a splitting crash over their heads, and ere they could leap aside a mass of falling beech tree had thundered down on them. Ulrich von Gradwitz found himself stretched on the ground, one arm numb beneath him and the other held almost as helplessly in a tight tangle of forked branches, while both legs were pinned beneath the fallen mass. His heavy shooting boots had saved his feet from being crushed to pieces, but if his fractures were not as serious as they might have been, at least it was evident that he could not move from his present position till someone came to release him. The descending twig had slashed the skin of his face, and he had to wink away some drops of blood from his eyelashes before he could take in a general view of the disaster. At his side, so near that under ordinary circumstances he could almost have touched him, lay Georg Znaeym, alive and struggling, but obviously as helplessly pinioned down as himself. All round them lay a thick-strewn wreckage of splintered branches and broken twigs.

Relief at being alive and exasperation at his captive plight brought a strange medley of pious thank-offerings and sharp curses to Ulrich's lips. Georg, who was nearly blinded with the blood which trickled across his eyes, stopped his struggling for a moment to listen, and then gave a short, snarling laugh.

"So you're not killed, as you ought to be, but you're caught, anyway," he cried; "caught fast. Ho, what a jest, Ulrich von Gradwitz snared in his stolen forest. There's real justice for you!"

And he laughed again, mockingly and savagely.

"I'm caught in my own forest land," retorted Ulrich. "When my men come to release us you will wish, perhaps, that you were in a better plight than caught poaching on a neighbor's land, shame on you."

Georg was silent for a moment; then he answered quietly, "Are you sure that your men will find much to release? I have men, too, in the forest tonight, close behind me, and *they* will be here first and do the releasing. When they drag me out from under these damned branches it won't need much clumsiness on their part to roll this mass of trunk right over on the top of you. Your men will find you dead under a fallen beech tree. For form's sake I shall send my condolences to your family."

"It is a useful hint," said Ulrich fiercely. "My men had orders to follow in ten minutes time, seven of which must have gone by already, and when they get me out—I will remember the hint. Only as you will have met your death poaching on my lands I don't think I can decently send any message of condolence to your family."

"Good," snarled Georg, "good. We fight this quarrel out to the death, you and I and our foresters, with no cursed interlopers to come between us. Death and damnation to you, Ulrich von Gradwitz."

"The same to you, Georg Znaeym, forest thief, game snatcher."

Both men spoke with the bitterness of possible defeat before them, for each knew that it might be long before his men would seek him out or find him; it was a bare matter of chance which party would arrive first on the scene.

Both had now given up the useless struggle to free themselves from the mass of wood that held them down; Ulrich limited his endeavors to an effort to bring his one partially free arm near enough to his outer coat pocket to draw out his wine flask. Even when he had accomplished that operation it was long before he could manage the unscrewing of the stopper or get any of the liquid down his throat. But what a Heaven-sent draught it seemed! It was an open winter, and little snow had fallen as yet, hence the captives suffered less from the cold than might have been the case at that season of the year; nevertheless, the wine was warming and reviving to the wounded man, and he looked across with something like a throb of pity to where his enemy lay, just keeping the groans of pain and weariness from crossing his lips.

"Could you reach this flask if I threw it over to you?" asked Ulrich suddenly; "there is good wine in it, and one may as well be as comfortable as one can. Let us drink, even if tonight one of us dies."

"No, I can scarcely see anything; there is so much blood caked round my eyes," said Georg, "and in any case I don't drink wine with an enemy."

Ulrich was silent for a few minutes, and lay listening to the weary screeching of the wind. An idea was slowly forming and growing in his brain, an idea that gained strength every time that he looked across at the man who was fighting so grimly against pain and exhaustion. In the pain and languor that Ulrich himself was feeling the old fierce hatred seemed to be dying down.

"Neighbor," he said presently, "do as you please if your men come first. It was a fair compact. But as for me, I've changed my mind. If my men are the first to come you shall be the first to be helped, as though you were my guest. We have quarreled like devils all our lives over this stupid strip of forest, where the trees can't even stand upright in a breath of wind. Lying here tonight thinking, I've come to think we've been rather fools; there are better things in life than getting the better of a boundary dispute. Neighbor, if you will help me to bury the old quarrel I—I will ask you to be my friend."

Georg Znaeym was silent for so long that Ulrich thought, perhaps, he had fainted with the pain of his injuries. Then he spoke slowly and in jerks.

"How the whole region would stare and gabble if we rode into the market-square together. No one living can remember seeing a Znaeym and a von Gradwitz talking to one another in friendship. And what peace there would be among the forester folk if we ended our feud tonight. And if we choose to make peace among our people there is none other to interfere, no interlopers from outside… You would come and keep the Sylvester night beneath my roof, and I would come and feast on some high day at your castle… I would never fire a shot on your land, save when you invited me as a guest; and you should come and shoot with me down in the marshes where the wildfowl are. In all the countryside there are none that could hinder if we willed to make peace. I never thought to have wanted to do other than hate you all my life, but I think I have changed my mind about things too, this last half-hour. And you offered me your wine-flask… Ulrich von Gradwitz, I will be your friend."

For a space both men were silent, turning over in their minds the wonderful changes that this dramatic reconciliation would bring about. In the cold, gloomy forest, with the wind tearing in fitful gusts through the naked branches and whistling round the tree trunks, they lay and waited for the help that would now bring release and succor to both parties. And each prayed a private prayer that his men might be the first to arrive, so that he might be the first to show honorable attention to the enemy that had become a friend.

Presently, as the wind dropped for a moment, Ulrich broke the silence. "Let's shout for help," he said; "in this lull our voices may carry a little way."

"They won't carry far through the trees and undergrowth," said Georg, "but we can try. Together, then."

The two raised their voices in a prolonged hunting call.

"Together again," said Ulrich a few minutes later, after listening in vain for an answering halloo.

"I heard nothing but the pestilential wind," said Georg hoarsely.

There was silence again for some minutes, and then Ulrich gave a joyful cry.

"I can see figures coming through the wood. They are following in the way I came down the hillside."

Both men raised their voices in as loud a shout as they could muster.

"They hear us! They've stopped. Now they see us. They're running down the hill towards us," cried Ulrich.

"How many of them are there?" asked Georg.

"I can't see distinctly," said Ulrich; "nine or ten."

"Then they are yours," said Georg; "I had only seven out with me."

"They are making all the speed they can, brave lads," said Ulrich gladly.

"Are they your men?" asked Georg. "Are they your men?" he repeated impatiently as Ulrich did not answer.

"No," said Ulrich with a laugh, the idiotic chattering laugh of a man unstrung with hideous fear.

"Who are they?" asked Georg quickly, straining his eyes to see what the other would gladly not have seen.

"*Wolves.*"

Property Condemned: A Story of Pine Deep
by
Jonathan Maberry

The house was occupied, but no one lived there.

That's how Malcolm Crow thought about it. Houses like the Croft place were never really empty.

Like most of the kids in Pine Deep, Crow knew that there were ghosts. Even the tourists knew about the ghosts. It was that kind of town.

All of the tourist brochures of the town had pictures of ghosts on them. Happy, smiling *Casper the Friendly Ghost* sorts of ghosts. Every store in town had a rack of books about the ghosts of Pine Deep. Crow had every one of those books. He couldn't braille his way through a basic geometry test or recite the U.S. presidents in any reliable order, but he knew about shades and crisis apparitions, church grims and banshees, crossroads ghosts and poltergeists. He read every story and historical account; saw every movie he could afford to see. Every once in a while Crow would even risk one of his father's frequent beatings to sneak out of bed and tiptoe down to the basement to watch *Double Chiller Theater* on the flickering old Emerson. If his dad caught him and took a belt to him, it was okay as long as Crow managed to see at least *one* good spook flick.

Besides, beatings were nothing to Crow. At nine-years-old he'd had so many that they'd lost a lot of their novelty.

It was the ghosts that mattered. Crow would give a lot—maybe everything he had in this world—to actually *meet* a ghost. That would be... well, Crow didn't know what it would be. Not exactly. *Fun* didn't seem to be the right word. Maybe what he really wanted was *proof.* He worried about that. About wanting proof that something existed beyond the world he knew.

He believed that he believed, but he wasn't sure that he was right about it. That he was aware of this inconsistency only tightened the knots. And fueled his need.

His *hunger.*

Ghosts mattered to Malcolm Crow because whatever they were, they clearly outlasted whatever had killed them. Disease, murder, suicide, war, brutality… abuse. The cause of their deaths was over, but they had survived. That's why Crow wasn't scared of ghosts. What frightened him—deep down on a level where feelings had no specific structure—was the possibility that they might *not* exist. That this world was all that there was.

And the Croft house? That place was different. Crow had never worked up the nerve to go there. Almost nobody ever went out there. Nobody really talked about it, though everyone knew about it.

Crow made a point of visiting the other well-known haunted spots—the tourist spots—hoping to see a ghost. All he wanted was a glimpse. In one of his favorite books on hauntings, the writer said that a glimpse was what most people usually got. "Ghosts are elusive," the author had written. "You don't form a relationship with one, you're lucky if you catch a glimpse out of the corner of your eye; but if you do, you'll know it for what it is. One glimpse can last you a lifetime."

So far, Crow had not seen or even heard a single ghost. Not one cold spot, not a single whisper of old breath, not a hint of something darting away out of the corner of his eye. Nothing, zilch. Nada.

However, he had never gone into the Croft place.

Until today.

Crow touched the front pocket of his jeans to feel the outline of his lucky stone. Still there. It made him smile.

Maybe now he'd finally get to see a ghost.

They pedaled through dappled sunlight, sometimes four abreast, sometimes in single file when the trail dwindled down to a crooked deer path. Crow knew the way to the Croft place and he was always out front, though he liked it best when Val Guthrie rode beside him. As they bumped over hard-packed dirt and whispered through uncut summer grass, Crow cut frequent covert looks at Val. Val was amazing. Beautiful. She rode straight and alert on her pink Huffy, pumping the pedals with purple sneakers. Hair as glossy black as crow feathers, tied in a bouncing ponytail. Dark blue eyes, and a serious mouth. Crow made it his life work to coax a smile out of her at least once a day. It was hard work, but worth it.

The deer path spilled out onto an old forestry service road that allowed them once more to fan out into a line. Val caught up and fell in beside him on the left, and almost at once Terry and Stick raced each other to be first on the right. Terry and Stick were always racing, always daring each other, always trying to prove who was best, fastest, smartest, strongest. Terry always won the strongest part.

"The Four Horsemen ride!" bellowed Stick, his voice breaking so loudly they all cracked up. Stick didn't mind his voice cracking. There was a fifty cent bet that he'd have his grown up voice before Terry. Crow privately agreed. Despite his size, Terry had a high voice that always sounded like his nose was full of snot.

Up ahead the road forked, splitting off toward the ranger station on the right and a weedy path on the left. On the left-hand side, a sign leaned drunkenly toward them.

PRIVATE PROPERTY
NO ADMITTANCE
TRESPASSERS WILL BE

That was all of it. The rest of the sign had been pinged off by bullet holes over the years. It was a thing to do. You shot the sign to the Croft place to show you weren't afraid. Crow tried to make sense of that, but there wasn't any end to the string of logic.

He turned to Val with a grin. "Almost there."

"Oooo, spooky!" said Stick, lowering the bill of his Phillies ball cap to cast his face in shadows.

Val nodded. No smile. No flash of panic. Only a nod. Crow wondered if Val was bored, interested, skeptical, or scared. With her you couldn't tell. She had enough Lenape blood to give her that stone face. Her mom was like that, too. Not her dad, though. Mr. Guthrie was always laughing, and Crow suspected that he, too, had a lifelong mission that involved putting smiles on the faces of the Guthrie women.

Crow said, "It won't be too bad."

Val shrugged. "It's *just* a house." She leaned a little heavier on the word "just" every time she said that, and she'd been doing that ever since Crow suggested they come out here. *Just* a house.

Crow fumbled for a comeback that would chip some of the ice off of those words, but as he so often did, he failed.

It was Terry Wolfe who came to his aide. "Yeah, yeah, yeah, Val, you keep saying that, but I'll bet you'll chicken out before we even get onto the porch."

Terry liked Val, too, but he spent a lot of time putting her down and making fun of whatever she said. Though, if any of that actually hurt Val, Crow couldn't see it. Val was like that. She didn't show a thing. Even when that jerk Vic Wingate pushed her and knocked her down in the schoolyard last April, Val hadn't yelled, hadn't cried. All she did was get up, walk over to Vic, and wipe the blood from her scraped palms on his shirt. Then, as Vic started calling her words that Crow had only heard his dad ever use when he was really hammered, Val turned and walked away like it was a normal spring day.

So Terry's sarcasm didn't make a dent.

Terry and Stick immediately launched into the Addams Family theme song loud enough to scare the birds from the trees.

A startled doe dashed in blind panic across their path. Stick tracked it with his index finger and dropped his thumb like a hammer.

"Pow!"

Val gave him a withering look, but she didn't say anything.

"...*So get a witch's shawl on, a broomstick you can crawl on...*"

They rounded the corner and skidded to a stop, one, two, three, four. Dust plumes rose behind them like ghosts and drifted away on a breeze as if fleeing from this place. The rest of the song dwindled to dust on their tongues.

It stood there.

The Croft house.

The place even *looked* haunted.

Three stories tall, with all sorts of angles jutting out for no particular reason. Gray shingles hung crookedly from their nails. The windows were dark and grimed, some were broken out. Most of the storm shutters were closed, but a few hung open and one lay half-buried in a dead rosebush. Missing slats in the porch railing gave it a gap-toothed grin. Like a jack-o'-lantern. Like a skull.

On any other house, Crow would have loved that. He would have appreciated the attention to detail.

But his dry lips did not want to smile.

Four massive willows, old and twisted by rot and disease, towered over the place, their long fingers bare of leaves even in the flush of summer. The rest of the forest stood back from the house as if unwilling to draw any nearer. Like people standing around a coffin, Crow thought.

His fingers traced the outline of the lucky stone in his jeans pocket.

"Jeeeez," said Stick softly.

"Holy moley," agreed Terry.

Val said, "It's *just* a house."

Without turning to her, Terry said, "You keep saying that, Val, but I don't see you running up onto the porch."

Val's head swiveled around like a praying mantis's and she skewered Terry with her blue eyes. "And when *exactly* was the last time you had the guts to even come here, Terrance Henry Wolfe? Oh, what was that? Never? What about you, George Stickler?"

"Crow hasn't been here, either," said Stick defensively.

"I know. Apparently three of the four Horsemen of the Apocalypse are sissies."

"Whoa, now!" growled Terry, swinging his leg off his bike. "There's a lot of places we haven't been. *You* haven't been here, either, does that make you a sissy, too?"

"I don't need to come to a crappy old house to try and prove anything," she fired back. "I thought we were out riding bikes."

"Yeah, but we're here now," persisted Terry, "so why don't you show everyone how tough you are and go up on the porch?"

Val sat astride her pink Huffy, feet on the ground, hands on the rubber grips. "You're the one trying to prove something. Let's see you go first."

Terry's ice-blue eyes slid away from hers. "I never said I wanted to go in."

"Then what *are* you saying?"

"I'm just saying that you're the one who's always saying there's no such thing as haunted houses, but you're still scared to go up there."

"Who said I was scared?" Val snapped.

91

"You're saying you're not?" asked Terry.

Crow and Stick watched this exchange like spectators at a tennis match. They both kept all expression off their faces, well aware of how far Val could be pushed. Terry was getting really close to that line.

"*Everyone's* too scared to go in there," Terry said, "and—"

"And *what?*" she demanded.

"And… I guess nobody should."

"Oh, chicken poop. It's just a stupid old house."

Terry folded his arms. "Yeah, but I still don't see you on that porch."

Val made a face, but didn't reply. They all looked at the house. The old willows looked like withered trolls, bent with age and liable to do something nasty. The Croft house stood, half in shadows and half in sunlight.

Waiting.

It wants us to come in, thought Crow, and he shivered.

"How do you know the place is really haunted?" asked Stick.

Terry punched him on the arm. "*Everybody* knows it's haunted."

"Yeah, okay, but… how?"

"Ask Mr. Halloween," said Val. "He knows everything about this crap."

They all looked at Crow. "It's not crap," he insisted. "C'mon, guys, this is Pine Deep. Everybody knows there are ghosts everywhere here."

"You ever see one?" asked Stick, and for once there was no mockery in his voice. If anything, he looked a little spooked.

"No," admitted Crow, "but a lot of people have. Jim Polk's mom sees one all the time."

They nodded. Mrs. Polk swore that she saw a partially formed figure of a woman in Colonial dress walking through the backyard. A few of the neighbors said they saw it, too.

"And Val's dad said that Gus Bernhardt's uncle Kurt was so scared by a poltergeist in his basement that he took to drinking."

Kurt Bernhardt was a notorious drunk—worse than Crow's father—and he used to be a town deputy until one day he got so drunk that he threw up on a town selectman while trying to write him a parking ticket.

"Dad used to go over to the Bernhardt place a lot," said Val, "but he never saw any ghosts."

"I heard not everybody sees ghosts," said Terry. He took a plastic comb out of his pocket and ran it through his hair, trying to look cool and casual, like there was no haunted house forty feet away.

"Yeah," agreed Stick, "and I heard that people sometimes see *different* ghosts."

"What do you mean 'different ghosts'?" asked Val.

Stick shrugged. "Something my gran told me. She said a hundred people can walk through the same haunted place, and most people won't see a ghost because they can't, and those who do will see their own ghost."

"Wait," said Terry, "what?"

Crow nodded. "I heard that, too. It's an old Scottish legend. The people who don't see ghosts are the ones who are afraid to believe in them."

"And the people who *do* see a ghost," Stick continued, "see the ghost of their own future."

"That's stupid," said Val. "How can you see your own ghost if you're alive?"

"Yeah," laughed Terry. "That's stupid, even for you."

"No, really," said Crow. "I read that in my books. Settlers used to believe that."

Stick nodded. "My gran's mom came over from Scotland. She said there are a lot of ghosts over there, and that sometimes people saw their own. Not themselves as dead people, not like that. Gran said people saw their own *spirits*. She said there were places where the walls between the worlds were so thin that past, present, and future were like different rooms in a house with no doors. That's how she put it. Sometimes you could stand in one room and see different parts of your life in another."

"That would scare the crap out of me," said Terry.

A sudden breeze caused the shutters on one of the windows to bang as loud as a gunshot. They all jumped.

"Jeeeeee-zus!" gasped Stick. "Nearly gave me a heart attack!"

They laughed at their own nerves, but the laughs died away as one by one they turned back to look at the Croft house.

"You really want me to go in there?" asked Val, her words cracking the fragile silence.

Sliding his comb back into his pocket, Terry said, "Sure."

"No!" yelped Crow.

Everyone suddenly looked at him: Val in surprise, Stick with a grin forming on his lips, Terry with a frown.

The moment held for three or four awkward seconds, and then Val pushed her kickstand down and got off her bike.

"Fine then."

She took three decisive steps toward the house. Crow and the others stayed exactly where they were. When Val realized she was alone, she turned and gave them her best ninja death stare. Crow knew this stare all too well; his buttocks clenched and his balls tried to climb up into his chest cavity. Not even that creep Vic Wingate gave her crap when Val had that look in her eyes.

"What I ought to do," she said coldly, "is make you three sissies go in with me."

"No way," laughed Terry, as if it was the most absurd idea anyone had ever said aloud.

"Okay!" blurted Crow.

Terry and Stick looked at him with a *Nice going, Judas* look in their eyes.

Val smiled. Crow wasn't sure if she was smiling at him or smiling in triumph. Either way, he put it in the win category. He was one smile up on the day's average.

Crow's bike had no kickstand, so he got off and leaned it against a maple, considered, then picked it up and turned it around so that it pointed the way they'd come. Just in case.

"You coming?" he asked Stick and Terry.

"If I'm going in," said Val acidly, "then we're *all* going in. It's only fair and I don't want to hear any different or so help me God, Terry…"

She left the rest to hang. When she was mad, Val not only spoke like an adult, she sounded like her mother.

Stick winced and punched Terry on the arm. "Come on, numbnuts."

The four of them clustered together on the lawn, knee deep in weeds. Bees and blowflies swarmed in the air around them. No one moved for over a minute. Crow could feel the spit in his mouth drying to paste.

I want to do this, he thought, but that lie sounded exactly like what it was.

The house glowered down at him.

The windows, even the shuttered ones, were like eyes. The ones with broken panes were like the empty eye-sockets of old skulls, like the ones in science class at school. Crow spent hours staring into those dark eye-holes, wondering if there was anything of the original owner's personality in there. Not once did he feel anything. Now, just looking at those black and empty windows made Crow shudder, because he was getting the itchy feeling that there *was* something looking back.

The shuttered windows somehow bothered him more than the open ones. They seemed... he fished for the word.

Sneaky?

No, that wasn't right. That was too cliché, and Crow had read every ghost story he could find. Sneaky wasn't right. He dug through his vocabulary and came up short. The closest thing that seemed to fit—and Crow had no idea *how* it fit— was *hungry*.

He almost laughed. How could shuttered windows look hungry?

"That's stupid."

It wasn't until Stick turned to him and asked what he was talking about that Crow realized he'd spoken the words aloud.

He looked at the others and all of them, even Val, were stiff with apprehension. The Croft house scared them. Really scared them.

Because they believed there was something in there.

They all paused in the yard, closer to their bikes and the road than they were to that porch.

They believed.

Crow wanted to shout and he wanted to laugh.

"Well," said Val, "let's go."

The Four Horseman, unhorsed, approached the porch.

The steps creaked.

Of course they did. Crow would have been disappointed if they hadn't. He suppressed a smile. The front door was going to creak, too; those old hinges were going to screech like a cat. It was how it was all supposed to be.

It's real, he told himself. *There's a ghost in there. There's something in there.*

It was the second of those two thoughts that felt correct. Not *right* exactly—but *correct*. There was some*thing* in that house. If they went inside, they'd find it.

No, whispered a voice from deeper inside his mind, *if we go inside, it will find us.*

"Good," murmured Crow. This time he said it so softly that none of the others heard him.

He wanted it to find them.

Please let it find them.

They crossed the yard in silence. The weeds were high and brown, as if they could draw no moisture at all from the hard ground. Crow saw bits of debris, half-hidden by the weeds. A baseball whose hide had turned a sickly yellow and whose seams had split like torn surgical sutures. Beyond that was a woman's dress shoe; just the one. There was a Triple-A road map of Pennsylvania, but the wind and rain had faded the details so that the whole state appeared to be under a heavy fog. Beyond that was an orange plastic pill-bottle with its label peeled halfway back. Crow picked it up, read the label, and was surprised to see that the pharmacy where this prescription had been filled was in Poland. The drug was called *Klozapol*, but Crow had no idea what that was or what it was used for. The bottle was empty, but it looked pretty new. Crow let it drop and touched the lucky stone in his pocket to reassure himself it was still safe.

Still his.

The yard was filled with junk. An empty wallet, a ring of rusted keys, a soiled diaper, the buckle from a seat belt, a full box of graham crackers that was completely covered with ants. Stuff like that. Disconnected things. Like junk washed up on a beach.

Val knelt and picked up something that flashed silver in the sunlight.

"What's that?" asked Terry.

She held it up. It was an old Morgan silver dollar. Val spit on her thumb and rubbed the dirt away to reveal the profile of Lady Liberty. She squinted to read the date.

"Eighteen-ninety-five," she said.

"Are you kidding me?" demanded Terry, bending close to study it. He was the only one of them who collected coins. "Dang, Val… that's worth a lot of money."

"Really?" Val, Crow, and Stick asked at the same time.

"Yeah. A *lot* of money. I got some books at home we can look it up in. I'll bet it's worth a couple of thousand bucks."

Crow goggled at him. Unlike the other three, Crow's family was dirt poor. Even Stick, whose parents owned a tiny TV repair shop in town, had more money. Crow's mom was dead and his father worked part-time at Shanahan's Garage, and then drank most of what he earned. Crow was wearing the same jeans this year that he'd worn all last season. Same sneakers, too. He and his brother Billy had learned how to sew well enough to keep their clothes from falling apart.

So he stared at the coin that might be worth a few thousand dollars.

Val turned the coin over. The other side had a carving of an eagle with its wings outstretched. The words UNITED STATES OF AMERICA arched over it and ONE DOLLAR looped below it. But above the eagle where IN GOD WE

TRUST should have been, someone had gouged deep into the metal, totally obscuring the phrase.

Terry gasped as if he was in actual physical pain.

"Bet it ain't worth as much like that," said Stick with a nasty grin.

Val shrugged and shoved the coin into her jeans pocket. "Whatever. Come on."

It was a high porch and they climbed four steep steps to the deck. Each step was littered with dried leaves and withered locust husks. Crow wondered where the leaves had come from; it was the height of summer. Except for the willows, everything everywhere was alive, and those willows looked like they'd been dead for years. Besides, these were dogwood leaves. He looked around for the source of the leaves, but there were no dogwoods in the yard. None anywhere he could see.

He grunted.

"What?" asked Val, but Crow didn't reply. It wasn't the sort of observation that was going to encourage anyone.

"The door's probably locked," said Terry. "This is a waste of time."

"Don't even," warned Val.

The floorboards creaked, each with a different note of agonized wood.

As they passed one of the big shuttered windows, Stick paused and frowned at it. Terry and Val kept walking, but Crow slowed and lingered a few paces away. As he watched, the frown on Stick's mouth melted away and his friend stood there with no expression at all on his face.

"Stick?"

Stick didn't answer. He didn't even twitch.

"Yo… Stick."

This time Stick jumped as if Crow had pinched him. He whirled and looked at Crow with eyes that were wide but unfocused.

"What did you say?" he asked, his voice a little slurred. Like Dad's when he was starting to tie one on.

"I didn't say anything. I just called your name."

"No," said Stick, shaking his head. "You called me 'daddy.' What's that supposed to mean?"

Crow laughed. "You're hearing things, man."

Stick whipped his ball cap off his head and slapped Crow's shoulder. "Hey… I *heard* you."

Terry heard this and he gave Stick a quizzical smile, waiting for the punch line. "What's up?"

Stick wiped his mouth on the back of his hand and stared down as if expecting there to be something other than a faint sheen of spit. He touched the corner of his mouth and looked at his fingers. His hands were shaking as he pulled his ball cap on and snugged it down low.

"What are you doing?" asked Terry, his smile flickering.

Stick froze. "Why? Do I have something on my face?"

"Yeah," said Terry.

Stick's face blanched white and he jabbed at his skin. The look in his eyes was so wild and desperate that it made Crow's heart hurt. He'd seen a look like that once when a rabbit was tangled up in some barbed wire by the Carby place. The little animal was covered in blood and its eyes were huge, filled with so much terror that it couldn't even blink. Even as Crow and Val tried to free it, the rabbit shuddered and died.

Scared to death.

For just a moment, Stick looked like that, and the sight of that expression drove a cold sliver of ice into Crow's stomach. He could feel his scrotum contract into a wrinkled little walnut.

Stick pawed at his face. "What is it?"

"Don't worry," said Terry, "it's just a dose of the uglies, but you had that when you woke up this morning."

Terry laughed like a donkey.

No one else did.

Stick glared at him and his nervous fingers tightened into fists. Crow was sure that he was going to smash Terry in the mouth. But then Val joined them.

"What's going on?" she demanded. Her stern tone broke the spell of the moment.

"Nothing," said Stick as he abruptly pushed past Terry and stalked across the porch, his balled fists at his sides. The others gaped at him.

"What—?" began Terry, but he had nowhere to go with it. After a moment he followed Stick.

Val and Crow lingered for a moment.

"Did they have a fight or something?" Val asked quietly.

"I don't know what that was," admitted Crow. He told her exactly what happened. Val snorted.

"Boys," she said, leaving it there. She walked across the porch and stood in front of the door.

Crow lingered for a moment, trying to understand what just happened. Part of him wanted to believe that Stick just saw a ghost. He wanted that very badly. The rest of him—*most* of him—suddenly wanted to turn around, jump on the bike that was nicely positioned for a quick escape, and never come back here. The look in Stick's eyes had torn all the fun out of this.

"Let's get this over with," said Val, and that trapped all of them in the moment. The three boys looked at her, but none of them looked at each other. Not for a whole handful of brittle seconds. Val, however, studied each of them.

"Boys," she said again.

Under the lash of her scorn, they followed her. The doors were shut, but even before Val touched the handle, Crow knew these doors wouldn't be locked.

It wants *us to come in.*

Terry licked his lips. "What do you suppose is in there?"

Val shook her head. Crow noted she was no longer saying that this was *just* a house.

Terry nudged Crow with his elbow. "You ever talk to anybody's been in here?"

"No."

"You ever know anyone who knows anyone who's been in here?"

Crow thought about it. "Not really."

"Then how do you know it's even haunted?" asked Val.

"I don't."

It was a lie and Crow knew that everyone read it that way. No one called him on it, though. Maybe they would have when they were still in the yard, but not now. There was a line somewhere and Crow knew—they all knew—they'd crossed it.

Maybe it was when Stick looked at the shuttered windows and freaked out.

Maybe it was when they came up on the porch.

Maybe, maybe...

Val took a breath, set her jaw, gripped the rusted and pitted brass knob, and turned it.

The lock clicked open.

A soft sound. Not at all threatening.

It wants us to come in, Crow thought again, knowing it to be true.

Then there was another sound, and Crow was sure only he heard it. Not the lock, not the hinges; it was like the small intake of breath you hear around the dinner table when the knife is poised to make the first cut into a Thanksgiving turkey. The blade gleams, the turkey steams, mouths water, and each of the ravenous diners takes in a small hiss of breath as the naked reality of hunger is undisguised.

Val gave the door a little push and let go of the knob.

The hinges creaked like they were supposed to. It was a real creak, too. Not another hungry hiss. If the other sound had been one of expectation, then the creak was the plunge of the knife.

Crow knew this even if he wasn't old enough yet to form the thoughts as cogently as he would in later years. Right now those impressions floated in his brain, more like colors or smells than structured thoughts. Even so, he understood them on a visceral level.

As the door swung open, Crow understood something else, too; two things, really.

The first was that after today he would never again need proof of anything in the unseen world.

And the second was that going into the Croft house was a mistake.

They went in anyway.

The door opened into a vestibule that was paneled in rotting oak. The broken globe light fixture on the ceiling above them was filled with dead bugs. There were no cobwebs, though, and no rat droppings on the floor.

In the back of Crow's mind he knew he should have been worried about that. But by the time the thought came to the front of his mind, it was too late.

The air inside was curiously moist, and it stank. It wasn't the smell of dust or the stench of rotting meat. That's what Crow had expected; this was different. It was a stale, acidic smell that reminded him more of his father's breath after he came home from the bar. Crow knew that smell from all of the times his father bent over him, shouting at him while he whipped his belt up and down, up and down. The words his father shouted seldom made any sense. The stink of his breath was what Crow remembered. It was what he forced his mind to concentrate on so he didn't feel the burning slap of the belt. Crow had gotten good at that over the years. He still felt the pain—in the moment and in the days following each beating—but he was able to pull his mind out of his body with greater ease each time, as long as he focused on something else. How or why that distraction had become his father's pickled breath was something Crow never understood.

And now, as they moved from the vestibule into the living room, Crow felt as if the house itself was breathing at him with that same stink.

Crow never told his friends about the beatings. They all knew—Crow was almost always bruised somewhere—but this was small town Pennsylvania in 1974, and nobody ever talked about stuff like that. Not even his teachers. Just as Stick never talked about the fact that both of his sisters had haunted looks in their eyes and never—*ever*—let themselves be alone with their father. Not if they could avoid it. Janie and Kim had run away a couple of times each, but they never said why. You just didn't talk about some things. Nobody did.

Nobody.

Certainly not Crow.

So he had no point of reference for discussing the stink of this house. To mention it to his friends would require that he explain what else it smelled like. That was impossible. He'd rather die.

The house wanted us to come in, he thought, *and now we're in.*

Crow looked at the others. Stick hung back, almost crouching inside the vestibule, and the wild look was back on his face. Terry stood with his hands in his pockets, but from the knuckly lumps under the denim Crow knew that he had his fists balled tight. Val had her arms wrapped around her chest as if she stood in a cold wind. No one was looking at him.

No one was looking at each other. Except for Crow.

Now we're inside.

Crow knew what would happen. He'd seen every movie about haunted houses, read every book. He had all the Warren *Eerie* and *Creepy* comics. He even had some of the old E.C. comics. He knew.

The house is going to fool us. It'll separate us. It'll kill us, one by one.

That's the way it always was. The ghost—or ghosts—would pull them apart, lead them into darkened cellars or hidden passages. They'd be left alone, and alone each one of them would die. Knives in the dark, missing stairs in a lightless hall, trapdoors, hands reaching out of shadows. They'd all die in here. Apart and alone. That was the way it always happened.

Except…

Except that it did not happen that way.

Crow saw something out of the corner of his eye. He turned to see a big mirror mounted on the wall. Dusty, cracked, the glass fogged.

He saw himself in the mirror.

Himself and not himself.

Crow stepped closer.

The reflection stepped closer, too.

Crow and Crow stared at each other. The boy with bruises, and a man who looked like his father. But it wasn't his father. It was Crow's own face, grown up, grown older. Pale, haggard, the jaws shadowy with a week's worth of unshaved whiskers, vomit stains drying on the shirt. A uniform shirt. A police uniform. Wrinkled and stained, like Kurt Bernhardt's. Even though it was a reflection, Crow could smell the vomit. The piss. The rank stink of exhaled booze and unbrushed teeth.

"Fuck you, you little shit," he said. At first Crow thought the cop was growling at him, but then Crow turned and saw Val and Terry. Only they were different. Everything was different, and even though the mirror was still there, nothing else was the same. This was outside, at night, in town. And the Val and Terry the cop was cursing were all grown up. They weren't reflections; they were real, they were here. Wherever and *whenever* here was.

Val was tall and beautiful, with long black hair and eyes that were filled with laughter. And she *was* laughing—laughing at something Terry said. There were even laugh lines around her mouth. They walked arm-in-arm past the shop windows on Corn Hill. She wore a dress and Terry was in a suit. Terry was huge, massive and muscular, but the suit he wore was expensive and perfectly tailored. He whispered to Val, and she laughed again. Then at the corner of Corn Hill and Baker Lane, they stopped to kiss. Val had to fight her laughs in order to kiss, and even then the kiss disintegrated into more laughs. Terry cracked up, too, and then they turned and continued walking along the street. They strolled comfortably. Like people who were walking home.

Home. Not home as kids on bikes, but to some place where they lived together as adults. Maybe as husband and wife.

Val and Terry.

Crow turned back to the mirror—the only part of the Croft house that still existed in this world. The cop—the older Crow—stood in the shadows under an elm tree and watched Val and Terry. Tears ran like lines of mercury down his cheeks. Snot glistened on his upper lip. He sank down against the trunk of the tree, toppling the last few inches as his balance collapsed. He didn't even try to stop his fall, but instead lay with his cheek against the dirt. Some loose coins and a small stone fell out of the man's pocket.

Crow patted his own pocket. The lucky stone was there.

Still there.

Still his.

The moment stretched into a minute and then longer as Crow watched the drunken man weep in wretched silence. He wanted to turn away, but he couldn't. Not because the image was so compelling, but because when Crow actually tried to turn… he simply could not make his body move. He was frozen into that scene.

Locked.

Trapped.

The cop kept crying.

"Stop it," said Crow. He meant to say it kindly, but the words banged out of him, as harsh as a pair of slaps.

The cop froze, lifting his head as if he'd heard the words.

His expression was alert but filled with panic, like a deer who had just heard the crunch of a heavy footfall in the woods. It didn't last, though. The drunken glaze stole over it and the tense lips grew rubbery and slack. The cop hauled himself to a sitting position with his back to the tree, and the effort winded him so that he sat panting like a dog, his face greasy with sweat. Behind the alcohol haze, something dark and ugly and lost moved in his eyes.

Crow recognized it. The same shapeless thing moved behind his own eyes every time he looked in the mirror. Especially after a beating. But the shape in his own eyes was smaller than this, less sharply defined. His usually held more panic, and there was none at all here. Panic, he would later understand, was a quality of hope, even of wounded hope. In the cop's eyes, there was only fear. Not fear of death—Crow was experienced enough with fear to understand that much. No, this was the fear that, as terrible as this was, life was as good as it would ever be again. All that was left was the slide downhill.

"No…" murmured Crow, because he knew what was going to happen.

The cop's fingers twitched like worms waiting for the hook. They crawled along his thigh, over his hip bone. They found the leather holster and the gnarled handle of the Smith and Wesson.

Crow could not bear to watch. He needed to not see this. A scream tried to break from him, and he *wanted* it to break. A scream could break chains. A scream could push the boogeyman away. A scream could shatter this mirror.

But Crow could not scream.

Instead he watched as those white, trembling fingers curled around the handle of the gun and pulled it slowly from the holster.

He still could not turn… but now his hands could move. Only a little, and with a terrible sluggishness, but they moved. His own fingers crawled along his thigh, felt for his pocket, wormed their way inside.

The click of the hammer being pulled back was impossibly loud.

Crow's fingers curled around the stone. It was cold and hard and so… *real*.

He watched the cylinder of the pistol rotate as the cop's thumb pulled the hammer all the way back.

Tears burned like acid in Crow's eyes and he summoned every ounce of will to pull the stone from his pocket. It came so slowly. It took a thousand years.

But it came out.

The cop lifted the barrel of the pistol and put it under his chin. His eyes were squeezed shut.

Crow raised his fist, and the harder he squeezed the stone the more power he had in his arm.

"I'm sorry," Crow said, mumbling the two words through lips bubbling with spit.

The cop's finger slipped inside the curled trigger guard.

"I'm so sorry…"

Crow threw the stone at the same moment the cop pulled the trigger.

The stone struck the mirror a microsecond before the firing pin punched a hole in the world.

There was a sound. It wasn't the smash of mirror glass and it wasn't the bang of a pistol. It was something vast and black and impossible, and it was the loudest sound Crow would ever hear. It was so monstrously loud that it broke the world.

Shards of mirror glass razored through the air around Crow, slashing him, digging deep into his flesh, gouging burning wounds in his mind. As each one cut him, the world shifted around Crow, buffeting him into different places, into different lives.

He saw Terry. The adult Terry, but now he was even older than the one who had been laughing with Val. It was crazy weird, but somehow Crow knew that this was as real as anything in his world.

Terry's face was lined with pain, his body crisscrossed with tiny cuts. Pieces of a broken mirror lay scattered around him. Each separate piece reflected Terry, but none of them were the Terry who stood in the midst of the debris. Each reflection was a distortion, a funhouse twist of Terry's face. Some were laughing— harsh and loud and fractured. Some were weeping. Some were glazed and catatonic. And one, a single large piece, showed a face that was more monster than man. Lupine and snarling and so completely *wrong*. The Terry who stood above the broken pieces screamed, and if there was any sanity left in his mind it did not shine out through his blue eyes. Crow saw a version of his best friend who was completely and irretrievably *lost*.

Terry screamed and screamed, and then he spun around, ran straight across the room and threw himself headfirst out of the window. Crow fell with him. Together they screamed all the way down to the garden flagstones.

The impact shoved Crow into another place. He was there with Val. They were in the cornfields behind Val's house. A black rain hammered down, the sky veined with red lightning. Val was older... maybe forty years old. She ran through the corn, skidding, slipping in the mud. Running toward a figure that lay sprawled on the ground.

"Dad!" screamed Val.

Mr. Guthrie lay on his stomach, his face pressed into the muck. In the brightness of the lightning, Crow could see a neat round bullet hole between his shoulder blades, the cloth washed clean of blood by the downpour.

"*No!*" shrieked Val. She dropped to her knees and clawed her father into her arms. His big old body resisted her, fighting her with limpness and weight and sopping clothes, but eventually Val found the strength to turn him onto his back.

"Daddy... Daddy?"

His face was totally slack, streaked with mud that clumped on his mustache and caught in his bushy eyebrows.

Val wiped the mud off his face and shook him very gently.

"Daddy... *please...*"

The lightning never stopped, and the thunder bellowed insanely. A freak eddy of wind brought sounds from the highway. The high, lonely wail of a police siren, but Crow knew the cops would be too late. They were already too late.

Crow spun out of that moment and into another. There were police sirens here, too, and the flashing red and blue lights, but no rain. This was a different place, a different moment. A different horror.

He was there.

He was a cop.

He was sober. Was he younger or older? He prayed that this was him as an older man, just as Val and Terry had been older.

Older. Sober.

Alive.

However, the moment was not offering any mercies.

Stick was there. He was on his knees and Crow was bent over him, forcing handcuffs onto his friend's wrists. They were both speaking, saying the same things over and over again.

"What did you do? Christ, Stick, what did you *do?*"

"I'm sorry," Stick said. "I'm sorry."

On the porch of the house a female cop and an EMT were supporting a ten-year-old girl toward a waiting ambulance. The girl looked a lot like Janie and Kim, Stick's sisters, but Crow knew that she wasn't. He knew this girl was Stick's daughter. Her face was bruised. Her clothes were torn. There was blood on her thighs.

"What did you do, Stick, what did you *do?*"

"I'm sorry," wept Stick. His mouth bled from where Crow had punched him. "I'm sorry."

Crow saw other images.

People he did not know. Some dressed in clothes from long ago, some dressed like everyone else. He stepped into sick rooms and cells, he crawled through the shattered windows of wrecked cars and staggered coughing through the smoke of burning houses.

Crow squeezed his eyes shut and clapped his hands over his ears. He screamed and screamed.

The house exhaled its liquor stink of breath at him.

Crow heard Val yell. Not the woman, but the girl.

He opened his eyes and saw the Morgan silver dollar leave her outstretched hand. It flew past him, and he turned to see it strike the mirror. The same mirror he'd shattered with his lucky stone.

For just a moment he caught that same image of her kneeling in the rain, but then the glass detonated.

Then he was running.

He wasn't conscious of when he was able to run. When he was *allowed* to run.

But he was running.

They were all running.

As Crow scrambled for the door, he cast a single desperate look back to see that the mirror was undamaged by either stone or coin. All of the restraints that had earlier held his limbs were gone, as if the house, glutted on his pain, ejected the table scraps.

And so they ran.

Terry shoved Stick so hard it knocked his ball cap off his head. No one stooped to pick it up. They crowded into the vestibule, burst out onto the porch, and ran for their bikes. They were all screaming.

They screamed as they ran and they screamed as they got on their bikes.

Their screams dwindled as the house faded behind its screen of withered trees.

The four of them tore down the dirt road, burst onto the access road, and turned toward town, pumping as hard as they could. They raced as hard and as fast as they could. Only when they reached the edge of the pumpkin patch on the far side of the Guthrie farm did they slow and finally stop. Panting, bathed in sweat, trembling, they huddled over their bikes, looking down at the frames, at their sneakered feet, at the dirt.

Not at each other.

Crow did not know if the others had seen the same things he'd seen. Or perhaps their own horrors.

Beside him, Terry seemed to be the first to recover. He reached into his pocket for his comb, but it wasn't there. He took a deep breath and let it out, then dragged trembling fingers through his hair.

"It must be dinner time," he said, and turned his bike toward town and pedaled off. He did not look back.

Stick dragged his forearm across his face and looked at the smear, just as he had done before. Was he looking for tears? Or for the blood that had leaked from the corners of his mouth when the older Crow had punched him? A single sob broke in his chest, and he shook his head. Crow thought he saw Stick mouth those same two terrible words. *I'm sorry.*

Stick rode away.

That was the last time he went anywhere with Crow, Val, or Terry. During the rest of that summer and well into the fall, Stick went deep inside of himself. Eight years later, Crow read in the papers that George Stickler had swallowed an entire bottle of sleeping pills, though he was not yet as old as he had been in the vision. Crow was heartbroken but not surprised, and he wondered what the line was between the cowardice of suicide and an act of bravery.

For five long minutes Crow and Val sat on their bikes, one foot each braced on the ground. Val looked at the cornfields in the distance and Crow looked at her. Then, without saying a word, Val got off her bike and walked it down the lane toward her house. Crow sat there for almost half an hour before he could work up the courage to go home.

None of them ever spoke about that day. They never mentioned the Croft house. They never asked what the others had seen.

Not once.

The only thing that ever came up was the Morgan silver dollar. One evening Crow and Terry looked it up in a coin collector's book. In mint condition it was valued at forty-eight-thousand dollars. In poor condition it was still worth twenty-thousand.

That coin probably still lay on the Croft house living room floor.

Crow and Terry looked at each other for a long time. Crow knew they were both thinking about that coin. Twenty-thousand dollars, just lying there. Right there.

It might as well have been on the dark side of the moon.

Terry closed his coin book and set it aside. As far as Crow knew, Terry never collected coins after that summer. He also knew that neither of them would ever go back for that silver dollar. Not for ten-thousand dollars. Not for ten-million. Like everything else they'd seen there—the wallet, the pill bottle, the diaper, all of it—the coin belonged to the house. Like Terry's pocket comb. Like Stick's ball cap. And Crow's lucky stone.

And what belonged to the house would stay there.

The house kept its trophies.

Crow went to the library and looked through the back issues of newspapers, through obituaries, but try as he might he found no records at all of anyone ever having died there.

Somehow it didn't surprise him.

There weren't ghosts in the Croft house. It wasn't that kind of thing.

He remembered what he'd thought when he first saw the old place.

The house is hungry.

Later, after Crow came home from Terry's house, he sat in his room long into the night, watching the moon and stars rise from behind the trees and carve their scars across the sky. He sat with his window open, arms wrapped around his shins, shivering despite a hot breeze.

It was ten days since they'd gone running from the house.

Ten days and ten nights. Crow was exhausted. He'd barely slept, and when he did there were nightmares. Never—not once in any of those dreams—was there a monster or a ghoul chasing him. They weren't those kinds of dreams. Instead he saw the image that he'd seen in the mirror. The older him.

The drunk.

The fool.

Crow wept for that man.

For the man he knew he was going to become.

He wept and he did not sleep. He tried, but even though his eyes burned with fatigue, sleep simply would not come. Crow knew it wouldn't come. Not tonight, and maybe not any night. Not as long as he could remember that house.

And he knew he could never forget it.

Around three in the morning, when his father's snores banged off the walls and rattled his bedroom door, Crow got up and, silent as a ghost, went into the hall and downstairs. Down to the kitchen, to the cupboard. The bottles stood in a row. Canadian Club. Mogen-David 20-20. Thunderbird. And a bottle of vodka without a label. Cheap stuff, but a lot of it.

Crow stood staring at the bottles for a long time. Maybe half an hour.

"No," he told himself.

No, agreed his inner voice.

No, screamed the drunken man in his memory.

No.

Crow reached up and took down the vodka bottle. He poured some into a Dixie cup.

"No," he said.

And drank it.

The Waxwork
by
A.M. Burrage

originally published in
Great Short Stories of Detection, Mystery and Horror, 1931

While the uniformed attendants of Marriner's Waxworks were ushering the last stragglers through the great glass-paneled double doors, the manager sat in his office interviewing Raymond Hewson.

The manager was a youngish man, stout, blond, and of medium height. He wore his clothes well and contrived to look extremely smart without appearing overdressed. Raymond Hewson looked neither. His clothes, which had been good when new and which were still carefully brushed and pressed, were beginning to show signs of their owner's losing battle with the world. He was a small, spare, pale man, with lank, errant brown hair, and though he spoke plausibly and even forcibly, he had the defensive and somewhat furtive air of a man who was used to rebuffs. He looked what he was, a man gifted somewhat above the ordinary, who was a failure through his lack of self-assertion.

The manager was speaking.

"There is nothing new in your request," he said. "In fact, we refuse it to different people—mostly young bloods who have tried to make bets—about three times a week. We have nothing to gain and something to lose by letting people spend the night in our Murderers' Den. If I allowed it, and some young idiot lost his senses, what would be my position? But your being a journalist somewhat alters the case."

Hewson smiled. "I suppose you mean that journalists have no senses to lose."

"No, no," laughed the manager, "but one imagines them to be responsible people. Besides, here we have something to gain: publicity and advertisement."

"Exactly," said Hewson, "and there I thought we might come to terms."

The manager laughed again.

"Oh," he exclaimed, "I know what's coming. You want to be paid twice, do you? It used to be said years ago that Madame Tussaud's would give a man a hundred pounds for sleeping alone in the Chamber of Horrors. I hope you don't think that we have made any such offer. Er—what is your paper, Mr. Hewson?"

"I am freelancing at present," Hewson confessed, "working on space for several papers. However, I should get no difficulty in getting the story printed. The *Morning Echo* would use it like a shot. 'A Night with Marriner's Murderers.' No live paper could turn it down."

The manager rubbed his chin. "Ah! And how do you propose to treat it?"

"I shall make it gruesome, of course, gruesome, with just a saving touch of humor."

The other nodded and offered Hewson his cigarette case. "Very well, Mr. Hewson," he said. "Get your story printed in the *Morning Echo*, and there will be a five pound note waiting for you here when you care to come and call for it. But first of all, it's no small ordeal that you're proposing to undertake. I'd like to be quite sure about you, and I'd like you to be quite sure of yourself. I own I shouldn't care to take it on. I've seen those figures dressed and undressed. I know all about the process of their manufacture. I can walk about in company downstairs as unmoved as if I were walking among so many skittles, but I should hate having to sleep down there alone among them."

"Why?" asked Hewson.

"I don't know. There isn't any reason, I don't believe in ghosts. If I did, I should expect them to haunt the scene of their crimes or the spot where the bodies were laid, instead of a cellar which happens to contain their waxwork effigies. It's just that I couldn't sit alone among them all night, with their seeming to stare at me in the way they do. After all, they represent the lowest and most appalling types of humanity, and, although I would not own it publicly, the people who come to see them are not generally charged with the very highest motives. The whole atmosphere of the place is unpleasant, and if you are susceptible to atmosphere I warn you that you are in for a very uncomfortable night."

Hewson had known that from the moment when the idea first occurred to him. His soul sickened at the prospect, even while he smiled casually upon the manager. But he had a wife and a family to keep, and for the past month he had been living on paragraphs, eked out by his rapidly dwindling store of savings. Here was a chance not to be missed—the price of a special story in the *Morning Echo*, with a five pound note to add to it. It meant comparative wealth and luxury for a week, and freedom from the worst anxieties for a fortnight. Besides, if he wrote the story well, it might lead to an offer of regular employment.

"The way of transgressors—and newspaper men—is hard," he said. "I have already promised myself an uncomfortable night because your Murderers' Den is obviously not fitted up as a hotel bedroom. But I don't think your waxworks will worry me much."

"You're not superstitious?"

"Not a bit," Hewson laughed.

"But you're a journalist; you must have a strong imagination."

"The news editors for whom I've worked have always complained that I haven't any. Plain facts are not considered sufficient in our trade, and the papers don't like offering their readers unbuttered bread."

The manager smiled and rose.

"Right," he said. "I think the last of the people have gone. Wait a moment. I'll give orders for the figures downstairs not to be draped, and let the night people know that you'll be here. Then I'll take you down and show you round."

He picked up the receiver of a house telephone, spoke into it, and presently replaced it.

"One condition I'm afraid I must impose on you," he remarked. "I must ask you not to smoke. We had a fire scare down in the Murderers' Den this evening. I don't know who gave the alarm, but whoever it was, it was a false one. Fortunately, there were very few people down there at the time, or there might have been a panic. And now, if you're ready, we'll make a move."

He led the way through an open barrier and down ill-lit stone stairs which conveyed a sinister impression of giving access to a dungeon. In a passage at the bottom were a few preliminary horrors, such as relics of the Inquisition, a rack taken from a medieval castle, branding irons, thumb screws, and other mementos of man's one-time cruelty to man. Beyond the passage was the Murderers' Den.

It was a room of irregular shape with a vaulted roof, and dimly lit by electric lights burning behind inverted bowls of frosted glass. It was, by design, an eerie and uncomfortable chamber—a chamber whose atmosphere invited its visitors to speak in whispers.

The waxwork murderers stood on low pedestals with numbered tickets at their feet. Seeing them elsewhere, and without knowing whom they represented, one would have thought them a dull looking crew, chiefly remarkable for the shabbiness of their clothes, and as evidence of the changes of fashions even among the unfashionable.

The manager, walking around with Hewson, pointed out several of the more interesting of these unholy notabilities.

"That's Crippen; I expect you recognize him. Insignificant little beast who looks as if he couldn't tread on a worm. And of course this—"

"Who's that?" Hewson interrupted in a whisper, pointing.

"Oh, I was coming to him," said the manager in a light undertone. "Come and have a good look at him. This is our star turn. He's the only one of the bunch that hasn't been hanged."

The figure, which Hewson had indicated, was that of a small, slight man not much more than five feet in height. It wore little waxed mustaches, large spectacles, and a caped coat. There was something so exaggeratedly French in his appearance that it reminded Hewson of a stage caricature. He could not have said precisely why the mild-looking face seemed to him so repellent, but he had already recoiled a step and, even in the manager's company, it cost him an effort to look again.

"But who is he?" he asked.

"That," said the manager, "is Dr. Bourdette."

Hewson shook his head doubtfully. "I think I've heard the name," he said, "but I forget in connection with what."

The manager smiled.

"You'd remember better if you were a Frenchman," he said. "For some long while the man was the terror of Paris. He carried on his work of healing by day, and of throat-cutting by night, when the fit was on him. He killed for the sheer devilish pleasure it gave him to kill, and always in the same way—with a razor. After his last crime, he left a clue behind him, which set the police upon his track. One clue led to another, and before very long they knew that they were on the track of the Parisian equivalent of our Jack the Ripper, and had enough evidence to send him to the madhouse or the guillotine on a dozen capital charges. But even then our friend here was too clever for them. When he realized that the toils were closing about him he mysteriously disappeared, and ever since the police of every civilized country have been looking for him."

Hewson shuddered and fidgeted with his feet.

"I don't like him at all," he confessed. "Ugh! What eyes he's got!"

"Yes, this figure's a little masterpiece. You find the eyes bite into you? Well, that's excellent realism, then, for Bourdette practiced mesmerism, and was supposed to mesmerize his victims before dispatching them. Indeed, had he not done so, it is impossible to see how so small a man could have done his ghastly work. There were never any signs of a struggle."

"I thought I saw him move," said Hewson with a catch in his voice.

The manager smiled. "You'll have more than one optical illusion before the night's out, I expect. You shan't be locked in. You can come upstairs when you've had enough of it. There are watchmen on the premises, so you'll find company. Don't be alarmed if you hear them moving about. I'm sorry I can't give you any more light, because all the lights are on. For obvious reasons we keep this place as gloomy as possible. And now I think you had better return with me to the office and have a tot of whisky before beginning your night's vigil."

The member of the night staff who placed the armchair for Hewson was inclined to be facetious.

"Where will you have it, sir?" he asked, grinning. "Just 'ere, so as you can have a little talk with Crippen when you're tired of sitting still? Say where, sir."

Hewson smiled. The man's chaff pleased him if only because, for the moment at least, it lent the proceedings a much desired air of the commonplace. Hewson wished the man good night. It was easier than he had expected. He wheeled the armchair—a heavy one upholstered in plush—a little way down the central gangway, and deliberately turned it so that its back was toward the effigy of Dr. Bourdette. For some undefined reason he liked Dr. Bourdette a great deal less than his companions. Busying himself with arranging the chair, he was almost lighthearted, but when the attendant's footfalls had died away and a deep hush stole over the chamber, he realized that he had no slight ordeal before him.

The dim unwavering light fell on the rows of figures, which were so uncannily like human beings that the silence and the stillness seemed unnatural and even ghastly. He missed the sound of breathing, the rustling of clothes, the hundred and one minute noises one hears when even the deepest silence has fallen upon a crowd. All was still to the gaze and silent to the ear.

"It must be like this at the bottom of the sea," he thought, and wondered how to work the phrase into his story on the morrow.

He faced the sinister figures boldly enough. They were only waxworks. So long as he let that thought dominate all other he promised himself that all would be well. It did not, however, save him long from the discomfort occasioned by the waxen stare of Dr. Bourdette, which, he knew, was directed upon him from behind. The eyes of the little Frenchman's effigy haunted and tormented him, and he itched with the desire to turn and look. At last, Hewson slewed his chair round a little and looked behind him. Among the many figures standing in stiff, unnatural poses, the effigy of the dreadful little doctor stood out with a queer prominence, perhaps because a steady beam of light beat straight down upon it.

"He's only a waxwork like the rest of you," Hewson muttered defiantly. "You're all only waxworks."

They were only waxworks, yes, but waxworks don't move. Not that he had seen the least movement anywhere, but it struck him that, in the moment or two while he had looked behind him, there had been the least subtle change in the grouping of the figures in front. Crippen, for instance, seemed to have turned at least one degree to the left. Or, thought Hewson, perhaps the illusion was due to the fact that he had not slewed his chair back into its exact original position.

He took a notebook from his pocket and wrote quickly.

"Mem.—Deathly silence and unearthly stillness of figures. Like being bottom of sea. Hypnotic eyes of Dr. Bourdette. Figures seem to move when not being watched."

He closed the book suddenly over his fingers and looked round quickly and awfully over his right shoulder. He had neither seen nor heard a movement, but it was as if some sixth sense had made him aware of one. He looked straight into the vapid countenance of Lefroy, which smiled vacantly back as if to say, "It wasn't I!"

Of course it wasn't he, or any of them; it was his own nerves.

Or was it? Hadn't Crippen moved again during that moment when his attention was directed elsewhere? You couldn't trust that little man! Once you took your eyes off him, he took advantage of it to shift his position. That was what they were all doing, if he only knew it, he told himself, and half rose out of his chair.

This was not quite good enough! He was going. He *wasn't* going to spend the night with a lot of waxworks which moved while he wasn't looking.

Hewson sat down again. This was very cowardly and very absurd. They were only waxworks and they couldn't move; let him hold to that thought and all would yet be well. Then why all that silent unrest about him? A subtle something in the air which did not quite break the silence and happened, whichever way he looked, just beyond the boundaries of his vision. He swung round quickly to encounter the mild but baleful stare of Dr. Bourdette. Then, without warning, he jerked his head back to stare straight at Crippen. Ha! He'd nearly caught Crippen that time!

"You'd better be careful, Crippen—and all the rest of you! If I do see one of you move, I'll smash you to pieces! Do you hear?"

He ought to go, he told himself. Already he had experienced enough to write his story, or ten stories, for the matter of that. Well, then, why not go? The

Morning Echo would be none the wiser as to how long he had stayed, nor would it care so long as his story was a good one. Yes, but that night watchman upstairs would chaff him. And the manager—one never knew—perhaps the manager would quibble over that five pound note which he needed so badly. He wondered if Rose were asleep, or if she were lying awake and thinking of him. She'd laugh when he told her what he had imagined!

This was a little too much! It was bad enough that the waxwork effigies of murderers should move when they weren't being watched, but it was intolerable that they should breathe. Somebody was breathing. Or was it his own breath which sounded to him as if it came from a distance? He sat rigid, listening and straining, until he exhaled with a long sigh. His own breath after all, or—if not, something had divined that he was listening, and had ceased breathing simultaneously.

This would not do! This distinctly would not do! He must clutch at something, grip with his mind upon something which belonged essentially to the workaday world, to the daylight London streets. He was Raymond Hewson, an unsuccessful journalist, a living and breathing man, and these figures grouped around him were only dummies, so they could neither move nor whisper. What did it matter if they were supposed to be life-like effigies of murderers? They were only made of wax and sawdust, and stood there for the entertainment of morbid sightseers and orange-sucking trippers. That was better! Now what was that funny story which somebody told him in the Falstaff yesterday?

He recalled part of it, but not all, for the gaze of Dr. Bourdette urged, challenged, and finally compelled him to turn. Hewson half turned, and then swung his chair so as to bring him face-to-face with the wearer of those dreadful hypnotic eyes. His own were dilated, and his mouth, at first set in a grin of terror, lifted at the corners in a snarl. Then Hewson spoke and woke a hundred sinister echoes.

"You moved, damn you!" he cried. "Yes, you did, damn you! I saw you!"

Then he sat quite still, staring straight before him, like a man found frozen in the Arctic snows.

Dr. Bourdette's movements were leisurely. He stepped off his pedestal with the mincing care of a lady alighting from a bus. The platform stood about two feet from the ground, and above the edge of it a plush-covered rope hung in arch-like curves. Dr. Bourdette lifted up the rope until it formed an arch for him to pass under, stepped off the platform, and sat down on the edge facing Hewson.

Then he nodded and smiled and said, "Good evening."

"I need hardly tell you," he continued, in perfect English, in which was traceable only the least foreign accent, "that not until I overhead the conversation between you and the worthy manager of this establishment, did I suspect that I should have the pleasure of a companion here for the night. You cannot move or speak without my bidding, but you can hear me perfectly well. Something tells me that you are—shall I say nervous? My dear sir, have no illusions. I am not one of these contemptible effigies miraculously come to life. I am Dr. Bourdette himself."

He paused, coughed, and shifted his legs.

"Pardon me," he resumed, "but I am a little stiff. And let me explain. Circumstances with which I need not fatigue you, have made it desirable that I should live in England. I was close to this building this evening when I saw a policeman regarding me a thought too curiously. I guessed that he intended to follow and perhaps ask me embarrassing questions, so I mingled with the crowd and came in here. An extra coin bought my admission to the chamber in which we now meet, and an inspiration showed me a certain means of escape. I raised a cry of fire, and when all the fools had rushed to the stairs, I stripped my effigy of the caped coat which you behold me wearing, donned it, hid my effigy under the platform at the back, and took its place on the pedestal. The manager's description of me, which I had the embarrassment of being compelled to overhear, was biased but not altogether inaccurate. Clearly I am not dead, although it is as well that the world thinks otherwise. His account of my hobby, which I have indulged for years, although, through necessity, less frequently of late, was in the main true, although not intelligently expressed. The world is divided between collectors and non-collectors. With the non-collectors we are not concerned. The collectors collect anything, according to their individual tastes, from money to cigarette cards, from moths to matchboxes. I collect throats."

He paused again and regarded Hewson's throat with interest mingled with disfavor.

"I am obliged to chance, which brought us together tonight," he continued, "and perhaps it would seem ungrateful to complain. From motives of personal safety, my activities have been somewhat curtailed of late years, and I am glad of this opportunity of gratifying my somewhat unusual whim. But you have a skinny neck, sir, if you will overlook a personal remark. I should have never selected you from choice. I like men with thick necks, thick red necks."

He fumbled in an inside pocket and took out something which he tested against a wet forefinger, and then proceeded to pass gently to and fro against the palm of his left hand.

"This is a little French razor," he remarked blandly. "They are not much used in England, but perhaps you know them? One strops them on wood. The blade, you will observe, is very narrow. They do not cut very deep, see for yourself. I shall ask you the little civil question of all the polite barbers. Does the razor suit you, sir?"

He rose up, a diminutive but menacing figure of evil, and approached Hewson with the silent, furtive step of a hunting panther.

"You will have the goodness," he said, "to raise your chin a little. Thank you, and a little more. Just a little more. Ah, thank you! *Merci, m'sieur. Ah, merci.*"

Over one end of the chamber was a thick skylight of frosted glass which, by day, let in a few sickly and filtered rays from the floor above. After sunrise these began to mingle with the subdued light from the electric bulbs, and this mingled illumination added a certain ghastliness to a scene which needed no additional touch of horror.

The waxwork figures stood apathetically in their places, waiting to be admired or execrated by the crowds who would presently wander fearfully among them. In their midst, in the center gangway, Hewson sat still, leaning far back in his armchair. His chin was uptilted as if he were waiting to receive attention from a barber, and although there was not a scratch upon his throat, nor anywhere upon his body, he was cold and dead. His previous employers were wrong in having him credited with no imagination.

Dr. Bourdette on his pedestal watched the dead man unemotionally. He did not move, nor was he capable of motion. But then, after all, he was only a waxwork.

No Man's Land
by
Nancy Hayden

Eroded and overgrown, the World War I trench zigzagged among beech and oak and vines before seeming to disappear within the Argonne Forest. The remains of the morning mist lingered in the trench and along the forest floor while the sun filtered in through moss-laden branches. Sarah took a deep breath and wondered how she let Anson talk her into another World War I adventure—rooting around a French forest, looking at hundred-year-old shell holes and a forgotten trench. She would much rather be strolling through a flower garden.

Anson stood next to her, mesmerized. His face flushed with excitement and eyes fixed, Sarah imagined he saw the whole scene in front of them: soldiers crouched in the trench, Enfield rifles at the ready, gas mask satchels hanging around their necks. Anson had been a World War I buff since he was a kid, but six months ago, when he found his great-grandfather's letters from the war, his enthusiasm had turned to obsession. Sarah had suggested the trip to France to get it out of his system. Thus far it hadn't worked. They'd toured battlegrounds, monuments, cemeteries, visited the World War I museum at Verdun, peered into porthole windows at skulls and bones at the Douaumont Ossuary, and it had all just fueled his fascination.

"This is it," Anson said. "This is where my great-grandfather fought and died. The Meuse-Argonne offensive, September twenty-sixth, nineteen-eighteen. Hey, that's tomorrow! Cool!"

"Cool." Sarah stared into the forest.

"And that," Anson waved his arm toward the trees in front of the trench. "That was No Man's Land."

Sarah shuddered. No Man's Land. The land between the Allies and the Germans that both sides filled with barbed wire entanglements, shells, and the dead. There were probably bones of some of the soldiers still beneath their feet, the ones they left in place. Supposedly, Anson's great-grandfather's remains had been buried with over 14,000 other American soldiers at the nearby Meuse-Argonne American Cemetery. She and Anson had wandered through rows and rows of white marble crosses and occasional Star of David grave markers that each bore the name, rank, division, home state, and date of death, but they couldn't find the great-grandfather's site. So many, and so young. Anson's great-grandfather was only twenty-five when he died.

Sarah looked over at Anson and was startled by the far-away look in his usually sparkling blue eyes. She'd fallen in love with those eyes two years ago, and couldn't believe her luck when they turned lovingly toward her. Lately, though, they hardly registered her as anything more than a map-reading companion. The romantic dinners in France she'd imagined had become monotonous history lessons. It wasn't that she didn't find World War I interesting. She'd learned a lot about the war that ushered in the twentieth century, but staring at the graves at dozens of French and American cemeteries, seeing the bones of hundreds of thousands of soldiers at the ossuary, and looking at pictures of the dead and wounded in the museum, had begun to weigh on her. This trench and the site of so much death made her stomach queasy.

"It would be amazing to go back there," Anson said, still staring at the trench. "Just for a day or two. Then I'd know what it was really like."

"And leave me here alone?" Sarah said. She could tell he'd really meant it, and that stung. In fact, the whole trip had turned sour. Anson acted like she didn't even exist.

"I wish you were done with this World War One insanity!"

"Come on," Anson said. "Let's go."

"Not this time," Sarah said, surprised at the firmness in her voice.

He stopped, looked at her, and seemed to see her for the first time that day.

"Ah," he said, smiling down on her and reaching for her hand. "Come here."

He pulled her close and kissed the top of her head.

"I'm sorry," he said. "I know I've been acting crazy about this stuff. I just can't help it. It's so interesting. But today is the last day of the World War One tour. We'll just take a few minutes to look at the trench. I'll get closure on my great-grandfather, and then we'll do what you want for the rest of the trip. Gardens, art museums, romantic dinners."

She looked up into his eyes and caught a glimpse of the old Anson. He kissed her sweetly.

"Promise?"

"I promise. Come on. Let's see where my great-grandfather spent his last few days."

He let go of her, and Sarah watched him run down the slope into the trench. She sighed. This was the kind of day she would have loved to spend in the woods back home, but it's not what she came to France for.

"I'm coming," she said. Anson had already turned the first corner of the trench and was out of sight. "Wait for me."

Sarah stumbled trying to catch up. Vines and brambles were thick in the bottom and sides of the trench, while branches littered the path. There were even a few large trees growing out of the bottom of the trench. This was more like bushwhacking than a walk in the woods. She turned the corner to the next section, only to find it empty.

"Anson, slow down," she called out.

She thought she heard something and stopped to listen.

"Stop it—no!" Anson shouted. "Get away!"

Sarah hurried around the next corner expecting to find Anson fighting with someone, but he was alone, staring in her direction, his face pale.

"Who are you talking to?" she asked.

He looked at her, but he didn't seem to see her. She hurried ahead and grabbed his hand.

"Honey, what is it? What's wrong?"

"Let's get out of here," he said, and pushed her back the way they'd come.

"What's going on?"

"Just go," he said, and something in his voice made her start running.

She felt him in close pursuit as she hopped a fallen branch, ducked under a vine, and turned the next corner. He was breathing loudly, as if in a panic. She started to turn to see what was wrong, but he pushed her forward.

"Go, go!"

Vines and branches seemed to be tripping her up as she ran, but finally she turned the last bend. There was the bank where they'd entered. They were almost there.

But halfway through the last stretch, something made her look back. Anson wasn't following anymore. He was running back down the trench.

"Anson!"

She was out of breath, sore and bleeding from scratches on her arm, but she stumbled after him, back through the trench, turned the corner and caught a blur of his shirt as he scrambled up the side and out of the trench.

"Anson, what are you doing?" she yelled out.

She tried to scramble up the bank but kept slipping back. When she was finally out, she looked all around the forest. He wasn't there.

"Anson, what's going on? Where are you?"

But he was gone.

Sarah was leaning back in her car seat, eyes closed, when she heard a car pull off the road. She'd spent hours roaming the woods, crying, shouting, searching, but there was no sign of Anson. She'd called the French police and spent a half hour pacing around the car. Exhausted and spent, she finally sat in the driver's seat and waited. Maybe she dozed, maybe she just lost track of the time; she was surprised to see it was almost four o'clock, hours since they'd started.

She looked out the window. A tall man emerged from the police car, and Sarah went to meet him. He introduced himself as a police detective. She followed his gaze, noticing for the first time how bloody and dirty her hands, pants, and shirt were.

"I don't speak French," she said. "I told the person on the phone."

"Yes, I know," the detective said.

Between sobs and tears, Sarah poured out her story. She showed the detective the trench; she'd walked it several times that afternoon and the woods around it, but she never saw any sign of Anson.

"I suppose I made a mess of the area," she said. "I spent hours wandering the woods, thinking that maybe Anson was lost or disoriented."

"Has that happened before?" the detective said.

"No. Today was the first time I'd ever seen him so upset."

"But he didn't say about what."

"There wasn't time. He wanted to get out of the trench."

They'd stopped near the place where Sarah had first found Anson so pale and frightened. "But then he ran back into the trench?"

"Yes," she said. "I don't understand why. We were almost out."

The detective looked around the trench. "And this is where he shouted?"

Sarah nodded. "It doesn't make sense," she said, her voice cracking again, tears welling up. "He just started acting…"

The detective stared down at her for a moment, his dark eyes narrowed. "Crazy?"

"Yes," she said softly.

It was almost dark by the time they left the forest. The detective escorted Sarah back to her hotel in Verdun. He said he'd alert the nearby village authorities, check with the local hospitals, and that she should contact him directly if she heard from Anson. He gave her an encouraging smile before he left.

Sarah didn't smile back.

She nodded and walked slowly up to her room. Partway up, she had an inkling that maybe Anson was already back at the hotel, that he had come back on his own, or maybe left a message. She ran up to their room and threw open the door. It was dark. She turned on the light. The room was clean and tidy. And no Anson.

Anson woke up with a jerk and looked around, hoping that everything was as it should be, that he was back with Sarah, telling her about his crazy dream or hallucination or whatever it was.

He choked back a sob when he saw he was still in the trench wearing the uniform of the American Expeditionary Forces and crowded in by other soldiers wearing the same. A shell exploded nearby and for a moment he forgot about his nausea from the stench of rot and feces and the quicklime used to mask it.

"This can't be happening."

Soil and stone rained down on him, making a plinking sound as they hit his metal helmet. For the hundredth time that day, he went through the events in his head. He and Sarah had been walking in the trench. He could hear voices and then a booming noise, like the sound of a shell. He'd stopped to listen and felt the earth and vines pulling on him. Sarah came to the spot where he waited. He felt something horrible was about to happen and panicked. They needed to get out of the goddamn trench. He stumbled behind her, felt himself being pulled, then they were coming at him from the other directions, soldiers all dressed in AEF uniforms, bayonets attached to their rifles and all aimed at him. He ran back through the trench again, but he had to get out of there. He climbed out and over the top, only to be knocked back in by an explosion. When he opened his eyes, the forest was gone, just blackened stumps and mud. He was in the trench and in his great-grandfather's boots.

He'd tried to get the sergeant and lieutenant to believe that he wasn't who they thought he was, that he didn't belong there.

"Enough of your bullshit, Private," the sergeant finally said. "Back to your post."

The lieutenant had deferred to his sergeant, but Anson had heard him asking whether he thought it was some kind of shock from the shell blast. If only it were. All day, Anson had thought of ways to escape, only to come back to the same thought. Escape to where?

"This isn't real," he said to himself. "It can't be real."

A soldier plopped down next to him, dressed in the uniform he knew so well from photographs of his great-grandfather. Anson even had his own World War I helmet, bought for five dollars at a flea market, hung up on the wall above his desk at home. Occasionally, he even tried it on and admired himself in the mirror.

"Of course this ain't real, Andy," the man said. "This here is Hell."

"I don't belong here," Anson said, more to himself than the soldier sitting next to him.

"None of us do," he said, and punched Anson in the arm. "Although I thought you was a goner when that shell hit this morning. I'm sure as hell glad you wasn't."

"What's your name?" Anson said.

"My name? That's a good one. Guess that blast knocked you a little cuckoo."

"Guess it did," Anson said.

The man turned his face toward Anson and smiled. "Come on. You know me."

In the dim light of dusk, Anson looked at him closely for the first time. He had a large nose and a big mouth, and he did recognize him. An older version, though, in a picture with his great-grandma Elizabeth. This man was her second husband, and stepdad to Anson's grandfather.

"Thomas," he said slowly. "Thomas Murdon."

"Damn straight, Andy. Your best friend, Tom," he said. "None of this Thomas shit. We been to high school together, I was best man at your wedding, helped you build your barn, was godfather to your first born, joined up with you when you said you wanted to go. We were at boot camp in Virginia together."

"That's right," Anson said, but he didn't know any of those things. He only knew the stories his father had told him about his granddad. How his granddad's stepfather was a crazy son-of-a-bitch. Warm one minute, cruel the next. They all said the war had done it to him, and losing his best friend.

"There you have it," Tom said. "Your memory's coming back."

"In fits and starts," Anson said.

The sound of metal clinking drew their attention.

"Let's get some chow," Tom said. "You remember slumgullion?"

Anson groaned.

Tom chuckled. "It's one of the things I'm trying to forget."

Food sounded good, though. Anson hadn't eaten since breakfast. Maybe food would calm him down, allow him to regain his sanity. Back to Sarah, back to what he'd taken for granted, back to life. He fought the stinging tears welling up in his eyes again and followed Tom to the marmite cans.

Anson kept at Tom all evening. Since Tom believed he had memory problems from the shell blast, Anson figured he could ask him anything: how to work the gas mask satchel, the rifle, the bayonet, and the thousand details Anson had only read about, never actually done. Tom didn't seem to mind. Anson asked him about his great-grandmother, Elizabeth, and what Tom thought of the boys. Anson's own grandfather was the third son, born shortly after the war. His great-grandfather never knew his third boy. Elizabeth had named him Thomas. Thomas Murdon, Jr.

"You're a lucky man, Andy. I always said that. Got yourself the prettiest gal in town, two young rascally boys. Wish I had kids like that."

"You married, Tom?"

"I'll say your memory's in fits and starts," Tom laughed. "No, I ain't married, and you know damn well you stole my gal."

"Sorry," Anson said.

"Oh, well. She weren't really my gal. Only ever had eyes for you. Lucky dog."

Tom liked talking and liked to laugh. After a few hours, Anson understood how this man was his great-grandfather's best friend.

"Tom," Anson said, knowing the truth of what he was about to ask. "If anything happens to me, I hope you'll look after Lizzy and the boys."

"Nothing's going to happen to you again," Tom said, and punched Anson's arm. "You got all the luck."

"I guess so," Anson said, but he had a feeling his luck had run out.

Sergeant Johnson called them together before midnight. A short, tough man with a nose that had obviously been broken a time or two, he'd been giving Anson a hard time all day.

"All right, boys," the sergeant said. "Shortly after midnight, our artillery will be letting loose with everything we've got. And Jerry will be giving some back. We'll be getting a hot meal after midnight. Eat it all, since we don't know when we'll be getting another. If you can sleep with the hellfire noise, do it. We go over the top at five-thirty."

The sergeant turned to each one of his men. In the darkness, his face and eyes were indiscernible with the blackness, but Anson was sure when they looked his way, his eyes narrowed.

"Dismissed. Except for you, Private."

Tom gave Anson a tap on the shoulder before he moved off. Anson watched him go, then turned back to the sergeant.

"Have a seat, Private." The sergeant sat down next to Anson. "Smoke?"

Anson shook his head. "Don't smoke." He didn't smoke, although his great-grandfather must have, by the looks the others had given him all day when he declined their invitations.

"How you feeling now?"

"Pretty much the same."

The sergeant lit a match and held it up toward Anson's face. He lit his cigarette and took a long drag.

"You ready?"

Anson swallowed hard. He wasn't ready. This was madness.

The sergeant looked over at him. "Well, boy?"

"I don't know," Anson finally said. "I think I'm crazy."

The sergeant took another drag and slowly exhaled. He stood up and so did Anson.

"It's crazy, Private. I'll grant you that, but we're in this together, and I don't want you doing anything stupid that puts the others in danger. You got that?"

Anson took a deep breath. "Got it."

"Got it, who," the sergeant said, jabbing his finger in Anson's chest.

"Got it, sir."

The sergeant walked off. Anson sat back down and instinctively fingered his wedding band. Sarah had it custom-made for him. Ivy etched into the gold wound around the band with heart-shaped leaves. Without either of them knowing, he'd had a band especially made for her, too, only he'd chosen tiny butterflies etched into the metal.

He wondered where she was now. How she was dealing with his disappearance. For the first time in his life, he was grateful his parents weren't alive to wonder about him, that there was no one else really to worry and feel sad. Only Sarah.

"I love you, Sarah," he whispered into his hands. "I'm so sorry you have to suffer like this."

He let his love for Sarah fill him and it sustained him all through the shelling, through his last meal, and as they lined up to go over the top. Tom was with him and gave him a reassuring smile.

"Tom," he said as they bunched in closer together. He put his mouth toward Tom's ear. The shelling had reached a roar like a thundering waterfall. "Listen to me. When this is all over, when you go home, make sure you tell them all how war is hell, how too many people died for no reason."

"Can't hear you," Tom shouted, and slapped Anson on the back.

The sergeant blew his whistle, high-pitched and barely audible with the booming artillery and screaming shells. Anson climbed onto the fire step and scrambled with the others out of the trench. Smoke and mist enveloped him as he fought his way through barbed wire entanglements, recently cut to allow the men through. Blackened stumps and snags loomed out of the gray dawn.

Anson looked right and then left. He saw Tom, the sergeant, and other men moving steadily forward. The artillery kept up a rolling barrage, screening them as they crossed No Man's Land. Anson's body tightened like a fist; he tried to think of Sarah again, but the tension stripped everything else from his mind. He tripped over a fallen log, caught himself, and stumbled into a large shell hole, bigger than their rental car. Tom was there with him. Anson felt a moment of relief knowing Tom would help, but when he looked up at his best friend, he was shocked to see the hateful determination on Tom's face and Tom's rifle pointed at him.

"You goddamn son of a bitch," Tom said.

Sarah gripped the steering wheel and stared into the dark forest lit only by the car's headlights. In the rearview mirror, she saw the dog, a big black Bouvier that looked more like a bear than a dog, sitting alert and staring ahead. Next to Sarah sat the woman, Lur, from Avocourt village. Short and thin with a lean wrinkled face, she looked about seventy but could have been older.

It had been almost two weeks since Anson disappeared. The police gave up inquiries after a week, and nothing Sarah said or did changed that. She was desperate. A few days earlier, she had started going house to house in the nearby villages with a hired French translator. No one told her anything. No one, that is, except Lur.

Lur had invited her in, listened to her sad story, and nodded her head knowingly. She told Sarah about other disappearances in the Argonne Forest, and how no one went there anymore because it was haunted. It sounded crazy. Some of Lur's neighbors said Lur was crazy, a crazy Basque witch. But Anson's disappearance was crazy, too.

Lur insisted they come at night. "During the day, I cannot see or hear anything, only faint echoes," she'd told Sarah in Spanish, a language they both spoke. "At night, though, the trees, the land, and even the wind will speak to me."

Sarah rolled down the windows and turned off the engine.

"Now, listen," Lur hissed. "Listen, listen."

Lur repeated the word several more times, in a lulling way that turned into the rhythm of marching feet, and then the rumble of thunder in the distance. No, not thunder. Artillery, booming in regular beats.

"I hear it," Sarah said as the artillery grew louder and shells exploded in the distance.

Lur went outside with her dog. "Come, Sarah. It's time."

Sarah stood next to the dog. It seemed the safest place. Shouting men and explosions echoed all around. Her stomach tightened. She stared at Lur's small but strong hands as she let the dog smell one of Anson's shirts.

"Go," Lur said, and the dog loped off, sniffing the ground, but in the opposite direction of the trench.

"The trench is that way," Sarah said. Lur paid no attention and followed the Bouvier with her powerful flashlight shining in front of her.

"This way, Sarah."

And it was at that moment, with the sounds of shelling and war like Sarah had heard in the museum movie, that terror took over. This was a trap. The old woman was taking her out to meet the same fate as Anson. She'd tricked her. Someone was hiding in the forest playing the recording from a movie.

"Hurry, Sarah." Lur stopped and shined the flashlight on Sarah. "What are you waiting for?"

Someone stepped out of the darkness behind the woman. Sarah shrieked. No, it was just the flashlight casting a strange light on the tree behind her. Not a tree, a burnt snag. Sarah looked up. There were no trees above anymore. Snags and blasted tree trunks were all that stood out against the starry night sky.

Lur moved toward the car. Sarah hurried to the driver's side. Her fingers fumbled to open the door latch, but she was too slow. Lur reached her and grabbed the handle.

"Stop it," Sarah shouted. "Get away."

"Quiet, you foolish girl," Lur said, shaking Sarah's arm. "I tell you we are safe. It is the fear and hate of the War that you are hearing and seeing. Dark shadows that seep into the mind if you let them. Do not let them."

"You're tricking me," Sarah cried out. "You killed Anson."

"Sarah, calm down," Lur said. The bear dog bounded back to the car and sat next to Sarah, leaning her body against Sarah's leg. Sarah's fingers reached for the soft curly fur.

"Listen to me, child," Lur continued. "You are letting all the horrible feelings of this place take you over. All the fear of those young men and the hatred and the suffering still lingers in the land, the rocks, soil and trees. This place will not let go of the War."

"Please, let's come back tomorrow," Sarah cried.

"We will find nothing in the daylight. Only now. I do not know why it is so. It just is."

The old woman reached out and held Sarah's hand. The war raged around them, but Sarah felt a little of her fear subside.

"Come," Lur said. "It's time."

They followed the dog through shell holes and over rubble piles, but it wasn't long before the dog stopped, loped down the slope of a shell crater, and started digging in the muck and detritus.

Sarah helped Lur down the steep slope. The old woman shined the flashlight on the dog. The dog barked.

"She has found him," Lur said, and hurried ahead. "Good girl."

Sarah walked behind, looking intently at the ground where Lur shined the light. It came to rest where the dog had dug.

For a moment, Sarah didn't know what she was looking at, so black and gnarled, but then something glistened in the light.

"No," Sarah gasped. She dropped down, her face twisting up with pain. "No. Anson."

She had hoped the old woman really was mad with her fantasies and haunted forests, but as Sarah stared down at the leathered flesh that still clung to the knuckles of the unearthed hand, she wished she wasn't seeing Anson's wedding band shining on the rotted finger.

The Bondage of Self
by
Holly Newstein

"You sure you'll be okay?"

If one more person asks me that, I'll scream, Stacy thought. She gritted her teeth and pasted a wan smile on her face.

"Sure. I'll be fine." She stood on the porch and waved to the last departing carload of mourners, then went back inside.

She looked around the room and sighed. Drink glasses and plates with half-eaten food were scattered around, and the kitchen was piled with dishes. Everyone had been so generous, bringing food and sodas and even a couple bottles of wine. But she was left with the mess.

Oh well, it will take my mind off things.

Derek had died suddenly five days ago. The doctor at the ER said it was a heart attack. They told her it was strange, because he had no history of high blood pressure or high cholesterol. Stacy declined an autopsy, and from that moment she hadn't had time to think about much of anything. She had dealt with the next thing in front of her—the ambulance crew, the coroner, the funeral home, Derek's employer, the cemetery, the lawyer, the family, the friends, the bank, on and on it went. With Derek's death, Stacy's world had exploded into a million unfamiliar pieces; documents, passwords, dates and numbers. All needing her attention and her signature.

But it kept her from thinking about the night Derek died.

She moved through the living room, gathering and stacking plates, taking them into the kitchen and putting them into the dishwasher. Back and forth. Clearing, scraping, wiping. Wrapping leftovers and placing them in the fridge.

Starting the dishwasher, with the next load waiting in neat piles on the counter. Finally, she picked up the framed photograph of Derek that someone had placed prominently on the dining room table, and went to replace it on the mantel in the living room. In front of the big gilt-framed mirror Derek had given her.

Stacy had never liked the mirror. Derek had brought it home as a housewarming gift for her.

Now you can always see how lovely you are, Derek had said with a smile. But the mirror always reflected her as smaller and darker, even almost ugly at times. It was a subtly different image than the ones she saw in the bathroom mirror and the full-length mirror in the bedroom. It might have been a trick of the light, but Stacy wasn't so sure.

As she moved to place the photograph, her foot caught on the edge of the Oriental rug on the hearth. She stumbled and the photograph flew out of her hand and crashed to the floor. Glass shattered and skittered on the wooden planks.

"Dammit," Stacy muttered, and knelt down to pick up the broken glass. A large shard sliced her forefinger deeply. Drops of blood fell from her hand onto the photo of Derek's face. They smeared over the half-smile he wore—the one she had once found so charming. And Stacy remembered the night he died.

Their marriage had followed an arc, like countless others before it. The bubbling ecstasy of newlyweds, into the contented comfort of habit and familiarity, through disillusion and finally contempt thinly veiled by civility. Stacy occasionally wondered if children would have made a difference, but finally decided that they wouldn't have, and was grateful she didn't have any to be held hostage in this deteriorating emotional dance between her and Derek.

Still, neither of them was brave enough to ask for a divorce. With both their incomes, they had a nice house, upmarket cars, and luxury vacations. Stacy knew that on her salary alone things would be very tight.

I'd be eating a lot of ramen noodles, she thought.

She found it easier to retreat into a fantasy world, a world where Derek simply wasn't there.

I'd sell this place and buy that cute Victorian house in the village, she thought. *The one with all the gingerbread scrollwork. Then I'd go to Rome and Paris and spend days in the museums. I'd get a cat. A Siamese cat.*

Stacy insulated herself in her dream world. Derek's actual existence, his comings and goings, became irrelevant. When he was there, she almost ignored him. They didn't talk much, and Stacy couldn't remember the last time they'd made love. The best times were when he worked late or went on a business trip. Waking up with the bed all to herself made her fantasy even more real—until he came home, as he always did. Sometimes she'd be startled to see him, so deeply engaged as she was in believing him gone.

It made her loveless marriage tolerable.

Then five days ago, reality slapped her in the face. She'd needed a fresh check register for her checkbook and had gone into Derek's desk. Under the boxes of checks she found a credit card in both their names that she did not know existed. With the card were several receipts. She took them out and looked them over. A couple were for restaurants in the city that she had never eaten in. Two entrees, some drinks, and one dessert. One was for the Four Seasons Hotel. The date was for a night Derek had told her he was traveling on business.

Her hands went ice-cold as her cheeks flamed red. She pulled the drawer out of the desk and upended it onto the floor. As she sorted out the receipts and papers, she pieced together enough to show that this affair had been going on for many months. Rage flashed through her body like a red-hot knife.

It wasn't so much that Derek didn't love her any more, but that now she had to deal with reality. And reality was a divorce, and it would be messy, and she would be so much worse off than she was now.

She slipped the receipts and the credit card into an envelope and cried, because her dream was over.

Derek's Mercedes pulled into the garage.

"Hi, Stace. What's for dinner?" he called as he entered the kitchen. He kissed her cheek perfunctorily.

"Come and have a seat at the table," she replied, keeping her voice light and pleasant. "It's a surprise."

Derek sat down at the bare kitchen table and looked around. "What is it?"

"This," she replied, and handed him a plate with the envelope on it.

He looked inside and stared at it for a few moments. Then he met Stacy's eyes, his face pale and guilty. He took the plate and set it on the counter.

"Let's get some wine and talk," he said.

"No, we'll talk now," she said, her voice rising with rage.

"All righty then," Derek replied with that little smile she had now grown to despise. "Her name is Renee, and I love her. I've been meaning to tell you..."

"'Meaning to tell me?' Tell me that you love her so much that you forge my name on a secret credit card and sneak around for months? All those nights you were working late? All those hotels you checked into as Mr. and Mrs. Coleman, no doubt."

Derek's cheeks flushed red. "Don't you think I've noticed how you ignore me? You hardly acknowledge my existence. What happened to us, Stace?" His face contorted as he struggled for self-control. "It's obvious you don't care anymore, and I can't live like that. Renee makes me happy. With her, I feel alive again."

Stacy was silent for a moment.

Maybe he's right. Maybe I haven't been fair.

But the self-righteous indignation at being the Wronged Spouse blazed up in her again.

"Fine, you cheating piece of shit. That's just fine. You can pack your bag and move in with your precious Renee. It would have been so much better for me if you had just *died*."

Derek's eyes widened. "What did you say?"

"Fine, I'll say it louder. *I wish you were dead!*"

He suddenly paled, and a fine sheen of sweat broke out on his forehead. He clutched his chest. Blood poured from his nose. Stacy went on, not noticing, too blinded by her anger.

"I can't believe you did this to me… Derek?"

Derek stared glassily at her. His face seemed to swell, and his lips drew back from his teeth.

"Very funny," she said. "You can stop being dramatic. Anytime now."

He tipped out of his chair and hit the floor with his face. Moments later there was a crimson puddle around his head.

"Derek!" Stacy knelt beside him. She rolled him onto his back, grabbed his shoulders, and shook him. His head bounced on the tile floor.

"*Derek!*"

Derek's open, unfocused eyes gazed at the ceiling. The gout of blood from his nose became a trickle, then stopped.

Stacy looked down into his face, stunned.

"Nooo," she moaned. "God, no."

She scrambled to her feet and called 911. But she burned the envelope before the paramedics arrived.

The sound of dripping brought her out of her reverie. She realized she was clutching the sharp piece of glass tightly in her hand, and blood was running all over the photograph.

"Shit!" she cried, dropping the piece of glass. Her fingers and palm were lacerated. She ran to the kitchen sink and grabbed the dishtowel, wrapping her hand tightly, and then went to finish cleaning up the mess. Derek's eyes, behind their bloody film, seemed to watch her as she carefully picked up the remaining glass with her uninjured hand. She glanced at the photo again as she carried it to the kitchen wastebasket. Instead of smiling, Derek now looked angry, even vengeful.

Stop it. It's the blood. You're giving yourself the heebie-jeebies.

She slid the photo and the glass shards into the trash. She unwrapped her hand and held it under cold running water in the sink. The cuts were deep, but not too bad, she decided. Already they were starting to clot. But they would probably leave scars.

"Bastard," she said out loud. But without much conviction.

"What do you mean, my luggage is lost? Stolen, more like. And my jewelry was in it!"

"I'm sorry, Mrs. Coleman, but airline liability policy limits us to two hundred dollars for the contents of your bag. You can download the claim form from our webs—"

Stacy clicked off the phone. She poured herself another drink and stared into the gilt-framed mirror. She saw herself, smaller and uglier than usual, with pasty skin and red-rimmed eyes. Her old nightgown, shapeless and stained, hung from her shoulders.

I should have thrown that stupid mirror away.

It had been a year since Derek died. She had just returned from her dream vacation, paid for with Derek's life insurance money. It had been a nightmare. Rome was hot and crowded, the traffic impossible, and the museums had long waits.

Six hours to see the Sistine Chapel. And it wasn't worth it.

In Paris, her wallet had been stolen and her hotel room had bedbugs. The hotel management did not share her horror and refused to refund her money. Her flights were delayed and her luggage lost on the flight home. Apparently for good, and with her mother's emerald ring inside.

Before she went on her trip, she'd sold the house she had shared with Derek and bought the cute little Victorian in the village. Immediately after she closed on it, the roof began to leak, the furnace gave out, and she discovered that the gingerbread trim had dry rot and termites were slowly destroying the parquet floor in the dining room. The repairs emptied her bank account.

Ming was the final insult. The Siamese kitten she bought had grown from an adorable seal-pointed ball of fluff into an unloving creature who refused to use the litter box and clawed the couch to ribbons. The day she returned from her European nightmare, Ming got out of the house and had not returned since.

Over time, burdened by her disillusions and a corroding undercurrent of guilt, she had begun to drink more than the occasional glass of wine with dinner. Too many bleary-eyed mornings at work had resulted in today's humiliating interview with her boss.

He had called her into his office and closed the door.

"Stacy, I know you have been through a lot this past year, but it has come to my attention that your performance has been subpar lately. And getting worse."

"I'm really sorry about that," she had said through her pounding headache. "But you see…"

He had cut her off. "You come in late almost every morning now, and I have noticed that you have been calling in sick on Mondays. I want you to make an appointment with Human Resources to see if you might have a substance abuse problem."

If you had my problems, you'd drink, too, she thought. But she said nothing, only nodded.

"I'm sorry, Stacy, but I can't have you dragging down the whole department. I need people who are willing to do their jobs one-hundred-percent. I am putting you on probation pending a report from HR. One more lateness or absence will be grounds for termination. Do you understand?"

"Yes, I do." Summoning what was left of her dignity, she said, "I understand, and I will make the appointment. I will do better."

She had left his office and cried in the ladies' room.

Rehab. They want to send me to rehab. Or I lose my job.

She flexed her hand and looked at the fine white scar on her palm from the glass cut. Derek's photograph. A year ago.

Cut my life line right in half, she thought, and laughed bitterly to herself.

A creak on the front porch roused her from her pitiful thoughts, and for a moment she thought perhaps Ming had returned. She moved to the front door, a little unsteadily, and opened it.

"Ming," she called—and her voice died in her throat.

A woman stood in the circle of light from the porch lamp. She was young, with long, curly dark hair and large dark eyes. She looked intently at Stacy.

"Who're you?" Stacy asked.

"My name is Renee," the woman answered.

Stacy swayed and grabbed the door jamb for support. "Renee? Derek's Renee?"

"That's me," she said with a twisted smile. "May I come in?"

Stacy looked her up and down.

Younger than me. Skinnier. Nice boots. Derek was always bugging me to grow out my hair. Now I know why.

She was suddenly conscious of her baggy old nightgown and her bare feet with chipped nail polish on her toes. The old, betrayed anger flashed up in her. She laughed bitterly.

"Sure, why not? We can talk about old times, and my dear departed cheating husband," she replied, and moved aside to let Renee pass.

"Can I get you something to drink? Wine, maybe?"

"Water would be nice," Renee replied politely. She sat down on the cat-shredded sofa, and Stacy got ice water for her and another gin and tonic for herself.

"Why are you here?" Stacy asked as she handed Renee her water.

"I want to know what happened to Derek. How he died."

"I don't know why that's any of your business, " Stacy replied tartly. "*I* was his wife. You must have known he was married."

"I did."

Stacy took a big swallow of her drink. "We were married for ten years, you know. I suppose he wined and dined you and promised he would leave me."

"He said you had left first. That you acted like he didn't exist. It's like living in a tomb, he told me. It hurt him so, the way you treated him."

"And of course you were the one who understood him," Stacy said, even as guilt clenched her stomach.

"How did he die? Please, tell me." Renee leaned forward.

Through the alcohol fog, Stacy sensed something was not right, but the gin pushed her on.

"The doctor said it was a heart attack," she said slowly. "But we were fighting—I had found out about you—and he just turned pale and fell over."

"What did he say?"

"He said you made him happy. I said I wished he was dead. And poof, he died."

"You wished he was dead," Renee repeated slowly.

"Yes," Stacy said. Tears ran down her cheeks. She gulped down the rest of her drink to keep from sobbing. The gin stung her throat. "I… I mean, you can't just wish and make someone die? I didn't mean it, really."

A minute or two of silence followed.

Renee spoke first. "Derek was the love of my life. I would have done anything for him. And rather than let him go, you just wanted him to die." Her face flushed an ugly red. "How selfish can you get?"

"I told you, I didn't mean it! And my life has been a perfect hell since he's been gone. My house is falling apart, I might lose my job, and my cat ran away."

"And you don't care that Derek is gone. You don't care that you practically killed him. You're too drunk to care."

"I didn't kill him!"

Renee stood up. Like an avenging angel, she pointed her finger at Stacy, her eyes burning.

"Well, I have a few wishes for you."

"Oh really? Do tell," Stacy retorted.

"I wish you a long and miserable life. I wish you pain and despair. I wish you bad luck and no joy, ever."

"Get out of my house," Stacy said. She pulled herself to her feet and glared at Renee.

"You killed him!" Renee shrieked, and threw her glass at the fireplace. It hit the mirror above it. Like a live thing, the mirror shuddered and twisted on its hook before splintering. Broken glass exploded all over the mantel and down onto the carpet. Jagged shards stuck up from the plush pile like stalagmites.

"You bitch! GET OUT!" Stacy shouted, and lunged at Renee. As she did, she lost her footing and fell hard into the glass shards. One long, sharp piece embedded itself in her thigh, and the force of her fall drove it into her femoral artery. Blood spouted up and out of the wound, showering the walls, the floor, and Stacy herself with bright red splatters. She stared stupidly at her leg, watching her life pulse away.

"Oh my God!" Renee cried. She frantically rummaged in her purse for her cell phone. As she begged the 911 operator to hurry, Stacy began to laugh.

"None of us got what we wanted, did we? Not me, not Derek, and not you."

A gout of blood choked off her bitter laughter. A red haze clouded her vision, and she lay back into the widening pool of blood.

The paramedics wheeled the gurney out. Renee tearfully told her story to the police, who noted the gin bottle in the kitchen and more in the trash, and believed her when she said it was an accident. As she was leaving, a Siamese cat darted out of the shrubbery and rubbed around her ankles.

"Well, hello there," she said, and bent down to stroke the cat. "Are you lost?"

Stacy said her cat ran away, she remembered.

The cat purred and looked up into Renee's face.

"Want to come home with me?"

Ming answered with a long meowing cry and butted Renee's face with his head.

"At least one of us should get what we wished for," Renee said, and took the cat in her arms.

That Other Place
by
Patrick Lacey

There was a window in the side of Mrs. Harrison's tree. It should not have been there. I had walked that route to and from school for five years and had never noticed it before. The oak was tall and sprawled against the front yard. It often reminded me of a hand reaching upward.

Pete Foster, who was walking alongside me, was going on about how he'd reached second base with Angela Pfeffer the previous night. I wanted to tell him this was no great feat, since I'd rounded third with her just last week. But I kept my mouth shut and stared at the window a few feet to my left.

The glass was smudged with dirt and the wood's paint had long since peeled away. It looked very old and the thought bothered me immensely.

I stopped and pointed.

"What's wrong?" Pete said. He was just getting to the part where he unclasped Angela's bra and exposed her miraculous tits.

"Do you see that?"

"The tree?"

"Yes, but do you see what's on the tree?"

"Branches and leaves? What the hell's gotten into you?"

I rubbed my eyes, squinted, and pinched myself to ensure I wasn't dreaming. The window was still there. I imagined what lay behind the panes, if it was just an odd decoration or if it was truly a window. And if that were the case, what would I see if I looked through it?

I thought about opening it and my body responded with shivers and tensing muscles. I decided to leave it be for the moment.

That night, before bed, there was a knock at my door.

"Come in." I was reading a fantasy novel when I should have been studying for my algebra quiz the next day.

"Time for your pills." My mother held in one hand a tall glass of water and in the other a handful of prescription medications, mostly for my ADD, but a couple were to combat my mood swings.

I imagined I wouldn't feel like a zombie once I swallowed the capsules. But it was a petty lie. Each time I took those pills, the world slipped away from me against my will.

She patted my head while I took the first few into my mouth and swallowed. "Open wide."

I opened my mouth and lifted my tongue to prove I'd taken them.

"That's a good boy. Just a few more."

I repeated the pattern and finished the glass of water, handing it back to her.

"How have you been feeling?"

"Foggy. The pills make me feel like I'm dreaming."

"That just means they're working. They're helping you be a normal boy."

"If this is normal, then I'm fine being crazy."

"You shouldn't say things like that." She looked at me like I was wearing a straightjacket and was covered with fresh blood. It was a look I'd grown used to.

After she left I tried to sleep, but it was impossible, perhaps a side effect of the meds, perhaps a side effect of the dread I felt.

Mrs. Harrison's house was three blocks to my left. I stood up reluctantly and went to my window. It was newly installed and nothing like the one I'd seen earlier. The one I told myself probably didn't exist.

I saw the tree from my position. At night it was less like a hand and more like a claw.

I'd never liked looking at that tree, but what bothered me was not the talon-like branches or the indentations and grooves that resembled bulging veins.

What bothered me was the glowing light.

The window was on the other side of the tree. There appeared to be some light source obscured by the base. At first I thought it was a reflection from the street lamp, but the angle didn't add up. The bulb wasn't strong enough, and the rest of the yard lay in thick darkness.

Perhaps someone had been walking their dog and had dropped their flashlight. It was a plausible theory except that the light flickered somehow, like a flame in the wind.

Every so often there was movement in the light, as if someone were obscuring the source for just a moment. Something beyond the window was giving off light and something inside the window was moving.

I considered forcing my fingers down my throat and puking up the pills, but I knew they'd already begun to dissolve, my body feeding on the contents. I wanted to turn away, but that brainwashed feeling came over me and I could not move from my viewpoint.

I watched the flickering and the shadows for most of the night.

I finally worked up the courage to get a closer look.

Every day, on the walk home from school, I made Pete swear he saw nothing out of the ordinary as we passed Mrs. Harrison's yard. He told me I was going off my rocker. He asked if I could spare him from my hit list when I shot up the school, and then would often go into a soliloquy about how Angela Pfeffer had gone down on him.

Finally I had to know for sure.

I did not want to investigate at night, but it seemed the safest time. No one would be out and no one would ask questions. It was no secret that I was the strange kid on the block, the one that had tantrums for no apparent reason, the one who seemed to stare at nothing for a bit too long, the one who ruined birthday parties and barbeques.

If my neighbors saw me standing inches away from the tree and looking into it as if there was a window there, it would not help my case. There would be more pills added to the nightly batch.

I stared at my ceiling until I was sure everyone was asleep, then I stood up, dressed, and descended the stairs slowly. I felt groggy from the meds and uneasy at the same time. From my front yard I could see the flickering light on the lawn. I took my time walking, stretching out the three-block distance in a mile.

Eventually I arrived. And I nearly fainted.

The light was blinding up close, like staring at the sun, though it was just past midnight. It was a long time before my eyes adjusted, and when they did I wished I *was* blind.

I'm sure everyone looking back on their life has a similar moment, where they tell themselves they should have just done this or that differently. The criminal who robs the delivery store and wonders why he chose to shoot the attendant between the eyes or the employee who calls his boss an asshole and wonders why he threw away his career.

And in my case, the boy who wonders why he chose to look through the window in the side of his neighbor's tree.

Because what that boy saw that night did indeed change everything.

The boy saw himself staring back from the other side of the aged glass.

But it wasn't me—not exactly.

It certainly resembled me, though its skin was much paler and its features were distorted like an abstract painting, a consequence of the physics of That Other Place.

But I'm getting ahead of myself.

I looked through the window several more times, but I did not open it until the Fourth of July that summer.

Earlier that day, I went to a massive party at my neighbor's house. Bill Archer, father of Miranda and Kelsey Archer, identical twins with severe freckles, and their older brother Andy, a menace to all those shorter and weaker, threw a party that drew in most of the people from my street. There were burgers and hot dogs, slush and ice cream, a pool, and even a jumpy house.

It all would have been fun had it not been next door to Mrs. Harrison's home.

The window side of the tree faced away from me, and every few moments I would wonder if that was good or bad. Good, because I couldn't see myself through the glass, or bad, because if the window was opened from the other side and my pale and misshapen twin came crawling out, I would have less time to flee.

"What the hell is so interesting?" It was Andy. He was a sophomore in high school, had taken an infinite amount of lunch money, and had given countless bloody noses. My balls receded at the sound of his voice.

"Nothing," I said. "I'm just spacing out."

"Well, keep that shit to a minimum. There are girls here."

"I'll try my best."

He slapped me in the back of the head. For a moment I saw white light and feared the tree had somehow turned around.

"Freak."

He walked away and left me staring and rubbing the oncoming pain. For a long time, the party continued without me until I heard approaching footsteps.

"What're you looking at?" There were two voices with identical pitches. It was the twins. They each held a plate with an identical piece of cake.

"What does that tree look like to you?"

"Nothing," one of them said. I wasn't sure which. "It just looks like a tree."

"Doesn't look like a hand to either of you? Or maybe a window?"

They shook their heads. "You should come eat," Miranda said. "Our dad says you're making him uneasy."

I looked toward the grill. Bill was drinking a beer and staring my way. "I guess I am a little hungry."

I ate two hamburgers, a hot dog, three pickles, and two slices of cake. I could not remember being so hungry. I wondered if the window was draining me somehow, taking away nutrients the closer I got.

A couple of hours later, while my parents were laughing with Bill and his wife, someone grabbed me from behind. They held a hand over my mouth and told me if I screamed they'd cut my fucking dick off. Then I was dragged away. I tried flailing and managed to bite the hand covering my lips. One of Andy's friends rewarded me with a punch to the kidney.

It was dark now and everyone was watching the sky for the fireworks to begin. No one noticed Andy and his buddies holding me against Mrs. Harrison's oak tree.

They chose the side with the window only I could see and placed me next to it. I winced at the light and one of them said I really was a nutcase.

"Were you talking to my sisters?" Andy said. He spit on my face as he spoke.

"Just in passing."

He punched me in the stomach.

"I bet you were coming on to them. I should snap your neck and do the neighborhood a favor. You're going to grow up and you're going to get a van and you're going to steal little ones and keep them in your basement, but none of them are going to be Miranda or Kelsey, because if I see you even looking at them again I'm going to shove one of these branches so far up your ass it'll come out your mouth. Got me?"

"We were just talking."

"I was looking for a yes." He punched me again in the stomach. This time much harder.

All the food I'd eaten earlier reversed its direction and I vomited onto him.

He gritted his teeth and wiped away half-digested meat from his shirt. "You little shit."

As if on cue, the fireworks began to go off. Everyone oohed and ahhed, heads toward the stars as Andy and his friends took turns beating the life out of the neighborhood freak.

My mother was drunk that night. She wobbled through the living room, my father holding her up, half in the bag himself. Neither of them noticed me holding an ice pack to my right eye or that my shirt was stained with blood and dirt.

"Don't stay up too late," my mother said as she was carried upstairs, giggling.

My father said something, but his voice slurred too much to make out details.

I sat in the living room with the television on mute until I realized it looked a bit like a window itself. I turned it off and paced.

After a few minutes, I realized I did not feel foggy or distant. My mother had forgotten to give me my meds. My mind worked quickly, and before I could stop myself I was marching outside and heading toward the tree.

One of my molars felt loose and my mouth tasted like copper. My ankle had swollen several sizes too large. It hurt to walk and breathe.

I'd had enough of this world. I decided whatever lay on the other side of that glass had to be better than this.

I marched, told myself I wasn't frightened, and stood in front of the window. My Other stared back at me, standing rigid as if he had not moved an inch since our last encounter. He studied me, wrinkled his brow, and tilted his pale head.

My pulse warned me to turn away, but I told it otherwise.

I reached out with a shaking hand. The window was stuck at first, unopened for an eternity. I put more strength into it, groaning against the pain in my abdomen. My Other seemed to will me on, nodding every so often until finally the wood gave and the window slid open.

The next morning I woke in my bed, thinking what a strange dream I'd had. I recalled being in an odd place, where the landscape was familiar yet distorted. My street was recognizable but deformed, the way things appear altered in a nightmare.

I had followed someone who looked like me, only more ghost-like, through the abandoned houses of my neighbors. Their living rooms and kitchens were ancient, filled with cobwebs and shadows. In fact, the entire world had been filled with shadows, no trace of the sun in the sky—or stars, for that matter.

Though I had been alone with myself—my other self—it had not felt that way. The darkness seemed to vibrate. I swore things moved in my peripherals, but each time I investigated, there was nothing there.

It went on like that for an eternity, my pale twin and I exploring another world, until I woke.

Some part of my right index finger flared with pain. I remembered Andy and his friends pummeling me. Perhaps there was a cut I had not noticed before. But the pain seemed fresher somehow, more recent. I looked at my hands and noticed dust, like they had touched something ancient, but that was not what made my nerves come alive like a jackhammer. I saw the source of my pain, the sharpness that was unaccounted for.

I knew then as I picked out the splinter.

"What're you looking at now?" Miranda asked.

"Still nothing." I stood in front of the window.

"You look at nothing an awful lot," Kelsey said. "Our dad says that's because there's nothing much going on in your brain."

"Your dad's a charming guy. So is your brother."

It was getting to be evening. My new favorite time of day. I was slowly turning nocturnal, sleeping most of the morning and afternoon and waking once the sky turned pink. At first my mother had protested, telling me it wasn't normal, as if that word meant anything when you knew what I did. But eventually she'd given up. So long as I took my pills like a good little boy, she said, I could stay awake for the entire summer.

"You two should get going," I warned. "The last time we spoke, I ended up bleeding a lot."

"We yelled at Andy for that," Kelsey said. At least I thought it was Kelsey. "You don't seem that creepy to us."

I looked away quickly from the window and caught Mrs. Harrison's glare from *her* window. She shook her head in disgust at the boy on her lawn and slid the curtain down.

"You're in the minority," I said. "Now if you don't mind, I'd like to be alone."

"But what're you looking at?" Miranda came closer to me, as did Kelsey, until there was one twin on either side.

"I told you. Nothing."

The sky had darkened and I could now see the bright light in the window. When my eyes adjusted, there was a shape there, moving closer. I stiffened, ready to see my Other. When the twins were gone and no one was looking, I would open the window and we would roam the alternate version of my neighborhood, where things were uneven and mismatched and much better.

But something was wrong. The shadow multiplied. There were two of them and they grew shorter.

I stepped back. It was not my Other but those of the twins, two pale forms that smiled and waved us on, beckoning.

I looked at the girls—the real girls. They were still seeing ancient bark. I saw the curiosity in their eyes, the longing to understand why I spent most evenings and nights in front of a tree while everyone slept. "Do you ever use your imagination?"

They nodded.

"Do you ever imagine other places?"

"Like other towns?" Kelsey or Miranda said.

"Like other worlds."

They nodded, this time hesitantly.

"Sometimes," one of them said, "I think about where fairies and goblins live. But that's all make believe, like in the books we read for school."

"But what if it wasn't? What if I could show you something else, something other than boring houses and schools? Would you want to go there?"

They looked at each other, eyes wide, and shrugged their shoulders.

I looked at their house to ensure Andy wasn't watching. "I want you to close your eyes really hard and count to three. Then I want you to open them again, and when you do you'll see a window on the side of this tree—a real window, one that you can reach out and touch for yourself. Can you do that?"

"Yes," they said.

"Good. Now close them tight." I looked at their Others, watching intently. "One."

Deeper inside That Other Place I could see my own twin, waiting for me, pacing back and forth on a street that was cracked and gouged as if an earthquake had shifted the landscape.

"Two."

It would be lovely to have someone else see for themselves. And who better than the twins? Children didn't know the word crazy. They hadn't yet become judgmental vermin.

"Three."

They opened their eyes and nearly turned as white as their Others. I knew immediately by the way their mouths hung open in shock. They could see the window and the place that lay beyond. They could see all of it.

"Do you want to go there?"

They nodded, no longer hesitant.

I took one last look around. The street was empty. It was as good a time as any. I reached for the window and opened it.

This time the frame slid easily upward.

"What is this place?"

It was Kelsey, mesmerized by the oddly formed shrubs in the yards we passed. There were flowers blooming that I'd never known to exist back home. What had once been a flat and boring sidewalk was now wavy and disjointed, like a cartoon.

"I'm not sure," I said, following my Other.

The Others did not speak. I'd asked mine countless questions. It never responded with anything more than a smile and perhaps a nod, as if any explanation would ruin the magic of that world.

"How did you find it?" Miranda kneeled down and traced her finger along an illustration in the pavement, something totally foreign to us yet wonderful at the same time.

"I think it found me." I looked in the distance and wondered how far that place went, if I could keep walking forever and never see another familiar sight again.

Something behind us moved. It sounded heavy and fast.

We spun around, us and our Others, but there was nothing there. Nothing obvious, at least. In my peripherals I could see something. It lay in the doorway of a house two blocks away. I could not see its eyes, though I knew it was watching. It was the first time I'd felt scared since I stepped through the window. I'd been uneasy on my first visit and part of me knew there were other things aside from me and my Other, but it had not been real fear.

Not until now.

The thing in the doorway stepped onto the street and began walking toward us.

"I think we'd better be going."

The twins didn't protest and neither did our Others, who followed behind us as we ran back to the tree. For a while it sounded as though our pursuer was gaining. I didn't risk a look until we were at the window. It was gone, though I knew it wasn't far.

The twins had a hard time reaching the window. The tree, much like everything else in that place, was shaped differently. The sill was roughly three feet higher. They jumped, but missed it by a few inches.

"Let me go first," I said. "You keep watch."

They looked around nervously at the shadows, which seemed to ripple like water. I pointed to my Other and told him to give the twins a lift when I was through.

I stepped back into the real world—a relative term at best—and reached back into the window. My Other got the twins' attention. Their Others were pointing at something in the distance.

I followed their line of sight. Miranda and Kelsey screamed. The thing from the shadows had appeared. It was not deformed or horned or scaled, as I had imagined. It was much worse than that.

It was Andy's Other.

He was paler and uglier than anything I'd ever known, with a set of knife-like teeth the size of daggers.

And he was a fast runner.

I yelled for the twins to hop onto my Other's shoulders, but my words were lost in their panic. Andy's Other snatched them up, hoisted them over his shoulder, and took them into the darkness, somewhere well hidden.

The window slammed shut onto my fingers. I fell onto the lawn, bleeding and crying.

So now you know.

I fled soon after and traveled for a while, but I never felt safe staying in one place for too long. My face had been on the news for quite some time. It felt like everyone I passed on the street recognized me. It was like being back home. There I had been the freak on the block, and to the rest of the world I was just a stranger that seemed familiar for some awful reason.

One night, between jobs and without a place to live, I spent the night in a shelter. I slept terribly and woke to see the man across the room watching me. His eyes were too still, never once blinking. He was sleeping, I realized, which calmed me down some. But then it hit me that somewhere out there, behind an invisible wall, was another version of him, one with the same features, albeit more pale. Did that other version sleep with its eyes open as well?

The man mumbled something and began snoring.

I gathered my things and left a few minutes later.

Eventually I took to the woods and found a structure that could have once been a cabin. I fixed it up as best I could, boarding up every window for good measure, and lived off squirrel and the occasional rabbit. I grew some vegetables and stole from the neighboring campground whenever I needed something in particular. It was not a glamorous life, but it felt good to be alone.

It was an illusion, of course. I would never again be alone.

Without my pills, the world sometimes went out of focus. It was hard to keep my attention on one thing for too long, but that was fine. The longer I looked at the world—trees, especially—the more I imagined everything becoming a doorway.

My thoughts, though, were painfully focused. I got to thinking of the twins, of where they'd been taken, of what else lay behind the curtain of this world and all the others that border it. Even now, it all sounds crazy to my own mind. Not crazy in the same way my mother and father and neighbors—everyone except Miranda and Kelsey—thought of me.

A different kind of crazy. The kind that makes you wonder if the bum you pass on the street may know something you don't, as if they've seen through this façade and into something much deeper and darker, which is why they now spend their days drooling and mumbling to themselves.

I try my best to live each day in ignorance, pretending I don't know things that would drive the average person to hang themselves. I try to stay busy and enjoy the emptiness of my life, the pure silence, save for that one thing that breaks it.

Every so often, when night falls, I wake to a sound. For a long time I thought it was an animal poking around outside or perhaps acorns falling onto the warped roof. But after a while it became obvious, proof that I am that other kind of crazy.

The sound is that of a soft tapping.

Like fingers against glass.

The Looking Glass
by
J.D. Beresford

originally published in *The Cornhill Magazine*, 1922

This was the first communication that had come from her aunt in Rachel's lifetime.

"I think your aunt has forgiven me, at last," her father said as he passed the letter across the table.

Rachel looked first at the signature. It seemed strange to see her own name there. It was as if her individuality, her very identity, was impugned by the fact that there should be two Rachel Deanes. Moreover there was a likeness between her aunt's autograph and her own, a characteristic turn in the looping of the letters, a hint of the same decisiveness and precision. If Rachel had been educated fifty years earlier, she might have written her name in just that manner.

"You're very like her in some ways," her father said, as she still stared at the signature.

Rachel's eyelids drooped and her expression indicated a faint, suppressed intolerance of her father's remark. He said the same things so often, and in so precisely the same tone, that she had formed a habit of automatically rejecting the truth of certain of his statements. He had always appeared to her as senile. He had been over fifty when she was born, and ever since she could remember she had doubted the correctness of his information. She was, she had often told herself, "a born sceptic; an ultra-modern." She had a certain veneration for the more distant past, but none for her father's period. "Victorianism" was to her a term of abuse. She had long since condemned alike the ethic and the aesthetic of the nineteenth century as represented by her father's opinions, so that even now, when his familiar comment coincided so queerly with her own thought, she instinctively disbelieved him. Yet, as always, she was gentle in her answer. She condescended from the heights of her youth and vigor to pity him.

"I should think you must almost have forgotten what Aunt Rachel was like, dear," she said. "How many years is it since you've seen her?"

"More than forty; more than forty," her father said, ruminating profoundly. "We disagreed, we invariably disagreed. Rachel always prided herself on being so modern. She read Huxley and Darwin and things like that. Altogether beyond me, I admit. Still, it seems to me that the old truths have endured, and will—in spite of all—in spite of all."

Rachel straightened her shoulders and lifted her head; there was disdain in her face, but none in her voice as she replied, "And so it seems that she wants to see me."

She was excited at the thought of meeting this traditional, this almost mythical aunt whom she had so often heard about. Sometimes she had wondered if the personality of this remarkable relative had not been a figment of her father's imagination, long pondered, and reconstructed out of half-forgotten material. But this letter of hers that now lay on the breakfast table was admirable in character. There was something of condescension and intolerance expressed in the very restraint of its tone. She had written a kindly letter, but the kindliness had an air of pity. It was all consistent enough with what her father had told her.

Mr. Deane came out of his reminiscences with a sigh.

"Yes, yes; she wants to see you, my dear," he said. "I think you had better accept this invitation to stay with her. She—she is rich, almost wealthy; and I, as you know, have practically nothing to leave you—practically nothing. If she took a fancy to you…"

He sighed again, and Rachel knew that for the hundredth time he was regretting his own past weakness. He had been so foolish in money matters, frittering away his once considerable capital in aimless speculations. He and his sister had shared equally under their father's will, but while he had been at last compelled to sink the greater part of what was left to him in an annuity, she had probably increased her original inheritance.

"I'll certainly go, if you can spare me for a whole fortnight," Rachel said. "I'm all curiosity to see this remarkable aunt. By the way, how old is she?"

"There were only fifteen months between us," Mr. Deane said, "so she must be, dear me, yes; she must be seventy-three. Dear, dear. Fancy Rachel being seventy-three! I always think of her as being about your age. It seems so absurd to think of her as *old*…"

He continued his reflections, but Rachel was not listening. He was asking for the understanding of the young, quite unaware of his senility, reaching out over half a century to try to touch the comprehension and sympathy of his daughter. But she was already bent on her own adventure, looking forward eagerly to a visit to London that promised delights other than the inspection of the mysterious, traditional aunt whom she had so long known by report.

For this invitation had come very aptly. Rachel pondered that, later in the morning, with a glow of ecstatic resignation to her charming fate. She found the guiding hand of a romantic inevitability in the fact that she and Adrian Flemming were to meet so soon. It had seemed so unlikely that they would see each other again for many months. They had only met three times; but they *knew*, although their friendship had been too green for either of them to admit the knowledge before he had gone back to town. He had, indeed, hinted far more in his two letters than he had ever dared to say. He was sensitive, he lacked self-confidence; but Rachel adored him for just those failings she criticized so hardly in her father. She took out her letters and re-read them, thrilling with the realization that in her answer she would have such a perfectly amazing surprise for him. She would refer to it quite casually, somewhere near the end. She would write, "By the way, it's just possible that we may meet again before long as I am going to stay with my aunt, Miss Deane, in Tavistock Square." He would understand all that lay behind such an apparently careless reference, for she had told him that she "never went to London," had only once in her life ever been there.

She was in her own room, and she stood before the cheval glass and studied herself, raising her chin and slightly pursing her lips, staring superciliously at her own image under half-lowered eyelids. Candidly, she admired herself; but she could not help that assumption of a disdainful criticism. It seemed to give her confidence in her own integrity, hiding that annoying shadow of doubt which sometimes fell upon her when she caught sight of her reflection by chance and unexpectedly.

But no thought of doubt flawed her satisfaction this morning. A sense of power came to her, a tranquil realization that she could charm Adrian as she would. With a graceful, habitual gesture she put up her hand and lightly touched her cheek with a soft, caressing movement of her fingertips.

II

The elderly parlor-maid showed Rachel straight to her bedroom when she arrived at Tavistock Square, indicating on the way the extensive-looking first floor drawing room, in which tea and her first sight of the wonderful aunt would await Rachel in half an hour. She had been eager and excited. The air and promise of London had thrilled her, but she found some influence in the atmosphere of the big house that was vaguely repellent, almost sinister.

Her bedroom was expensively furnished and beautifully kept; some of the pieces were, she supposed, genuine antiques, perhaps immensely valuable. But how could she ever feel at home there? She was hampered by the necessity of moving circumspectly among this aged delicate stuff, so wonderfully preserved and yet surely fragile and decrepit at the heart. That spindling escritoire, for instance, and that mincing Louis Quinze settee, ought to be taking their well-earned leisure in some museum. It would be indecent to write at the one or sit on the other. They were relics of the past, foolishly pretending an ability for service when their life had been sapped by dry rot and their original functions outlived.

"Well, if ever I have a house of my own," Rachel thought, regarding these ancient splendors, "I'll furnish it with something I shan't be afraid of."

With a gesture of dismissal she turned and looked out of the window. From the square came the sounds of a motor drawing up at a neighboring house; she heard the throbbing of the engine, the slam of the door, and then the strong, sonorous tones of a man's voice. That was her proper *milieu*, she reflected, among the strong vital things. Even after twenty minutes in that bedroom she had begun to feel enervated, as if she herself were also beginning to suffer from dry rot.

She was anxious and uneasy as she went slowly downstairs to the drawing room. Her anticipations of this meeting with her intimidating, wealthy aunt had changed within the last half hour. Her first idea of Miss Deane had been of a robust, stout woman, frank in her speech and inclined to be very critical of the newly found niece whom she had chosen to inspect. Now, she was prepared rather to expect a fragile, rather querulous old lady, older even than her years; an aunt to be talked to in a lowered voice and treated with the same delicate care that must be extended to her furniture.

Rachel paused with her hand on the drawing room door, and sighed at the thought of all the repressions and nervous strains that this visit might have in store for her.

She entered the room almost on tiptoe, and then stood stock-still, suddenly shocked and bewildered with surprise. Whatever she had expected, it was not this. For a moment she was unable to believe that the sprightly, painted and bedizened figure before her could possibly be that of her aunt. Her head was crowned with an exuberant brown wig, her heavy eyebrows were grotesquely blackened, her hollow cheeks stiff with powder, her lips brightened to a fantastic scarlet. And she was posed there, standing before the tea table with her head a little back, looking at her niece with a tolerant condescension, with the air of a superb young beauty, self-conscious and proud of her charms.

"Hm! So you're my semi-mythical niece," she said, putting up her lorgnette. "I'm glad at any rate to find that you're not, after all, a fabulous creature." She spoke in a high, rather thin voice that produced an effect of effort, as if she were playing on the top octave of a flute.

Rachel had never in her life felt so gauche and awkward.

"Yes—I—you know, aunt, I had begun to wonder if you were not fabulous, too," she tried, desperately anxious to seem at ease. She was afraid to look at that, to her, grotesque figure, afraid to show by some unconscious reflex her dislike for its ugliness. As she took the bony, ring-bedecked hand that was held out to her, she kept her eyes away from her aunt's face.

Miss Deane, however, would not permit that evasion.

"Hold your head up, my dear, I want to look at you," she said, and when Rachel reluctantly obeyed, continued, "Yes, you're more like my father than your own, which means that you're like me, for I took after him, too, so everyone said."

Rachel drew in her breath with a little gasp. Was it possible that her aunt could imagine for one instant that there was any likeness between them?

"Our—our names are the same," she said nervously.

Miss Deane nodded. "There's more in it than that," she said with a touch of complacence; "and there's no reason why there shouldn't be. It's good Mendelism that you should take after an aunt rather than either of your parents."

"And you really think that we are alike?" Rachel asked feebly, looking in vain for any sign of a quizzical humor in her aunt's face.

Miss Deane looked down under her half-lowered eyelids with a proud air of tolerance. "Ah, well, a little without doubt," she said, as though the advantages of the difference were on her own side. "Now sit down and have your tea, my dear."

Rachel obeyed with a vague wonder in her mind as to why that look of tolerance should be so familiar. It seemed to her as if it was something she had felt rather than seen; and as tea progressed she found herself half furtively studying the raddled ugliness of her aunt's face in the search for possible relics of a beautiful youth.

"Ah, I think you're beginning to see it, too," Miss Deane said, marking her niece's scrutiny. "It grows on one, doesn't it?"

Rachel shivered slightly. "Yes, it does," she said experimentally, watching her aunt's face for some indication of a malicious teasing humor. It seemed to her so incredible that this hideous parody of her own youth could honestly believe that any physical likeness *still* existed.

Miss Deane, however, was faintly simpering. "I have been told that I've changed very little," she said; and Rachel suppressed a sigh of impatience at the reflection that she was expected to play up to this absurd fantasy.

"Of course, I can't judge of that," she said, "as we met for the first time five minutes ago."

"No, no, you can't judge of *that*," her aunt replied, with the half-bashful emphasis of one who awaits a compliment.

Rachel decided to plunge. "But you do look extraordinarily young for your age still," she lied desperately.

Miss Deane straightened her back and toyed with a teaspoon. "I have always taken great care of myself," she said.

Unquestionably she believed it, Rachel decided. This was no pose, but a horrible piece of self-deception. This raddled, repulsive creature had actually persuaded herself into the delusion that she still had the appearance of a young girl. Heaven help her if that delusion were ever shattered!

Yet outside this one obsession Miss Deane, as Rachel soon discovered, had a clear and well-balanced mind. For, now that she had received her desired assurance from this new quarter, she began to talk of other things. Her boasted "modernism," it is true, had a smack of the stiff, broadcloth savor of the eighties, but she had a point of view that coincided far more nearly with Rachel's own than did that of her father. Her aunt, at least, had outlived the worst superstitions and inanities of the mid-Victorians.

Indeed, by the time tea was finished Rachel's spirits were beginning to revive. She would have to be very careful in her treatment of her aunt, but on the whole it would not perhaps be so bad; and presently she would see Adrian again. She would almost certainly get a letter from him by the last post, making some appointment to meet her, and after that she would introduce him to Miss Deane. She had a feeling that Miss Deane would not raise any objection; that she might even welcome the visit of a young man to her house.

The time was passing so easily that Rachel was surprised when she heard the gong sound.

"Does that mean it's time to dress already?" she asked.

Miss Deane nodded. "You've an hour before dinner," she said, "but I'll go up now. I like to be leisurely over my toilet."

She rose as she spoke, but as she crossed the room, she paused with what seemed to be a little jerk of surprise as she caught sight of her own reflection in a tall mirror above one of the gilt-legged console tables against the wall. Then she deliberately stopped, turned and surveyed herself, half contemptuously, under lowered eyelids, with a set of her head and back that belied plainly enough the pout of her critical lips. And having admired that haggard image, she lifted her wasted hand and delicately touched her whitened, hollow cheeks with the tips of her heavily jeweled fingers.

Rachel stared in horror. It seemed to her just then as if the reflection of her aunt in the mirror was indeed that of herself grown instantly and mysteriously old. For now, whether because the reversal of the image by the mirror or because of that perfect duplication of her own characteristic pose and gesture, the likeness had flashed out clear and unmistakable. She saw that her father had been right. Once, incalculable ages ago, this repulsive old woman might have been very like herself.

She slipped quickly out of the room and ran upstairs. She felt that she must instantly put that question to the test; search herself for the signs of coming age as she had so recently searched her aunt's face for the indications of her former youth.

But when, with an effect of challenge, she scrutinized her reflection in the tall cheval glass, the likeness appeared to have vanished. She saw her head thrust a little forward, her arms stiff, and in her whole pose an air of vigorous defiance. She was prepared to admit that she was ugly at that moment, if the ugliness was of another kind than that she had seen downstairs. No! She drew herself up, more than a little relieved by the result of her test. The likeness was all a fancy, the result of suggestions, first by her father and then by Miss Deane herself. And she need at least have no fear that she was ugly. Why...

She paused suddenly, and the light died out of her face. Her image was looking back at her stiffly, superciliously, with, so it seemed to her, the contemptible simper of one who still fatuously admires the thing that has long since lost its charm. She caught her breath and clenched her hands, drawing down her rather heavy eyebrows in an expression of angry scorn. "Oh! never, never, never again, will I look at myself like that," Rachel vowed fiercely.

She was to find, however, before this first evening was over, that the mere avoidance of that one pose before the mirror would not suffice to lay the ghost of the suspicion that was beginning to haunt her.

At the very outset a new version of the likeness was presented to her when, during the first course of dinner, Miss Deane, with a lowering frown of her blackened eyebrows, found occasion to reprimand the elderly parlor-maid. For a moment Rachel was again puzzled by the intriguing sense of the familiar, before she remembered her own scowl at the looking glass an hour before.

"Do I really frown like that?" she thought. And on the instant found herself *feeling* like her aunt.

That, indeed, was the horror that, despite every effort of resistance, deepened steadily as the evening wore on. Miss Deane had, without question, lost every trace of her beauty; but her character, her spirit was unchanged, and it was, so Rachel increasingly believed, the very spit and replica of her own.

They had the same characteristic gestures and expressions; the look of kindly tolerance with which her aunt regarded Rachel was precisely the same as that with which Rachel regarded her father. When her aunt's voice dropped in speaking from the rather shrill, strained tone that was obviously not natural to her, Rachel heard the inflexions of her own voice. And as her knowledge of Miss Deane grew, so, also, did that haunting unpleasant feeling of looking and speaking in precisely the same manner. It seemed to her as if she were being invaded by an alien personality; as if the character she had known and cherished all her life were no longer her own, but merely a casual inheritance from some unknown ancestor. Her very integrity was threatened by her consciousness of that likeness, her pride of individuality. She was not, after all, a unique personality, but merely another version—if she were even that?—of a Miss Rachel Deane born in the middle of the previous century.

Moreover, with that growing recognition of likeness in character, there came the thought that she in time might look even as her aunt looked at this present moment. She also would lose her beauty, until no facial resemblance could be traced between the hag she was and the beauty she had once been. For, through all her torment, Rachel proudly clung to the certainty that, physically at least, there was no sort of likeness between her aunt and herself.

Miss Deane's belief in that matter, however, was soon proved to be otherwise; for when they were alone together in the drawing room after dinner, and the topic so inevitably present to both their minds came to the surface of conversation, she unexpectedly said, "But we're evidently the poles apart in character and manner, my dear."

"Oh! do you think so?" Rachel exclaimed. "I—it's a queer thing to say perhaps—but I curiously feel like you, aunt; when you speak sometimes and—and when I watch the way you do things."

Miss Deane shook her head. "I admit the physical resemblance," she said; "otherwise, my dear, we are utterly different."

Did she too, Rachel wondered, resent the aspersion of her integrity?

By the last post Rachel received her expected letter from Adrian Flemming. Her aunt separated it from the others brought in by her maid and passed it across to her niece with a slight hint of displeasure in her face. "Miss Rachel Deane, *junior*," she said. "Really, it hadn't occurred to me how difficult it will be to distinguish our letters. I hope my friends won't take to addressing me as Miss Deane, *senior*. Properly, of course, I am Miss Deane, and you Miss Rachel, but I'll admit there's sure to be some confusion. Now, my dear, I expect you're tired. You'd better run up to bed."

Rachel was willing enough to go. She was glad to have an opportunity to read her letter in solitude; she was even more glad to get away from the company of this living echo of herself. "I believe I should go mad if I had to live with her," she reflected. "I should get into the way of copying her. I should begin to grow old before my time."

When she reached her bedroom, she put down her letter unopened on the toilet-table and once more stared searchingly at her own reflection in the mirror. Was there any least trace of a physical likeness, she asked herself; and began in imagination to follow the possible stages of the change that time would inevitably work upon her. She shrugged her shoulders. If there were indeed any sort of facial resemblance between herself and her aunt, no one would ever see it except in Miss Deane, and she was obsessed with a senile vanity. Yet was it, after all, Rachel began to wonder, an unnatural obsession? Might she not in time suffer from it herself? The change would be so slow, so infinitely gradual; and always one would be cherishing the old, loved image of youth and beauty, falling in love with it, like a deluded Hyacinth, and coming to be deceived by the fantasy of an unchanging appearance of youth. Looking always for the desired thing, she would suffer from the hallucination that the thing existed in fact, and imagine that the only artifice needed to perfect the illusion was a touch of paint and powder. No doubt her aunt—perhaps searching her own image in the mirror at this moment—saw not herself but a picture of her niece. She was hypnotized by the suggestion of a pose and the desire of her own mind. In time, Rachel herself might also become the victim of a similar illusion!

Oh, it was horrible! With a shudder, she picked up her letter and turned away from the looking glass. She would forget that ghastly warning in the thought of the joys proper to her youth. She would think of Adrian and of her next meeting with him. She opened her letter to find that he had, rather timorously, suggested that she should meet him the next afternoon—at the Marble Arch at three o'clock, if he heard nothing from her in the meantime.

For a few minutes she lost herself in delighted anticipation, and then slowly, insidiously, a new speculation crept into her mind. What would be the effect upon Adrian if he saw her and her aunt together? Would he recognize the likeness and, anticipating the movement of more than half a century, see her in one amazing moment as she would presently become? And, in any case, what a terrible train of suggestion might not be started in his mind by the impression left upon him by the old woman? Once he had seen Miss Deane, Rachel's every gesture would serve to remind him of that repulsive image of raddled, deluded age. It might well be that, in time, he would come to see Rachel as she would presently be rather than as she was. It would be a hideous reversal of the old romance; instead of seeing the girl in the old woman, he would foresee the harridan in the girl!

That picture presented itself to Rachel with a quite appalling effect of conviction. She suddenly remembered a case she had known that had remarkable points of resemblance—the case of a rather pretty girl with an unpleasant younger brother who, so she had heard it said, "put men off his sister" because of the facial likeness between them. She was pretty and he was ugly, but they were unmistakably brother and sister.

It would be nothing less than folly to let Adrian and her aunt meet, Rachel decided. In imagination, she could follow the process of his growing dismay; she could see his puzzled stare as he watched Miss Deane, and struggled to fix that tantalizing suggestion of likeness to someone he knew; his flash of illumination as he solved the puzzle and turned with that gentle, winning smile of his to herself; and then the progress of his disillusionment as, day by day, he realized more plainly the intriguing similarities of expression and gesture, until he felt that he was making love to the spirit of an aged spinster temporarily disguised behind the appearance of beauty.

III

Rachel had believed on the first night of her arrival in Tavistock Square that, so far as her love affair was concerned, she would be able to avoid all danger by keeping her lover and her aunt unknown to each other. She very soon found, however, that the spell Miss Deane seemed to have put upon her was not to be laid by any effect of mere distance.

She and Adrian met rather shyly at their first appointment. Both of them were a little conscious of having been overbold, one for having suggested, and the other for having agreed to so significant an assignation. And for the first few minutes their talk was nothing but a quick, nervous reminiscence of their earlier meetings. They had to recover the lost ground on which they had parted before they could go on to any more intimate knowledge of each other. But for some reason she had not yet realized, Rachel found it very difficult to recover that lost ground. She knew that she was being unnecessarily distant and cold, and though she inwardly accused herself of "putting on absurd airs," her manner, as she was uncomfortably aware, remained at once stilted and detached.

"I suppose it's because I'm self-conscious before all these people," she thought, and, indeed, Hyde Park was very full that afternoon.

And it was Adrian who first, a little desperately, tried to reach across the barrier that was dividing them.

"You're different, rather, in town," he began shyly. "Is it the effect of your aunt's grandeurs?"

"Am I different? I feel exactly the same," Rachel replied mechanically.

"You didn't think it was rather impudent of me to ask you to meet me here, did you?" he went on anxiously.

She shook her head emphatically. "Oh, no, it wasn't that," she said.

"But then you admit that it was—something?" he pleaded.

"The people, perhaps," she admitted. "I—I feel so exposed to the public view."

"We might walk across the Park if you preferred it," he suggested; "and have tea at that place in Kensington Gardens? It would be quieter there."

She agreed to that willingly. She wanted to be alone with him. The crowd made her nervous and self-conscious this afternoon. Always before, she had delighted in moving among a crowd, appreciating and enjoying the casual glances of admiration she received. Today she was afraid of being noticed. She had a queer feeling that these smart, clever people in the Park might see through her, if they stared too closely. Just what they would discover she did not know; but she suffered a disquieting qualm of uneasiness whenever she saw any one observing her with attention.

They cut across the grass and, leaving the Serpentine on their left, found two chairs in a quiet spot under the trees. Here, at least, they were quite unwatched, but still Rachel found it impossible to regain the relations that had existed between her and Adrian when they had parted a month earlier. And Adrian, too, it seemed, was staring at her with a new, inquisitive scrutiny.

"Why do you look at me like that?" she broke out at last. "Do you notice any difference in me, or what? You—you've been staring so!"

"Difference!" he repeated. "Well, I told you just now, didn't I, that you were different this afternoon?"

"Yes, but in what way?" she asked. "Do I—do I look different?"

He paused a little judiciously over his answer. "N—no," he hesitated. "There's something, though. Don't be offended, will you, if I say that you don't seem to be quite yourself today; not quite natural. I miss a rather characteristic expression of yours. You've never once looked at me with that rather tolerating air you used to put on."

"It was a horrid air," she said sharply. "I've made up my mind to cure myself of it."

"Oh! No, don't," he protested. "It wasn't at all horrid. It was—don't think I'm trying to pay you a compliment—it was, well, charming. I've missed it dreadfully."

She turned and looked at him, determined to try an experiment. "This sort of air, do you mean?" she asked, and with a sickening sensation of presenting the very gestures and appearance of her aunt, she regarded him under lowered eyelids with an expression of faintly supercilious approval.

His smile at once thanked and answered her.

"But it's an abominable look," she exclaimed. "The look of an old, old, painted woman, vain, ridiculous."

He stared at her in amazement. "How absurd!" he protested. "Why, it's *you*, and you're certainly not old or painted nor unduly vain, and no one could say you were ridiculous."

"And you want me to look like that?" she asked.

"It's—it's so *you*," he said shyly.

"But, just suppose," she cried, "that I went on looking like that after I'd grown old and ugly. Think how hateful it would be to see a hideous old woman posturing and pretending and making eyes. And, you see, if one gets a habit, it's so hard to get rid of it. Think of me at seventy, all painted and powdered, trying to seem as if I hadn't altered and really believing that I hadn't."

He laughed that pleasant, kind laugh of his which had been one of the first things in him that had so attracted her.

"Oh, I'll chance the future," he said. "Besides if—if it could ever happen that—that your growing old came to me gradually, that I should be seeing you every day, I mean, I shouldn't notice it. I should be old too; and *I* should think you hadn't altered either." He was afraid, as yet, to be too plain spoken, but his tone made it quite clear that he asked for no greater happiness than that of seeing her grow old beside him.

She did not pretend to misunderstand him. "Would you? Perhaps you would," she said. "But, all the same, I don't think you need insist on that particular—pose."

He passed that by, too eager at the moment to claim the concession she had offered him. "Is there any hope that I may be allowed to—to watch you growing old?" he asked.

"Perhaps—if you'll let me do it in my own way," Rachel said.

Adrian shyly took her hand. "You mean that you will—that you don't mind?" He put the question as if he had no doubt of its intelligibility to her.

She nodded.

"When did you begin to know?" he asked, awed by the wonder of this stupendous thing that had happened to him.

"From the beginning, I think," Rachel murmured.

"So did I, from the very beginning," he agreed, and from that they dropped into sacred reminiscences and comparisons concerning the innumerable things they had adoringly seen in each other and had had as yet no opportunity to glory in.

And in the midst of all these new and bewildering, embarrassing, delightful revelations and discoveries, Rachel completely forgot the shadow that was haunting her, forgot how she looked or felt or acted, forgot that there was or had ever been a terrible old woman who lived in Tavistock Square and whose hold on life was maintained by her horrible mimicry of youth. And then, in a moment, she was lifted out of her dream and cruelly set down on the hard, unsympathetic earth by the sound of her lover's voice.

"I suppose I'll have to meet your aunt?" he was saying. "Shall we go back there now, and tell her?"

Rachel flushed, as if he had suggested some startling invasion of her secret life. "Oh! No," she ejaculated impulsively.

Adrian looked his surprise. "But why not?" he asked. "I'm—I'm a perfectly respectable, eligible party."

"I wasn't thinking of that," Rachel said.

"Is she a terrible dragon?" he inquired with a smile.

Rachel shook her head, rejecting the excuse offered in favor of a more probable modification. "She's odd rather. She might prefer my giving her some kind of notice," she said.

He accepted that without hesitation. "Will you warn her then?" he replied. "And I'll come and do my duty tomorrow. I understand she's a lady to be propitiated."

"Not tomorrow," Rachel said.

The irk and disgust of it all had returned to her with renewed force at the first mention of her aunt's name. The thought of Miss Deane had revived the repulsive sense of acting, speaking, looking like that aged caricature of herself. Yet she wanted, strangely enough, to get back to Tavistock Square; for only there, it seemed to her, was she safe from the examination of an inquisitive stare that might at any moment penetrate her secret and reveal her as a posturing hag masquerading in the alluring freshness of a young girl.

"I ought to be going back to her now," she said.

"But you promised that we should have tea together," Adrian remonstrated.

"Yes, I know; but please don't pester me. I'll see you again tomorrow," Rachel returned with a touch of elderly hauteur. And, despite all his entreaties, she would not be persuaded to change her mind. Already he was looking at her with a touch of suspicion, she thought; and as she checked his remonstrances, she was aware of doing it with the air, the tone, the very look that were her inheritance from endless generations of precisely similar ancestors.

IV

If she could but have lived a double life, Rachel thought, her present position might have been endurable, and then, in a few months or even weeks, the problem would be solved forever by her marriage with Adrian and the final obliteration of Miss Deane from her memory. But she could not live a double life. Day by day, as her intimacy with her aunt increased, Rachel found it more difficult to forget her when she was away from Tavistock Square. In the deepest and most beautiful moments of her intercourse with Adrian, she was aware now of practicing upon him a subtle deception, of pretending that she was other than she was in reality—an awareness that was constantly pricked and stimulated by the continually growing consciousness of her likeness to Miss Deane.

Miss Deane on her part evidently took a great pleasure in her niece's society. The fortnight of her original invitation had already been exceeded, but she would not hear of Rachel's return to Devonshire.

"Why should you go back?" she demanded scornfully. "Your father doesn't want you. Richard is one of those slipshod people who prefer to live alone. I used to try to stir him up, and he ran away from me. He'll run away from you, my dear, in a few years' time. He hasn't the courage to stand up to women like us."

Miss Deane unquestionably wanted her niece to stay with her. She was even beginning to hint at the desirability of making the present arrangement a permanent one.

Rachel, however, was not flattered by this display of pleasure in her society. She knew that it was due to no individual charm of her own, but to the fact that she had become her aunt's mirror. For Miss Deane no longer, in Rachel's presence at least, gazed at herself in the looking glass; she gazed at her niece instead. And as Rachel endured the posings and simperings, the alternate adoration and fond contempt with which her aunt regarded her, she was unable to resist the impulse to reflect them. Every day she fell a little lower in that weakness, and however slight the likeness had once been, she knew that now it must be patent to every observer. She copied her aunt, mimicked, duplicated her. It was easier to do that than fight the resemblance, against her aunt's determination; and so, by unnoticed degrees, she had permitted herself to become a lay figure upon which was dressed the image of Miss Deane's youth. She had even come to desire the look of almost sensual gratification on her aunt's face when she saw her niece so perfectly reflecting her own well-remembered airs.

And Rachel, too, had come to avoid the looking glass, dreading to see there the poses and gesticulations of the old, repulsive woman whose every feature and expression had become so sickeningly familiar.

And, in all that time, Adrian had not once been to the house in Tavistock Square. Rachel had kept him away by what she felt had become all too transparent excuses. That terror, at least, she felt must be kept at bay. For she could not conceive it possible that, once he had seen her and her aunt together, he could retain one spark of his admiration. He would, he must, see her then as she was, see that her contemptible vanity was the essential enduring thing, all that would remain when time had stripped her of youth's allurement.

Nevertheless, the day came when Rachel could no longer endure to deceive him. He had challenged her, at last, with hiding something from him. Inevitably, he had become increasingly curious about her strange reticences concerning the Miss Deane whom he, in turn, had grown to regard as almost mythical; and all his suppressed suspicions had suddenly found expression in a question.

"What are you hiding? Do you really live with your aunt in Tavistock Square?" he had asked that day, with all the fierce intensity of a jealous lover.

Rachel had been stirred to a quick response. "Oh, if you don't believe me, you'd better come and see for yourself," she had said. "Come this afternoon—to tea."

And afterwards, even when Adrian had humbly sought to make amends for his unwarrantable jealousy, she had stuck to that invitation. The moment that she had issued it, she had had a sense of relief, a sense of having gratefully confessed her weakness. Adrian's visit would consummate that confession, and thereafter she would have no further secrets from him. And if he found that he could no longer love her after he had seen her as she was, well, it would be better in the end than that he should marry a simulacrum and make the discovery by slow degrees.

"Yes, come this afternoon. We'll expect you about four" had been her last words to him. And now she had to tell her aunt, who was still unaware that such a person as Adrian Flemming existed. Rachel postponed the telling until after lunch.

Her knowledge of Miss Deane, though in some respects it equaled her knowledge of her own mind, did not tell her how her aunt would take this particular piece of news. She might possibly, Rachel thought, be annoyed, fearful lest her beloved looking glass should be stolen from her. But she could wait no longer. In half an hour Miss Deane would go upstairs to rest, and Adrian himself would be in the house before she appeared again.

"I've something to tell you, aunt," Rachel began abruptly.

Miss Deane put up her lorgnette and surveyed her lovely portrait with an interested air.

"Aunt—I've never told you and I know I ought to have," Rachel blurted out. "But I'm—I'm engaged to a Mr. Adrian Flemming, and he's coming here to call on you—to call on us, this afternoon at four o'clock."

Miss Deane closed her eyes and gave a little sigh.

"You might have given me *rather* longer notice, dear," she said.

"It isn't two yet," Rachel replied. "There are more than two hours to get ready for him."

Miss Deane bridled slightly. "I must have my rest before he comes," she said, and added, "I suppose you've told him about us, dear?"

"About *you*?" Rachel asked.

Miss Deane nodded, complacently.

"Well, not very much," Rachel admitted.

Miss Dean's look, as she playfully threatened Rachel with her long-handled lorgnette, was distinctly sly.

"Then he doesn't know yet that there are two of us?" she simpered. "Won't it be just a little bit of a shock to him, my dear?"

Rachel drew a long breath and leaned back in her chair. "Yes," she said curtly. "I expect it will."

Never before had the realization of that strange likeness seemed so intolerable as at that moment. Even now her aunt was looking at her with the very air and gesture which had once charmed her in her own reflection, and that she knew still charmed and fascinated her lover. It was an air and gesture of which she could never break herself. It was natural to her, a true expression of something ineradicable in her being. Indeed, one of the worst penalties imposed upon her during the past month had been the omission of those pleasant ceremonies before the mirror. She had somehow missed herself, lost the sweetest and most adorable of companions!

Miss Deane got up, and holding herself very erect, moved with a little mincing step towards the tall mirror over the console table. Rachel held her breath. She saw that her aunt, suddenly aroused by this thought of the coming lover, was returning mechanically to her old habit of self-admiration. Was it possible, Rachel wondered, that the sight of the image she would see in the looking glass, contrasted now with the memories of the living reflection she had so intimately studied for the past four weeks, might shock her into a realization of the starkly hideous truth?

But it seemed that the aged woman must be blind. She gave no start of surprise as she paused before the glass; she showed no sign of anxiety concerning the vision she saw there. Her left hand, in which she held her lorgnette, had fallen to her side, and with the fingertips of her right she daintily caressed the hollows of her sunken cheeks. She stayed there until Rachel, unable to endure the sight any longer, and with some vague purpose of defiance in her mind, jumped to her feet, crossed the room, and stood shoulder by shoulder with her aunt staring into the glass.

For a moment Miss Deane did not move; then, with a queer hesitation, she dropped her right hand and slowly lifted her lorgnette.

Rachel felt a cold chill of horror invading her. Something fearful and terrible was happening before her eyes; her aunt was shrinking, withering, growing old in a moment. The stiffness had gone out of her pose, her head had begun to droop; the proud contempt in her face was giving way to the moping, resentful reminiscence of the aged. She still held up her lorgnette, still stared half fearfully at the glaring contrast that was presented to her, but her hand and arm had begun to tremble under the strain, and instant by instant, all life and vigor seemed to be draining away from her.

Then suddenly, with a fierce effort she turned away her head, straightened herself, and walked over to the door, passing out with a high, thin cackle of laughter that had in it the suggestion of a vehement, petulant derision; of a bitterness outmastering control.

Rachel shivered, but held her ground before the mirror. She had nothing to fear from that contemplation. As for her aunt, she had had her day. It was time she knew the truth.

"She *had* to know," Rachel repeated, addressing the dear likeness that so proudly reflected her.

V

She found consolation in that thought. Her aunt *had* to know and Rachel herself was only the chance instrument of the revelation. She had not *meant*, so she persisted, to do more than vindicate her own integrity.

Nevertheless, her own passionate problem was not yet solved. Her aunt would not, so Rachel believed, give way without a struggle. Had she not made a gallant effort at recovery even as she left the room, and would she not make a still greater effort while Adrian was there, assert her rivalry if only in revenge?

She must meet that, Rachel decided, by presenting a contrast. She would be meek and humble in her aunt's presence. Adrian might recognize the admired airs and gestures in those of the old woman, but he should at least have no opportunity to compare them.

And it was with this thought and intention in her mind that Rachel received him, when he arrived with a lover's promptness a little before four o'clock.

"Are you so dreadfully nervous?" he asked her, when they were alone together in the drawing room. "You're like you were the first day we met in town—different from your usual self."

"Oh! What a memory you have for my looks and behavior," she replied pettishly. "Of course, I'm nervous."

He tried to argue with her, questioning her as to Miss Deane's probable reception of him, but she refused to answer. "You'll see for yourself in a few minutes," she said; but the minutes passed and still Miss Deane did not come.

At a quarter to five the elderly parlor-maid brought in tea. "Miss Deane said you were not to wait for her, Miss Rachel," was the message she delivered. "She'll be down presently, I was to say."

Rachel could not suppress a scornful twist of her mouth. She had no doubt that her aunt was taking very special pains with her toilet; trying to obliterate, perhaps, her recent vision before the console glass. Rachel saw her entrance in imagination, stiff-necked and proud, defying the criticisms of youth and the suggestions of age.

"Oh! Why doesn't she come and let me get it over?" she passionately demanded, and even as she spoke she heard the sounds of someone coming down the stairs, not the accustomed sounds of her aunt's finicking, high-heeled steps, but a shuffling and creaking, accompanied by the murmurs of a weak, protesting voice.

Rachel jumped to her feet. She knew everything then—before the door opened, and she saw first of all the shocked, scared face of the elderly parlor-maid who supported the crumpled, palsied figure of the old, old woman who, three hours before, had been so miraculously young, magically upheld and supported then by the omnipotent strength of an idea.

She only stayed in the drawing room for five minutes; a querulous, resentful old lady, malignantly jealous, so it seemed, of their vigor and impatient of their sympathy.

When the parlor-maid had been sent for and Miss Deane had gone, Rachel stood up and looked down at Adrian with all her old hauteur.

"Can you realize," she asked, "that once my aunt was supposed to be very, very like me?"

He smiled and shook his head, as if the possibility was too absurd to contemplate.

Rachel turned and looked at herself in the glass, raising her chin and slightly pursing her lips, staring superciliously at her own image under half-lowered eyelids.

"Someday I may be as she is now," she said, with the superb contemptuous arrogance of youth.

Adrian was watching her with adoration. "You will never grow old," he said.

"So long as one does not get the idea of growing old into one's head," Rachel began speculatively.

But Miss Deane had got the idea so strongly now that she died that night. Rachel was with her at the last.

The old woman was trying to mouth a text from the Bible.

"What did you say, dear?" Rachel murmured, bending over her, and caught enough of the answer to guess what Miss Deane was mumbling again and again: "Now we see through a glass darkly, but then face to face."

Lead Us Not Into Temptation
by
Joe Powers

He was asking for trouble just being there. He had no business being anywhere near that kind of establishment, and he knew it. Toy stores were on the lengthy list of places he was to specifically avoid, along with playgrounds, schools, and malls. These were very explicitly laid out among the many conditions attached to his parole, and they were non-negotiable.

If he was spotted and reported by the wrong person it would surely mean a return trip to prison, as unpleasant a place as there was for a man with his proclivities. He wanted no part of that and had gone to considerable lengths to avoid it. He'd diligently behaved himself for most of the past ten months, minding his own business and keeping as low a profile as possible under the circumstances—a tricky proposition in a town in which he'd never previously been, but where everyone was fully aware of his presence and who he was. He did his best, and for a while he thought he'd kicked it. But on some level he knew better. Sooner or later the ugly beast within would rear its head. He was drawn to his old ways as surely as a moth is drawn to a flame. And then, as if on cue, he saw her.

Not that he was doing much to maintain obscurity on this day. For reasons he couldn't completely fathom or explain—a random impulse, a rare moment of indulgence, perhaps—he'd dressed in possibly the gaudiest clothes he'd ever worn. A bright yellow and orange Hawaiian shirt that was several sizes too big hung past his waist, giving him the illusion of being much smaller than he actually was. White cotton slacks paired with baby blue golf shoes and a ridiculous straw hat rounded out an ensemble that flew in the face of the whole concept of anonymity. On some level, he thought it might represent the early stages of feeling human again; the drab earth tones felt constrictive and held him back, if only on a psychological level. The outfit fairly screamed of change, of new beginnings beyond a shadowy past, and for all his longings and temptations, moving beyond was exactly what he wanted to do.

He'd heard it said that a predator—and that was what he unquestionably was—was never cured, his urges always bubbling just beneath the surface, threatening to boil over at any time. A leopard never changes its spots, they said. A monster is a monster. All it would take was the right trigger and they'd fall right back into their old ways. Through those doors of the big box store he'd spotted the very catalyst in question, in the form of a five-year-old girl.

She was tiny but not fragile, more delicate than anything, and moving with a grace and beauty reserved for children of a certain age. She had a face he could only describe as angelic, framed with shimmering blond hair, arrow-straight and tied back in a neat ponytail with a red ribbon. Her bright blue eyes shone as she looked around eagerly at the vast array of toys. She was smiling, and he noticed she still had all of her baby teeth—not a single one missing. She was absolutely perfect: uncannily similar to the one which always appeared when his dreams turned to the forbidden pleasures. He was instantly smitten—ten months of careful diligence thrown away in an instant.

More and more often the images returned unbidden from the folds of his subconscious mind. When he closed his eyes he could see, hear, and smell the experience as though it were still fresh instead of merely a whisper of a distant past. Even when the prison shrinks were working on getting to the root of his obsessions, when he was really making an effort to exorcise the memories, the dreams would come. He would savor the sensation as long as he could, then drift up from the depths of sleep and lie there, perfectly still, trying vainly to cling to the last vestiges of the swiftly fading images.

He had always assumed the girl was a manifestation of his deepest desires. The thought never crossed his mind he might someday encounter someone that so closely resembled the vision of perfection in his mind's eye. All he could think of was that fate had brought the two of them to the same place—a toy store, of all places. He took it as a sign.

He'd found himself standing by the doors entirely by accident. He was on his way home, driving the rusty minivan he'd bought not long after he got to town, as he did every day. After ten months he still struggled with the seemingly illogical street system, which forced him to take numerous side streets and off-ramps that made no sense, over a distance of just twenty miles. He missed one of his turnoffs while preoccupied with a strange pinging noise under the hood. In an effort to get off the road and check things out, he pulled into the first parking lot he came to, where the van sputtered and gasped its last. Despondent and frustrated, he looked around, saw with alarm where he was, and almost ran away in fear. But something compelled him to stand his ground.

"You're not hurting anyone," he'd reasoned. "You've got a perfectly legitimate excuse for being where you are. Take a few minutes and gather your thoughts, then call Triple A."

That line of reasoning had led him to see if he could walk up to the doors and look in, just to test his resilience. He'd taken several shaky steps, all the while feeling burning pangs of guilt gnawing at his sensibilities. He knew on some level what he was doing was not only tempting fate, but inherently wrong. But he'd fought the inner turmoil, convinced if he could touch the door and not be tempted to go inside and look around, he'd actually be on the road to recovery. And then there he was, his hand pressed against the cool brick façade of the building, his eyes nervously scanning the parking lot as if he were being watched. For all he knew, maybe he was. But he'd made it, and even allowed himself a tiny sliver of pride—until he saw her, and his resolve melted away in an instant.

All thoughts of logic and reason were cast aside as he stepped through the automatic doors into the artificial chill of the air-conditioned toy store. He feigned subtlety and disinterest, only keeping the girl peripherally within his line of sight as he pretended to look for something at the far end of the aisle she walked along. All of his predatory instincts had kicked in immediately, he noted with far more pleasure than dismay. He stepped past the aisle to the next one, planning his approach. Just as she passed from his sight he thought he saw her look in his direction. His breath caught in his throat, but he quickly diverted his glance and kept walking.

He strolled casually along the next aisle over, desperately hoping the girl would still be unaccompanied by a parent by the time he reached her. He wiped his sweaty palms on his pants and gave his head a little shake as he began to get into character. He reached back into the forgotten recesses of his mind for one of his opening lines, trying to recall which ones had worked the best for him in the past. Despite the long layoff, he was back in his element once again, doing the only thing he'd ever been any good at.

He'd gone to prison for molesting four young girls over a ten year period. The oldest had been thirteen, and she had been the one who finally blew the whistle on him. As is often the case in such matters, the other three quickly came forward once his arrest and the nature of his crime became public knowledge. Almost immediately, he was found guilty in the court of public opinion, and the judicial system didn't take long to concur. He received a twelve year sentence, and following a brief but ugly period in a holdover facility where he was taunted, threatened, and attacked, he was transferred to the protective custody unit in an undisclosed and distant maximum security prison.

He spent just over five years there, gradually responding to intense therapy and counselling, until he was declared a likely candidate for early release by the psychiatric staff. While he openly regretted his past choices and agreed what he'd done was unforgivable, there remained a small part of him that always clung to the idea that a lot of people were making a really big deal out of nothing—an opinion he fastidiously kept to himself. What they didn't know, and what he certainly never volunteered, was that there were more girls that didn't come forward. He considered it a testament to his skill, coupled with a broad stroke of luck, that nobody ever made the connection between him and the eight missing girls—the ones whose bodies had never been recovered.

Relief at having dodged that particular bullet didn't translate to the anticipation of a lifetime of immunity. He approached his state-enforced rehabilitation with an open mind and a willingness to be cured. Only, they told him, there was no cure. It was up to him to get a grip on his perversions and to keep them under control. And for the most part, he did.

For nearly a year he'd been wandering around a free man, or as free as a convicted sex offender can ever truly be. He'd abided by the court-appointed stipulations and stayed on the straight and narrow, never wavering or even thinking all that much about his former lifestyle. Until the present day, when that little girl with the bright smile dragged him backwards through time.

He needn't have worried about his approach: as he rounded the corner, he nearly collided with her. He jumped back in surprise and grabbed at a nearby shelf to regain his balance, narrowly avoiding bowling her over in the process. She skidded to a halt, her eyes widening at the near miss, her mouth forming a tiny 'o' of surprise. She quickly recovered, however, composing herself and treating him to a broad smile.

"Oh, hello," she said.

He was so caught off guard that it took a second for him to realize she was looking at him expectantly, waiting for him to say something. He cleared his throat and returned her smile. "Well, hello there, young lady," he said. "What are you doing in here, all by yourself? Where's your mommy?"

"She went in there with a man," she said without hesitation, gesturing toward the rear of the store. "She told me to look at the toys, and she'd come find me later."

He mulled over the situation. Was it possible the girl's mother was dating one of the employees, and had snuck into the back for a little action while her daughter wandered around out front? He decided he didn't much care about the whats, hows, or whys. Opportunity was knocking loudly; he barely hesitated before he stepped beyond the point of no return and decided to answer.

"Well now, it wouldn't be right for a young lady to have to spend such a lovely day all alone. Would you like some company? Believe it or not, I'm pretty good at picking out the best toys." He braced himself for the possibility of a negative reaction, ready to make a run for it if she caused a scene and drew unwanted attention. Instead she seemed to embrace the idea immediately, her eyes flashing with excitement.

Within a few short minutes he'd managed to persuade her to accompany him outside. The girl wasn't shy in the least, as it turned out, and combined a rare mixture of maturity and naiveté that made his approach work perfectly. It had taken very little convincing; she seemed more than happy to put her complete trust in him. He was almost uncontrollably pleased with himself; for better or worse, he still had the touch.

"It's almost too easy," he thought with an inward smile.

Almost too easy, indeed. The culmination of a lifetime of searching for that exact set of conditions, only to have it fall into his lap so smoothly, gave him cause for suspicion. A terrible thought flashed through his mind: maybe he was being set up. The idea occurred to him that he'd been recognized and followed, and that the girl was planted by someone trying to entrap him. He subtly scanned the area for anything that looked out of the ordinary. For a moment he considered just calling it quits and getting out before any such ambush could take place. But in the end the urge was too strong. He forced aside any thoughts of stopping; he'd come too far to turn back now.

He took extra care to avoid detection, knowing that he'd reached a critical juncture of his mission. He was so close to being in the clear, almost deathly afraid of raising suspicion among the staff or numerous other shoppers in the store. Luck was with him—she was so at ease with him, chatting amiably and even holding his hand, acting very comfortable and natural enough in his company that nobody gave them so much as a second glance. They made it to the front door, casually staying out of sight of the security cameras—a trick he'd picked up and never quite put down—and they were on their way.

As the van door opened, he roughly shoved her inside. She gave a small cry and landed hard, face down. He reached back to grab the handle, took a final look around to make sure nobody had seen him, and pulled it firmly shut. When he turned back to face her, he saw she'd already gained her footing and was crouched on the van floor facing him, sporting a look he wasn't expecting. Was it confusion, sadness, or fear? No, he knew those expressions very well. This was something different, something he couldn't quite put his finger on. Defiance? Yes, that was it. She may have been small, but she had spirit. By the time he pulled the door closed, he'd decided this one was going to be one of those they never found.

Had anyone passed nearby, they might have been drawn to stop and listen, curiously, as some very strange and suspicious sounds came from within the confines of the old rusted van sprawled at a haphazard angle across two parking spaces. At first there were shuffling sounds, as if someone were moving around the cramped space. These were quickly accompanied by cries of fear, followed by the unmistakable sounds of a struggle. The distinct ripping sounds of clothing being torn asunder. The muffled bumps as something struck the inside walls of the van, sometimes violently enough to rock it back and forth, eliciting sounds of protest from the vehicle's sagging suspension. The pleading cries softened to silence after just a few minutes, interspersed only by brief bursts of pain-filled anguish.

Had the passerby crept closer still, she might have heard a faint, wet sloshing sound coming from within, accompanied by soft moans of pleasure. An astute observer might even have noticed that the fresh oil spill under the van wasn't oil at all, wasn't anywhere near the motor, in fact. But nobody passed close enough to hear any of these sounds or take in these sights. The rest of the world remained oblivious, and within minutes the noises had ceased; the encounter had ended, missed completely by the outside world.

The van door shuddered open and she stepped lightly to the ground, her tiny feet touching down delicately on the pavement. She seemed completely unconcerned at the prospect of potential onlookers, possibly because she had a good idea if they hadn't stepped forward before now there weren't any nearby. As she wiped her hands and dabbed at a red smudge at the corner of her mouth with a torn piece of yellow and orange cloth, she was completely unrecognizable from the way she'd appeared just minutes earlier. The greenish gray scales covering her body were already reverting to the pale, pinkish hue she'd sported earlier. The steely claws retracted, leaving delicate little fingernails in their place. An impossibly long tongue danced across the rows of jagged, bloody fangs, removing the last traces of his blood even as they morphed into the tiny, pearly white deciduous teeth of a five-year-old girl.

She stopped in front of the set of large glass doors and checked her reflection for any evidence she might have missed. Yellow, pupil-less eyes stared back at her. She blinked once, and the sparkling, sky-blue eyes were back in place. Satisfied that the illusion was once again complete, she flashed herself the innocent, child-like smile she'd perfected over time for occasions such as this.

She'd tried to be good for so long. She did her best to keep as low a profile as possible under the circumstances in a town she'd never previously been to. But she was always drawn back, as surely as a moth to a flame. She'd always heard that a predator, no matter how determined or resolved to change, was never truly cured. And when presented with such a tempting target, she couldn't resist. A monster, after all, is a monster.

"It's almost too easy," she muttered in a lilting, whispery voice, pushing her way back inside the store.

The Weathermaker
by
K. Trap Jones

I consider myself a rational person with a good head on my shoulders, but I have stumbled upon something that I shouldn't have. I have seen things that even my own eyes cannot justify. Everything that I have been taught has fled my thoughts like the shifting tides. I find myself randomly wandering without a single thought in my head as if my mind does not exist anymore. If I could only go back, if I could only breathe my own existence once again, I would trade everything. If I could just be myself for one last day, I would gladly sacrifice my sanity and embrace the confusion gifted to me on the day that I met the *Weathermaker*.

Some called us risk-takers, but we considered ourselves to be adrenaline junkies, obsessed with the extreme challenges that life had to offer. My friends and I were always seeking out the next rush. It didn't matter whether it was from cliff jumping or sky diving, as long as the risk was there. We each had broken many bones in our day, but pain was always included under the fine print of the adrenaline contract. I didn't fear death; I had no reason to until the day it walked up and introduced itself.

There is not much I can recall about my past life. I know the memories are there, locked away in the back of my mind, but I am no longer in possession of the key. I remember my arms burning as I held the paddle. Little Pigeon River, western Tennessee is the last memory I am granted.

White water rafting in category five currents was the next on the checklist and we were well prepared for the feat—or so we believed. There were five of us in the raft along with our guide, but even he couldn't see the jagged, submerged boulder. The current had always been brutal, but the water was especially tormented that day, and the raft collided with the boulder. Through the lingering fog, I remember looking down at my friends as we were being tossed like rag dolls.

I fell deep into the freezing water. The chill stung my eyes as I tried to keep my head above water. My muscles quickly tightened and my lungs begged for air, but I could not help either of them. The fog made it difficult to see, but I could decipher the orange vests of my friends floating ahead of me. My heart quickened, but failed to provide warm blood to my shivering limbs. The fog thickened as I lost sight of my friends. The current carried me around a bend as I tried desperately to keep my legs from dragging against the rocks. I was too numb for physical pain, but nothing in my life would prepare me for what I encountered next.

My mind would never be the same again.

The rapids calmed and the fog vanished as the water temperature increased. My muscles loosened and my teeth no longer clattered. Up ahead, I saw a lone cabin where the river ended. Smoke was siphoning through a chimney and snaking through the dense trees. Hope conjured up courage as my arms began to swim toward the shoreline. All of my friends were floating aimlessly and swaying with the current. Their lifeless stares brutalized my mind as I pulled each of them up to the shore. As I dragged the last one from the water, I noticed that the embankment was comprised of bones. Speckled throughout were helmets, vests, and paddles. It was some sort of sadistic graveyard for rafters. I know my words will seem odd at first. I wish they weren't that way, but obscurity does not work in that manner.

"Hello?" I yelled toward the cabin, but received no response.

I treaded lightly on the skulls and bones of the shoreline as I made my way to the porch of the cabin. I noticed someone in the window from the way the curtain was being pulled back.

"I need help!" I shouted, prompting the curtains to fall back into place.

Tired, I sat upon the porch steps as my eyes embraced the vision of my dead friends. Sadness crept up my spine and dug its claws deep into my heart.

"Why aren't you dead?" a disgruntled voice rang out from inside the cabin.

The words startled me as I turned around and stood up.

"You're not supposed to be alive! Why are you still alive?"

I had no response. I couldn't form any words.

"Go back into the river and die. The currents are only allowed to bring corpses upon my land."

"There's been a terrible accident."

The front door opened just a crack.

"Do not mistake me for someone who cares about your problems. I was told that I would not have to deal with your kind, and yet every so often one of you contaminates my land. I am not happy!"

"I need…"

"We all need something, but few ever receive it. Now, as I said before, go back into the river and die already."

"I will not!" I said angrily. The confusion and frustration of not truly understanding the situation was draining my rationale.

The cabin door swung fully open to reveal a small, frail man. He couldn't have been but about three feet in height. Jabbing his cane into my chest, he pushed me backward off the porch.

"Don't use that tone of voice with me!" he shouted in unison with a thunderous roar from the sky.

Lightning streaked across the sky and splintered trees that buckled into the river. The piles of bones shook uncontrollably beneath my feet as I was forced back to the shoreline. The clouds let loose a heavy rain that blinded my vision.

"See what you've done? You've upset me," the old man stated, pointing his cane to the clouds. "Now I have to fix all this. I do not like visitors, especially live ones."

"Please, I need your help," I pleaded with the man as he walked back up to the porch.

"I cannot help you. I cannot help the living or the dead. You have strayed from the path, one that you must return to."

"Am I dead?"

"Unfortunately, no."

The door slammed shut. Alone with only my confused thoughts and the corpses of my friends, I sat upon a rock on the riverbank. Even with the current of the river moving the corpses of my friends around, I could not fully grasp the situation. I could sense that the strange old man was looking at me through the window. The wind became angry and showed its vengeance by abnormally bending the trees. The crackling of the bark howled and frightened the fog. I was no longer afraid, as I truly believed that I was already dead.

"Stubbornness will get you nowhere," he said through the cracked door.

"I don't know what has happened," I replied through my choked throat.

"You belong with the dead. You should not be here. She will not be happy unless you rectify the situation. You must kill yourself."

"I cannot kill myself. How could I possibly do that?"

"Well, I can't do it either; it's not part of my job. Although I wish I could," he added sarcastically.

Thunder roared from the horizon.

"Dammit, the storm's early. See what happens when I get distracted? She's not going to be happy."

"God?"

"Ha, no! Mother Nature. I have to work with her, but I don't have to like her."

"Where am I?"

"You are where no human should ever be; behind the veil of the planet. If you had just hit your head on a jagged rock like the others, you would've been well on your way, fulfilling whatever predetermined destiny was meant for you."

The thunder grew louder as the leaves fled the branches of the trees.

"I can smell your stubbornness. Your human skin is covered with it. After the storm subsides, you must return to the path. Once you die, you will remember nothing."

I was at a loss for words. Whatever courage I had remaining was left on that raft. The lightning was intensifying as the electric serpents split apart the trees with no effort. I looked to my friends. Their corpses were being dragged back into the river by the wakes creeping upon the shoreline. For a moment, I wished I was like them; dead and gone with their minds at ease. Instead, I was the lone survivor, stricken from the path that was to be my destiny.

"What if I cannot do it?"

"It's not a matter of if; it's a matter of when. I do not like that you are upon my land, but I have to deal with it, now don't I?"

"Is there no other way?"

"No, you cheated death. It is the only fair way to settle the score. I see plenty of your kind; high-energy seeking people taking every risk that comes your way. Well, guess what? You took a risk that you failed. All of you did. Now you must deal with the aftermath. There is no such thing as a risk without consequences."

"Why only me?"

"If I knew that, I wouldn't be standing here talking to you, now would I? I would use that knowledge to make sure that everyone dies, so that I never get interrupted again. Maybe you shouldn't have been obsessed with risks in the first place. Have you ever thought of that? There are plenty of people who don't enter a vessel and allow their lives to be at the mercy of Mother Nature's wrath."

"I... I..."

"Up there beyond the ridge is a tree; the tallest in the mountains. Upon the sturdiest of limbs, I have attached a noose made from the strongest of threads. After the storm subsides, you are to climb that tree and place that noose around your neck. You do not have to jump, as I will control the winds of death for you."

"And if I do not?" I replied stubbornly, which sent the old man walking toward his door.

"Be it as it may, but there are things much worse than a peaceful death by one's own hand."

Insanity was swinging from my rib cage, desperately making its way to my heart. Inside, the old man started to close the door.

My panic betrayed me by the tone of my voice. "Alright, alright."

"Now that everything is in order, come inside, the storm is approaching."

Agreeing to kill myself took a toll upon my mind. Rapid visions of what death would be like plagued my thoughts. Anticipating death was difficult to comprehend. On the porch, I looked back to the river and surrounding mountains. The darkest of clouds were rolling into the valley, suffocating the horizon. The thunder roared like a pack of starved lions.

"Close the door behind you; seal it tight. I don't care for the unpredictability of rain. Those falling droplets are mischievous; always sneaking in through the cracks, causing mold and whatnot. It makes it very difficult to breathe if they are allowed to run rampart."

After ducking under the doorframe and closing the door, my eyes were met with wonder. I had to bend my neck downward and squat my knees in order to avoid hitting the ceiling. It was as if I had walked into a historical gallery of a museum. Beautiful relics were mounted to the wooden walls. Large bookshelves were packed to the brim, but what caught my eye the most was the sheer amount of globes hanging from the ceiling. I tried my best to avoid colliding into one, but my fascination with the beautiful copper telescopes blinded me. My forehead struck one of the globes ever so slightly.

"Mind your manners! Do not touch anything!"

"I'm sorry," I replied, trying my best to avoid any others.

"Your huge forehead could tip the scales off balance."

I tried to follow him to the center of the cabin. I moved slowly, as it was difficult to see where I was stepping. I felt that if I knocked over one item, it would cause a domino effect. I could sense his frustration with me as the thunder outside grew louder. Lightning occurred whenever his stress spiked. Trying to shuffle my feet within the cabin, my eyes were focused downward as my head collided with another hanging globe. The whole cabin swayed from side to side with the movement of the globe.

"Why must you be so clumsy? Are human minds not capable of following simple instructions? No wonder your kind is always killing themselves."

With a pipe in his mouth, he put on a small pair of spectacles. Rolling up his sleeves, two globes floated down from the ceiling. My eyes widened as one was a replica of Earth and the other was the Moon.

"What is…" I started to ask.

"Silence! Don't speak! One slip and mass chaos ensues," he said from behind the globes.

Spinning the Moon with one hand, he slowly rotated the Earth while staring deep into the globe. His eyes turned a shade of grey as small streaks of lightning extended from his fingertips. Outside, lightning cracked alongside the sound of rain.

"Every cloud must be controlled; every element must be watched. The atmospheric pressure must be contained at all times," he said, spinning the globe.

His hand halted the rotation. With his index finger stuck within the globe, he began spinning it. I leaned forward and saw him creating a hurricane. When the storm was moving under its own free will, he exhaled, blowing the system on a direct course. Rotating the globe again, he gave it a hit from his pipe. Releasing small puffs of the grey smoke, he forged darkened clouds within the atmosphere.

"That should suffice for now," he said, sitting back and taking off his glasses.

Looking to the ceiling, I couldn't help but see other globes of different colors.

"Are those…"

"Different planets? Yes. You didn't think you were the only ones, did you?" he said with a smirk.

"How many are there?" I asked, not truly believing what I was seeing.

"A dozen or so, each with its own environment and capable of holding life, but also capable of destroying it, as well. Life is a delicate equation that no mortal mind can contemplate."

"Where will death take me?" I nervously asked, hearing the storm outside.

"I do not know. There are many things that I am not given knowledge about. Never fret, think of it as another risk involving the unknown," he said, laughing.

He spoke the truth with regard to death. Never before had I feared it. Every time I stood on a ledge or looked out the open door of a plane, I never gave death an ounce of thought. I assumed I would live through any action; I assumed I would be alive when the opportunity for another risk revealed itself.

"One should always fear death; it should never be taken for granted, especially by those who are able to die," he said with confidence.

The simple act of swallowing became difficult.

"However, death is by no means the end of your existence; it is merely a detour. Like most paths, the directions can go astray and that is why you are here. Although you were supposed to die, you didn't; a questionable blockade of sorts."

"If I am not alive or dead, then what am I?" I said with a dry throat.

"Nothing; a speck of sand that clings to the walls of an hourglass instead of falling through like the others. You will eventually fall, but it is your choice as to whether you want to jump or not in order to speed up the process."

The storm was lessening. As the thunder was fading, he allowed the globes to hover back up to the ceiling.

"There, those storms should appease her for a while."

I didn't want to get up from the table; I didn't want to walk out that door.

"Unfortunately, it has come time for you to leave. For what it's worth, I do not confide in many people, but there is a brave soul within you that I admire. Most of those who stumble upon my land lack courage, but you are different. You may not even need my wind at your back."

I didn't know what to say as I didn't feel brave, and my courage level felt like it was running low.

"You must go before she notices. Like I said, there are worse things to fear than a normal death," he said, standing from the table.

My knees were trembling as I stood and I needed the support of my arms to help keep my body upright. He opened the door for me as fresh air flowed inside.

"Will there be pain?" I said, looking back.

"Nothing that you can't handle," he said with a smile before closing the door.

I walked toward the shoreline where the bodies of my friends were rolling in the wakes. The raft had made it ashore, and memories of how excited we were to enter it rehashed within my mind. We didn't have a care in the world. Our only complaint was how cold the water was.

A path led me up the hillside, high above the river. The tree which he spoke of was directly in front of me. The trunk was massive and the height could not be determined by my eyes as the clouds hung low. Small pieces of tree limbs were nailed to the bark and formed a ladder. Each reaching hand shook uncontrollably; each stepping foot had no energy. I kept my eyes looking up as if I was climbing toward the Heavens. With no more steps to grab, I looked to the right and saw a thick tree limb. Just above was the noose, swaying in the wind.

I tried not to think about it; I tried not to allow it to consume my thoughts. Instead, I focused on the memories and all of the great times I had during my life. I had come so close to death on many occasions, but I was so blinded by the obsession of adrenaline that I did not even offer a blink of hesitation. The fear I should have had conjured itself all at once as I stepped out on that limb. Holding the rope for support, I looked down, much like I always did before jumping.

I was becoming unstable out on the limb. The wind instantly died down; I believed the Weathermaker was watching me. The rope fibers were rough as they slid around my neck. The clouds parted and allowed the sun to shine through. The sting of the rays felt good against my skin and renewed my courage. He was right— I *was* brave. I could feel the adrenaline pumping though my veins and my heart racing. I looked to either side and saw my friends; each one had their own rope.

"Are we doing this or what?"

"This is crazy!"

"How are we possibly going to top this next year?"

"On the count of three, we all go!"

"You ready?"

"One!"

"Two!"

"Three!"

The Rocking Horse Winner
by
D.H. Lawrence

originally published in
The Woman Who Rode Away and Other Stories, 1928

There was a woman who was beautiful, who started with all the advantages, yet she had no luck. She married for love, and the love turned to dust. She had bonny children, yet she felt they had been thrust upon her, and she could not love them. They looked at her coldly, as if they were finding fault with her. And hurriedly she felt she must cover up some fault in herself. Yet what it was that she must cover up she never knew. Nevertheless, when her children were present, she always felt the center of her heart go hard. This troubled her, and in her manner she was all the more gentle and anxious for her children, as if she loved them very much. Only she herself knew that at the center of her heart was a hard little place that could not feel love, no, not for anybody. Everybody else said of her, "She is such a good mother. She adores her children." Only she herself, and her children themselves, knew it was not so. They read it in each other's eyes.

There were a boy and two little girls. They lived in a pleasant house, with a garden, and they had discreet servants, and felt themselves superior to anyone in the neighborhood.

Although they lived in style, they felt always an anxiety in the house. There was never enough money. The mother had a small income, and the father had a small income, but not nearly enough for the social position which they had to keep up. The father went in to town to some office. But though he had good prospects, these prospects never materialized. There was always the grinding sense of the shortage of money, though the style was always kept up.

At last the mother said, "I will see if *I* can't make something." But she did not know where to begin. She racked her brains, and tried this thing and the other, but could not find anything successful. The failure made deep lines come into her face. Her children were growing up, they would have to go to school. There must be more money, there must be more money. The father, who was always very handsome and expensive in his tastes, seemed as if he never *would* be able to do anything worth doing. And the mother, who had a great belief in herself, did not succeed any better, and her tastes were just as expensive.

And so the house came to be haunted by the unspoken phrase: *There must be more money! There must be more money!* The children could hear it all the time, though nobody said it aloud. They heard it at Christmas, when the expensive and splendid toys filled the nursery. Behind the shining modern rocking horse, behind the smart doll's house, a voice would start whispering, "There *must* be more money! There *must* be more money!" And the children would stop playing, to listen for a moment. They would look into each other's eyes, to see if they had all heard. And each one saw in the eyes of the other two that they too had heard. "There *must* be more money! There *must* be more money!"

It came whispering from the springs of the still-swaying rocking horse, and even the horse, bending his wooden, champing head, heard it. The big doll, sitting so pink and smirking in her new pram, could hear it quite plainly, and seemed to be smirking all the more self-consciously because of it. The foolish puppy, too, that took the place of the teddy bear, he was looking so extraordinarily foolish for no other reason but that he heard the secret whisper all over the house, "There *must* be more money."

Yet nobody ever said it aloud. The whisper was everywhere, and therefore no one spoke it. Just as no one ever says, "We are breathing!" in spite of the fact that breath is coming and going all the time.

"Mother!" said the boy Paul one day. "Why don't we keep a car of our own? Why do we always use uncle's, or else a taxi?"

"Because we're the poor members of the family," said the mother.

"But why *are* we, mother?"

"Well—I suppose," she said slowly and bitterly, "it's because your father has no luck."

The boy was silent for some time.

"Is luck money, mother?" he asked, rather timidly.

"No, Paul! Not quite. It's what causes you to have money."

"Oh!" said Paul vaguely. "I thought when Uncle Oscar said *filthy lucker,* it meant money."

"*Filthy lucre* does mean money," said the mother. "But it's lucre, not luck."

"Oh!" said the boy. "Then what *is* luck, mother?"

"It's what causes you to have money. If you're lucky you have money. That's why it's better to be born lucky than rich. If you're rich, you may lose your money. But if you're lucky, you will always get more money."

"Oh! Will you! And is father not lucky?"

"Very unlucky, I should say," she said bitterly.

The boy watched her with unsure eyes. "Why?" he asked.

"I don't know. Nobody ever knows why one person is lucky and another unlucky."

"Don't they? Nobody at all? Does *nobody* know?"

"Perhaps God! But He never tells."

"He ought to, then. And aren't you lucky either, mother?"

"I can't be, if I married an unlucky husband."

"But by yourself, aren't you?"

"I used to think I was, before I married. Now I think I am very unlucky indeed."

"Why?"

"Well—never mind! Perhaps I'm not really," she said.

The child looked at her, to see if she meant it. But he saw, by the lines of her mouth, that she was only trying to hide something from him.

"Well, anyhow," he said stoutly, "I'm a lucky person."

"Why?" said his mother, with a sudden laugh.

He stared at her. He didn't even know why he had said it. "God told me," he asserted, brazening it out.

"I hope He did, dear!" she said, again with a laugh, but rather bitter.

"He did, mother!"

"Excellent!" said the mother, using one of her husband's exclamations.

The boy saw she did not believe him; or rather, that she paid no attention to his assertion. This angered him somewhere, and made him want to compel her attention.

He went off by himself, vaguely, in a childish way, seeking for the clue to "luck." Absorbed, taking no heed of other people, he went about with a sort of stealth, seeking inwardly for luck. He wanted luck, he wanted it, he wanted it. When the two girls were playing dolls, in the nursery, he would sit on his big rocking horse, charging madly into space, with a frenzy that made the little girls peer at him uneasily. Wildly the horse careered, the waving dark hair of the boy tossed, his eyes had a strange glare in them. The little girls dared not speak to him.

When he had ridden to the end of his mad little journey, he climbed down and stood in front of his rocking horse, staring fixedly into its lowered face. Its red mouth was slightly open, its big eye was wide and glassy bright.

"Now!" he would silently command the snorting steed. "Now take me to where there is luck! Now take me!"

And he would slash the horse on the neck with the little whip he had asked Uncle Oscar for. He *knew* the horse could take him to where there was luck, if only he forced it. So he would mount again, and start on his furious ride, hoping at last to get there. He knew he could get there.

"You'll break your horse, Paul!" said the nurse.

"He's always riding like that! I wish he'd leave off!" said his elder sister Joan.

But he only glared down on them in silence. Nurse gave him up. She could make nothing of him. Anyhow he was growing beyond her.

One day his mother and his Uncle Oscar came in when he was on one of his furious rides. He did not speak to them.

"Hallo! You young jockey! Riding a winner?" said his uncle.

"Aren't you growing too big for a rocking horse? You're not a very little boy any longer, you know," said his mother.

But Paul only gave a blue glare from his big, rather close-set eyes. He would speak to nobody when he was in full tilt. His mother watched him with an anxious expression on her face.

At last he suddenly stopped forcing his horse into the mechanical gallop, and slid down.

"Well, I got there!" he announced fiercely, his blue eyes still flaring, and his sturdy long legs straddling apart.

"Where did you get to?" asked his mother.

"Where I wanted to go to," he flared back at her.

"That's right, son!" said Uncle Oscar. "Don't you stop till you get there. What's the horse's name?"

"He doesn't have a name," said the boy.

"Gets on without all right?" asked the uncle.

"Well, he has different names. He was called Sansovino last week."

"Sansovino, eh? Won the Ascot. How did you know his name?"

"He always talks about horse races with Bassett," said Joan.

The uncle was delighted to find that his small nephew was posted with all the racing news. Bassett, the young gardener who had been wounded in the left foot in the war, and had got his present job through Oscar Cresswell, whose batman he had been, was a perfect blade of the "turf." He lived in the racing events, and the small boy lived with him.

Oscar Cresswell got it all from Bassett.

"Master Paul comes and asks me, so I can't do more than tell him, sir," said Bassett, his face terribly serious, as if he were speaking of religious matters.

"And does he ever put anything on a horse he fancies?"

"Well—I don't want to give him away—he's a young sport, a fine sport, sir. Would you mind asking him himself? He sort of takes a pleasure in it, and perhaps he'd feel I was giving him away, sir, if you don't mind."

Bassett was serious as a church.

The uncle went back to his nephew, and took him off for a ride in the car. "Say, Paul, old man, do you ever put anything on a horse?" the uncle asked.

The boy watched the handsome man closely.

"Why, do you think I oughtn't to?" he parried.

"Not a bit of it! I thought perhaps you might give me a tip for the Lincoln."

The car sped on into the country, going down to Uncle Oscar's place in Hampshire.

"Honor bright?" said the nephew.

"Honor bright, son!" said the uncle.

"Well, then, Daffodil."

"Daffodil! I doubt it, sonny. What about Mirza?"

"I only know the winner," said the boy. "That's Daffodil!"

"Daffodil, eh?" There was a pause. Daffodil was an obscure horse comparatively.

"Uncle!"

"Yes, son?"

"You won't let it go any further, will you? I promised Bassett."

"Bassett be damned, old man! What's he got to do with it?"

"We're partners! We've been partners from the first! Uncle, he lent me my first five shillings, which I lost. I promised him, honor bright, it was only between me and him: only you gave me that ten shilling note I started winning with, so I thought you were lucky. You won't let it go any further, will you?"

The boy gazed at his uncle from those big, hot, blue eyes, set rather close together. The uncle stirred and laughed uneasily.

"Right you are, son! I'll keep your tip private. Daffodil, eh! How much are you putting on him?"

"All except twenty pounds," said the boy. "I keep that in reserve."

The uncle thought it a good joke.

"You keep twenty pounds in reserve, do you, you young romancer? What are you betting, then?"

"I'm betting three hundred," said the boy gravely. "But it's between you and me, Uncle Oscar! Honor bright?"

The uncle burst into a roar of laughter.

"It's between you and me all right, you young Nat Gould," he said, laughing. "But where's your three hundred?"

"Bassett keeps it for me. We're partners."

"You are, are you! And what is Bassett putting on Daffodil?"

"He won't go quite as high as I do, I expect. Perhaps he'll go a hundred and fifty."

"What, pennies?" laughed the uncle.

"Pounds," said the child, with a surprised look at his uncle. "Bassett keeps a bigger reserve than I do."

Between wonder and amusement, Uncle Oscar was silent. He pursued the matter no further, but he was determined to take his nephew with him to the Lincoln races.

"Now, son," he said, "I'm putting twenty on Mirza, and I'll put five for you on any horse you fancy.

What's your pick?"

"Daffodil, uncle!"

"No, not the fiver on Daffodil!"

"I should if it was my own fiver," said the child.

"Good! Good! Right you are! A fiver for me and a fiver for you on Daffodil."

The child had never been to a race meeting before, and his eyes were blue fire. He pursed his mouth tight, and watched. A Frenchman just in front had put his money on Lancelot. Wild with excitement, he flayed his arms up and down, yelling "*Lancelot! Lancelot!*" in his French accent.

Daffodil came in first, Lancelot second, Mirza third. The child, flushed and with eyes blazing, was curiously serene. His uncle brought him five five pound notes: four to one.

"What am I to do with these?" he cried, waving them before the boy's eyes.

"I suppose we'll talk to Bassett," said the boy. "I expect I have fifteen hundred now and twenty in reserve and this twenty."

His uncle studied him for some moments.

"Look here, son!" he said. "You're not serious about Bassett and that fifteen hundred, are you?"

"Yes, I am. But it's between you and me, uncle! Honor bright!"

"Honor bright all right, son! But I must talk to Bassett."

"If you'd like to be a partner, uncle, with Bassett and me, we could all be partners. Only you'd have to promise, honor bright, uncle, not to let it go beyond us three. Bassett and I are lucky, and you must be lucky, because it was your ten shillings I started winning with…"

Uncle Oscar took both Bassett and Paul into Richmond Park for an afternoon, and there they talked.

"It's like this, you see, sir," Bassett said. "Master Paul would get me talking about racing events, spinning yarns, you know, sir. And he was always keen on knowing if I'd made or if I'd lost. It's about a year since, now, that I put five shillings on Blush of Dawn for him: and we lost. Then the luck turned, with that ten shillings he had from you: that we put on Singhalese. And since that time, it's been pretty steady, all things considering. What do you say, Master Paul?"

"We're all right when we're *sure*," said Paul. "It's when we're not quite sure that we go down."

"Oh, but we're careful then," said Bassett.

"But when are you *sure*?" smiled Uncle Oscar.

"It's Master Paul, sir," said Bassett, in a secret, religious voice. "It's as if he had it from heaven. Like Daffodil now, for the Lincoln. That was as sure as eggs."

"Did you put anything on Daffodil?" asked Oscar Cresswell.

"Yes, sir. I made my bit."

"And my nephew?"

Bassett was obstinately silent, looking at Paul.

"I made twelve hundred, didn't I, Bassett? I told uncle I was putting three hundred on Daffodil."

"That's right," said Bassett, nodding.

"But where's the money?" asked the uncle.

"I keep it safe locked up, sir. Master Paul, he can have it any minute he likes to ask for it."

"What, fifteen hundred pounds?"

"And twenty! And *forty,* that is, with the twenty he made on the course."

"It's amazing!" said the uncle.

"If Master Paul offers you to be partners, sir, I would, if I were you: if you'll excuse me," said Bassett.

Oscar Cresswell thought about it. "I'll see the money," he said.

They drove home again, and sure enough, Bassett came round to the garden house with fifteen hundred pounds in notes. The twenty pounds reserve was left with Joe Glee, in the Turf Commission deposit.

"You see, it's all right, uncle, when I'm *sure!* Then we go strong, for all we're worth. Don't we, Bassett?"

"We do that, Master Paul."

"And when are you sure?" said the uncle, laughing.

"Oh, well, sometimes I'm *absolutely* sure, like about Daffodil," said the boy; "and sometimes I have an idea; and sometimes I haven't even an idea, have I, Bassett? Then we're careful, because we mostly go down."

"You do, do you! And when you're sure, like about Daffodil, what makes you sure, sonny?"

"Oh, well, I don't know," said the boy uneasily. "I'm sure, you know, uncle;

that's all."

"It's as if he had it from heaven, sir," Bassett reiterated.

"I should say so!" said the uncle.

But he became a partner. And when the Leger was coming on, Paul was "sure" about Lively Spark, which was a quite inconsiderable horse. The boy insisted on putting a thousand on the horse, Bassett went for five hundred, and Oscar Cresswell two hundred. Lively Spark came in first, and the betting had been ten to one against him. Paul had made ten thousand.

"You see," he said, "I was absolutely sure of him."

Even Oscar Cresswell had cleared two thousand. "Look here, son," he said, "this sort of thing makes me nervous."

"It needn't, uncle! Perhaps I shan't be sure again for a long time."

"But what are you going to do with your money?" asked the uncle.

"Of course," said the boy, "I started it for mother. She said she had no luck, because father is unlucky, so I thought if *I* was lucky, it might stop whispering."

"What might stop whispering?"

"Our house! I *hate* our house for whispering."

"What does it whisper?"

"Why—why," the boy fidgeted. "Why, I don't know! But it's always short of money, you know, uncle."

"I know it, son, I know it."

"You know people send mother writs, don't you, uncle?"

"I'm afraid I do," said the uncle.

"And then the house whispers like people laughing at you behind your back. It's awful, that is! I thought if I was lucky—"

"You might stop it," added the uncle.

The boy watched him with big blue eyes, that had an uncanny cold fire in them, and he said never a word.

"Well then!" said the uncle. "What are we doing?"

"I shouldn't like mother to know I was lucky," said the boy.

"Why not, son?"

"She'd stop me."

"I don't think she would."

"Oh!" and the boy writhed in an odd way, "I *don't* want her to know, uncle."

"All right, son! We'll manage it without her knowing."

They managed it very easily. Paul, at the other's suggestion, handed over five thousand pounds to his uncle, who deposited it with the family lawyer, who was then to inform Paul's mother that a relative had put five thousand pounds into his hands, which sum was to be paid out a thousand pounds at a time, on the mother's birthday, for the next five years.

"So she'll have a birthday present of a thousand pounds for five successive years," said Uncle Oscar. "I hope it won't make it all the harder for her later."

Paul's mother had her birthday in November. The house had been "whispering" worse than ever lately, and even in spite of his luck, Paul could not bear up against it. He was very anxious to see the effect of the birthday letter, telling his mother about the thousand pounds.

When there were no visitors, Paul now took his meals with his parents, as he was beyond the nursery control. His mother went into town nearly every day. She had discovered that she had an odd knack of sketching furs and dress materials, so she worked secretly in the studio of a friend who was the chief "artist" for the leading drapers. She drew the figures of ladies in furs and ladies in silk and sequins for the newspaper advertisements. This young woman artist earned several thousand pounds a year, but Paul's mother only made several hundreds, and she was again dissatisfied. She so wanted to be first in something, and she did not succeed, even in making sketches for drapery advertisements.

She was down to breakfast on the morning of her birthday. Paul watched her face as she read her letters. He knew the lawyer's letter. As his mother read it, her face hardened and became more expressionless. Then a cold, determined look came on her mouth. She hid the letter under the pile of others, and said not a word about it.

"Didn't you have anything nice in the post for your birthday, mother?" said Paul.

"Quite moderately nice," she said, her voice cold and absent. She went away to town without saying more.

But in the afternoon Uncle Oscar appeared. He said Paul's mother had had a long interview with the lawyer, asking if the whole five thousand could not be advanced at once, as she was in debt.

"What do you think, uncle?" said the boy.

"I leave it to you, son."

"Oh, let her have it, then! We can get some more with the other," said the boy.

"A bird in the hand is worth two in the bush, laddie!" said Uncle Oscar.

"But I'm sure to *know* for the Grand National; or the Lincolnshire; or else the Derby. I'm sure to know for *one* of them," said Paul.

So Uncle Oscar signed the agreement, and Paul's mother touched the whole five thousand. Then something very curious happened. The voices in the house suddenly went mad, like a chorus of frogs on a spring evening. There were certain new furnishings, and Paul had a tutor. He was *really* going to Eton, his father's school, in the following autumn. There were flowers in the winter, and a blossoming of the luxury Paul's mother had been used to. And yet the voices in the house, behind the sprays of mimosa and almond-blossom, and from under the piles of iridescent cushions, simply trilled and screamed in a sort of ecstasy, "There *must* be more money! Oh-h-h! There *must* be more money! Oh, now, now-w! Now-w-w—there *must* be more money! More than ever! More than ever!"

It frightened Paul terribly. He studied away at his Latin and Greek with his tutors. But his intense hours were spent with Bassett. The Grand National had gone by. He had not "known," and had lost a hundred pounds. Summer was at hand. He was in agony for the Lincoln. But even for the Lincoln he didn't "know," and he lost fifty pounds. He became wild-eyed and strange, as if something were going to explode in him.

"Let it alone, son! Don't you bother about it!" urged Uncle Oscar.

But it was as if the boy couldn't really hear what his uncle was saying.

"I've got to know for the Derby! I've *got* to know for the Derby!" the child reiterated, his big blue eyes blazing with a sort of madness.

His mother noticed how overwrought he was.

"You'd better go to the seaside. Wouldn't you like to go now to the seaside, instead of waiting? I think you'd better," she said, looking down at him anxiously, her heart curiously heavy because of him.

But the child lifted his uncanny blue eyes.

"I couldn't possibly go before the Derby, mother!" he said. "I couldn't possibly!"

"Why not?" she said, her voice becoming heavy when she was opposed. "Why not? You can still go from the seaside to see the Derby with your Uncle Oscar, if that's what you wish. No need for you to wait here. Besides, I think you care too much about these races. It's a bad sign. My family has been a gambling family, and you won't know till you grow up how much damage it has done. But it has done damage. I shall have to send Bassett away, and ask Uncle Oscar not to talk racing to you, unless you promise to be reasonable about it: go away to the seaside and forget it. You're all nerves!"

"I'll do what you like, mother, so long as you don't send me away till after the Derby," the boy said.

"Send you away from where? Just from this house?"

"Yes," he said, gazing at her.

"Why, you curious child, what makes you care about this house so much, suddenly? I never knew you loved it!"

He gazed at her without speaking. He had a secret within a secret, something he had not divulged, even to Bassett or to his Uncle Oscar.

But his mother, after standing undecided and a little bit sullen for some moments, said, "Very well, then! Don't go to the seaside till after the Derby, if you don't wish it. But promise me you won't let your nerves go to pieces! Promise you won't think so much about horse racing and *events,* as you call them!"

"Oh no!" said the boy, casually. "I won't think much about them, mother. You needn't worry. I wouldn't worry, mother, if I were you."

"If you were me and I were you," said his mother, "I wonder what we should do!"

"But you know you needn't worry, mother, don't you?" the boy repeated.

"I should be awfully glad to know it," she said wearily.

"Oh, well, you *can,* you know. I mean you *ought* to know you needn't worry!" he insisted.

"Ought I? Then I'll see about it," she said.

Paul's secret of secrets was his wooden horse, that which had no name. Since he was emancipated from a nurse and a nursery governess, he had had his rocking horse removed to his own bedroom at the top of the house.

"Surely you're too big for a rocking horse!" his mother had remonstrated.

"Well, you see, mother, 'til I can have a *real* horse, I like to have *some* sort of animal about," had been his quaint answer.

"Do you feel he keeps you company?" she laughed.

"Oh yes! He's very good, he always keeps me company, when I'm there," said Paul.

So the horse, rather shabby, stood in an arrested prance in the boy's bedroom.

The Derby was drawing near, and the boy grew more and more tense. He hardly heard what was spoken to him, he was very frail, and his eyes were really uncanny. His mother had sudden strange seizures of uneasiness about him. Sometimes, for half an hour, she would feel a sudden anxiety about him that was almost anguish. She wanted to rush to him at once, and know he was safe.

Two nights before the Derby, she was at a big party in town, when one of her rushes of anxiety about her boy, her first-born, gripped her heart till she could hardly speak. She fought with the feeling, might and main, for she believed in common sense. But it was too strong. She had to leave the dance and go downstairs to telephone to the country. The children's nursery governess was terribly surprised and startled at being rung up in the night.

"Are the children all right, Miss Wilmot?"

"Oh yes, they are quite all right."

"Master Paul? Is he all right?"

"He went to bed as right as a trivet. Shall I run up and look at him?"

"No!" said Paul's mother reluctantly. "No! Don't trouble. It's all right. Don't sit up. We shall be home fairly soon."

She did not want her son's privacy intruded upon.

"Very good," said the governess.

It was about one o'clock when Paul's mother and father drove up to their house. All was still. Paul's mother went to her room and slipped off her white fur cloak. She had told her maid not to wait up for her. She heard her husband downstairs, mixing a whisky-and-soda.

And then, because of the strange anxiety at her heart, she stole upstairs to her son's room.

Noiselessly she went along the upper corridor. Was there a faint noise? What was it?

She stood, with arrested muscles, outside his door, listening. There was a strange, heavy, and yet not loud noise. Her heart stood still. It was a soundless noise, yet rushing and powerful. Something huge, in violent, hushed motion. What was it? What in God's name was it? She ought to know. She felt that she *knew* the noise. She knew what it was.

Yet she could not place it. She couldn't say what it was. And on and on it went, like a madness. Softly, frozen with anxiety and fear, she turned the door handle.

The room was dark. Yet in the space near the window, she heard and saw something plunging to and fro. She gazed in fear and amazement.

Then suddenly she switched on the light, and saw her son, in his green pajamas, madly surging on his rocking horse. The blaze of light suddenly lit him up, as he urged the wooden horse, and lit her up, as she stood, blonde, in her dress of pale green and crystal, in the doorway.

"Paul!" she cried. "Whatever are you doing?"

"It's Malabar!" he screamed, in a powerful, strange voice. "It's Malabar!"

His eyes blazed at her for one strange and senseless second, as he ceased urging his wooden horse. Then he fell with a crash to the ground, and she, all her tormented motherhood flooding upon her, rushed to gather him up.

But he was unconscious, and unconscious he remained, with some brain-fever. He talked and tossed, and his mother sat stonily by his side.

"Malabar! It's Malabar! Bassett, Bassett, I *know*: it's Malabar!"

So the child cried, trying to get up and urge the rocking horse that gave him his inspiration.

"What does he mean by Malabar?" asked the heart-frozen mother.

"I don't know," said the father, stonily.

"What does he mean by Malabar?" she asked her brother Oscar.

"It's one of the horses running for the Derby," was the answer.

And, in spite of himself, Oscar Cresswell spoke to Bassett, and himself put a thousand on Malabar: at fourteen to one.

The third day of the illness was critical: they were watching for a change. The boy, with his rather long, curly hair, was tossing ceaselessly on the pillow. He neither slept nor regained consciousness, and his eyes were like blue stones. His mother sat, feeling her heart had gone, turned actually into a stone.

In the evening, Oscar Cresswell did not come, but Bassett sent a message, saying could he come up for one moment, just one moment? Paul's mother was very angry at the intrusion, but on second thought she agreed. The boy was the same. Perhaps Bassett might bring him to consciousness.

The gardener, a shortish fellow with a little brown moustache and sharp little brown eyes, tiptoed into the room, touched his imaginary cap to Paul's mother, and stole to the bedside, staring with glittering, smallish eyes at the tossing, dying child.

"Master Paul!" he whispered. "Master Paul! Malabar came in first all right, a clean win. I did as you told me. You've made over seventy thousand pounds, you have; you've got over eighty thousand. Malabar came in all right, Master Paul."

"Malabar! Malabar! Did I say Malabar, mother? Did I say Malabar? Do you think I'm lucky, mother? I knew Malabar, didn't I? Over eighty thousand pounds! I call that lucky, don't you, mother? Over eighty thousand pounds! I knew, didn't I know I knew? Malabar came in all right. If I ride my horse 'til I'm sure, then I tell you, Basset, you can go as high as you like. Did you go for all you were worth, Bassett?"

"I went a thousand on it, Master Paul."

"I never told you, mother, that if I can ride my horse, and *get there*, then I'm absolutely sure—oh, absolutely! Mother, did I ever tell you? I *am* lucky!"

"No, you never did," said the mother.

But the boy died in the night.

And even as he lay dead, his mother heard her brother's voice saying to her: "My God, Hester, you're eighty-odd thousand to the good, and a poor devil of a son to the bad. But, poor devil, poor devil, he's best gone out of a life where he rides his rocking horse to find a winner."

One More
by
Gregory L. Norris

Another nickel. Just five more cents.

Five more cents is enough for a loaf of bread. Bottles today are scarce at the beach. A late summer chill infuses the air. Few people come to the rides and arcades at the seaside amusement park when it's raining. For two days, huddled beneath the pier and reading a dog-eared novel someone left in a garbage can with three returnables, he's sat dreaming of bread. Soft bread, fresh bread, the kind that sticks to your teeth, his fantasies set to a baleful soundtrack of calliope music.

For days, it has rained. The boy, seventeen, is now past waiting for sunlight to return so, in the rain, he combs the purple sands of Hollings Head, Rhode Island, in search of one more bottle, one more lifeline. The tumbled, ground-down shells of mussels in the bay lend the sand its pale lavender color; the rain and hunger chill his fingertips to the verge of blue. Five more cents. Just one more nickel will silence his hunger and save his life.

With his hoodie up and his backpack slung around his shoulders, a plastic garbage bag filled with eleven cans and a handful of plastic liter bottles, he roams the beach. Hollings Head is fast becoming a place for the well-to-do, million-dollar condos replacing the tarpaper summer cottages and concession stands like a merciless occupying army. Boys turned out to the streets by abusive hands and lamentable circumstances get swept under the pier, where no one sees them. For two months, this is how it has been. Every day, he looks for cans and bottles, turns them in at the little groceria nestled on Atlantic Avenue, across from the Tilt-a-Whirl. And if he collects enough, he eats. Every day, the same.

He used to love this beach, the boy remembers when he reaches the closest garbage barrel. Back then, he came here as a visitor, happy and well-fed, a boy with a name. At some point over the last few weeks, he either forgot his name or it was taken from him, like the remains of the tropical storm that had once been a named hurricane now soaking the coastline with its tears on its slow amble past.

Since nobody has come to the beach in two days except for a few adrenaline junkies eager to challenge the waves, the barrel is as empty as the last time he checked. The boy sets off to his next destination, farther up along the beach. Wet sand collapses awkwardly beneath his sneakers, which are soaked through. Since the start of the storm, the pain in his gut has dulled to an ever-present burning sensation. That scares him almost more than the looming specter of the changing season, summer cooling to autumn; the fear that he might somehow be surrendering to his hunger before the coldness can have a go at his marrow.

You're giving up, a voice in his head taunts as he trudges a hundred yards through driving rain to another barrel. It, too, is filled with a soup of rainwater and empty food wrappers. The beaches at Hollings Head are kept immaculate, because the condo owners have taken over. No candy wrappers or cigarette butts, no cans, no bottles. No half-eaten burgers or funnel cakes. *No food*, the voice adds.

Just five more cents.

The nameless boy plods on, shivering with every step as icy rain pelts him, a clear testament to the death of summer. The air stinks of ocean, churning and seething in the remnants of the storm. The rain falling before his eyes creates a gray veil, obscuring the way ahead, as if to telegraph the days to come will be turbulent.

He walks on.

The boy knows the routine well: barrels at every hundred yards, one beside the payphones, another near the dunes. He has walked this route every day, mostly in sunlight, but now in the rain. The music from the amusement park drags down, slows, warped by the downpour. All the barrels are empty. His journey ends at the base of the dunes, as do his hopes. There are no bottles. That means no bread. Without bread, the dull burn that was once a clawing pain might short out completely, signaling oblivion.

The boy stops and stands beside the barrel, his tears hidden in the rain. He has reached the end of the beach. Beyond this part of Hollings Head, the dunes give way to castles, expensive homes set behind a gate dominating stretches of private beach. Do not enter. It's no place for homeless boys. He can't go forward. In some ways, he can't go back to that place beneath the pier where he huddles and tries to steal sleep, his dreams populated by bells, whistles, and the calliope music from the merry-go-round.

He gazes across the ocean. Silver-capped swells crash against the shore, leaving fresh purple bruises upon the sand. Behind him, the dunes rise up. Blankets of windblown marsh grass and sea roses obscure what lies beyond, though he knows what he will find on the other side: a house, tall and sinister, its gabled peak peering over the tops of the dunes.

Don't ever go near that house, he hears his mother warn, perhaps ten years ago when they sat on this same beach, when there was an abundance of food, warmth, dryness. The same hand that would force him from his home earlier in the summer adds in a whisper, *It's a dangerous place.*

Another voice, this from a fellow vagrant under the pier, joins in. "Whatever you do, stay clear of that place. He'll try to lure you inside. There ain't nothing good about it."

The nameless boy stands frozen in the rain, staring at the two visible windows of the house's gabled roof. The windows gaze back, like eyes made of glass. He hasn't thought about this place much until now, hasn't considered that twice in his young life, he has been warned away. What he can see of the house from the beach is framed by roiling storm clouds. Curiously, the big house on the beach is colored the same pale purple as the sand. He stares, unable to break his gaze until the wind gusts. Over its howl, he hears the hollow metallic clatter of a can dislodged by the gale, rolling somewhere up in those dunes.

Five more cents.

Before he can talk himself out of it or consider the implications, he tromps through the sand and into the tangle of reeds and thorns. Clumps of roots and sand give way and tumble; eventually, he finds firm footing. The perfume of the marsh roses is sweet, intoxicating, but the enormous clusters, washed ashore hundreds of years earlier from a wrecked Chinese merchant ship, block his path. He picks his way carefully around them, tracking the metal clatter. In his haste to find the can—and possibly save his life—he stumbles face-first into a tangle of thorns. Fresh agony ignites across his left cheek and forehead.

The boy picks himself up and looks down, realizing that he has tripped over the weathered planks of an old boardwalk. The boardwalk meanders, forming a thin channel through the roses. Wiping his face, he sets off along the path. Roses have grown over one another, a wild tangle, a modern Hydra. He ducks under the brambles, his backpack snagging on thorns. After an arduous near-crawl, he emerges again on a stretch of level sand, directly in front of the purple house.

The house was built here long ago, that much is clear. Instead of rising up from the beach like the McMansions behind the gate, the three-story house with the gabled roof gives the boy the impression that it's either slowly sinking into the earth or was buried until the tropical depression exhumed it. No illusion created by the storm, the house matches the color of the sand. It evaporates before his wide-open eyes. He blinks. The house pulls back into cohesion, but barely.

White sheers hang in every window. One set of impressive French doors dominates the first floor, at eye level. The boy focuses on the doors, sees one is slightly ajar. A figure stands among the curtains, indistinct. Fear slithers over his flesh, only to break at the sound of an aluminum can, skipping across the sand. A flash of darker purple teases his eyes. An empty grape soda can rolls to a jarring stop right at his well-traveled left sneaker.

He scrambles for it before the wind can steal the can from him, falling to his knees on the ancient boardwalk. There, with the key to his survival clutched in both hands, he notices the latticework of additional planks leading from different directions through the dunes, all ending at the French doors of the purple house.

At staggered distances along each of the pathways, soda cans and bottles jut up from the sand, dozens of them. Some unaffected part of the boy's consciousness notes their labels—orange soda, strawberry soda, chocolate soda, grape. All sugary-sweet, anchored into the sand at intervals along every stretch of time-eroded plank.

A jolt of fresh coldness trips down the boy's spine. He hastily stuffs the soda can in with his others and races from the dunes.

As he savors the warm, moist heaven of fresh bread in the cloistered cold beneath the pier that night, he ponders the bottles and cans. In his memory, they take on an ominous pattern, becoming a trail of glass and aluminum crumbs scattered through the dunes. He knows but doesn't focus on the malevolent design behind the arrangement; he only sees his next meal. A dozen bottles or cans add up to sixty cents. Two dozen, enough for a cheeseburger at the corner grill in the amusement park—a fat, juicy cheeseburger pink in the middle, dripping with grease and smothered in mayonnaise and ketchup, with lettuce, tomato, pickles, and a slice of red onion. The bottles and cans are there for the taking. All he need do is take them.

He thinks of the figure standing just inside that one open door, not much of a deterrent in the face of starvation. Still, the warnings nag at him, tease his dreams amid the echo of crashing waves.

Stay away from that house!

If it's sunny, he won't need those cans and bottles. He'll get more than enough for a cheeseburger picking through the barrels at the amusement park and on Hollings Head Beach.

But morning comes, gray and raw. Rain falls in thin curtains, little more than a steady drizzle but enough to keep the crowds away. There is no warmth to the day. Cold and hungry, the nameless boy clutches the empty garbage bag in one hand and slings the backpack containing the fragments of all he owns in the world onto his shoulder. He must return to that mysterious house in the dunes one more time.

Just once more.

The clouds are breaking. The day grows lighter. Rain lets up, but in its place a cold and numbing wind blows. Nobody comes to the beach at Hollings Head; nobody except a nameless, hungry boy, a thin figure, gray and ghostly, like a wisp of smoke, fading more with every second. Soon he'll be lost from sight.

He picks his way carefully through the marsh roses, finds another of the plank paths running between them. Coming back here isn't so much about survival as luxury—he's risking his life for something more than the basics. It would be so good to have a hot meal, and those empty cans are the ticket. He exits the dunes and falls beneath the gaze of the pale purple house once more. Broken sunlight spills through a lapse in the clouds, illuminating the weathered exterior. The boy's mind drifts, and he wonders about its age. Like a relic born of the same ocean that stained the sands purple, how long has this house brooded over the beach? Did it wash ashore as an ancient shipwreck that transformed itself into a house, adapting to the land like the roses from China? Or is it actually the skull of some primeval sea monster, its windows really empty eye sockets?

The brief flash of sunlight does little to warm his skin. The house possesses his eyes. Only the hunger in his belly breaks the trance.

Leaning down, he wrests the first soda can out of the sand, stuffs it into the garbage bag, and moves on to the next, a yard ahead of him. One yard closer to the purple house. The one after that lures him even nearer. The bag grows heavy. He can taste his next meal. He grabs cans, advancing up the boardwalk, unaware he's gotten almost to those French double doors until a shadow sweeps over the sand, engulfing him. The boy looks up. Something tall and dark blocks what little sun there is. He staggers away, trips.

"Don't be afraid," the man says, his voice deep but soothing. "I was hoping you'd return."

The nameless boy realizes that in his haste to collect cans, he hasn't kept an eye on the French doors or seen the man wander out of the house, a handsome man with short silver hair and a mustache, dressed in well-tailored clothes. The man leans down and extends his hand.

"It's all right, don't be frightened. Let me help you."

The boy freezes, his spine on the sand, at first too stunned to move. Yes, the silver-haired man is handsome, even fatherly. With the rise and fall of the boy's chest, he smells a trace of the man's cologne, robust and comforting. He doesn't take the offered hand right away. Clearly sensing the boy's distrust, the silver-haired man flashes a sad smile, showing a length of perfect white teeth.

"I understand, son, really I do," he continues, withdrawing his outstretched hand. "I just want to help you. I see you out here every day collecting cans and bottles and it breaks my heart. Don't you have a home to go to? Doesn't anybody miss you?"

"No," the boy says. It's been days since he's heard his own voice instead of all the voices in his head playing their verbal tug of war in counterpoint against the calliope music, and it sounds alien to him.

The silver-haired man slowly shakes his head. "No one at all? What a shame. I'd like to help you. That's why I left you the cans. Are you hungry?"

The aching pain in the nameless boy's stomach seems to double by addressing it. Yes, he is hungry, almost starving. Bread just isn't enough. Yes, he wants to eat and be warm and not live this miserable transient existence.

"Let me help you," the silver-haired man says, again extending his hand.

The boy looks up and sees the trustworthy smile. Although unsure as to why, since he stopped trusting anyone weeks ago, he reaches his frail fingers out. Hands touch. At the instant of contact, something icy-hot ignites across the boy's skin. He faces the man and sees the sun has vanished from sight behind a veil of storm clouds, and a shadow has fallen over his benefactor, lending his skin an unsettling pale purple tinge.

Then thunder crashes, not from the dying storm but a door slamming in place. The boy blinks. When his vision focuses, he is no longer outside, sitting on the dunes, but inside the house, standing.

How did I get in here? a voice in his head demands. Another answers, *He pulled you inside.* But as shocking as that concession may be, it pales against the vision that greets him in the vast open space of the house's first floor, which captures all of his attention. He has never seen anything like it.

A pale purple carpet covers the little of the floor that is visible. Elegant furniture fills the living area—overstuffed Victorian velvet settees and mahogany tables carved with wings, claws, and lion heads. Some pieces look ready to take flight or run away or lunge for his throat under their own power. Bronze statues and torchieres crowd between the furniture, but there are no lights on, and an oppressive stagnancy barely broken by the glow seeping in from the windows hangs over the open space.

More curious are the stacks of books, thousands of them, their spines piled on the floor, all around the edges. In some places, the books rise to three times a man's height. They're old books, hardcover editions; big books heavy with weight and age. Strung across those books is the most unexpected of all the strange sights inside the house: a series of tracks, like the tracks of toy trains, only bigger, more complex. The metal tracks wind and dip around the edges of the room, rising in some spots where the books are piled highest and plunging down to loop over the lower stacks.

"You must be hungry," the silver-haired man says. The boy whips around to face the shadow at his back, an action that stirs a column of dust. "Would you like to eat?"

The man aims his hand and the boy follows it. Unseen until that moment, he faces a banquet table. A light snaps on, illuminating trays of cream-filled pastries, cakes and cookies, fresh fruit, hamburgers, whole piles of them, three high on a serving platter. Cans and bottles of soda line the table.

Like a rabid animal, the boy lunges for the spread, grabbing and biting until his mouth is caked with a mess of half-eaten food. Barely chewing, he rips into the meat and chokes down finger pastries. He has become a primitive, notions of civilization lost to hunger. Lost, forever.

The weight of all that food in so fragile a stomach alters his pain. A sour sensation shudders through him. The boy reaches for a soda can. Grape. The can is purple. He notices that all the cans, like the ones left for him on the beach, are sugary-sweet concoctions. He hesitates.

"Is something wrong?" the voice over his shoulder says, more an acknowledgment than a question.

Slowly, the boy turns, and a second shiver wracks his body. In the bald glow of the lamp beside the banquet table, the silver-haired man's features come clearly to him now. His skin has absorbed the dusty pallor of the surrounding room. Purple veins rise in spider webs along his neck, and his perfect white teeth, the boy notices, appear unusually sharp.

"You've eaten too much, too fast," the man says.

The words wash over the boy without a name, sour and repulsive. It isn't cologne he's smelled, but an odor of decay, covered up.

"You need to slow down, enjoy yourself," the man continues. "Everybody who visits loves to take a ride in my roller coaster."

The man smiles, and as the *clunk-clunk* noise of movement along the tracks forming a necklace around the vast room reaches the boy's ears, a jolt of terror unlike anything he's ever experienced cramps his guts. *The doors*, both voices in his head shriek in unison. *Where are those French doors?*

The nameless boy looks behind him, sees the doors and something else. From the shadows along those tracks comes a collection of wagons, strewn together like a makeshift roller coaster. In the moody gray glow it's difficult to be sure, but he thinks he sees other people, seated in the wagons.

Escape, now! the voices urge.

Yes, run back to the dunes, run and keep running, as far away from this house as possible.

He attempts to run.

And finds that he cannot move.

Paralyzed, the boy sits behind the silver-haired man, propped into one of the wagons. Tears stream from his eyes, which stare straight ahead, unable to do more than water.

"They wouldn't let me ride the one in the park after the rumors started, so I built my own. You'll love this—it's so much fun!" the silver-haired monster chuckles, a boy in some ways himself.

The ride begins and the wagons clunk along the tracks, building momentum each time the roller coaster plunges downward. At the corners of the room, the wagons take wide, sweeping arcs, nearly jumping the tracks before breaking with a jolt, resuming the climb upward for another terrifying plunge down. Each pass around the room dislodges more books from the stacks, gives the boy with no name a better look at the house, his eyes unable to blink.

There are no white curtains in the windows, as he earlier thought. Only cobwebs.

Apart from the purple-skinned monster with silver hair, there are no people in the ride with him, only skeletons wearing the rags of old clothes.

But there also isn't any pain. He isn't hungry any more. In fact, he doesn't feel anything. The poison he has eaten has freed him from his hunger.

The ride coasts to a stop, and the boy is dead.

The silver-haired man feels sated, gorged on what he has done, but also horrified. He wants the killing to stop, but knows his hunger to feed in the days and weeks ahead will again grow all-consuming.

He'll tell himself it will be for the last time. That he'll stop after one more.

Just one more.

The Morgue
by
Aaron Gudmunson

I could read the change on Ken's face after just a month on the job. It looked like someone had dabbed dark paint beneath his eyes and whittled lines around his lips. His hair, which had been ink-black since I'd known him, was now threaded through with white. Not even the divorce, which had practically killed him, had made him look so old.

"You need a vacation already?"

Even his smile looked exhausted. "The last thing I want is more time off."

I leaned forward and leveled with him. "You look like death, man. You're not back on the sauce, are you?"

"Hell, no," he said over the rim of his mug.

"Don't jerk me around, Ken."

"Swear on my grave. I've just been busy at work."

"How *is* the new gig, anyway?" I didn't want to discuss it further, but I *really* didn't want to talk about booze anymore. Thinking about it for too long brought about that old familiar yearning. That old familiar *burning*.

"It's a blast," Ken said through a lopsided smile.

"Hollering at some kid when he throws the evening edition through old lady Klingman's window is a blast?"

"There's more to it than that," Ken said, smile vanishing. "I'm responsible for organizing the morgue."

The morgue, my friend informed me, was the place old newspapers went after their publication date. In essence, the place they went to die. Ten copies of each edition were kept onsite as a backlog. All newspapers have a morgue, according to Ken. The Devon's Hollow *Register*, the state's second-oldest continually running weekly journal, was housed in a squat brick building on the town's east end.

All of this Ken told me with slightly elevated superiority. I let him talk. If it meant leaving Jill and the damned divorce out of the picture, it was okay by me. He'd discovered she'd had an affair and when confronted, she first confirmed it and then demanded a divorce. It was the booze, she'd claimed, that had driven her to do it. Not long after that, Ken begged me to attend AA with him. A diehard rumhead, I'd shrugged him off. Losing my drinking buddy sounded like the worst idea in the world. But he'd been insistent. Only I could save him, he'd begged. But that wasn't the whole truth. After I'd finally agreed to the meetings, it soon became clear that we'd saved *each other.*

"So what do you do in this morgue?"

Ken stared out at the snow. "Organize it. It was a mess when they hired me on. Papers strewn around, completely out of order. Mouse turds everywhere. I've managed to get most of it put together again, but there's still a lot of work to be done."

For my part, I thought it weird that my friend had applied to be the circulation manager for the weekly rag of our little burg. What qualified a former associate professor of American history to shuffle around dead papers in a backroom basement? He was smarter than this. He deserved better.

"Ken, you shouldn't be working in some knucklehead job like that. You should be teaching. I mean, isn't that what you always said you were born to do?"

He waved this off. "To hell with teaching. I'm *learning* down there. I didn't know how much I didn't know until I started working in the morgue. There are things about the Hollow most people have forgotten, things I'm sure no living soul even knows about."

Here came the old argument again. It was one we'd shared for the past two decades, ever since we'd been professing together. Ever since we'd become after-hours drinking buddies.

"I've said it once and I'll say it again. History is the past. Let it die in peace."

"And I've told *you* that to ignore history is a mistake."

We volleyed on for another hour, drinking refills and watching the snow. It felt good to converse with my friend again rather than console him. Holding in pain is suicide of the soul.

I only wish now I'd taken his haggard looks for what they really were and not mistaken them for fallout from the divorce. God, do I wish.

Usually Ken and I found time every weekend to drink coffee and play chess after our AA meetings. We kept each other clear of the bottle and I can honestly say that without him, I'd probably be an alley bum, sipping Boone's Farm out of paper sacks. Our relationship was a symbiosis. He needed me and I needed him, if for no other reason than to keep each other sober. And he needed me because he no longer had Jill or his job (his real job, not this simpering little circulation thing). Hell, if I'd lost my wife and my work in the same month, I'd have hit the bottle again, too.

But Ken dropped clean off the radar. One cold January Saturday, he just didn't show up to the café and I did not see him again until the last weekend in March. After his first AA no-show, I sincerely considered following his lead. But I hung on. I'd been sober this long and I wasn't about to fall off the wagon now.

Many times during this hiatus it had been my intention to drop by his apartment, but I always resisted. (Jill had gotten their Cape Cod in the settlement, which was strange because it was *she* who had the affair, not Ken). He needed time, I determined, and I was going to give him all he needed. I did try calling a few times, but his cell had been deactivated. Emails bounced back. I asked a cop friend of mine to do a wellness check as a courtesy and was told Ken had been spotted entering his residence, apparently fine as fiddlesticks.

It so happened that when I was on the verge of giving up our friendship, a chance encounter brought Ken back into my life. Or was it chance? Is anything random? As a mathematician, probabilities are my forte… but who can ever really know? There's no formula for something like this, no method by which to reach a solution.

It occurred as I was coming out of the coffee shop we frequented once upon a time, having enjoyed three refills and an apple fritter. He was coming around the corner of the building with his head down and his hands shoved deep into the pockets of his coat. I nearly ran him down.

"Ken, good God," I said, flabbergasted at his appearance. The brackets around his lips had deepened. The eyes were bloodshot and drooping, the skin of his face pulled taut over the contours of his skull. He had shed twenty pounds. He reeked of booze and… something else, I'm not sure what. Like a morgue, maybe.

"Hello, Bruce," he rasped.

"What happened to you?"

When he grinned I saw some of his teeth had vanished and his gums were mottled black. He looked like a war refugee seeking succor after escaping some unspeakable torment. It was evident some vital piece of him was missing. I silently damned Jill for what she'd done. It was much easier to blame a person than the bottle. Hell, it always is.

"I've been busy," Ken replied. "Organizing the morgue, remember?"

"Jesus, pal, you're not finished yet?"

"Not even close. You want to see? Come, I'll show you." And because I was too scared to leave him alone, I followed.

"I work every day now. There's just so much to do," he told me. We tromped to the old building that sheltered the Devon's Hollow *Register*.

He held the door for me, then locked it behind us. He kept the lights off, maneuvering around the shadows of editorial desks on sheer habit. He opened an interior door with a skeleton key on his ring and we stepped down a cramped, narrow staircase.

There was little heat in the cellar of the old place. The walls were cinderblock, uninsulated, and the floors were scarred planks. A bare 60-watt bulb hung from the ceiling, casting more places in shadow than illuminating them. Boxes lay heaped against the walls like caskets. A few had dates scrawled across them in grease-pencil: *May 1966-Jun 1967*, *Sep 1974*, *Feb 1952-Mar 1954*, *Oct 1977*. The dates were in no discernible order.

"It's through here," Ken said, indicating a door that at one time might have been red; the paint had faded to a dusky pink and had chipped in places. Suddenly I wanted no part of Ken's morgue.

Already, though, he was laying open the door and reaching inside. My heart thundered and sweat sprang out across my face and chest. For one terrible instant, I was certain that when the light came on there would be corpses hanging from homemade nooses by the open rafters, or perhaps severed heads in jars of formaldehyde.

But then the room came awash in dingy yellow light and I saw what my friend had been up to these months past. The walls were lined with wooden racks as tall as the ceiling. Each of these contained neat stacks of ten papers, beneath which a hand-labeled date had been taped. The place smelled of mildew and turpentine.

I strolled to the nearest rack and plucked down a random paper, this one from November 1969.

"Good issue," Ken said, leaning over my shoulder. "It has the story about Donnie Hanson's kidnapping."

"I remember that," I said. My idea was to keep as collected as possible and to avoid alarming Ken in any way. He needed help, I understood. The man was on the verge of collapse.

"Drink?" Ken asked. He reached into a cubby behind a shelf and removed a bottle of whiskey and a shooter. "Sorry, I only have one glass."

"That's okay. Thanks anyway."

"I insist," he said, eyes black in the dimness.

I relented. It wasn't hard. I told myself it was because I was afraid of his reaction if I didn't. Which, of course, was a lie. I always was a sucker for a good bourbon, and to hell with AA.

Ken poured and handed it over. He swigged straight from the bottle. I swallowed. The shot hit me in the gut like a playful slug from an old friend. In a single burning moment, my years of sobriety fell away like a line of dominoes.

"Refill," Ken said. It was not a question. I held out the glass, he poured, I swallowed. Suddenly his morgue project didn't seem quite so insane. Not nearly as, say, my time on the wagon.

"Let me show you something," he said. He was grinning and his eyes shone now with something malicious. I can't rightly say they sparkled, because that would denote life. There was nothing alive about his eyes.

He shouldered aside an empty filing cabinet and crouched. At first I thought he was vanishing into the wall until I saw a tiny recessed door leading into some hidden root cellar. I followed, grabbing the bottle of bourbon.

The ceiling of our new compartment was barely shoulder-height, forcing us to duck-walk. In the center of the room, Ken clicked on a lamp that looked fashioned during the last world war, all ornate bronze and beveled glass. Its shade was crumpled and provided little of the function for which it was designed. Like the bulb in the main cellar, this one spun weird shadows in the corners like black webs.

But the areas it illuminated caught my breath up short. Every inch of wall and ceiling was covered with newspaper clippings, meticulously held in place by squares of Scotch tape.

"Isn't it wonderful?" Ken asked, peering around at his project. "All the history of our little hamlet out on display."

"It's amazing," I whispered, and took a sip. "This should be a museum."

"Here, see?" Ken indicated a yellowed article near the door. The headline read: *Farmer Daniel Hollister Settles Dispute at Bud's Tavern: Shots Fired!* "This is from 1887, the year after the town was incorporated."

He'd set up an honest-to-God historical timeline. As the taped articles progressed, the paper grew less-yellowed and more legible. In a snippet dated August 12, 1913, I was able to make out that downtown Devon's Hollow had been gutted by a fire started by a carelessly-flicked cigar.

"The place where we're standing burned to cinders, along with damn near the rest of town," Ken said. "Took a decade to rebuild."

"Jesus," I muttered, scrubbing my chin with my knuckles.

"How about this one?" Ken touched a column from 1937 in which a man had murdered his entire family with a hammer and chisel. After coming home from the bar, Will Allister had simply walked room to room and cracked each skull like he was opening coconuts. If there had been a motive, he'd taken it with him to his grave.

After scanning a dozen more blurbs, I no longer required Ken's narration. I dove into them on my own.

Another article discussed a flood that had covered all low-lying areas in

1946. Six people had gone missing and had never been recovered. In 1953, a busload of school kids was driven off a ridge by their driver, who had been sneaking nips of Scotch from a flask in his lap. There had been no survivors. In 1964, a murder-suicide by a preacher who shot a woman, claiming she was possessed by "the devil hisself." I actually remembered that one, in a deep back-pocket memory.

"The weirdest shit happens in the Hollow, Bruce. This town, man, it *swallows* people."

"Maybe it's something in the firewater," I said, half-joking, and took another swig.

"The Hollow is almost like a sentient creature. Conscious. *Knowing*."

"And the *Register* documents it all before getting shuffled off to the morgue. Is that what you're telling me?"

"That's it exactly, old friend."

Here was an article that rang clearer. In 1987, a man drowned in his swimming pool after weeks of claiming it was haunted. "He said he saw things swimming in it," the wife was quoted as saying. "But Tommy was drunk most of the time and I'm pretty sure he just fell in and forgot to swim." The pool had been cemented over after the death without further investigation. The wife had not been named a suspect and had eventually moved out of the area with her two young children.

Another I remembered, from 1994: a Boy Scout troop leader had vanished without a trace after a night of campfire ghost stories. The scouts had hiked eight miles back to town to report the incident. The man had never been found.

"This is great work, Ken. Does your boss know what you're doing down here?"

I had not realized the room had grown silent except for my own murmuring as I read aloud. When I turned, I was alone with my friend's bottle. I started for the small door and realized I could not find it. Between reading and drinking, I'd lost the way.

But how was that possible? The room was no larger than ten-by-ten. The first tinges of panic hit, but they were fuzzy from my buzz. I called out for Ken, but there was no answer. I crawled toward the place where I was certain I recalled the door—no, just empty wall space. I fumbled behind me and grabbed the lamp, yanking it as far as the cord would allow, but careful not to unplug it. I did not want to be left alone in the dark. Not here, in this room of the dead.

In the arc of light, something caught my eye. An article printed on clean, white newspaper. The date was today's. The headline read:

Former Professor Found Dead in Workplace
Colleague Missing

I scanned the article, moaning, knowing already what it would say. The names were Ken MacDormand and Bruce Diercks. MacDormand and Diercks, the article claimed, were recovering alcoholics who had been seen together around town. MacDormand had been found hanged in his place of employment (which was prudently left unnamed). Foul play had not been ruled out. Police had no leads. The search for Diercks, the article stated, was ongoing.

This was not the end, though, and I knew it. Beside this article was attached another. The tape holding it to the wall was so fresh I could see the fingerprint left on its adhesive side.

Whose? I wondered, and decided I did not really want the answer.

The article was dated a week from today. What day was it? I tried to recall, but couldn't. Maybe today was next week. Or next month, next year, next millennium. I read the article, word for word, three times through:

Death of Professor Ruled Suicide

DEVON'S HOLLOW, Ill.— Investigation continues into the death of former North Central University professor Ken MacDormand, who was found hanged last Saturday in the cellar of his workplace. Results of an autopsy cited alcohol was found in his system and the cause of death was asphyxiation. MacDormand's only family was estranged ex-wife Jill Brenner, who had not returned interview requests by press time. The coroner is expected to rule the death a suicide.

A colleague, Bruce Diercks, has gone missing since the discovery of MacDormand's body. While not officially named a suspect of any crime, Diercks is sought by authorities for questioning. The two had reportedly been witnessed entering the place where the incident occurred. Sources revealed the two met during their tenure at NCU, where

MacDormand taught history and Diercks mathematics.

If anyone has information relevant to this case, or of the current whereabouts of Bruce Diercks, they are urged to phone Devon's Hollow Police Department or their local authorities.

Some final, rational part of my mind moved me to seek a subsequent article, insisting there must be a conclusion to the story. It was my only hope for salvation, I understood. But there was nothing. The blurb I'd just read was the last.

For several hours, or perhaps days, I crawled in the glow of that sickly light, in search of the doorway back to the morgue. In search of new articles that may have been recently added. In search of anything. Thwarted, I collapsed on my back and finished off the bottle my friend had left behind.

How had he escaped? How had he gotten out from one morgue to the next? I stared at the timeline of history hung all around and waited for something to happen. When, sometime later, the filament inside the ancient light bulb exploded, I lay alone in the dark and wept. And wondered. And prayed.

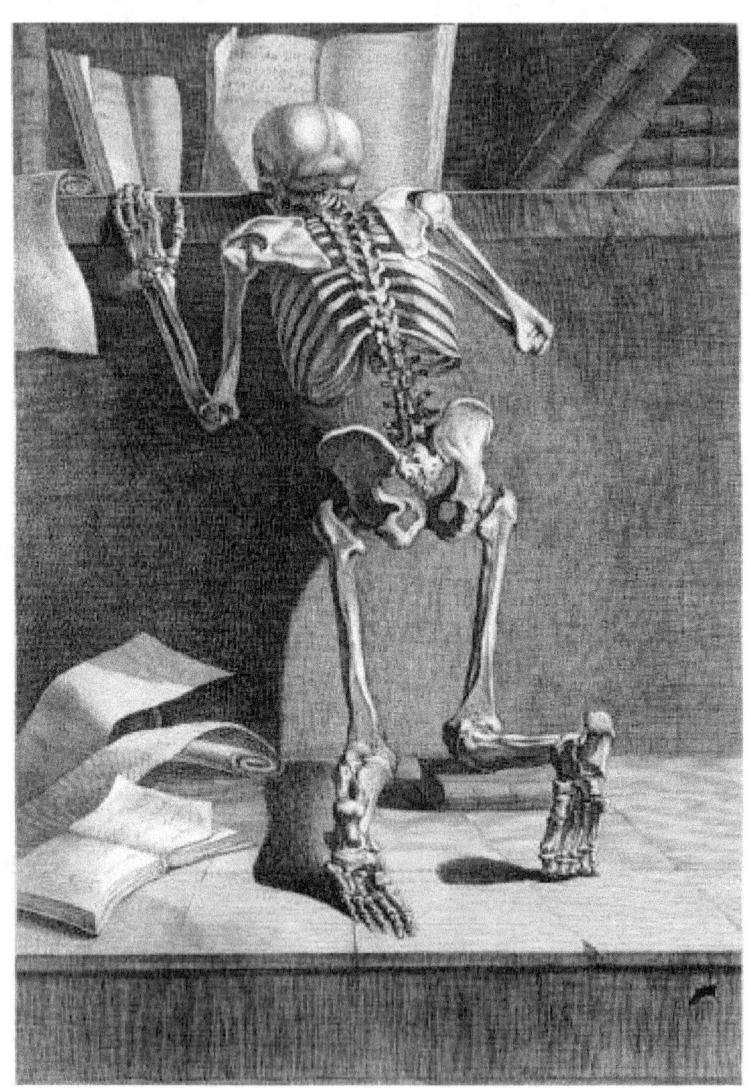

The New Catacombs
by
Sir Arthur Conan Doyle

originally published in *Tales of Terror and Mystery*, **1922**

"Look here, Burger," said Kennedy. "I do wish that you would confide in me."

The two famous students of Roman remains sat together in Kennedy's comfortable room overlooking the Corso. The night was cold, and they had both pulled up their chairs to the unsatisfactory Italian stove which threw out a zone of stuffiness rather than of warmth. Outside under the bright winter stars lay the modern Rome, the long, double chain of the electric lamps, the brilliantly lighted cafes, the rushing carriages, and the dense throng upon the footpaths. But inside, in the sumptuous chamber of the rich young English archaeologist, there was only old Rome to be seen. Cracked and timeworn friezes hung upon the walls, grey old busts of senators and soldiers with their fighting heads and their hard, cruel faces peered out from the corners. On the center table, amidst a litter of inscriptions, fragments, and ornaments, there stood the famous reconstruction by Kennedy of the Baths of Caracalla, which excited such interest and admiration when it was exhibited in Berlin. Amphorae hung from the ceiling, and a litter of curiosities strewed the rich red Turkey carpet.

And of them all there was not one which was not of the most unimpeachable authenticity, and of the utmost rarity and value; for Kennedy, though little more than thirty, had a European reputation in this particular branch of research, and was, moreover, provided with that long purse which either proves to be a fatal handicap to the student's energies, or, if his mind is still true to its purpose, gives him an enormous advantage in the race for fame. Kennedy had often been seduced by whim and pleasure from his studies, but his mind was an incisive one, capable of long and concentrated efforts which ended in sharp reactions of sensuous languor. His handsome face, with its high, white forehead, its aggressive nose, and its somewhat loose and sensual mouth, was a fair index of the compromise between strength and weakness in his nature.

Of a very different type was his companion, Julius Burger. He came of a curious blend, a German father and an Italian mother, with the robust qualities of the North mingling strangely with the softer graces of the South. Blue Teutonic eyes lightened his sun-browned face, and above them rose a square, massive forehead, with a fringe of close yellow curls lying round it. His strong, firm jaw was clean-shaven, and his companion had frequently remarked how much it suggested those old Roman busts which peered out from the shadows in the corners of his chamber. Under its bluff German strength there lay always a suggestion of Italian subtlety, but the smile was so honest, and the eyes so frank, that one understood that this was only an indication of his ancestry, with no actual bearing upon his character.

In age and in reputation, he was on the same level as his English companion, but his life and his work had both been far more arduous. Twelve years before, he had come as a poor student to Rome, and had lived ever since upon some small endowment for research which had been awarded to him by the University of Bonn. Painfully, slowly, and doggedly, with extraordinary tenacity and single-mindedness, he had climbed from rung to rung of the ladder of fame, until now he was a member of the Berlin Academy, and there was every reason to believe that he would shortly be promoted to the Chair of the greatest of German Universities.

But the singleness of purpose which had brought him to the same high level as the rich and brilliant Englishman, had caused him in everything outside their work to stand infinitely below him. He had never found a pause in his studies in which to cultivate the social graces. It was only when he spoke of his own subject that his face was filled with life and soul. At other times he was silent and embarrassed, too conscious of his own limitations in larger subjects, and impatient of that small talk which is the conventional refuge of those who have no thoughts to express.

And yet for some years there had been an acquaintanceship which appeared to be slowly ripening into a friendship between these two very different rivals. The base and origin of this lay in the fact that in their own studies each was the only one of the younger men who had knowledge and enthusiasm enough to properly appreciate the other. Their common interests and pursuits had brought them together, and each had been attracted by the other's knowledge. And then gradually something had been added to this. Kennedy had been amused by the frankness and simplicity of his rival, while Burger in turn had been fascinated by the brilliancy and vivacity which had made Kennedy such a favorite in Roman society.

I say "had," because just at the moment the young Englishman was somewhat under a cloud. A love affair, the details of which had never quite come out, had indicated a heartlessness and callousness upon his part which shocked many of his friends. But in the bachelor circles of students and artists in which he preferred to move there is no very rigid code of honor in such matters, and though a head might be shaken or a pair of shoulders shrugged over the flight of two and the return of one, the general sentiment was probably one of curiosity and perhaps of envy rather than of reprobation.

"Look here, Burger," said Kennedy, looking hard at the placid face of his companion, "I do wish that you would confide in me."

As he spoke he waved his hand in the direction of a rug which lay upon the floor. On the rug stood a long, shallow fruit basket of the light wickerwork which is used in the Campagna, and this was heaped with a litter of objects, inscribed tiles, broken inscriptions, cracked mosaics, torn papyri, rusty metal ornaments, which to the uninitiated might have seemed to have come straight from a dustman's bin, but which a specialist would have speedily recognized as unique of their kind. The pile of odds and ends in the flat wickerwork basket supplied exactly one of those missing links of social development which are of such interest to the student. It was the German who had brought them in, and the Englishman's eyes were hungry as he looked at them.

"I won't interfere with your treasure trove, but I should very much like to hear about it," he continued, while Burger very deliberately lit a cigar. "It is evidently a discovery of the first importance. These inscriptions will make a sensation throughout Europe."

"For everyone here there are a million there!" said the German. "There are so many that a dozen savants might spend a lifetime over them, and build up a reputation as solid as the Castle of St. Angelo."

Kennedy sat thinking with his fine forehead wrinkled and his fingers playing with his long, fair moustache.

"You have given yourself away, Burger!" said he at last. "Your words can only apply to one thing. You have discovered a new catacomb."

"I had no doubt that you had already come to that conclusion from an examination of these objects."

"Well, they certainly appeared to indicate it, but your last remarks make it certain. There is no place except a catacomb which could contain so vast a store of relics as you describe."

"Quite so. There is no mystery about that. I have discovered a new catacomb."

"Where?"

"Ah, that is my secret, my dear Kennedy. Suffice it that it is so situated that there is not one chance in a million of anyone else coming upon it. Its date is different from that of any known catacomb, and it has been reserved for the burial of the highest Christians, so that the remains and the relics are quite different from anything which has ever been seen before. If I was not aware of your knowledge and of your energy, my friend, I would not hesitate, under the pledge of secrecy, to tell you everything about it. But as it is I think that I must certainly prepare my own report of the matter before I expose myself to such formidable competition."

Kennedy loved his subject with a love which was almost a mania—a love which held him true to it, amidst all the distractions which come to a wealthy and dissipated young man. He had ambition, but his ambition was secondary to his mere abstract joy and interest in everything which concerned the old life and history of the city. He yearned to see this new underworld which his companion had discovered.

"Look here, Burger," said he, earnestly, "I assure you that you can trust me most implicitly in the matter. Nothing would induce me to put pen to paper about anything which I see until I have your express permission. I quite understand your feeling and I think it is most natural, but you have really nothing whatever to fear from me. On the other hand, if you don't tell me I shall make a systematic search, and I shall most certainly discover it. In that case, of course, I should make what use I liked of it, since I should be under no obligation to you."

Burger smiled thoughtfully over his cigar.

"I have noticed, friend Kennedy," said he, "that when I want information over any point you are not always so ready to supply it."

"When did you ever ask me anything that I did not tell you? You remember, for example, my giving you the material for your paper about the temple of the Vestals."

"Ah, well, that was not a matter of much importance. If I were to question you upon some intimate thing would you give me an answer, I wonder! This new catacomb is a very intimate thing to me, and I should certainly expect some sign of confidence in return."

"What you are driving at I cannot imagine," said the Englishman, "but if you mean that you will answer my question about the catacomb if I answer any question which you may put to me, I can assure you that I will certainly do so."

"Well, then," said Burger, leaning luxuriously back in his settee, and puffing a blue tree of cigar smoke into the air. "Tell me all about your relations with Miss Mary Saunderson."

Kennedy sprang up in his chair and glared angrily at his impassive companion.

"What the devil do you mean?" he cried. "What sort of a question is this? You may mean it as a joke, but you never made a worse one."

"No, I don't mean it as a joke," said Burger, simply. "I am really rather interested in the details of the matter. I don't know much about the world and women and social life and that sort of thing, and such an incident has the fascination of the unknown for me. I know you, and I knew her by sight—I had even spoken to her once or twice. I should very much like to hear from your own lips exactly what it was which occurred between you."

"I won't tell you a word."

"That's all right. It was only my whim to see if you would give up a secret as easily as you expected me to give up my secret of the new catacomb. You wouldn't, and I didn't expect you to. But why should you expect otherwise of me? There's Saint John's clock striking ten. It is quite time that I was going home."

"No; wait a bit, Burger," said Kennedy; "this is really a ridiculous caprice of yours to wish to know about an old love affair which has burned out months ago.

You know we look upon a man who kisses and tells as the greatest coward and villain possible."

"Certainly," said the German, gathering up his basket of curiosities, "when he tells anything about a girl which is previously unknown he must be so. But in this case, as you must be aware, it was a public matter which was the common talk of Rome, so that you are not really doing Miss Mary Saunderson any injury by discussing her case with me. But still, I respect your scruples; and so good night!"

"Wait a bit, Burger," said Kennedy, laying his hand upon the other's arm; "I am very keen upon this catacomb business, and I can't let it drop quite so easily. Would you mind asking me something else in return—something not quite so eccentric this time?"

"No, no; you have refused, and there is an end of it," said Burger, with his basket on his arm. "No doubt you are quite right not to answer, and no doubt I am quite right also—and so again, my dear Kennedy, good night!"

The Englishman watched Burger cross the room, and he had his hand on the handle of the door before his host sprang up with the air of a man who is making the best of that which cannot be helped.

"Hold on, old fellow," said he; "I think you are behaving in a most ridiculous fashion; but still; if this is your condition, I suppose that I must submit to it. I hate saying anything about a girl, but, as you say, it is all over Rome, and I don't suppose I can tell you anything which you do not know already. What was it you wanted to know?"

The German came back to the stove, and, laying down his basket, he sank into his chair once more.

"May I have another cigar?" said he. "Thank you very much! I never smoke when I work, but I enjoy a chat much more when I am under the influence of tobacco. Now, as regards this young lady, with whom you had this little adventure. What in the world has become of her?"

"She is at home with her own people."

"Oh, really—in England?"

"Yes."

"What part of England—London?"

"No, Twickenham."

"You must excuse my curiosity, my dear Kennedy, and you must put it down to my ignorance of the world. No doubt it is quite a simple thing to persuade a young lady to go off with you for three weeks or so, and then to hand her over to her own family at—what did you call the place?"

"Twickenham."

"Quite so—at Twickenham. But it is something so entirely outside my own experience that I cannot even imagine how you set about it. For example, if you had loved this girl your love could hardly disappear in three weeks, so I presume that you could not have loved her at all. But if you did not love her why should you make this great scandal which has damaged you and ruined her?"

Kennedy looked moodily into the red eye of the stove.

"That's a logical way of looking at it, certainly," said he. "Love is a big word, and it represents a good many different shades of feeling. I liked her, and—well, you say you've seen her. You know how charming she could look. But still I am willing to admit, looking back, that I could never have really loved her."

"Then, my dear Kennedy, why did you do it?"

"The adventure of the thing had a great deal to do with it."

"What! You are so fond of adventures!"

"Where would the variety of life be without them? It was for an adventure that I first began to pay my attentions to her. I've chased a good deal of game in my time, but there's no chase like that of a pretty woman. There was the piquant difficulty of it also, for, as she was the companion of Lady Emily Rood, it was almost impossible to see her alone. On the top of all the other obstacles which attracted me, I learned from her own lips very early in the proceedings that she was engaged."

"*Mein Gott!* To whom?"

"She mentioned no names."

"I do not think that anyone knows that. So that made the adventure more alluring, did it?"

"Well, it did certainly give a spice to it. Don't you think so?"

"I tell you that I am very ignorant about these things."

"My dear fellow, you can remember that the apple you stole from your neighbor's tree was always sweeter than that which fell from your own. And then I found that she cared for me."

"What—at once?"

"Oh, no, it took about three months of sapping and mining. But at last I won her over. She understood that my judicial separation from my wife made it impossible for me to do the right thing by her—but she came all the same, and we had a delightful time, as long as it lasted."

"But how about the other man?"

Kennedy shrugged his shoulders.

"I suppose it is the survival of the fittest," said he. "If he had been the better man she would not have deserted him. Let's drop the subject, for I have had enough of it!"

"Only one other thing. How did you get rid of her in three weeks?"

"Well, we had both cooled down a bit, you understand. She absolutely refused, under any circumstances, to come back to face the people she had known in Rome. Now, of course, Rome is necessary to me, and I was already pining to be back at my work—so there was one obvious cause of separation. Then, again, her old father turned up at the hotel in London, and there was a scene, and the whole thing became so unpleasant that really—though I missed her dreadfully at first—I was very glad to slip out of it. Now, I rely upon you not to repeat anything of what I have said."

"My dear Kennedy, I should not dream of repeating it. But all that you say interests me very much, for it gives me an insight into your way of looking at things, which is entirely different from mine, for I have seen so little of life. And now you want to know about my new catacomb. There's no use my trying to describe it, for you would never find it by that. There is only one thing, and that is for me to take you there."

"That would be splendid."

"When would you like to come?"

"The sooner the better. I am all impatience to see it."

"Well, it is a beautiful night—though a trifle cold. Suppose we start in an hour. We must be very careful to keep the matter to ourselves. If anyone saw us hunting in couples they would suspect that there was something going on."

"We can't be too cautious," said Kennedy. "Is it far?"

"Some miles."

"Not too far to walk?"

"Oh, no, we could walk there easily."

"We had better do so, then. A cabman's suspicions would be aroused if he dropped us both at some lonely spot in the dead of the night."

"Quite so. I think it would be best for us to meet at the Gate of the Appian Way at midnight. I must go back to my lodgings for the matches and candles and things."

"All right, Burger! I think it is very kind of you to let me into this secret, and I promise you that I will write nothing about it until you have published your report. Goodbye for the present! You will find me at the Gate at twelve."

The cold, clear air was filled with the musical chimes from that city of clocks as Burger, wrapped in an Italian overcoat, with a lantern hanging from his hand, walked up to the rendezvous. Kennedy stepped out of the shadow to meet him.

"You are ardent in work as well as in love!" said the German, laughing.

"Yes; I have been waiting here for nearly half an hour."

"I hope you left no clue as to where we were going."

"Not such a fool! By Jove, I am chilled to the bone! Come on, Burger, let us warm ourselves by a spurt of hard walking."

Their footsteps sounded loud and crisp upon the rough stone paving of the disappointing road which is all that is left of the most famous highway of the world. A peasant or two going home from the wine shop, and a few carts of country produce coming up to Rome, were the only things which they met. They swung along, with the huge tombs looming up through the darkness upon each side of them, until they had come as far as the Catacombs of St. Calistus, and saw against a rising moon the great circular bastion of Cecilia Metella in front of them. Then Burger stopped with his hand to his side.

"Your legs are longer than mine, and you are more accustomed to walking," said he, laughing. "I think that the place where we turn off is somewhere here. Yes, this is it, round the corner of the trattoria. Now, it is a very narrow path, so perhaps I had better go in front and you can follow."

He had lit his lantern, and by its light they were enabled to follow a narrow and devious track which wound across the marshes of the Campagna. The great Aqueduct of old Rome lay like a monstrous caterpillar across the moonlit landscape, and their road led them under one of its huge arches, and past the circle of crumbling bricks which marks the old arena. At last Burger stopped at a solitary wooden cow house, and he drew a key from his pocket. "Surely your catacomb is not inside a house!" cried Kennedy.

"The entrance to it is. That is just the safeguard which we have against anyone else discovering it."

"Does the proprietor know of it?"

"Not he. He had found one or two objects which made me almost certain that his house was built on the entrance to such a place. So I rented it from him, and did my excavations for myself. Come in, and shut the door behind you."

It was a long, empty building, with the mangers of the cows along one wall. Burger put his lantern down on the ground, and shaded its light in all directions save one by draping his overcoat round it.

"It might excite remark if anyone saw a light in this lonely place," said he. "Just help me to move this boarding."

The flooring was loose in the corner, and plank by plank the two savants raised it and leaned it against the wall. Below there was a square aperture and a stair of old stone steps which led away down into the bowels of the earth.

"Be careful!" cried Burger, as Kennedy, in his impatience, hurried down them. "It is a perfect rabbit warren below, and if you were once to lose your way there the chances would be a hundred to one against your ever coming out again. Wait until I bring the light."

"How do you find your own way if it is so complicated?"

"I had some very narrow escapes at first, but I have gradually learned to go about. There is a certain system to it, but it is one which a lost man, if he were in the dark, could not possibly find out. Even now I always spin out a ball of string behind me when I am going far into the catacomb. You can see for yourself that it is difficult, but every one of these passages divides and subdivides a dozen times before you go a hundred yards."

They had descended some twenty feet from the level of the barn, and they were standing now in a square chamber cut out of the soft tufa. The lantern cast a flickering light, bright below and dim above, over the cracked brown walls. In every direction were the black openings of passages which radiated from this common center.

"I want you to follow me closely, my friend," said Burger. "Do not loiter to look at anything upon the way, for the place to which I will take you contains all that you can see, and more. It will save time for us to go there direct."

He led the way down one of the corridors, and the Englishman followed closely at his heels. Every now and then the passage bifurcated, but Burger was evidently following some secret marks of his own, for he neither stopped nor hesitated. Everywhere along the walls, packed like the berths upon an emigrant ship, lay the Christians of old Rome. The yellow light flickered over the shriveled features of the mummies, and gleamed upon rounded skulls and long, white arm bones crossed over fleshless chests. And everywhere as he passed Kennedy looked with wistful eyes upon inscriptions, funeral vessels, pictures, vestments, utensils, all lying as pious hands had placed them so many centuries ago. It was apparent to him, even in those hurried, passing glances, that this was the earliest and finest of the catacombs, containing such a storehouse of Roman remains as had never before come at one time under the observation of the student.

"What would happen if the light went out?" he asked, as they hurried onwards.

"I have a spare candle and a box of matches in my pocket. By the way, Kennedy, have you any matches?"

"No; you had better give me some."

"Oh, that is all right. There is no chance of our separating."

"How far are we going? It seems to me that we have walked at least a quarter of a mile."

"More than that, I think. There is really no limit to the tombs—at least, I have never been able to find any. This is a very difficult place, so I think that I will use our ball of string."

He fastened one end of it to a projecting stone and he carried the coil in the breast of his coat, paying it out as he advanced. Kennedy saw that it was no unnecessary precaution, for the passages had become more complex and tortuous than ever, with a perfect network of intersecting corridors. But these all ended in one large circular hall with a square pedestal of tufa topped with a slab of marble at one end of it.

"By Jove!" cried Kennedy in an ecstasy, as Burger swung his lantern over the marble. "It is a Christian altar—probably the first one in existence. Here is the little consecration cross cut upon the corner of it. No doubt this circular space was used as a church."

"Precisely," said Burger. "If I had more time I should like to show you all the bodies which are buried in these niches upon the walls, for they are the early popes and bishops of the Church, with their miters, their croziers, and full canonicals. Go over to that one and look at it!"

Kennedy went across, and stared at the ghastly head which lay loosely on the shredded and moldering miter.

"This is most interesting," said he, and his voice seemed to boom against the concave vault. "As far as my experience goes, it is unique. Bring the lantern over, Burger, for I want to see them all."

But the German had strolled away, and was standing in the middle of a yellow circle of light at the other side of the hall.

"Do you know how many wrong turnings there are between this and the stairs?" he asked. "There are over two thousand. No doubt it was one of the means of protection which the Christians adopted. The odds are two thousand to one against a man getting out, even if he had a light; but if he were in the dark it would, of course, be far more difficult."

"So I should think."

"And the darkness is something dreadful. I tried it once for an experiment. Let us try it again!" He stooped to the lantern, and in an instant it was as if an invisible hand was squeezed tightly over each of Kennedy's eyes. Never had he known what such darkness was. It seemed to press upon him and to smother him. It was a solid obstacle against which the body shrank from advancing. He put his hands out to push it back from him.

"That will do, Burger," said he, "let's have the light again."

But his companion began to laugh, and in that circular room the sound seemed to come from every side at once.

"You seem uneasy, friend Kennedy," said he.

"Go on, man, light the candle!" said Kennedy impatiently.

"It's very strange, Kennedy, but I could not in the least tell by the sound in which direction you stand. Could you tell where I am?"

"No; you seem to be on every side of me."

"If it were not for this string which I hold in my hand I should not have a notion which way to go."

"I dare say not. Strike a light, man, and have an end of this nonsense."

"Well, Kennedy, there are two things which I understand that you are very fond of. The one is an adventure, and the other is an obstacle to surmount. The adventure must be the finding of your way out of this catacomb. The obstacle will be the darkness and the two thousand wrong turns which make the way a little difficult to find. But you need not hurry, for you have plenty of time, and when you halt for a rest now and then, I should like you just to think of Miss Mary Saunderson, and whether you treated her quite fairly."

"You devil, what do you mean?" roared Kennedy. He was running about in little circles and clasping at the solid blackness with both hands.

"Goodbye," said the mocking voice, and it was already at some distance. "I really do not think, Kennedy, even by your own showing that you did the right thing by that girl. There was only one little thing which you appeared not to know, and I can supply it. Miss Saunderson was engaged to a poor ungainly devil of a student, and his name was Julius Burger."

There was a rustle somewhere, the vague sound of a foot striking a stone, and then there fell silence upon that old Christian church—a stagnant, heavy silence which closed round Kennedy and shut him in like water round a drowning man.

Some two months afterwards the following paragraph made the round of the European Press:

"One of the most interesting discoveries of recent years is that of the new catacomb in Rome, which lies some distance to the east of the well-known vaults of St. Calixtus. The finding of this important burial place, which is exceeding rich in most interesting early Christian remains, is due to the energy and sagacity of Dr.

Julius Burger, the young German specialist, who is rapidly taking the first place as an authority upon ancient Rome. Although the first to publish his discovery, it appears that a less fortunate adventurer had anticipated Dr. Burger. Some months ago Mr. Kennedy, the well-known English student, disappeared suddenly from his rooms in the Corso, and it was conjectured that his association with a recent scandal had driven him to leave Rome. It appears now that he had in reality fallen a victim to that fervid love of archaeology which had raised him to a distinguished place among living scholars. His body was discovered in the heart of the new catacomb, and it was evident from the condition of his feet and boots that he had tramped for days through the tortuous corridors which make these subterranean tombs so dangerous to explorers. The deceased gentleman had, with inexplicable rashness, made his way into this labyrinth without, as far as can be discovered, taking with him either candles or matches, so that his sad fate was the natural result of his own temerity. What makes the matter more painful is that Dr. Julius Burger was an intimate friend of the deceased. His joy at the extraordinary find which he has been so fortunate as to make has been greatly marred by the terrible fate of his comrade and fellow worker."

Graveyard
by
Lawrence Buentello

When Joe Campbell bought the house he was very much aware of the small cemetery occupying the field across the chain link fence from the backyard. As an older man, he had no need for busy neighborhoods, or children shouting in the street, or young people playing painfully inharmonious music during late-night parties. The graveyard, a relic from a time when the area was part of a small town, yet unincorporated into the city limits, was bordered on one side by his house, on another by a wooded ravine, and on another by an empty field used as a dump by unprincipled people from other parts of the city.

Campbell, long divorced from Lorraine, hadn't known anything close to a successful relationship since his only marriage ended. He was also childless, specifically because he never wanted the responsibility of children. This was certainly one of the reasons for his ex-wife's abiding resentment. His only living relatives resided in California, refusing to visit Texas, or perhaps only refusing to visit him. He felt this no significant loss.

Lorraine always called him an intolerant man; not intolerant of another creed or nationality, but of people in general, an increasingly hermitic soul who did little other than drive to work every day and then home again, only to linger long hours in front of the television or listening to old jazz records on an antiquated stereo. Now that he was retired, he no longer had to suffer the indignity of subservience to those who signed his paycheck. His pension installments were deposited into his bank account every month, and every evening he sat listening to long-dead musicians and drinking cold beer, thankful he no longer had to endure the absurd preoccupations of others.

Though retired, and disinclined to uproot himself, he'd realized he had to sell the house he and Lorraine had bought twenty years prior; too many young families were moving into the neighborhood, and he simply had to find some peace and quiet. Find this for me, he'd told his realtor—she'd complied with the drab little house by the graveyard, and he was happy, at least as much as a man of his nature could manage.

Campbell's new neighbors were mostly elderly—none bothered him, and seemed to accept him as one of their own, though he was still only in his sixties and the homeowners on his street seemed nearer the grave.

The back porch overlooked the graveyard. He quickly found that he enjoyed sitting in a chair beneath the overhang with the patio door slightly opened so the music of Hawkins and Parker could echo quietly behind him. The alignment of the stones only let him see the markers edge-on, but he found counting them a meditative experience, noting their shapes and materials. Some days, though rarely, someone would enter the cemetery and lay flowers at one of the stones, but in the evenings no one came, and he was alone with his solitude and the affectations of the dead.

However others may see him, to Campbell this was satisfactory, and something his ex-wife would never have understood.

He wasn't particularly intelligent, or inquisitive about the universe, or motivated by discovery. He enjoyed being by himself, surrounded by his own admittedly limited interests. He didn't understand people, or human psychology, and didn't believe it was his obligation to try to. Why should a man spend what limited time he had on Earth trying to solve the riddle of other people?

Campbell would have continued this psychologically Spartan existence indefinitely if it hadn't been for ambivalent feelings that suddenly overwhelmed him one evening while studying the graveyard.

As difficult as he found people to understand, he did miss having occasional conversations with them, if only to express his feelings about the state of the world. Therein lay his ambivalence. He'd like to talk to people occasionally, but he didn't want to *know* them, something that ensured future intrusions on his life, and something he'd fought against all his working years.

Still, the feeling pressed on him and fostered regret in his heart, but he knew his displeasure with people would always prevent him from voluntarily moving among them again.

But after rising from his chair and stepping across the yard to the fence, a thought occurred to him that seemed perfect for his needs. Why not walk among the gravestones and talk to the dead? He could say all he pleased, and no one would interrupt him or ask him to listen to an opposing opinion. And he certainly wouldn't have to worry about offending anyone or trying to interpret the mystery of an alien psychology.

As he stood with his fingers slipped through the links of the fence, he thought this was a wonderful idea, perhaps the best he'd ever conjured in a life full of mediocre thoughts. Now he would have to decide how to visit the cemetery, and how best to avoid confrontations with anyone objecting to his presence on the grounds.

At the end of the day, a day spent mulling over his strange dilemma, he found a pair of wire cutters and carefully snipped a door into the fence. He affixed some makeshift fasteners to the mesh so he could maintain the impression of an unbroken span, but at any time he chose he could pull away the fencing and step from his yard onto the cemetery grounds.

But even after he cut this portal, he still hesitated entering the graveyard.

He stood shifting the wire cutters from one hand to the other, as if uncomfortable holding an implement used to commit such an ambiguous crime, wondering if he could possibly enter the grounds unnoticed during daylight hours. Very few mourners ever came to the grounds, and the groundskeeper only came monthly to attack the weeds with a handheld grass cutter.

But his caution overrode his eagerness, preventing him from acting until twilight, when only the distant streetlights played across the gravestones and he had the best chance of remaining unnoticed.

Only then did he peel back the fencing and enter the cemetery.

When his self-consciousness diminished, he began walking easily between the markers, his hands in his pockets, studying the engravings in the gloom.

He'd been to cemeteries before, but only as a matter of obligation, and never paused to actually appreciate the stones. But the stones were beautiful in the twilight, especially those hewn from crystalline rock, glimmering and shining. When the sun faded completely on the horizon and the evening breeze intensified, he felt a wonderful peace of mind as the grass whispered at the wind's passing and the heat of the day surrendered to the coming night.

Campbell finally came to the conclusion that his presence in the cemetery wasn't going to raise any alarms, and eventually he relaxed and enjoyed his walks.

Night after night he moved in silence, reading the names on the stones and wondering who these people were, and what they were like in life. Often he would think of his own life, of his minimal triumphs and his ultimate failures, and feel better or worse about his circumstances depending on the night and the mood that accompanied his visits.

About the time the autumn winds blew across the stones, and he dressed in a light jacket and gloves before stepping through the hole in the fence, he began feeling a subtle urge to actually communicate with someone about his visits to the graveyard, to tell them of his observations and feelings. But there was no one to tell, lest he invite the wrong kind of scrutiny and be prosecuted for trespassing.

But one night, when the chill of the season manifested itself in the frosty breath he exhaled as he walked among the stones, he simply began speaking to the markers as if he were holding a conversation with living people.

"Hello, Mr. Kropp, how are you tonight?" he said aloud after reading the name on the nearest stone. At first, the salutation seemed odd to him, as if he were talking to himself, but as he continued commenting on the weather and the coming holidays, the act felt more natural, more comfortable.

That first night, he spoke to the deceased Mr. Kropp for a few minutes before moving on to Mrs. Ward, and then Mr. Garcia. Since these people couldn't respond or enlighten him of their own lives, he imagined lives for them, family histories, past jobs and experiences. The oddity of speaking to dead people quickly changed into the comfort of confiding in those who could never betray his confidence. This inspired him to speak of himself as he never did to the living, and he found it to be a thoroughly cathartic experience.

"I'm retired now," he found himself saying before Harvey Dorsett's small granite marker. "But I've worked most of my life. I was married once, too, but she left me a long time ago. Lorraine didn't deserve to be burdened by a man like me, I guess. In fact, if I thought about it long enough, I might come to believe that I drove her away intentionally. But maybe that's only hindsight."

He crossed his arms against the cold and swallowed self-consciously. Mr. Dorsett wasn't bound to judge him, but it seemed as if he was judging himself. The feeling this observation produced chilled him more, and he shivered, stamping his feet.

"It's just the way I am," he said in the way of defending himself. "I've never been comfortable with people, so why should I have to be burdened by their company? I'm sorry about that, but what can I do? It's my nature."

He laughed, expelling a misty breath.

"I don't have to worry about that anymore. It's a relief to be by myself. I don't know how many years I have left before I join you people, but right now you're all the company I need."

Just as he spoke these words, his eye caught a light bobbing in the distance by the cemetery gate. He ducked down instinctively, realizing someone with a flashlight was playing the beam over the headstones.

Someone's seen me, he thought, and immediately began moving toward the fence. He didn't bother waiting to discover who might be flashing a light into the cemetery, or if they were actually searching for an intruder. He found the hole in the fence and quickly moved into his own yard, closing the gap and breathing fearfully. Did they see him? His pulse rushed in his ears. He certainly didn't want anyone disturbing his peace.

Chastened by his foolishness, he crossed the patio and stepped into his living room, closing the sliding glass door and drawing the curtain.

Campbell stopped visiting the cemetery after that night, convinced that his ramblings over the graves of the dead were symptomatic of a disturbed mind. Why else would a man risk prosecution over so bizarre a preoccupation? He listened to his music nightly, drank his beer, and sat on his patio gazing on the headstones standing just beyond his house. Whenever some small regret came to his mind, he lectured it away as if it were an illicit impulse.

Then one night, waking from dark, undefined dreams, he walked through the hallway toward the kitchen for some water, only to see a figure sitting in his recliner by the mute television.

He stopped, stricken with fear of what this intruder might do.

But the figure remained seated, neither moving nor making a sound, and for a moment Campbell wondered if he were still dreaming. He stepped cautiously forward, uncertain what he might do if the person rose to attack him, and then said, almost in a whisper, "Who's there?"

The figure didn't reply.

"What do you want?" Campbell said, puzzled by the person's demeanor. If it were an intruder, wouldn't he be moving to hurt him, or at least leave the house in a panic?

For a long, curious moment Campbell stood gazing on the shadowy figure sitting in his chair, until he heard the words, or thought he heard: "How are you?"

With these whispered words Campbell's paralysis left him, and he turned toward the wall to find the light switch.

But when he flipped the switch and the ceiling fixture bathed the room in bright, white light, he found the recliner empty. There was no dark figure sitting there, no one who might speak to him, or ask him any questions

Puzzled, he searched the rest of the house, checked the locks on the doors and windows, but found nothing out of place.

That night he slept with the lights on, but the next morning he convinced himself that he'd suffered some waking nightmare, that he'd only dreamed he'd seen someone sitting in his chair and some undefined illness was probably to blame.

For days after the incident he saw no more phantoms, heard no more voices, and returned to his normal habits.

But then he woke one night to find a short, shadowy figure standing by his bed. He was too shocked by this person's appearance to do anything but lie frozen in place, but even in the shadows he sensed that the shape belonged to a woman, though why she'd suddenly appeared in his bedroom he had no idea.

"I'm not feeling well," he heard a voice say, far away, as if in a gravelly whisper. "Lucy won't take me to the doctor. Why won't she take me to the doctor?"

"Who are you?" Campbell managed to say, though he was frightened, uncertain.

"Won't you tell Lucy to take me to the doctor?" the woman's voice said. "Please, won't you tell her?"

"I don't know you," he said. "I don't know Lucy."

"I must see the doctor, I'm not feeling well. Please, tell Lucy."

For some reason he suddenly reached out to grab the woman, to make her stop talking to him, but when his hand reached the place where her body should have been he touched nothing.

The figure disappeared in that second, though a terrible, agonized moan echoed in the bedroom for a few seconds, as if a sick old woman were groaning pitifully.

Slowly he sat up in bed, gazing around the darkened bedroom before turning on the bedside lamp. Alone in the room, he waited until his nerves ceased playing their jangled music down his spine, and then he drew a deep breath and wondered why he was seeing such things.

A superstitious man might think they were ghosts, the phantasms of the bodies interred in the graveyard by his house. But that was too simple, too sensational an explanation; no, a much more frightening theory came to mind. Could he be suffering delusions? Hallucinations wrought from some undiagnosed mania? No, no, it wasn't that; he wasn't losing his mind. These apparitions must be some form of waking dream, a kind of nightmare he only perceived as real.

He refused to believe his self-imposed isolation was the catalyst for some psychosis. The opposite was true—he would be entertaining some psychosis were he still suffering the company of others. His isolation was his refuge from anxiety.

He lay back down, though he left the light burning as a shield against further dreams.

He closed his eyes, but he didn't sleep.

The next day he found himself repeatedly staring at the gravestones through the kitchen window. But he finally left the window, determined to lead the life he wanted to live, despite any dreams.

Thereafter, whenever his eye caught a drifting shadow in the corner of the room, he closed his eyes and turned away from it. He wrapped his days in ritual, sitting at the kitchen table with his morning coffee, watching the news on the television, reading the books by the chair in the living room. For a while no more unwanted entities disturbed his peace.

But then one evening, as he gazed up from the book he held against his knee, his eyes met the eyes of an old man standing before him, the deathly face of someone consumed by a withering illness. Dressed in a hazy gown that may have been a shroud or hospital garment, the old man raised a hand with upturned palm toward Campbell, his lips moving silently.

Campbell let the book fall to the floor. The apparition took no notice of the noise. *Is this a dream?* he found himself thinking. *Am I sleeping now?*

But he knew he was awake, and he knew he was seeing something that shouldn't be.

Then he thought he heard the old man say, in a voice as dry as dust, "Why have you stopped coming?"

"Who are you?" Campbell said, though he didn't move from the chair.

"Why have you stopped coming?" the old man said again. "I thought you wanted to see me."

"No, I *don't* want to see you. I don't—"

"Don't you love me?"

"You're just a dream, a nightmare. You're not real."

"Why have you stopped coming?"

Campbell closed his eyes. When he opened them again, the old man was gone.

I'm suffering some mania, he thought, and then pushed the thought away. He wouldn't see a doctor, he wouldn't. All through his marriage, Lorraine pushed him to see a therapist, someone who could help him overcome his anxiety, his social phobia. Of course, he refused. If she were with him now, she would have told him he was reaping what he'd sown.

I'm perfectly fine, he thought, as forcefully as possible. *This will pass, it's just a temporary fugue.*

But the apparitions continued appearing despite his attempts to dismiss them as a mental aberration, sometimes speaking to no one in particular, sometimes seeming to speak directly to him, and always desperately, or sadly, or breathing through a misery that somehow formed words only he could hear.

He couldn't raise the volume of the television loud enough to drown out their imprecations, nor could he find earplugs effective enough to keep himself from hearing their words at night when he tried to sleep. They begged him for attention, they implored him to listen, they regurgitated their fears and needs until he couldn't endure their company any longer.

If these ghosts were an aberration, then he might not be able to dismiss them at all. But even if they were, or if they were something else entirely, perhaps he could finally be rid of them if he engaged them directly.

The dying winter left the air uncomfortably cool. Campbell stepped onto the patio, rubbing his hands together nervously, before deciding to find the place in the fencing where he could enter the graveyard again.

The stars shone in a moonless sky; the distant streetlights threw long shadows across the field of headstones. He walked among the graves quietly, trying to hear the voices of the dead rising from the earth, but all he heard was an occasional passing vehicle. Even the insects were silent, which intimidated him, made him afraid to hear his voice breaking the silence.

But as he turned among the graves, he knew he must say his piece or be plagued by the voices forever.

"Please, stop," he began, the sound of his voice echoing through the grounds. He didn't know which name to implore; Mr. Kropp, or Mrs. Ward—did it really matter? He would never know which voice belonged beneath which stone.

"Please, stop speaking to me," he continued, raising his outstretched hands to the graves. "I just want to be left alone. I don't like being among people, I don't. I need to live in silence, in peace. I don't want to have to listen to people any more. I've worked hard all my life, and I've earned that right. So, please, just leave me alone. Leave me alone!"

Campbell lowered his hands, turning his head from one side of the cemetery to the other, wondering if his words had had any effect on the voices. He stood in the middle of the graveyard for several minutes before becoming self-conscious about his presence there and quietly returning to his own property.

He sat staring from his chair on the patio well into the night, fearful of entering the house again. When he finally did, he was met by silence.

That night Campbell slept without being disturbed, and the next day passed in silence as well. He kept to his daily rituals as closely as possible, and after a few days without a recurrence of the phenomenon he felt he'd finally succeeded in ridding himself of his unwanted visitors.

Then one night, while standing by the patio door and gazing out over the cemetery, he thought he heard a voice, though mutely. He turned immediately, fearful of another invasion of phantasms, but perceived nothing more. Perhaps he hadn't heard anything to begin with; but he *thought* he heard—

No, it was just a mirage, a mistaken impression.

You're already dead—

No, it was just the wind, or a blackbird calling from across the graveyard, or water flowing through pipes.

Campbell closed the door, intending to sleep. But he slept fitfully that night, and entertained unpleasant dreams.

The Mortal Immortal
by
Mary Shelley

originally published in *The Keepsake*, 1833

July 16, 1833

This is a memorable anniversary for me; on it I complete my three hundred and twenty-third year!

The Wandering Jew? Certainly not. More than eighteen centuries have passed over his head. In comparison with him, I am a very young Immortal.

Am I, then, immortal? This is a question which I have asked myself, by day and night, for now three hundred and three years, and yet cannot answer it. I detected a gray hair amidst my brown locks this very day—that surely signifies decay. Yet it may have remained concealed there for three hundred years—for some persons have become entirely white headed before twenty years of age.

I will tell my story, and my reader shall judge for me. I will tell my story, and so contrive to pass some few hours of a long eternity, become so wearisome to me. Forever! Can it be? To live forever! I have heard of enchantments, in which the victims were plunged into a deep sleep, to wake, after a hundred years, as fresh as ever: I have heard of the Seven Sleepers—thus to be immortal would not be so burthensome: but, oh! The weight of never-ending time—the tedious passage of the still-succeeding hours! How happy was the fabled Nourjahad! But to my task.

All the world has heard of Cornelius Agrippa. His memory is as immortal as his arts have made me. All the world has also heard of his scholar, who, unawares, raised the foul fiend during his master's absence, and was destroyed by him. The report, true or false, of this accident, was attended with many inconveniences to the renowned philosopher. All his scholars at once deserted him—his servants disappeared. He had no one near him to put coals on his ever-burning fires while he slept, or to attend to the changeful colors of his medicines while he studied. Experiment after experiment failed, because one pair of hands was insufficient to complete them: the dark spirits laughed at him for not being able to retain a single mortal in his service.

I was then very young, very poor, and very much in love. I had been for about a year the pupil of Cornelius, though I was absent when this accident took place. On my return, my friends implored me not to return to the alchemist's abode. I trembled as I listened to the dire tale they told; I required no second warning; and when Cornelius came and offered me a purse of gold if I would remain under his roof, I felt as if Satan himself tempted me. My teeth chattered. My hair stood on end. I ran off as fast as my trembling knees would permit.

My failing steps were directed where for two years they had every evening been attracted, a gently bubbling spring of pure living waters, beside which lingered a dark-haired girl, whose beaming eyes were fixed on the path I was accustomed each night to tread. I cannot remember the hour when I did not love Bertha; we had been neighbors and playmates from infancy. Her parents, like mine, were of humble life, yet respectable. Our attachment had been a source of pleasure to them. In an evil hour, a malignant fever carried off both her father and mother, and Bertha became an orphan. She would have found a home beneath my paternal roof, but, unfortunately, the old lady of the near castle, rich, childless, and solitary, declared her intention to adopt her. Henceforth Bertha was clad in silk, inhabited a marble palace, and was looked on as being highly favored by fortune. But in her new situation among her new associates, Bertha remained true to the friend of her humbler days; she often visited the cottage of my father, and when forbidden to go thither, she would stray towards the neighboring wood, and meet me beside its shady fountain.

She often declared that she owed no duty to her new protectress equal in sanctity to that which bound us. Yet still I was too poor to marry, and she grew weary of being tormented on my account. She had a haughty but an impatient spirit, and grew angry at the obstacles that prevented our union. We met now after an absence, and she had been sorely beset while I was away; she complained bitterly, and almost reproached me for being poor.

I replied hastily, "I am honest, if I am poor! Were I not, I might soon become rich!"

This exclamation produced a thousand questions. I feared to shock her by owning the truth, but she drew it from me; and then, casting a look of disdain on me, she said, "You pretend to love, and you fear to face the Devil for my sake!"

I protested that I had only dreaded to offend her, while she dwelt on the magnitude of the reward that I should receive. Thus encouraged, shamed by her, led on by love and hope, laughing at my late fears, with quick steps and a light heart, I returned to accept the offers of the alchemist, and was instantly installed in my office.

A year passed away. I became possessed of no insignificant sum of money. Custom had banished my fears. In spite of the most painful vigilance, I had never detected the trace of a cloven foot; nor was the studious silence of our abode ever disturbed by demoniac howls. I still continued my stolen interviews with Bertha, and Hope dawned on me—Hope—but not perfect joy; for Bertha fancied that love and security were enemies, and her pleasure was to divide them in my bosom. Though true of heart, she was somewhat of a coquette in manner; and I was jealous. She slighted me in a thousand ways, yet would never acknowledge herself to be in the wrong. She would drive me mad with anger, and then force me to beg her pardon. Sometimes she fancied that I was not sufficiently submissive, and then she had some story of a rival, favored by her protectress. She was surrounded by silk-clad youths—the rich and gay. What chance had the sad-robed scholar of Cornelius compared with these?

On one occasion, the philosopher made such large demands upon my time, that I was unable to meet her as I was wont. He was engaged in some mighty work, and I was forced to remain, day and night, feeding his furnaces and watching his chemical preparations. Bertha waited for me in vain at the fountain. Her haughty spirit fired at this neglect; and when at last I stole out during the few short minutes allotted to me for slumber, and hoped to be consoled by her, she received me with disdain, dismissed me in scorn, and vowed that any man should possess her hand rather than he who could not be in two places at once for her sake. She would be revenged! And truly she was. In my dingy retreat I heard that she had been hunting, attended by Albert Hoffer. Albert Hoffer was favored by her protectress, and the three passed in cavalcade before my smoky window. Methought that they mentioned my name—it was followed by a laugh of derision, as her dark eyes glanced contemptuously towards my abode.

Jealousy, with all its venom, and all its misery, entered my breast. Now I shed a torrent of tears, to think that I should never call her mine; and, anon, I imprecated a thousand curses on her inconstancy. Yet, still I must stir the fires of the alchemist, still attend on the changes of his unintelligible medicines.

Cornelius had watched for three days and nights, nor closed his eyes. The progress of his alembics was slower than he expected. In spite of his anxiety, sleep weighed upon his eyelids. Again and again he threw off drowsiness with more than human energy; again and again it stole away his senses. He eyed his crucibles wistfully.

"Not ready yet," he murmured; "will another night pass before the work is accomplished? Winzy, you are vigilant. You are faithful. You have slept, my boy. You slept last night. Look at that glass vessel. The liquid it contains is of a soft rose color. The moment it begins to change its hue, awaken me—till then I may close my eyes. First, it will turn white, and then emit golden flashes; but wait not till then; when the rose color fades, rouse me."

I scarcely heard the last words, muttered, as they were, in sleep. Even then he did not quite yield to nature.

"Winzy, my boy," he again said, "do not touch the vessel. Do not put it to your lips; it is a filter—a filter to cure love; you would not cease to love your Bertha—beware to drink!"

And he slept. His venerable head sunk on his breast, and I scarce heard his regular breathing. For a few minutes I watched the vessel—the rosy hue of the liquid remained unchanged. Then my thoughts wandered. They visited the fountain, and dwelt on a thousand charming scenes never to be renewed—never! Serpents and adders were in my heart as the word "Never!" half-formed itself on my lips. False girl! False and cruel! Never more would she smile on me as that evening she smiled on Albert. Worthless, detested woman! I would not remain unrevenged. She should see Albert expire at her feet. She should die beneath my vengeance. She had smiled in disdain and triumph. She knew my wretchedness and her power. Yet what power had she? The power of exciting my hate—my utter scorn—my—oh, all but indifference! Could I attain that? Could I regard her with careless eyes, transferring my rejected love to one fairer and more true, that were indeed a victory!

A bright flash darted before my eyes. I had forgotten the medicine of the adept; I gazed on it with wonder. Flashes of admirable beauty, more bright than those which the diamond emits when the sun's rays are on it, glanced from the surface of the liquid; an odor the most fragrant and grateful stole over my sense; the vessel seemed one globe of living radiance, lovely to the eye, and most inviting to the taste. The first thought, instinctively inspired by the grosser sense, was, I will—I *must* drink. I raised the vessel to my lips.

"It will cure me of love of torture!"

Already I had quaffed half of the most delicious liquor ever tasted by the palate of man, when the philosopher stirred. I started—I dropped the glass—the fluid flamed and glanced along the floor, while I felt Cornelius's grip at my throat, as he shrieked aloud, "Wretch, you have destroyed the labor of my life!"

The philosopher was totally unaware that I had drunk any portion of his drug. His idea was, and I gave a tacit assent to it, that I had raised the vessel from curiosity, and that, frightened at its brightness, and the flashes of intense light it gave forth, I had let it fall. I never undeceived him. The fire of the medicine was quenched—the fragrance died away—he grew calm, as a philosopher should under the heaviest trials, and dismissed me to rest.

I will not attempt to describe the sleep of glory and bliss which bathed my soul in paradise during the remaining hours of that memorable night. Words would be faint and shallow types of my enjoyment, or of the gladness that possessed my bosom when I woke. I trod air—my thoughts were in heaven. Earth appeared heaven, and my inheritance upon it was to be one trance of delight.

"This it is to be cured of love," I thought; "I will see Bertha this day, and she will find her lover cold and regardless: too happy to be disdainful, yet how utterly indifferent to her!"

The hours danced away. The philosopher, secure that he had once succeeded, and believing that he might again, began to concoct the same medicine once more. He was shut up with his books and drugs, and I had a holiday. I dressed myself with care; I looked in an old but polished shield, which served me for a mirror; methought my good looks had wonderfully improved. I hurried beyond the precincts of the town, joy in my soul, the beauty of heaven and earth around me. I turned my steps towards the castle. I could look on its lofty turrets with lightness of heart, for I was cured of love. My Bertha saw me afar off, as I came up the avenue. I know not what sudden impulse animated her bosom, but at the sight, she sprung with a light fawn-like bound down the marble steps, and was hastening towards me. But I had been perceived by another person. The old high-born hag, who called herself her protectress, and was her tyrant, had seen me, also; she hobbled, panting, up the terrace; a page, as ugly as herself, held up her train, and fanned her as she hurried along, and stopped my fair girl with a, "How, now, my bold mistress? Whither so fast? Back to your cage—hawks are abroad!"

Bertha clasped her hands. Her eyes were still bent on my approaching figure. I saw the contest. How I abhorred the old crone who checked the kind impulses of my Bertha's softening heart. Hitherto, respect for her rank had caused me to avoid the lady of the castle; now I disdained such trivial considerations. I was cured of love, and lifted above all human fears; I hastened forwards, and soon reached the terrace. How lovely Bertha looked, her eyes flashing fire, her cheeks glowing with impatience and anger. She was a thousand times more graceful and charming than ever—I no longer loved—oh! No, I adored—worshipped—idolized her!

She had that morning been persecuted, with more than usual vehemence, to consent to an immediate marriage with my rival. She was reproached with the encouragement that she had shown him. She was threatened with being turned out of doors with disgrace and shame. Her proud spirit rose in arms at the threat; but when she remembered the scorn that she had heaped upon me, and how, perhaps, she had thus lost one whom she now regarded as her only friend, she wept with remorse and rage. At that moment, I appeared.

"Oh, Winzy!" she exclaimed, "take me to your mother's cot; swiftly let me leave the detested luxuries and wretchedness of this noble dwelling. Take me to poverty and happiness."

I clasped her in my arms with transport. The old lady was speechless with fury, and broke forth into invective only when we were far on our road to my natal cottage. My mother received the fair fugitive, escaped from a gilt cage to nature and liberty, with tenderness and joy; my father, who loved her, welcomed her heartily; it was a day of rejoicing, which did not need the addition of the celestial potion of the alchemist to steep me in delight.

Soon after this eventful day, I became the husband of Bertha. I ceased to be the scholar of Cornelius, but I continued his friend. I always felt grateful to him for having, unawares, procured me that delicious draught of a divine elixir, which, instead of curing me of love (sad cure! solitary and joyless remedy for evils which seem blessings to the memory), had inspired me with courage and resolution, thus winning for me an inestimable treasure in my Bertha.

I often called to mind that period of trance-like inebriation with wonder. The drink of Cornelius had not fulfilled the task for which he affirmed that it had been prepared, but its effects were more potent and blissful than words can express.

They had faded by degrees, yet they lingered long, and painted life in hues of splendor. Bertha often wondered at my lightness of heart and unaccustomed gaiety; for, before, I had been rather serious, or even sad, in my disposition. She loved me the better for my cheerful temper, and our days were winged by joy.

Five years afterwards I was suddenly summoned to the bedside of the dying Cornelius. He had sent for me in haste, conjuring my instant presence. I found him stretched on his pallet, enfeebled even to death; all of life that yet remained animated his piercing eyes, and they were fixed on a glass vessel, full of a roseate liquid.

"Behold," he said, in a broken and inward voice, "the vanity of human wishes! A second time my hopes are about to be crowned, a second time they are destroyed. Look at that liquor. You remember five years ago I had prepared the same, with the same success; then, as now, my thirsting lips expected to taste the immortal elixir—you dashed it from me! And at present it is too late."

He spoke with difficulty, and fell back on his pillow. I could not help saying, "How, revered master, can a cure for love restore you to life?"

A faint smile gleamed across his face as I listened earnestly to his scarcely intelligible answer. "A cure for love and for all things—the Elixir of Immortality. Ah! If now I might drink, I should live forever!"

As he spoke, a golden flash gleamed from the fluid; a well-remembered fragrance stole over the air; he raised himself, all weak as he was—strength seemed miraculously to re-enter his frame—he stretched forth his hand—a loud explosion startled me—a ray of fire shot up from the elixir, and the glass vessel which contained it was shivered to atoms! I turned my eyes towards the philosopher; he had fallen back—his eyes were glassy—his features rigid—he was dead!

But I lived, and was to live forever! So said the unfortunate alchemist, and for a few days I believed his words. I remembered the glorious drunkenness that had followed my stolen draught. I reflected on the change I had felt in my frame—in my soul. The bounding elasticity of the one—the buoyant lightness of the other. I surveyed myself in a mirror, and could perceive no change in my features during the space of the five years which had elapsed. I remembered the radiant hues and grateful scent of that delicious beverage—worthy the gift it was capable of bestowing——I was, then, IMMORTAL!

A few days after I laughed at my credulity. The old proverb, that "a prophet is least regarded in his own country," was true with respect to me and my defunct master. I loved him as a man. I respected him as a sage, but I derided the notion that he could command the powers of darkness, and laughed at the superstitious fears with which he was regarded by the vulgar. He was a wise philosopher, but had no acquaintance with any spirits but those clad in flesh and blood. His science was simply human; and human science, I soon persuaded myself, could never conquer nature's laws so far as to imprison the soul forever within its carnal habitation. Cornelius had brewed a soul-refreshing drink—more inebriating than wine— sweeter and more fragrant than any fruit. It possessed probably strong medicinal powers, imparting gladness to the heart and vigor to the limbs; but its effects would wear out; already were they diminished in my frame. I was a lucky fellow to have quaffed health and joyous spirits, and perhaps long life, at my master's hands; but my good fortune ended there. Longevity was far different from immortality.

I continued to entertain this belief for many years. Sometimes a thought stole across me—was the alchemist indeed deceived? But my habitual credence was, that I should meet the fate of all the children of Adam at my appointed time—a little late, but still at a natural age. Yet it was certain that I retained a wonderfully youthful look. I was laughed at for my vanity in consulting the mirror so often, but I consulted it in vain—my brow was untrenched—my cheeks—my eyes—my whole person continued as untarnished as in my twentieth year.

I was troubled. I looked at the faded beauty of Bertha. I seemed more like her son. By degrees our neighbors began to make similar observations, and I found at last that I went by the name of the scholar bewitched. Bertha herself grew uneasy. She became jealous and peevish, and at length she began to question me. We had no children; we were all in all to each other; and though, as she grew older, her vivacious spirit became a little allied to ill-temper, and her beauty sadly diminished, I cherished her in my heart as the mistress I had idolized, the wife I had sought and won with such perfect love.

At last our situation became intolerable. Bertha was fifty—I twenty years of age. I had, in very shame, in some measure adopted the habits of a more advanced age; I no longer mingled in the dance among the young and gay, but my heart bounded along with them while I restrained my feet; and a sorry figure I cut among the Nestors of our village. But before the time I mention, things were altered—we were universally shunned; we were, at least I was, reported to have kept up an iniquitous acquaintance with some of my former master's supposed friends. Poor Bertha was pitied, but deserted. I was regarded with horror and detestation.

What was to be done? We sat by our winter fire. Poverty had made itself felt, for none would buy the produce of my farm; and often I had been forced to journey twenty miles, to some place where I was not known, to dispose of our property. It is true we had saved something for an evil day—that day was come.

We sat by our lone fireside—the old-hearted youth and his antiquated wife. Again Bertha insisted on knowing the truth; she recapitulated all she had ever heard said about me, and added her own observations. She conjured me to cast off the spell; she described how much more comely grey hairs were than my chestnut locks; she descanted on the reverence and respect due to age—how preferable to the slight regard paid to mere children. Could I imagine that the despicable gifts of youth and good looks outweighed disgrace, hatred, and scorn? Nay, in the end I should be burnt as a dealer in the black art, while she, to whom I had not deigned to communicate any portion of my good fortune, might be stoned as my accomplice. At length she insinuated that I must share my secret with her, and bestow on her like benefits to those I myself enjoyed, or she would denounce me, and then she burst into tears.

Thus beset, methought it was the best way to tell the truth. I revealed it as tenderly as I could, and spoke only of a very long life, not of immortality, which representation, indeed, coincided best with my own ideas. When I ended, I rose and said, "And now, my Bertha, will you denounce the lover of your youth? You will not, I know. But it is too hard, my poor wife, that you should suffer from my ill luck and the accursed arts of Cornelius. I will leave you. You have wealth enough, and friends will return in my absence. I will go; young as I seem, and strong as I am, I can work and gain my bread among strangers, unsuspected and unknown. I loved you in youth; God is my witness that I would not desert you in age, but that your safety and happiness require it."

I took my cap and moved towards the door; in a moment Bertha's arms were round my neck, and her lips were pressed to mine.

"No, my husband, my Winzy," she said, "you shall not go alone. Take me with you; we will remove from this place, and, as you say, among strangers we shall be unsuspected and safe. I am not so very old as quite to shame you, my Winzy; and I dare say the charm will soon wear off, and, with the blessing of God, you will become more elderly-looking, as is fitting; you shall not leave me."

I returned the good soul's embrace heartily. "I will not, my Bertha; but for your sake I had not thought of such a thing. I will be your true, faithful husband while you are spared to me, and do my duty by you to the last."

The next day we prepared secretly for our emigration. We were obliged to make great pecuniary sacrifices. It could not be helped. We realized a sum sufficient, at least, to maintain us while Bertha lived; and, without saying adieu to any one, quitted our native country to take refuge in a remote part of western France.

It was a cruel thing to transport poor Bertha from her native village, and the friends of her youth, to a new country, new language, new customs. The strange secret of my destiny rendered this removal immaterial to me; but I pitied her deeply, and was glad to perceive that she found compensation for her misfortunes in a variety of little ridiculous circumstances. Away from all tell-tale chroniclers, she sought to decrease the apparent disparity of our ages by a thousand feminine arts—rouge, youthful dress, and assumed juvenility of manner. I could not be angry. Did not I myself wear a mask? Why quarrel with hers, because it was less successful? I grieved deeply when I remembered that this was my Bertha, whom I had loved so fondly, and won with such transport—the dark eyed, dark-haired girl, with smiles of enchanting archness and a step like a fawn—this mincing, simpering, jealous old woman. I should have revered her gray locks and withered cheeks; but thus! It was my work, I knew; but I did not the less deplore this type of human weakness.

Her jealousy never slept. Her chief occupation was to discover that, in spite of outward appearances, I was myself growing old. I verily believe that the poor soul loved me truly in her heart, but never had woman so tormenting a mode of displaying fondness. She would discern wrinkles in my face and decrepitude in my walk, while I bounded along in youthful vigor, the youngest looking of twenty youths. I never dared address another woman. On one occasion, fancying that the belle of the village regarded me with favoring eyes, she bought me a gray wig. Her constant discourse among her acquaintances was, that though I looked so young, there was ruin at work within my frame; and she affirmed that the worst symptom about me was my apparent health. My youth was a disease, she said, and I ought at all times to prepare, if not for a sudden and awful death, at least to awake some morning white-headed, and bowed down with all the marks of advanced years. I let her talk—I often joined in her conjectures. Her warnings chimed in with my never-ceasing speculations concerning my state, and I took an earnest, though painful, interest in listening to all that her quick wit and excited imagination could say on the subject.

Why dwell on these minute circumstances? We lived on for many long years. Bertha became bed-ridden and paralytic. I nursed her as a mother might a child. She grew peevish, and still harped upon one thing—of how long I should survive her. It has ever been a source of consolation to me, that I performed my duty scrupulously towards her. She had been mine in youth, she was mine in age, and at last, when I heaped the sod over her corpse, I wept to feel that I had lost all that really bound me to humanity.

Since then how many have been my cares and woes, how few and empty my enjoyments! I pause here in my history. I will pursue it no further. A sailor without rudder or compass, tossed on a stormy sea—a traveler lost on a wide-spread heath, without landmark or star to guide him—such have I been. More lost, more hopeless than either. A nearing ship, a gleam from some far cot, may save them; but I have no beacon except the hope of death.

Death! Mysterious, ill-visaged friend of weak humanity! Why alone of all mortals have you cast me from your sheltering fold? Oh, for the peace of the grave! The deep silence of the iron-bound tomb! That thought would cease to work in my brain, and my heart beat no more with emotions varied only by new forms of sadness!

Am I immortal? I return to my first question. In the first place, is it not more probable that the beverage of the alchemist was fraught rather with longevity than eternal life? Such is my hope. And then be it remembered that I only drank half of the potion prepared by him. Was not the whole necessary to complete the charm? To have drained half the Elixir of Immortality is but to be half immortal— my forever is thus truncated and null.

But again, who shall number the years of the half of eternity? I often try to imagine by what rule the infinite may be divided. Sometimes I fancy age advancing upon me. One gray hair I have found. Fool! Do I lament? Yes, the fear of age and death often creeps coldly into my heart; and the more I live, the more I dread death, even while I abhor life. Such an enigma is man—born to perish—when he wars, as I do, against the established laws of his nature.

But for this anomaly of feeling surely I might die. The medicine of the alchemist would not be proof against fire—sword—and the strangling waters. I have gazed upon the blue depths of many a placid lake, and the tumultuous rushing of many a mighty river, and have said, peace inhabits those waters; yet I have turned my steps away, to live yet another day. I have asked myself, whether suicide would be a crime in one to whom thus only the portals of the other world could be opened. I have done all, except presenting myself as a soldier or duelist, an object of destruction to my—no, not my fellow mortals, and therefore I have shrunk away. They are not my fellows. The inextinguishable power of life in my frame, and their ephemeral existence, place us wide as the poles asunder. I could not raise a hand against the meanest or the most powerful among them.

Thus I have lived on for many a year—alone, and weary of myself— desirous of death, yet never dying—a mortal immortal. Neither ambition nor avarice can enter my mind, and the ardent love that gnaws at my heart, never to be returned—never to find an equal on which to expend itself—lives there only to torment me.

This very day I conceived a design by which I may end all—without self-slaughter, without making another man a Cain—an expedition, which mortal frame can never survive, even endued with the youth and strength that inhabits mine. Thus I shall put my immortality to the test, and rest forever—or return, the wonder and benefactor of the human species.

Before I go, a miserable vanity has caused me to pen these pages. I would not die, and leave no name behind. Three centuries have passed since I quaffed the fatal beverage. Another year shall not elapse before, encountering gigantic dangers—warring with the powers of frost in their home—beset by famine, toil, and tempest—I yield this body, too tenacious a cage for a soul which thirsts for freedom, to the destructive elements of air and water. Or, if I survive, my name shall be recorded as one of the most famous among the sons of men; and, my task achieved, I shall adopt more resolute means, and, by scattering and annihilating the atoms that compose my frame, set at liberty the life imprisoned within, and so cruelly prevented from soaring from this dim earth to a sphere more congenial to its immortal essence.

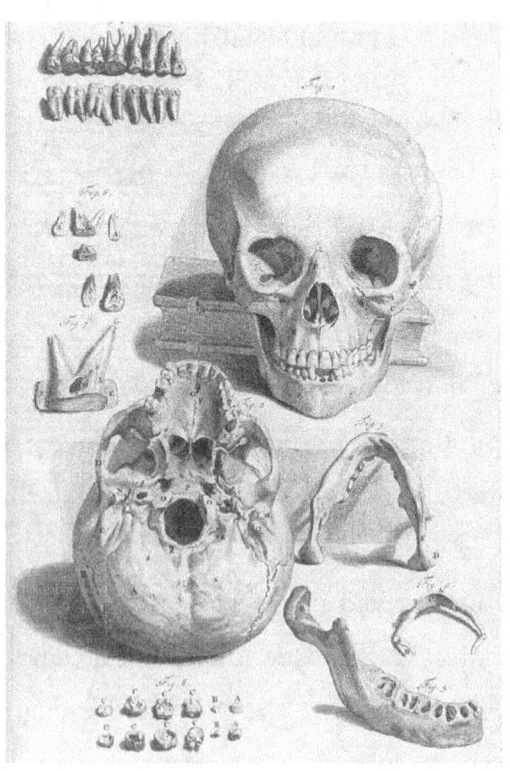

Shelley Unbound
by
Bo Balder

The Monster

I fashioned her body from graves in and around Geneva. It seemed to me that as long as it was a young woman, it wouldn't matter much what shape or color the limbs were. I did pay particular attention to matching up the legs, as the slight limp my maker gave me has never ceased to bother me.

This time has marvelous, colorless thread and machines that will stitch for you. And electricity! No need to channel lightning, as my maker had. I would simply plug a *cord* into a *socket* and out would flow power my maker couldn't have dreamed of—nor she who wrote him.

If I had known life could be like this, full of light and warmth and ease, I wouldn't have stayed on the North Pole such a length of time. Although that land has its own beauty. I learned to hunt like a polar bear, shooting up from below through the icy waters, and covered myself in white furs to hide from humanity.

For her head, I took a great deal of time and care. Whether my face has beauty is debatable, but still I wouldn't like to see it changed for another one. So although I'd started out with the object not to kill anyone, for her face I had to. Not surprisingly, I found an English woman resembling her. Mary had no direct descendants, but her facial type was not distinctive.

Her brain was another matter. It was unique among women of her time. She was strong, smart, imaginative, politically sophisticated, unconventional. How could I possibly hope to duplicate that? Science couldn't help me, so I used magic for that part. I chose the right hemisphere of a great female poet, the left hemisphere of a great scholar. I steeped the dead brains in a tea I'd infused from her writings, chips of her grave, a lock from her hair I stole from a museum. I read her works out loud, and her husband's poems. I'd pulverized and boiled photographs of her likenesses in the tea, Shelley's and their son's. It would have to be enough.

So here she lay in the conservatory of that same villa in Geneva where she conceived of me.

Now I will return the favor and conceive of her.

Not for her a stormy night and the human scientist peering down at me. I chose a tranquil summer evening, at dusk. The sounds of busy Geneva and boats on the lake were audible but not intrusive.

I attached clips to the conductors beneath her jaw. The harsh lighting makes the stitches in her neck seem more prominent than they really are, what with wound glue, invisible line, and some beautiful overhand stitching.

I dim those harsh overhead lights, lights in thin glass poles, very nifty for close work but not very nice to be born under, I would think. So now when she wakes she will see the sunset gilding the lake to her left, a few candles to her right. I'd have loved to be born under lighting like that, and since she created me, I feel confident she will, too.

I take one last look as she lies there in beautiful repose under her linen sheet, and then plug in.

Mary

I woke with soft moonlight lapping my face. I knew at once where I was. Lying on a table, of all peculiar circumstances, in that villa on the lake. I couldn't conceive of a reason for it. The men might drink themselves to stupefaction and find themselves in undignified positions in the morning, but I never did.

I sat up with an ease that surprised me. How smooth my hands looked. And how odd. I turned and massaged them to loosen them up, then realized I needn't. Why did I expect my hands to be stiff upon waking?

I put my feet down on the floor. They tingled, each with a different, distinct prickling. The left as if it had been asleep for a while, the right wobbly, as if after a sprain. I pushed myself off the table and stood, swaying, forced to hold onto the table until the dizziness passed.

I only wore a loose dressing gown, with nothing underneath. The weight of my breasts seemed heavier than expected. One of my feet was quite dark. I searched for candles or a lamp to light, but although I found two candelabras on the window sill, they were burnt out. They still felt warm.

The doors to the garden, past the pillars, were open. Although I could see the moonlight reflected off the lake, the view was obscured by a row of trees. Strange buzzing sounds whooshed past beyond those trees, growling and menacing. I became afraid, as in a dream one knows is turning into a nightmare, but unable to avert it.

My tingling, unsure feet bore me to the edge of the flag-stoned terrace. Not the same flagstones as before. Silhouetted against the trees stood a tall dark figure with a square head. I did not know him.

But since he was the only living soul here I spoke to him. "Sir? May I trouble you to ask where I am and why?"

My voice sounded not like my voice at all. It was deeper, rougher, and the tongue had trouble with the "r's." A dreadful suspicion leapt into my heart. I was not me. I was not Mary Wollstonecraft Shelley, but someone else. But who? Claire? A maid? This had to be a dream. I prayed it was. I pinched myself to wake up, but all I felt was a cottony ball of pain somewhere far away. As if I pinched myself through a thick blanket. Perhaps that was indeed the case.

The tall man turned. His square, marred visage frightened me so the blood rushed from my head, and I swayed. I clung to a white lawn chair that almost toppled when I leaned on it, much less sturdy than I had expected.

He opened his mouth and bared his teeth at me. Did he imagine it a smile?

"What is your name?" a booming, rushing, windy voice spoke, as if from the tatters of ruptured vocal chords.

"My name is Mary Wollstonecraft Shelley," I said. "Who are you and why are you trespassing on these grounds? Lord Byron rented this villa for the whole summer."

"I know this," the person spoke, and creaked in laughter. "You wrote about me here, did you not? Perhaps on a beautiful summer evening like this?"

It had rained all that summer.

Behind his misshapen face the sky shone violet, and continuous buzzing and growling noises could be heard in the distance. This was not the same place. It seemed to me I had been old, had seen a son, Percy, grow up and go to university. Yet here, now, I was young again, though my grasp on youth and memory seemed feeble, full of inexplicable gaps and fuzziness.

"Who are you?" I croaked out. The effort was making me faint. I did not want to show weakness to this madman or freak or whatever he was.

"You may give me a name, if you wish. You never did before. Clara, perhaps, or William?"

These names brought burning pain. Yet it seemed old pain, and at the same time, it seemed I was a young woman who'd had no children yet. I touched my stomach with my free hand, unable to stop even while I was in a nightdress out here, alone and vulnerable. Should I not be in a delicate condition?

The grass that had seemed so soft and woolly to my numb feet a moment ago rose up to meet me.

The Monster, named Clara, perhaps, or William.

I am debating with myself. Should I be masterful and press on? Should I be merciful and have patience? One never knows with one's children. She, who was in a way my mother, now is my child and in my care. I have seen humans both beat their children and rock them. I must choose wisely.

Mary

I woke again, brought up above the seas of sleep sharply aware of what had happened last night. I sat bolt upright and found myself bound to a wicker chair in the sunroom. The late afternoon light glittered on what must be the lake behind the trees. The northern shores looked far more normal than they had last night in their blanket of light and their cover of lurid purple sky. I could now far more readily believe I was awake.

I looked around, noticing in the back of my mind how easily I could crane my head, without any pain or grinding noises in my vertebrae. The monster stood in the farthest corner of the room, its head tilted back, contemplating the ceiling or God knows what inhuman vistas. In the light of day it was clear it could not be a human being, but then what? It had faded stitch marks all over its bony, square face and strange stubs stuck out behind its jaws.

I grimaced, pulling the muscles in my neck to test a theory. I felt a tautness behind my own jaws, but with my hands bound I couldn't verify my suspicion.

My glance fell on my hands. One of them was noticeably darker than the other, of a more Mediterranean, perhaps southern Swiss complexion. A red, inflamed ridge encircled the wrist. The other hand was much paler, and in fact the hand was of a different, sturdier shape.

My suspicions, nay, my fears, became much stronger. The creature's body was stitched together, rather clumsily, from different, ill-matching parts. As my creation, Dr. Frankenstein, had done.

Was I, as I had suspected before, not me, but rather a cobbled together facsimile of me? I spread my two different hands. I didn't want to know what else of me had been stitched out of other people. Imagining it was horrible enough.

The novel I wrote that summer. My mind groped after that thought as after a slippery fish. That summer. Not this summer. Then, not now. I was sure of it.

The monster stood in the corner, staring at the summer sky, thinking thoughts I couldn't fathom. Or couldn't I? Take our stitched-together hands, for example. We might have more in common with each other than I'd like.

"What's your name?" I asked. "What do you want?"

It turned its dull eyes to me. Although presumably it could see with them, they lacked the shine and brightness of human eyes.

"You asked before," it said. "Don't you remember?"

I did, when he said that. And that he'd wished to be named after one of my dead infants. I would not dishonor their memory. "I shall call you Adam," I said, regretting the choice immediately after it had left my tongue. For what mind would not now leap to Eve? And procreation?

"I'd like something to eat," I said. Surely with a full stomach I'd be able to whittle my thoughts to sharper points.

He turned and showed his teeth. He really oughtn't to, it made him look even less human. I vowed not to look in a mirror if I passed one. I didn't want to know. It would only upset me, I suspected, and I needed a clear head.

"We do not need to eat, unless we wish to," he said. A memory of diving into icy water, surging upward and tearing a great, double-fanged beast apart from below, skittered over the dull orbs in his skull.

Did that mean he could see my thoughts moving over my eyes as well? His countenance didn't change. Maybe he couldn't.

"Has your confusion passed? Are you ready to go out into the world with me, mother?" it asked. *He* asked.

"I am clear of mind. But I would know more about this world before I agree to entering it."

Adam seemed to ponder this. "As you indicate, this world is not the same one you left. Centuries have passed. Your name and your husband's are well remembered, but you would find the society that remembers it alien, perhaps even repellent."

The words deluged me like a bucket of icy water in the face. My head swam. Centuries had passed. I had joined Percy in heaven. My son Percy would be dead as well. Had he left any children? It didn't matter. I could hardly seek out my descendants and be hailed as a long-lost grandmother—I, the abomination, the warped version of who I once had been. Did I even want to be here, now that I knew? The answer rose up swift and piercing. I wanted to be back in heaven and be joined with my husband and son.

"This world has persevered on the course of science you imagined. It has tamed the oceans and the skies and driven away the night. All I saw seemed prosperous and healthy, if not at leisure."

This told me not enough. Not that I cared, not that I intended to stay. "Untie me, then," I said, daring him. "Show me the world through your eyes."

His eyes lit up from within. "Yes. Together, daughter, you and I will populate this world with our children, the better to remind mankind of nature's dangers."

I shivered on the inside. He'd called me both mother and daughter, yet intended to take me as a wife. Apart from these names, which I considered metaphorical rather than literal, I could only shudder at the thought of bearing children. Three dead babes were enough. Whatever womb he'd created for me would remain empty.

Even if he meant us to rob graves together and choose matching limbs for our changeling children, I would not do it.

The setting sun outside sent a shard of splintering, lake-reflected light into my eyes. And then I knew. The means for my escape and salvation lay close at hand, for Lac Leman is terrifyingly deep.

Adam

Her thoughts shoot over her irises like shoals of silvery fish. I cannot read them fast enough. Yet something tells me she does not welcome my suit. I shall not give up so easily. I untie her, extend my hand, which she accepts, and pull her forth into the new world. I will show her automobiles, flying coaches and moving pictures. She will be entranced.

Mary

I told him I wished to cross the lake in one of the large, white sailless boats I'd seen rumbling past. His heavy brow wrinkled. It would be very dangerous to venture forth among so many ordinary people. He wore a hat, I, a veil and a coat over my nightdress. He'd forgotten or omitted to bring me decent clothes. I saw a few women as we walked over the smooth hard road. I would not have dared wear their clothing—trousers, tight little shirts. What strange times.

The much expanded city of Geneva lay like a fallen galaxy upon the hills across the lake. So much light! For a moment I thought to ask the monster how much time had passed, but then I dismissed the thought. It would not help me, knowing the date, it would not sway me from my resolve.

We walked a very long time. My feet hurt, but in such a distant and cottony way, as if they weren't my feet at all. Which I suppose was the truth.

The monster, or Adam, led me to a dock where a gleaming white soup tureen of a ship lay. It had no sails, no rowlocks. I marveled at its beauty and oddness. The monster led me onto the gangplank, a common object that made me feel a little more at home in this world.

The gangplank was the last such thing, though. All surfaces of the boat shone like porcelain or silver, so clean, no splinters or rust anywhere. A passenger could truly feel at leisure on such a boat, made for royalty. A lady's silk skirts would not sag or get dirty, her gloves would remain pristine. Not that I had any such accoutrements. I clutched my coat around me.

"How will you sail it?" I said.

Adam shrugged. "I will cast off and let currents and chance take us where they will."

Adam heaved the great coils of rope over their bollards, broke the chains, and pushed the boat off with a great heave of his thick legs. He vaulted over the railing like a circus elephant and loped to the bridge.

I took one last look at the dark lake with its glittering skirt of light under the purple sky, the ever-present zooming and buzzing and occasional flashes of disturbing, pounding music. This world was not for me.

I shook off my coat, clambered over the railing, and debated how to minimize my splash. But then I realized I couldn't just slip away, cowardly. I had a duty to these people, my descendants, perhaps. I couldn't leave the monster loose upon the world. He would only make more of me or other gruesome facsimiles.

He had to die.

My hands were clenched upon the cool silvery railing. When I lifted them, my hands had made prints in it as if it was made of wax. The sight didn't even surprise me. Perhaps I didn't have the full range of human emotion. But it made a tiny, faraway spark of hope jump off my leaden brain. If the monster was strong, so was I.

I walked back to the gap in the railing where the gangplank had been. Beside it, bollards, or whatever these were called on a boat, were bolted to the steel deck. I wrenched one loose.

I couldn't subdue my numb feet into a silent approach, but the banging and clanging Adam made in his labors seemed enough to mask my approach. I rounded a corner and found him heaving mightily on enormous coils of rope. I identified pulleys and chains I imagined were used to manage this in daily life. Hefting the unwieldy bollard over my head, I took the last step and smashed the thing down on Adam's brains.

He inadvertently helped me by rising just at that moment, perhaps finally alarmed by my silent approach. Gouts of yellowy blood oozed from his burst skull.

He went down like a log, hanging half over the railing. I dropped the bloody bollard and finished the thing off by pushing him overboard. He sank like a stone, dead already.

I walked over to the other end of the boat, for some reason reluctant to follow him into the deeps in the same spot. For one moment I teetered outside the railing, saying goodbye to the lake and its memories, goodbye to the world.

The water was cold.

I blew out my breath the way I'd heard one was supposed to do when drowning oneself.

The water darkened rapidly. I hung in it, suspended, while the bright spot above me sped away.

I was gathering my courage to inhale the lake water as a booming sound buffeted my ears. Something was coming. A huge shadow rising from below, shooting upward toward me in a rush of water pressure.

I opened my mouth wide and breathed in.

The Son Who Shattered His Father's Dream
by
B.E. Scully

Gold watch, Armani suit, pockets full of cash. Black BMW with heated leather seats, conspicuously parked on a dead-end street in the most crime-ridden neighborhood in the city. This time, he'd even cracked open the passenger side door to make it easier.

The first time, he'd left all four doors unlocked, but they hadn't done the obvious thing and just tried to open one of them. Instead, one of the kids—and they *had* been kids, no more than fifteen, sixteen-years old, from the looks of them—had actually pointed a gun at the rolled-up window and shouted, "Open up, motherfucker, or your new interior will be brains and blood!" or some such Hollywood tough-guy phrase. He'd wanted to tell them the car already *was* opened up, in four different places! But he'd been too nervous, that first time.

The second time, he rolled his windows down, but it was ten-degrees below zero at this time of year, and he'd sat there for almost two hours, rubbing his hands together and turning on the heat just long enough to thaw out before finally giving up and going home. He had come to the alleyway to die, yes, but hypothermia wasn't going to be the method. He never had been able to stand the cold.

It occurred to him that because he was dark-skinned, the criminals might think the flashy clothes and car meant he was a drug-dealer, and were afraid of him. So the third time out, he'd dressed more casually and driven his sensible Toyota instead of the BMW, but still nothing. Maybe then they thought he was too poor to have anything worth killing for.

He'd been at it for almost three weeks now, and all he had to show for his trouble was two missing watches, three beatings—one severe enough to send him to the hospital for the night—and a bank account about seven-thousand-dollars lighter.

He'd have thought it would be easier for a man to get himself killed.

But then again, unlike his son, for whom everything had been easy—correction, for whom everything had been *made* easy, and by him, to think!—nothing had ever been easy for Mohanlal Malhorta. Not since leaving Kerala, India, at eighteen-years old with two-hundred dollars in his pocket and not many more words of English in his head. Not the twelve years working sixteen-hour days in one clattering, hellishly hot laundry after another, sleeping on a mattress in a filthy apartment with five other young men as smelly, tired, and homesick as he was. Not since scrimping and saving every cent until he could open his own dry-cleaning business. Not since almost losing everything in those first few sleepless years of expansion, until the franchise started making money.

No, despite the big house and the even bigger bank account that he enjoyed now, nobody could ever say that things had been easy for Mohanlal Malhorta.

Maybe that's why he'd been so cautious about marrying. He was forty-six-years old then—his own father had died of a heart-attack at age forty-nine, only three more years to go! But he hadn't wanted some young wife looking for American citizenship and an air-conditioned house. He'd tried courting a few of those types—silly, insubstantial things. No, he'd wanted a real wife, a real woman. A woman who understood the world and knew how to handle herself in it. He wanted a partner, not a dependent. And so he'd married Amrita—bold, funny Amrita, with her quick, knowing eyes and even quicker laugh, and they'd been happy. Amrita, dead nine years now from an artery that just opened up in her head one day like a blooming night jasmine and killed her instantly. Amrita had been thirty-eight when they'd married, and so they only had one child, a son. They'd named him Matthew—a good, solid American name, even though it sounded strange and unwieldy on his and Amrita's tongues, like the name of someone else's child. But names, Mohanlal knew, were important—names were destiny!

Matthew had been named for a great destiny, his father's greatest dream.

Mohanlal closed his eyes and leaned his head back against the leather headrest, trying, as he always did, to forget what could never be forgotten. One simple mistake had undone the entire thing, just like in the children's stories Mohanlal used to read to Matthew when he was a child. The wolf throws a rope to the fox, the pig makes a house of straw instead of bricks. In Matthew's case, it had been the money—always the money!

His son had somehow managed to get thirty-five-thousand dollars in untraceable cash, with another twenty-thousand paid up front. Apparently, he would then pay another fifty-thousand afterward. Later, Mohanlal found out that Matthew had arranged to be out of the country when the murder occurred, visiting relatives back in Kerala—imagine the nerve, the very same relatives his mother had spent years sending copies of every one of Matthew's graduation announcements, newspaper articles, and awards!

But his son never got the chance to make the trip.

Matthew never *had* understood the importance of community, of friends one trusts with one's very life. Mohanlal had such a friend at the bank where he'd conducted his business for over forty years, the same bank he urged his son to do business with when he became his own man of the world. Which is why his friend called him one afternoon to discreetly inquire about the large amounts of money Matthew had been withdrawing from his account for the past six months (after the untraceable cash ran out, no doubt). Was Matthew in some kind of financial trouble, his friend wanted to know? Or perhaps there was some secret investment opportunity Matthew knew about from his job, which Mohanlal could perhaps share with a very old family friend?

Secret investment opportunity, indeed.

Mohanlal had wanted to ask his son directly about the money, he really had. But then he remembered—as if he could ever forget!—"The Incident." In graduate school, Matthew had certainly never intended to doctor his grades on the transcripts he'd sent out when he'd been trying to secure an internship. Mohanlal had never questioned Matthew's claim that he had altered the transcripts, had changed a few "Bs" into "As," for *him*—for Mohanlal. On the night before his first day of kindergarten, Mohanlal had sat his son down and explained to him that nothing less than top-notch would do.

"In America especially," he'd said, "people love a winner. Now tell me, in a running competition, does the second-place runner win the race?"

His small son, his child, could only shake his head wordlessly.

"That's right!" Mohanlal had boomed. "Only first-place wins the race. Everyone else is a loser, no matter how fast they run."

In the photograph of his first day of school, Matthew is grinning widely—perhaps, Mohanlal can see now, a bit *too* widely—his hands folded in front of him as if in prayer, wearing a miniature three-piece suit. In middle school, Matthew had started a lucrative lawn mowing operation by outsourcing the mowing to other kids. When Matthew graduated from high school as co-valedictorian, Mohanlal was certain he would go to Harvard—only the best! But he'd ended up going to Duke instead. On the day Matthew left for college, Mohanlal presented him with a plaque inscribed with the words "Son Who Shattered His Father's Dream."

Which, of course, made Matthew work even harder. He graduated a year early from Duke, summa cum laude, and was accepted at Harvard Law School.

Mohanlal was so pleased that he only mildly chastised his son for not going to medical school and becoming a doctor, as Mohanlal had always dreamed.

"Dad," his son had chastised him back, "you've always taught me that America loves winners, right? And who are the winners in today's world? The ones who control the money, that's who." When his father didn't look convinced, Matthew added, "Listen, can you tell me who Anthony Fauci is? No? He's a doctor who did ground-breaking work on HIV. How about Mildred Dresselhaus? She pioneered work on graphite, the substance about ready to change the world. Seiji Ogawa, who helped revolutionize MRI technology—doesn't ring a bell, does it? I could go on, but you get the point. Now, I don't even have to ask the same question about Bill Gates, Warren Buffett, or the Koch brothers, do I?"

Mohanlal Malhorta could only shake his head wordlessly.

At Harvard, the right internship was the next step on the upward climb, and certainly Matthew had simply mixed up the transcripts meant for his father with the correct ones he had meant to send those judges and law firms. But Harvard, not quite as convinced, had expelled Matthew anyway. Which hadn't prevented him from landing a job with a hedge fund company founded by a billionaire who within ten years—ten years, less time than it had taken Mohanlal to even get out of the back rooms of all those laundromats!—within ten years, this billionaire had turned his company into a fourteen billion dollar empire. The company did background checks on every potential employee, of course, but Matthew's expulsion from Harvard hadn't seemed to hurt. In fact, it might have even helped—Matthew had told his father that the billionaire was always looking for hungry young portfolio managers with "edge."

And Matthew, apparently, had a lot of edge. In less than two years, his son was one of the company's fastest rising stars. Matthew married and had two kids, a boy and then a girl, one right after the other. Like his father, Matthew had married a woman whose family had come from India—Padma, as smart and capable as she was poised and graceful. Also like his father, Matthew had given both children solid American names. The young family had seemed happy and prosperous, but the work—my god, the work! Unrelenting even by Mohanlal's standards, the work eventually took its toll. Portfolio managers were given obscene amounts of money to work with—"pots of gold," as Matthew called them. If their investments were consistently profitable, those pots of gold could multiply astonishingly fast. But if their investments lost money, the gold disappeared along with their jobs. As far as the billionaire who ran the company was concerned, it was prosper or die.

Somewhere along the line, Mohanlal guessed, his son's pot of gold had come up empty, and he needed to find a new one, fast. His rainbow, it seemed, had begun at his own bank account—but where did it end?

In spite of "The Incident," Mohanlal *had* wanted to ask his son directly about the missing money. But after three decades in business, Mohanlal didn't need a Harvard law degree to know when an "A" is really a "B." Or worse.

He'd hired a private investigator and prayed every night that there was some simple explanation. In less than two weeks, the detective called him and asked to meet privately one otherwise exceptional autumn day. The investigator was a brusque mountain of a man, bald-headed and alarming, but he was as tentative as a child when he handed over a manila envelope so thick the flap wouldn't close and said, "I sure hope you have other kids, Mr. Malhorta."

No, Mr. Malhorta did not have other kids. Instead he had a son who had very methodically withdrawn large amounts of money from his bank account in order to pay a man named Aria Black—Aria Black, no less, like a gangster in a Hollywood movie!—to discreetly assassinate one Mohanlal Malhorta, aged sixty-eight, widowed for nine years, owner and operator of the Quick N' Clean dry-cleaning franchise, and father to one son. One son who wanted him dead.

Prosper or die—or make sure someone else does it for you. Even your own father. Sitting in his office with the late afternoon light streaming through the cut-glass windows, Mohanlal understood that *he* was the end of his son's rainbow.

Mohanlal wasn't worth as much as the billionaire, but if he sold off the dry cleaning franchise, he'd be worth enough to help Matthew out of trouble. Correction: if *Matthew* sold off the dry cleaning business after inheriting it from his father, *Matthew* would be worth enough to get *himself* out of trouble Not to mention the million dollar life insurance policy he stood to collect. That is, once Mohanlal died. Or was killed. By his own child—his *only* child! Even the fact that Matthew had hired someone else to do the job rankled him—shot down by a complete stranger, like a mad dog in the street! If he was going to be murdered by his own child, then that child should look him in the face and do it himself, like a man of honor.

Even the private investigator had known that, and Mohanlal still burned with shame at the memory of "The Afternoon Everything Changed."

Mohanlal could perfectly remember the mechanical motions of paying the detective and somehow mumbling, "Thank you for your time," and "No, no, I don't wish to notify the authorities just yet." Almost as awful as what was in the big thick envelope was the expression in the man's eyes as Mohanlal shook his big, beefy hand, as thick and weighty as the envelope he'd delivered—the look of pure, unmistakable *pity*. "How unthinkable," the eyes said, "to have a son like that!"

How unthinkable indeed. Unbearable. Unsurvivable. Mohanlal didn't even know if that was a real word—unsurvivable. If it wasn't, then it should be.

On "The Afternoon Everything Changed," the sun went down and evening passed into darkest night, and still Mohanlal sat at his desk, unable to think, unable to act. For the first time in his life, he didn't know what to do, how to proceed. If Matthew would have just come to him for the money! Of course he would have been disappointed. Of course he might have lectured a bit, chastised a bit. But if Matthew was in trouble, he would have gotten the money somehow, no matter how large the amount.

As if Matthew was right there in the office with him, his son's voice suddenly filled the empty air. "Yes, father, but would you also have given me another plaque?"

And suddenly he understood that Matthew would never have asked him for the money for the same reason he would never accept it, even if Mohanlal found a way to disguise it as a gift—pride. But no, perhaps something even more awful than pride—its wounded co-joined twin, self-protection. And what was Matthew protecting himself from—or, more to the point, whom?

Mohanlal, that's *whom*.

And in that instant, the solution appeared, opening in the darkness like the night jasmine that had killed his wife. If his son despised him, or, at the very least, disregarded him enough to want to kill him—even for money, even to save himself!—how could Mohanlal wish to continue to live? It would have been different if Amrita was still with him, but he had been alone for a long time—too long. He was an old man now, and tired. He could not go on living through the even more barren years to come without the love of his only child—and *with* the knowledge that had come in that hateful, fateful (how alike those two words sounded in English!) manila envelope.

And yet he could not kill himself. The shame for his family back in Kerala! Such a thing might even put a stain on Matthew's future—who knows, his son might rise up to be a great politician someday, making laws and policies that changed the world. Mohanlal would never wish to jeopardize a future like that. Not to mention that if he committed suicide, Matthew wouldn't get a penny of the life insurance money. He couldn't wait around for death to come naturally, either.

Matthew was in trouble, and Mohanlal, with no artery to blossom open without warning, might live for years to come. Even decades, maybe. No, his death had to be completely random, with no questions, no confusion, no staged "accident" that might lead to an investigation. There could be no connection to Matthew, and it had to be now.

It had to be murder.

Which is Mohanlal was sitting in an alleyway with his passenger side door propped open, waiting for the criminal to come along who was both bold and desperate enough to shoot him dead right there on his heated leather seat. Mohanlal glanced at his watch—almost midnight—and then at himself in the rearview mirror. He saw a tired old man looking back at him—a broken man—and he quickly looked away.

Suddenly, two stories from long ago came into his mind. The first was one of the stories Mohanlal used to read to Matthew when his son was still a small child. In the story, a monkey gets hold of a looking-glass and goes around showing it to all of the other animals. The bear looks into the glass and says he's very sorry he has such an ugly face. The wolf says he wishes for the face of the stag, with its beautiful horns. So every beast felt sad that it didn't have the face of some other animal. When the monkey took the looking-glass to the owl, who had been observing the whole scene, the owl said, "No, I will not look into it, for in cases such as this, knowledge is but a source of pain."

Or as the Americans might say, "Ignorance is bliss."

The second story was one he'd read in an American history book long ago, when he was still a boy in India struggling to learn the strange words and unfamiliar rhythms of this mysterious new language. The story was about a man named Morris Birkbeck, a nineteenth-century pioneer and successful businessman in a place called Illinois. One day, while fording a stream with his twenty-three year old son, Birkbeck got caught in the current. His son, having crossed safely to the other side, plunged back in to save his father. However, upon reaching him, his son discovered he was too weighed down by his father and his own clothes to fight the strong current and bring them both back to shore. Birkbeck, grasping the situation, gave up his hold on his son and, smiling, motioned him away. The son survived, and when the father's body was found later, his face still wore a serene smile.

Mohanlal had been so taken with this story that one of the first things he did in America was go to a library and check out a book about Birkbeck's life. He had been dismayed to learn, however, that the man's death had devastated the family's financial well-being, and the son he had given his life to save died a broken man less than fifteen years later.

A car pulled into the alleyway and turned off its engine, jerking Mohanlal out of his stories. This was it! This was his chance at last!

He wondered if he should get out of the car, perhaps even approach the other vehicle. Once, after two hours with only one vodka-fumed bum panhandling for spare change, he'd considered that he might achieve his goal more easily by getting out of his car and walking around. After all, what was more vulnerable than a lone man at night in an unfamiliar, dangerous neighborhood (except, of course, a lone woman)? And yet it was so hard to will himself out of the warm safety of his car, away from the toasty comfort of the heated seats and the familiar smell of clean leather. How strange and fearful death is, even when one wishes to die!

But it was time. Or as the Americans said, "Now or never." Mohanlal got out of his car before he had time to stop himself and walked toward the end of the alleyway, head down against both the cold and his own cowardice. Only when he reached the menacingly dark and silent car did he stop and look up. His potential murderer had gotten out of his car, too—a BMW, like his own!—and was standing with his arms folded across his chest as if waiting. Waiting for him?

And then Mohanlal saw that the man was in fact waiting for him, because he also saw, with bewildered astonishment, that the man was his own son.

"Hi, dad," Matthew said. "I know you've been coming here almost every night for the past three weeks. It's easy to track people these days. Though of course you already know that."

And all of a sudden, Mohanlal knew that his son knew *he* knew—about the missing money, about the private investigator. About the fateful envelope and what had been inside. And also all of a sudden, Mohanlal wanted to tell his son that there was still time—that they could come up with the money somehow, no matter how much it was. That he could quit working for that greedy huckster and do something worthwhile with his life, that there was still time for him and Padma and the kids. That Mohanlal forgave him—

But Matthew was pulling something from the inside pocket of his coat. A gun. A big, menacing-looking, American gun.

"What?" Matthew smiled, his voice coming to his father from far-away, as if from across a very big, very empty room. "You think your foolish friends are loyal to you, father? They're loyal to money, just like everyone else. When you wouldn't tell your friend at the bank what all of my missing money was for, he called me. Was sure I had some hot stock tip to pass along. Funny, isn't it? Didn't take too long after that to find out about the private investigator. I kept waiting for you to call me into your office like you used to do when I was a kid, to sit me down and pull your eyebrows together the way you always did when you were *really* about to let me have it. But I guess I'm not a kid anymore, am I, dad?"

"Matthew, listen—"

"Of course, I had to scrap the whole plan after that. Too risky. To be honest, I didn't know what the hell I was going to do. But then I found out you were driving way across town and just sitting here in this alleyway every night, almost as if you *wanted* something bad to happen to you!"

"Matthew, please listen—!"

"I kind of wanted to wait around just to see what would happen. Maybe fate would work things out okay, one way or another. But I don't have any more time, dad. Time's been up for me for quite some time, actually. It's not just the house and all the rest. It's... it's everything. I could go to prison, dad, if I don't come up with a lot of money in a lot of hurry. Of course, Padma knows nothing about any of this."

Matthew gave his eyes a savage swipe with the sleeve of his coat, and Mohanlal saw that he was crying. He couldn't recall the last time he'd seen his son crying, not even when his mother had died. Come to think of it, Mohanlal hadn't cried then, either, wanting to be strong for (as strong as?) his son.

Thoughts, memories, stories rushed Mohanlal's over-worked brain—the monkey with the looking glass! The dead man with a smile on his face! He pressed his hands against the side of his head to steady himself, but the delay had been a fateful one—that word again!

Matthew was pointing the gun straight at his father's chest.

"No missing money to account for now, dad, especially after a big chunk went to that private investigator of yours to get him out of the picture. No shady hit men or suspicious phone calls. Just an old man in an alleyway in the wrong part of town. Maybe lost his way, or who knows? Maybe out looking for a prostitute. Happens every hour of every day in alleyways just like this one, all across the country."

All of a sudden—and what was it with these "all of a sudden" realizations, when suddenly, they're all too late?—Mohanlal saw his son on trial for his life. He saw that the cops and the police detectives would put it all together—of course they would! They'd uncover both the private investigator and whatever financial trouble Matthew had gotten into. They'd trace the money—always the money!—all the way back to its source. To a million dollar life insurance policy with only one beneficiary. He saw—actually *saw*, not imagined, not feared, but *saw*—his son sitting in prison, and not some cushy federal one for white-collar frauds and crooks, either.

Mohanlal raised his hands in the air like a criminal in one of the cops-and-robbers shows his wife used to watch on television. He had to make his son listen. He had to make him understand—

But he knew that it was suddenly, fatefully too late.

"Maybe I dreamed too much," was all that Mohanlal could say.

"No, dad. Maybe you just dreamed the wrong dream," was all that his son could reply.

The next day, when they found Mohanlal Malhorta's body, there wasn't even the faintest trace of a smile on the dead man's face.

Heart of Stone
by
Roxanne Dent

When I traveled to Europe for the first time, I did all the typical tourist things. I enjoyed the local cuisine, sat in cafes sipping cappuccinos as I read guide books, and visited art museums and churches. In Rome, I greatly admired Michelangelo's *David*, but as far as I was concerned it was nothing more than a beautiful piece of sculpture. It wasn't until I went to France that a bizarre obsession overtook me.

Chantelle, my cheerful tour guide, knew of my interest in mysteries and all things supernatural. She suggested I visit the hilltop church at Rennes le-Chateau dedicated to St. Mary Magdalene.

"The church is in the south, near the village of Couiza. You can take a train or a bus and a taxi will take you the rest of the way." She smiled. "It's the one mentioned in *The Da Vinci Code*."

Like a zillion others, I'd avidly read the book. "Have you been there?" I asked, intrigued.

"Once," she admitted.

"What did you think?"

She gave me a Gallic shrug. "It has a certain... how do you say? Atmosphere."

"It sounds intriguing."

"There is much controversy, but if you like such things, you will enjoy it, and the countryside is beautiful with many Roman ruins and limestone caves."

My curiosity aroused, I arrived two days later.

It was late afternoon and foggy. The extensive stone buildings were spread out across the top of a hill. The fog made it appear as if they were resting in the clouds, a veritable Shangri La.

Inside the church on the left was a crouching statue of the horned-demon Asmodeus. He wore a green tunic and gold belt. He had cloven hoofs and his membranous wings were half-opened, supporting the Holy Water Stoup. He guarded what was supposed to be the accursed treasures of King Solomon. Above his head was a base decorated with two salamanders and a red oval cartouche. It read, *Par Ce Signe Tu Le Vaincras*—By This Sign You Will Conquer Him. The statue was absolutely terrifying. Adults on the tour looked away. Little children whimpered and begged to leave.

As the group moved off, I stood still, mesmerized. It was only a statue made by man, but I felt its charisma. Asmodeus' eyes were piercing and seemed to follow me about. I recalled the King of Demons aroused anger and vengeful desires, inciting humans to evil acts. He also had a reputation as a demon of lust. I fell under his spell that fall afternoon.

I'm not a Satanist, nor do I belong to a cult, but I kept going back. I would stare at the statue for hours. At times, I swore his hideous features softened toward me. The locals thought me mad.

I was.

I didn't care about the scrolls or hidden treasures Abbe' Beranger Sauniere supposedly discovered while renovating the church. There were times when I swore Asmodeus' cruel lips parted in a lustful grin. It was crazy. I was in love with the King of Demons.

Eventually, I had to go home. The time I spent away from Asmodeus was bleak, devoid of color or life. I saw friends, went to work, watched television and read, but I couldn't concentrate. All I could think about was the next time I would see him.

Tormented, I called Beth, a friend from college. We met for dinner. Over a glass of wine, I related what happened to me in France. I admitted I couldn't rid myself of my fixation. Her eyebrows shot up. After more wine, she told me, "You should see a therapist, Jane. This obsession could be dangerous."

Sadly, I didn't take her advice. I decided the only way to break my bizarre fantasy was to give myself over to it completely. I went online and purchased the Rosetta Stone Series. Learning to speak fluent French, I cashed in my IRA and all my savings. The following year, I moved to the little village of Couiza, where I visited the church of St. Mary Magdalene every day.

I'd been in Couiza for two months when it happened. Asmodeus spoke to me. It was nearly closing time, my favorite time of day when the church was empty and full of shadows.

An amused voice asked, "Do you love me?"

Startled, I looked around, but saw no one. When I looked up, Asmodeus' eyes gleamed in the semi-darkness of the church. I blinked, thinking I was imagining things.

"Do you love me?" he repeated in a booming voice.

I fell to my knees. "I do."

"It's been a while since anyone loved me, and even longer since I loved anyone."

"You loved someone?" I asked, surprised.

"You find it hard to believe?"

"Well, you are the King of Demons."

"And as such I have a heart of stone?" he bellowed.

"Who was she?" I asked, jealous.

"Sarah, daughter of Rachel."

"From biblical times. That was a long time ago. She must have been beautiful."

"She was. And her heart was pure, purer than yours."

I felt an irrational surge of anger and jealousy. "What happened to her?"

"Her family disapproved, as you may imagine," he said dryly. "They called on my enemy, the angel Raphael, who used trickery to banish me. Sarah was forced to marry another."

"Did you ever love again?" I asked breathlessly, my heart pounding in my ribs so I could hardly breathe.

He stared at me with those devilish eyes that seared my soul. "Stand up, Jane."

I stood trembling before him. I was thrilled he knew my name, yet at the same time wanted to turn away and race out of the church.

"Look at me."

His eyes bore into me, stripping away layers of defense until his black soul touched mine. I cried out in horror. It felt like hundreds of insects were crawling all over me.

"I know what your dreams are, what you lust after," he leered.

"I... I'm not after the treasure," I sobbed.

I felt dirty, nauseas and violated, unable to move.

I heard a soft, fluttering sound, as if Asmodeus was stretching his wings. The doors of the church swung open and a cold wind blew down the aisles.

"Your arrogance knows no bounds," he said scornfully.

The candles flickered. I could hear the saints and angels praying for my soul, their voices like the murmuring of hundreds of medieval monks.

For the first time in my life, I fainted.

A guard on his rounds found me sprawled on the floor. He called for an ambulance, but I woke up and insisted on going home. As I staggered out of the church, I risked a look back. In the dark I saw only the form of a crouching, plaster statue.

It took me three days before I returned, drawn by a force within I couldn't control.

The church was crowded with tourists and parishioners who eventually departed. The statue never moved. I nearly left with the last tourist, convinced I'd imagined the bizarre episode. I rose from the pew, but as I reached the entrance, I sensed movement by the door and froze.

"Back, I see," Asmodeus said dryly. I let out a shriek and dropped my shoulder bag, the contents spilling all over the marble floor.

"Tell me, Jane, how many men have you loved who were liars, abusers, thieves, and even murderers?"

"I… I don't know what you mean," I stammered.

"Poor, plain Jane. You told yourself you were ignorant of their true nature until it was too late. Admit it, you loved the danger, the excitement, the thrill you got from believing your love could reform them." His voice turned soft, sensuous. "Think what a coup it would be if your love reformed the King of Demons."

I gasped. "Impossible."

"Is it? Then why did you give up everything to come here and spend hours staring at me with love-sick eyes?"

I backed away. "You're not real. This isn't happening."

"Coward! You awakened me, and now I need your help."

I was shaking, but he had my attention. "My help?"

"When that fool Sauniere first ordered the statue and the artist Giscard, a Freemason, created it, the priest did it to bind my spirit so he could access the treasures." He bent toward me. "You will free me by your sacrifice."

Terror gripped me. It was hard to speak. "What sacrifice?"

"What sacrifice could be greater, Jane, then releasing me from my plaster prison in this morbid place, so I can begin my reign on earth again with you by my side?"

"No," I whimpered.

Chuckling, he whispered, "Don't be afraid."

I wanted to run, but against my will, my feet brought me closer to him. I felt his wings encircle me, the smell of mold and crushed hopes smothering me.

"Together, we shall travel the world. I shall reveal to you a tapestry of such terrible beauty you will weep, Jane. You will see things no human has ever seen, be a witness to such evil, such filth you will want to pluck out your eyes. But you won't be able to turn away. And you will have all eternity to reform me if you wish. Isn't that what you envisioned?" His mocking laughter reverberated around the church, making the stained-glass windows rattle.

I managed to break his hold and run, but it was too late.

The doors slammed shut and locked. I pounded on them, screaming and sobbing, but no one came.

As I turned around, I nearly fainted a second time. Out of the mouth of Asmodeus came a swirling red mist that stank of sulphur and rotting flesh. I retched. Everywhere the mist went, it left drops of blood that sizzled when they hit the floor. I whimpered. It was coming for me.

I ran, ducking between the pews, but the evil vapor snaked along the icy floor, taking its time, knowing I was trapped, leaving bloody, cloven hoof prints behind.

I tried the door that led into the back, but it was locked. I kept moving just out of reach.

Avoiding the pools of blood as best I could, I knew I couldn't keep it up much longer. When I stepped close to the gore, the stinking mess bubbled up, hissing, reaching out as if to pull me in.

The image of Asmodeus suddenly rose up from the festering blood to tower over me.

"Am I not a handsome fellow? Do I not make your heart beat faster, plain Jane?" he mocked.

"Stop calling me that," I screamed. "Keep away from me!"

He reached out a claw-like hand. I climbed over the raised dais where the sacraments were given and collapsed at the feet of an angel.

The sound of peeling bells rent the air, nearly shattering my eardrums. The doors flew open, letting in the last rays of the late afternoon sun. I thought I saw an angel holding a golden sword. I heard the demon howl with rage as the red mist rolled backward and into the statue's mouth.

A guard stepped in and crossed himself. Two late tourists looked in behind him and gasped.

Now that Asmodeus was gone, I felt the pain of what I'd done. I lay crouched in a pool of my own blood. In my hand was a jagged chunk of Asmodeus' tunic, which I'd used to cut myself. My arms, legs, and neck were bleeding from dozens of wounds. I was laughing and crying at the same time and couldn't stop. It took two burly men to pry the piece of plaster I'd used to slash myself out of my hands.

They took me to the nearest hospital and shot me full of drugs. It took a while for me to stop screaming. When they finally released me a few months later, I discovered they hadn't charged me with destruction of property, but I was forbidden to enter the church again. I left France and returned to Boston.

Once home, I made an appointment with a therapist, eventually admitting Asmodeus was a figment of my imagination. She assured me it was a symptom of my illness, which had its roots in an unhappy childhood, and brutal and unrequited love affairs, triggering a mental collapse.

I almost believed it.

When I was home, I left the television on. In order to sleep through the night, I took sleeping pills, ignoring the chilling voice in my dreams that called to me to return to Rennes le-Chateau.

Yellow Bullet
by
Joe Sherry

It wasn't so bad at first. If nothing else, he still got to be behind the twenty-inch wheel of Bullet. To everyone else, she was just Bus 33, but to Tom Walsch, she—yes, *she*, was Bullet. Most of the company's buses had been retired and replaced with newer models, but Tom had fought to keep Bullet, and he had won the battle. At the end of the day, if a driver's bus ran, and he wanted to keep driving it, there was no reason to spend eighty-thousand dollars on a new one. They were always trying to stay under budget anyway, so Tom was doing them a favor. And Tom had no shame in admitting that he was attached to her. Bullet was sturdy and dependable, and for a fifteen-ton school bus, she could go when she wanted to. She could really *go*.

But why did that moron Emma, in the office, have to give him the one route that went down Ontario Street and turned onto Bradley Road? Didn't she know what she was putting him through? Didn't she know what he had to deal with? It wasn't even that he just had to pass his house, his *old* house, *her* house. *Their* house. But he had to stop at the sign at the end of Ontario and stare at the house directly across from him while he waited for an opening in traffic. It was torture and it made him sick. Some mornings he even saw Don, Jenn's new husband. He had a mustache, and not even a good one. It was sparse and looked half-assed. How could a guy who couldn't even grow a proper mustache be living in his house with his wife and his daughter? Well, his *ex*-house and his *ex*-wife. But Colleen would still be Tom's daughter and they couldn't take that from him, although they tried their best, telling the courts that he was unbalanced, that he—

"Mr. Walsch?"

"Hmm?" he said, hearing the small voice in the seat behind him.

"You, um, passed Tara's house."

Damn, he thought. *See what they did? They made me mess up. I never missed a kid before, not in sixteen years of driving.* Tom used the cul-de-sac on Broadway to turn around and pick up Tara, the small redhead that lived on Grimly Lane.

When he came out of the outlet onto Main, Tom saw his daughter, Colleen. He raised his hand to wave, but she wasn't looking toward him, and he didn't want to startle her by honking. Colleen was peddling leisurely to school on the pink bike that Don had bought her, her purple backpack bouncing merrily and, dammit, where was the backpack he had bought her? The bag was only a year old, and it couldn't have been worn out. But they had to replace it. They had to try and erase all signs of him from his daughter's life. And the gray sky threatened rain at any moment, why wasn't she on his bus? She was on his route. It would be nice driving her to school. She could have sat in the seat right behind him and talked to him, telling him about her day. But *they* probably wouldn't let her. *They*—

"Mr. Walsch?" this time the voice was louder, not so timid.

"WHAT?" he asked, louder than he'd expected to.

"It's just—"

"I'm sorry," he said, "I didn't mean to shout." He took the volume of his voice down and tried to sound cheerful. "What is it?" He had always been one of the kids' favorite drivers, and he didn't want to risk his reputation just because he was dealing with some… personal issues.

"You passed Tara's house." The girl paused before adding, "Again."

Tom gritted his teeth and took a deep breath before speaking.

"No. I didn't. I just wanted to pick her up in the same direction that I have been for the rest of the week. Okay?"

"Okay, I guess," the little girl said, relenting.

"You don't need to guess, Susan, I've been doing this for longer than you've been alive. I think I can do it without your help."

"You don't need to be so mean, Mr. Walsch. We're going to be late—"

"We are NOT going to be late," he said, opening his service door and activating the red stop lights to let Tara onto the bus.

"Fine," Susan said curtly.

Tom felt bad. He had only been Susan's driver for a week, but he was already fond of her. He was fond of them all. But if she was mad at him, fine. He had forty-six other children on the bus—he couldn't be too worried about a single student.

"Good morning, Tara," he said to the small red-headed girl.

"Good morning, Mr. Walsch," she said cheerily, "you got here just in time. It's starting to rain."

See, he thought. *At least Tara still likes me.* Then he thought about Colleen, and hoped she got out of the rain before it got worse.

Tom turned onto Oak Street and picked up a freckled boy wearing a Patriots hoodie.

"Nice sweatshirt, Kevin," he said.

"Thanks, Mr. Walsch."

"Going to watch the game Sunday?"

"I guess so," he said, shrugging, "if I can't play Madden."

"It should be a good game," Tom said. Kevin didn't answer. He had already walked to the rear of the bus and sat down.

Kevin's in a mood today, Tom thought. He glanced into his overhead mirror and looked at the heads that sprung up between the seats like gophers popping up from their holes. They all looked so young. Tom had started driving before Jenn even got pregnant with Colleen. It was supposed to be a temporary job, something he'd do until he could save up enough money to open up his own business, a sports card store. The twelve dollars an hour he'd been paid when he first started driving bus seemed good enough, but the hours were never there. As soon as he'd get a little ahead on bills, there would be a snow day, or a weeklong vacation, and he'd have to spend the little money he'd saved in order to stay afloat. It was the perfect job to keep a man and a small family in permanent financial stasis. It was no wonder his wife had finally decided to walk away from their marriage. Don had his own business. A construction business, of all things. Don had Tom's wife. Don had *everything*. Except for a decent mustache.

Tom had driven enough years to see kids grow up, go to college, and then return home for Christmas and summer vacations, where he would invariably run into them at the supermarket or, a couple times, at Rick's Tavern. It was strange. He could always see the ghosts of the kids he'd driven in his forty-foot bus, and when he'd run into former riders he would walk over and say hello, trying to make small talk and see what they'd been doing with their lives. If they were alone, they were usually cordial, although they rarely remembered his name (or pretended not to), but God forbid if they were with friends. They looked mortified that their old *bus driver* would have the audacity to actually approach them as they sucked down their pissy little Bud Lights. After the third time, Tom had learned his lesson and nursed his Pabst in the dark corner of Rick's, not even acknowledging the kids he had watched grow up on either side of the school day.

Tom stopped and picked up Phil, a boy who was plump for his age, but who was always quick with a joke or passing around a gag or prop: sometimes a rubber spider that made the girls scream, or maybe rubber vomit that grossed everyone out. Tom had seen his type pass through the aisle of Bullet many times in sixteen years, and although they would probably annoy most drivers trying to keep order on the bus, they were usually Tom's personal favorites. Phil, and some of the other boys like him—and they were always boys—developed their senses of humor and repertoires in an effort to deflect attention from their weight. In most cases, it worked. If a boy was funny, charming, and made you laugh, the fact that he wore jeans made for husky boys meant little to his peers.

"Mr. Walsch is being a total ass this morning," Susan whispered.

Tom heard her, and thought of reprimanding her for language, but stopped himself. He wanted to hear what she had to say. He was surprised to hear Tara giggle.

"He's so funny," Tara whispered back. "Do you see the way he combs his hair over the top? Does he think no one notices that he's a total cue ball under those four long hairs?"

They weren't even being subtle! Tom wanted to say something, to let them know he could hear them, but he didn't. He felt like a fool. He gripped Bullet's wheel tighter, and as his knuckles grew whiter, his face grew redder.

Tom thought about the ridiculous way youth inoculated children to the aging process: they giggled and laughed at parents and older people, not realizing that the gun of life fired them in the same forward direction, and the only possible protection they would have from growing old was dying when they were still young. There was a disconnect where kids didn't understand that grown-ups had been kids themselves. They made fun of adults and then they fell into the same trap of adulthood and responsibility. They didn't get it—they never did, until it was too late, and only the mist of youth remained.

Tom let his mind wander about the children. He wondered if Phil would grow up and resent his weight, becoming one of those people that overcompensated for being the fat guy: working out (probably too much), eating healthy (but probably too little) in an effort to never be big again. Or maybe Phil would grow into one of those jolly, fat adults who was actually comfortable with his weight and who he was.

Tom glanced into his overhead mirror again and wished he could tell them all that they weren't safe, ahead of them life held heartbreak, lost jobs, the deaths of people they loved and their own deaths, but it would do no good. They would laugh and look down at their phones—they never put them down—and they would use their time like they had an infinite amount to spend. He could almost hear them whispering, *We'll never be old like you, Mr. Walsch. We'll never be bald like you. We'll never have wives, and even if we did, they would never leave us.*

Tom took his left hand off the wheel to run it through the wisps of black hair that remained on his crown and sighed deeply. It seemed like everyone behind him was laughing, and he wondered how many of them were laughing at him. Everything seemed so loud. The high androgynous voices of the children blurred together and his head started to ache. He imagined a volume knob that he could turn down, clipping their voices, but it didn't work. If anything, they seemed even louder.

Tom went down Ontario and stopped at the stop sign. He realized that he had circled back without thinking about it—his mind and the bus were in an orbit around his house. His *ex*-house. Tom looked straight ahead and saw that both Jenn's Prius and Don's Ford F-350, the one with the stupid magnets on the side reading *Don's Home Improvements*, sat in the driveway. Tom loved the way some men were about their trucks, especially the big ones like 350s, obviously trying to prove something to themselves and the world. They always thought they were riding high. He liked to look down at them from Bullet's throne with a smile that said, *Mine is bigger than yours.* Don's truck wouldn't stand a chance against Bullet. It must be nice having your own business, not having to get up at five in the morning and turning on the TV just to find out that school had been canceled, and that your check was going to be twenty percent less than you wanted—hell, than you *needed*—it to be.

It was 7:28. He bet Don and Jenn were inside the kitchen right at the front of the house, listening to the gentle rain patter against the window while he drove a bunch of unappreciative little boogers to school.

"Mr. Walsch," Susan said, "it's already seven-thirty, and I told you we were going to be late. This isn't even the right direction!"

"Shut up," he said quietly.

"But—"

"Shut. Up." he repeated, softly but with finality.

Susan and the rest of the bus didn't push their luck: they shut up. Tom passed his ex-wife's house and drove around to the school as the light drizzle gave way to a downpour.

"Base to bus thirty-three, over," the CB radio squelched.

"This is bus thirty-three," Tom said.

"Tom, where are you? The vice-principal of Kennedy Middle just called."

"Are you kidding? I'm only running five minutes behind."

"Well, when the bell rings and the kids aren't in school, they tend to get worried. Over."

"Whatever. I'm pulling in now."

"Fine. Come by the office after you park your bus. Over."

Tom couldn't help glancing into the overhead mirror at the kids. A couple of them snickered at the reprimand. Tom depressed the brake pedal hard, stopping abruptly in front of the red brick middle school. The kids, not seat belted in, jerked forward. Alan, a constant pain in the ass, spilled some of the orange juice he was drinking onto the front of his shirt and then onto the floor of the bus. Tom was responsible for cleaning his own bus, but it was worth cleaning a sticky floor to see the smug look wiped off the boy's face.

A tall teacher stood in the rain, ushering the kids out of the bus while still finding time to send angry looks at Tom. Tom shrugged in a 'sorry, couldn't be helped' manner. When the bus was empty, Tom didn't bother doing his post-bus inspection. He wasn't in the mood.

Tom pulled the bus away from the curb and listened to the heavy rain drops pound the metal of Bullet's roof.

It wasn't enough to take my wife, my house, and daughter from me, he thought. *Now Don is causing me to mess up at work.*

Tom didn't want to admit it to himself, but the job was all he had left. Without Jenn, and without Colleen, Bullet was the only woman in his life. When he left work to go home, his studio apartment was actually smaller than Bullet's interior cabin. He didn't think they would let him go for being a little late, but he was going to get hell for it. Even an older bus like Bullet had a GPS installed so the office could keep an eye on the exact routes and even the speed at which the buses traveled. Normally, he didn't mind. Tom Walsch did what he was supposed to do, and when you do what you're supposed to, who cares if you're being watched? The same went for the small camera affixed at the front of the bus. He looked up and smiled at it.

Tom didn't go straight back to the lot. He didn't feel like talking to Emma, his supervisor, and he didn't feel like being talked down to by a woman half his age who said all the right things and made all the right political decisions to climb the ranks and become the manager. Hell, it was her fault for putting him on this run in the first place.

He circled the small town a final time before coming back to Ontario Street. He left the bus running and put Bullet into neutral. Even from a quarter mile he could see the happy couple's driveway, and the two vehicles still parked there. The driveway he had spent a hot summer day patching with black asphalt.

Sitting at the table in the house, that he, Tom, had borrowed the money from his parents to buy, and where Don now lived, and slept with his wife, and sat at the kitchen table sipping coffee, probably using the coffee maker that Tom bought when—

Enough, Tom thought. *My problem is I never act, I only react, isn't that what Jenn told me? Isn't that why she couldn't be with a bus driver anymore? Maybe it's time I acted.*

"What do you say, sweetheart?" Tom said, lovingly patting Bullet's dash. "Want to have a little fun?" Tom gave her a little gas, and she purred approvingly.

Part of Tom felt bad. Odds were Bullet wouldn't be salvaged, but really, that was the least of his worries. She was old and had run a good life, and she wouldn't last forever anyway. They would go out together. All four of them. The rain came down harder, and it felt like even the rain was egging him on. Tom shifted Bullet into drive and pressed the metal pedal all the way to the floor. The orange needle of the speedometer jumped clockwise as Tom fired Bullet toward his ex-wife's house.

The wheels found traction on the wet pavement and her speed climbed to 20 miles per hour, and then 30. Tom thought of his daughter and felt a twinge of regret. She would be an orphan—he and her mother would be gone. And Don. Well, at least his daughter wouldn't be raised by that scum bucket. It was worth it.

Bullet was all the way up to 45 as she crossed Bradley. Time slowed down, and Tom realized he was grinning. He was finally doing what he wanted to do, what he *needed* to do. And he wouldn't even be stuck cleaning up that brat Alan's orange juice!

As the bus jumped the curb in front of the house at 50 miles per hour, he caught a glimpse of the pink bike with a flat tire by the side of the house. Time slowed to a crawl as Tom's mind reeled. She shouldn't be home, she should be at school. She should be—

Tom slammed his foot on the brake, but even if it hadn't been raining, he wouldn't have had a chance of slowing the bus, let alone stopping it. Bullet could go when she wanted to. She could really *go*.

The Outsider
by
H.P. Lovecraft

originally published in *Weird Tales*, 1926

Unhappy is he to whom the memories of childhood bring only fear and sadness. Wretched is he who looks back upon lone hours in vast and dismal chambers with brown hangings and maddening rows of antique books, or upon awed watches in twilight groves of grotesque, gigantic, and vine-encumbered trees that silently wave twisted branches far aloft. Such a lot the gods gave to me—to me, the dazed, the disappointed; the barren, the broken. And yet I am strangely content and cling desperately to those sere memories, when my mind momentarily threatens to reach beyond to the other.

I know not where I was born, save that the castle was infinitely old and infinitely horrible, full of dark passages and having high ceilings where the eye could find only cobwebs and shadows. The stones in the crumbling corridors seemed always hideously damp, and there was an accursed smell everywhere, as of the piled-up corpses of dead generations. It was never light, so that I used sometimes to light candles and gaze steadily at them for relief, nor was there any sun outdoors, since the terrible trees grew high above the topmost accessible tower. There was one black tower which reached above the trees into the unknown outer sky, but that was partly ruined and could not be ascended save by a well-nigh impossible climb up the sheer wall, stone by stone.

I must have lived years in this place, but I cannot measure the time. Beings must have cared for my needs, yet I cannot recall any person except myself, or anything alive but the noiseless rats and bats and spiders. I think that whoever nursed me must have been shockingly aged, since my first conception of a living person was that of somebody mockingly like myself, yet distorted, shriveled, and decaying like the castle. To me there was nothing grotesque in the bones and skeletons that strewed some of the stone crypts deep down among the foundations. I fantastically associated these things with everyday events, and thought them more natural than the colored pictures of living beings which I found in many of the moldy books. From such books I learned all that I know. No teacher urged or guided me, and I do not recall hearing any human voice in all those years—not even my own; for although I had read of speech, I had never thought to try to speak aloud. My aspect was a matter equally unthought of, for there were no mirrors in the castle, and I merely regarded myself by instinct as akin to the youthful figures I saw drawn and painted in the books. I felt conscious of youth because I remembered so little.

Outside, across the putrid moat and under the dark mute trees, I would often lie and dream for hours about what I read in the books; and would longingly picture myself amidst gay crowds in the sunny world beyond the endless forests. Once I tried to escape from the forest, but as I went farther from the castle the shade grew denser and the air more filled with brooding fear; so that I ran frantically back lest I lose my way in a labyrinth of nighted silence.

So through endless twilights I dreamed and waited, though I knew not what I waited for. Then in the shadowy solitude my longing for light grew so frantic that I could rest no more, and I lifted entreating hands to the single black ruined tower that reached above the forest into the unknown outer sky. And at last I resolved to scale that tower, fall though I might; since it were better to glimpse the sky and perish, than to live without ever beholding day.

In the dank twilight I climbed the worn and aged stone stairs till I reached the level where they ceased, and thereafter clung perilously to small footholds leading upward. Ghastly and terrible was that dead, stairless cylinder of rock; black, ruined, and deserted, and sinister with startled bats whose wings made no noise. But more ghastly and terrible still was the slowness of my progress; for climb as I might, the darkness overhead grew no thinner, and a new chill as of haunted and venerable mold assailed me. I shivered as I wondered why I did not reach the light, and would have looked down had I dared. I fancied that night had come suddenly upon me, and vainly groped with one free hand for a window embrasure, that I might peer out and above, and try to judge the height I had once attained.

All at once, after an infinity of awesome, sightless crawling up that concave and desperate precipice, I felt my head touch a solid thing, and I knew I must have gained the roof, or at least some kind of floor. In the darkness I raised my free hand and tested the barrier, finding it stone and immovable. Then came a deadly circuit of the tower, clinging to whatever holds the slimy wall could give; till finally my testing hand found the barrier yielding, and I turned upward again, pushing the slab or door with my head as I used both hands in my fearful ascent. There was no light revealed above, and as my hands went higher I knew that my climb was for the nonce ended; since the slab was the trapdoor of an aperture leading to a level stone surface of greater circumference than the lower tower, no doubt the floor of some lofty and capacious observation chamber. I crawled through carefully, and tried to prevent the heavy slab from falling back into place, but failed in the latter attempt. As I lay exhausted on the stone floor, I heard the eerie echoes of its fall, hoped when necessary to pry it up again.

Believing I was now at prodigious height, far above the accursed branches of the wood, I dragged myself up from the floor and fumbled about for windows, that I might look for the first time upon the sky, and the moon and stars of which I had read. But on every hand I was disappointed; since all that I found were vast shelves of marble, bearing odious oblong boxes of disturbing size. More and more I reflected, and wondered what hoary secrets might abide in this high apartment so many eons cut off from the castle below. Then unexpectedly my hands came upon a doorway, where hung a portal of stone, rough with strange chiseling. Trying it, I found it locked; but with a supreme burst of strength I overcame all obstacles and dragged it open inward. As I did so there came to me the purest ecstasy I have ever known; for shining tranquilly through an ornate grating of iron, and down a short stone passageway of steps that ascended from the newly found doorway, was the radiant full moon, which I had never before seen save in dreams and in vague visions I dared not call memories.

Fancying now that I had attained the very pinnacle of the castle, I commenced to rush up the few steps beyond the door; but the sudden veiling of the moon by a cloud caused me to stumble, and I felt my way more slowly in the dark. It was still very dark when I reached the grating, which I tried carefully and found unlocked, but which I did not open for fear of falling from the amazing height to which I had climbed. Then the moon came out.

Most demoniacal of all shocks is that of the abysmally unexpected and grotesquely unbelievable. Nothing I had before undergone could compare in terror with what I now saw; with the bizarre marvels that sight implied. The sight itself was as simple as it was stupefying, for it was merely this: instead of a dizzying prospect of treetops seen from a lofty eminence, there stretched around me on the level through the grating nothing less than the solid ground, decked and diversified by marble slabs and columns, and overshadowed by an ancient stone church, whose ruined spire gleamed spectrally in the moonlight.

Half unconscious, I opened the grating and staggered out upon the white gravel path that stretched away in two directions. My mind, stunned and chaotic as it was, still held the frantic craving for light; and not even the fantastic wonder which had happened could stay my course. I neither knew nor cared whether my experience was insanity, dreaming, or magic; but was determined to gaze on brilliance and gaiety at any cost. I knew not who I was or what I was, or what my surroundings might be; though as I continued to stumble along I became conscious of a kind of fearsome latent memory that made my progress not wholly fortuitous. I passed under an arch out of that region of slabs and columns, and wandered through the open country; sometimes following the visible road, but sometimes leaving it curiously to tread across meadows where only occasional ruins bespoke the ancient presence of a forgotten road. Once I swam across a swift river where crumbling, mossy masonry told of a bridge long vanished.

Over two hours must have passed before I reached what seemed to be my goal, a venerable ivied castle in a thickly wooded park, maddeningly familiar, yet full of perplexing strangeness to me. I saw that the moat was filled in, and that some of the well-known towers were demolished, whilst new wings existed to confuse the beholder. But what I observed with chief interest and delight were the open windows, gorgeously ablaze with light and sending forth sound of the gayest revelry. Advancing to one of these I looked in and saw an oddly dressed company indeed; making merry, and speaking brightly to one another. I had never, seemingly, heard human speech before and could guess only vaguely what was said. Some of the faces seemed to hold expressions that brought up incredibly remote recollections, others were utterly alien.

I now stepped through the low window into the brilliantly lighted room, stepping as I did so from my single bright moment of hope to my blackest convulsion of despair and realization. The nightmare was quick to come, for as I entered, there occurred immediately one of the most terrifying demonstrations I had ever conceived. Scarcely had I crossed the sill when there descended upon the whole company a sudden and unheralded fear of hideous intensity, distorting every face and evoking the most horrible screams from nearly every throat. Flight was universal, and in the clamor and panic several fell in a swoon and were dragged away by their madly fleeing companions. Many covered their eyes with their hands, and plunged blindly and awkwardly in their race to escape, overturning furniture and stumbling against the walls before they managed to reach one of the many doors.

The cries were shocking; and as I stood in the brilliant apartment alone and dazed, listening to their vanishing echoes, I trembled at the thought of what might be lurking near me unseen. At a casual inspection the room seemed deserted, but when I moved towards one of the alcoves I thought I detected a presence there, a hint of motion beyond the golden-arched doorway leading to another and somewhat similar room. As I approached the arch I began to perceive the presence more clearly; and then, with the first and last sound I ever uttered, a ghastly ululation that revolted me almost as poignantly as its noxious cause. I beheld in full, frightful vividness the inconceivable, indescribable, and unmentionable monstrosity which had by its simple appearance changed a merry company to a herd of delirious fugitives.

I cannot even hint what it was like, for it was a compound of all that is unclean, uncanny, unwelcome, abnormal, and detestable. It was the ghoulish shade of decay, antiquity, and dissolution; the putrid, dripping eidolon of unwholesome revelation, the awful baring of that which the merciful earth should always hide. God knows it was not of this world, or no longer of this world, yet to my horror I saw in its eaten-away and bone-revealing outlines a leering, abhorrent travesty on the human shape; and in its moldy, disintegrating apparel an unspeakable quality that chilled me even more.

I was almost paralyzed, but not too much so to make a feeble effort towards flight; a backward stumble which failed to break the spell in which the nameless, voiceless monster held me. My eyes bewitched by the glassy orbs which stared loathsomely into them, refused to close; though they were mercifully blurred, and showed the terrible object but indistinctly after the first shock. I tried to raise my hand to shut out the sight, yet so stunned were my nerves that my arm could not fully obey my will. The attempt, however, was enough to disturb my balance; so that I had to stagger forward several steps to avoid falling. As I did so I became suddenly and agonizingly aware of the nearness of the carrion thing, whose hideous hollow breathing I half fancied I could hear. Nearly mad, I found myself yet able to throw out a hand to ward off the fetid apparition which pressed so close; when in one cataclysmic second of cosmic nightmarishness and hellish accident my fingers touched the rotting outstretched paw of the monster beneath the golden arch.

I did not shriek, but all the fiendish ghouls that ride the night wind shrieked for me as in that same second there crashed down upon my mind a single fleeting avalanche of soul-annihilating memory. I knew in that second all that had been; I remembered beyond the frightful castle and the trees, and recognized the altered edifice in which I now stood; I recognized, most terrible of all, the unholy abomination that stood leering before me as I withdrew my sullied fingers from its own.

But in the cosmos there is balm as well as bitterness, and that balm is nepenthe. In the supreme horror of that second I forgot what had horrified me, and the burst of black memory vanished in a chaos of echoing images. In a dream I fled from that haunted and accursed pile, and ran swiftly and silently in the moonlight. When I returned to the churchyard place of marble and went down the steps I found the stone trapdoor immovable; but I was not sorry, for I had hated the antique castle and the trees. Now I ride with the mocking and friendly ghouls on the night wind, and play by day amongst the catacombs of Nephren-Ka in the sealed and unknown valley of Hadoth by the Nile. I know that light is not for me, save that of the moon over the rock tombs of Neb, nor any gaiety save the unnamed feasts of Nitokris beneath the Great Pyramid; yet in my new wildness and freedom I almost welcome the bitterness of alienage.

For although nepenthe has calmed me, I know always that I am an outsider; a stranger in this century and among those who are still men. This I have known ever since I stretched out my fingers to the abomination within that great gilded frame; stretched out my fingers and touched a cold and unyielding surface of polished glass.

An Interview with Samuel X. Slayden
by
Kurt Fawver

Today on *Horror Gateway* we have an ultra-exclusive in-depth interview with Samuel X. Slayden, pseudonym of the reclusive owner and managing editor of Tantalus Press. Tantalus is the publisher of the award-winning and supposedly cursed fiction anthology *Desire*. As of this interview, four of *Desire*'s contributors have committed suicide, three have been institutionalized, two have altogether retired from writing, and one murdered his entire family.

In the following interview, Slayden explains a bit about the anthology's genesis, its curation, and his take on the misfortune that hangs over its pages.

WARNING: Spoilers ahead for anyone who hasn't yet read Desire.

Horror Gateway: At this point, *Desire* has become one of the most recognized works of horror fiction of the last decade. The *New York Times* wrote a piece on it, it's recently entered its third printing, and it's swept every genre award it's been nominated for. So, how did it all begin?

Samuel X. Slayden: As many anthologies do. With a submissions call.

HG: But I assume the call didn't work out as you'd planned, given that you eventually transitioned to invitation?

SXS: The guidelines couldn't have been any clearer: we wanted stories about wanting. Terrible, erosive wanting. The kind of wanting that launches a thousand ships, that topples kingdoms, that drives men and women to slit throats and burn homes.

We wanted to know how far people would go to fulfill a dream and what tainted colors they might see at the end of their rainbows, after they'd shredded their souls to get there. We wanted horror, torment, infernal desire. We wanted irony and the subversive twist of expectation you never saw coming. We wanted Burgess Meredith crying out "It's not fair!" over a pair of broken glasses amidst apocalyptic rubble.

HG: So the problem with the original submissions was substance?

SXS: Style, too. Even the meaning of all existence would be rendered impotent if it was written in incomprehensible gibberish. There was, as most in human endeavor, a tremendous mound of spastic idiocy.

HG: What did you do then? Since the first submissions call didn't work out as well as you'd planned?

SXS: As champions of genre literature and knights of quality fiction for the ages, we at Tantalus Press did what we felt necessary to create our anthology: we selected several of the most prominent and promising writers from the horror writing world and, to make sure the stories they submitted might contain truth beyond truth and wisdom beyond wisdom, we provided them the rare opportunity to experience the darkest shades of desire at our exclusive Tantalus Writer's Retreat and Workshop.

HG: Which is what, exactly?

SXS: An all-expenses paid opportunity for writers to explore the dark corners of themselves and human experience.

HG: Can you give us any details? Did all the writers in *Desire* attend the retreat?

SXS: They did. The first writer we chose to invite to Tantalus was Dane Bushnell. Bushnell was, of course, already quite famous in the horror community, having written the story collections *Cicadrix* and *The Grinding Place* as well as the novel *Bloodstains in a Well-Lit Room*. Bushnell's style is incomparable; he writes like an armored, 800-pound gorilla on a bender, which is to say without reservation and with a brutality rarely seen in prose. No one can package nihilism as well as Bushnell. We had to have him in the anthology. But he didn't take our invitation seriously at first.

HG: Bushnell is a burly guy and, like his characters, has something of a reputation as a churlish strongman. How did you convince him to come?

SXS: Two darts tipped with horse tranquilizer to the neck and he was comfortably bound and gagged in the back on a van, on his way to the retreat.

HG: Isn't that kidnapping?

SXS: No, it's editing. Of the most complex text.

HG: What text is that?

SXS: "Reality." Note the quotation marks. We're all flash fiction.

HG: And you say Bushnell's the nihilist. In any case, he arrived at your retreat. What then?

SXS: At the retreat complex, we strapped him face-down to a table and tore the shirt from his back. Once every hour, we let in visitors—hulking, steroid-enhanced visitors with equally hulking fists—to see him. They were paid to massage Mr. Bushnell the way one of his anti-heroes might massage a confession out of a weaker character. At first, he held his composure, his portly frame steady and unyielding as a steel plate. But over the course of several weeks, the bruises on Bushnell's back ruptured and re-ruptured so many times that the color of his flesh changed from talcum white to the purple-black of death's foul tongue. By the fourth week, Mr. Bushnell cried out for mercy when the fists landed against that hump of clotted blood, pulverized muscle, and shattered bone. But we had to keep pushing. We had to make him not just *cry* for mercy but *desire* mercy in every thought and breath and bead of sweat from his brow. Only then would he be able to pen the sort of story that tilts the axis of the world. So we made sure that Mr.

Bushnell's massage therapy continued for another month. It was our solemn obligation to art.

HG: Do you realize what you're describing?

SXS: A writer's retreat and workshop. And a very successful one, at that.

HG: Also, torture.

SXS: Every writer worth reading would admit that sometimes the creative act must necessarily be torture. Art demands it.

HG: Would you say art is of the highest value to you?

SXS: Art is the only value.

HG: What about human life? Did you cause your authors undue pain and suffering?

SXS: There can be no art without pain, without suffering. It's the great catalyst. Philosophers used to talk about a "Prime Mover" shaping the universe. That mover is suffering.

HG: *Desire* is an incredible anthology, unlike anything I've ever read. But the cost seems steep.

SXS: Our authors didn't understand the dark depths of yearning when they came to us. When they left, they were masters of want. And now you reap the benefits of their understanding in every story.

HG: But Dane Bushnell shot himself after finishing "Machismo" (his story which appears in *Desire*).

SXS: We wanted art for the ages. He gave us such art. A tale of an effeminate boy beaten by bullies so terribly that he desires to grow to gargantuan proportions. A realization of the boy's wish, and his subsequent transformation to a kaiju of sorts. His rampage, his destruction—of not just his oppressors, but his entire town, his loved ones, everything. And that final scene, where he pounds his fists against Mt.

Rainier, bringing it down upon him. *That's* a desire for mercy. It's brilliant. The immortality of Mr. Bushnell's work should be recompense enough for his fate.

HG: I'm not denying the quality of the story—we can feel every ounce of the horrible yearning that throbs from young Tolliver Vix (the main character of "Machismo")—but do you believe your retreat contributed to Mr. Bushnell's suicide?

SXS: As much as anything else in his life. He was a tormented individual.

HG: Did any of the other retreat invitees have an experience similar to Bushnell's?

SXS: Of course. Julian Larchmont was the second writer we invited to the Tantalus workshop.

Note: Larchmont, a professor of creative writing at Cardley College, works exclusively in short form and has released two collections, Lachrymose Retinae and Darwin's Oversight.

SXS: Larchmont's a man of big ideas in small packages. His fiction doesn't sell especially well and is rarely understood, but is always mentioned as some of the most intellectually stimulating in the genre. For instance, in his "Bloodletting," he writes from the perspective of a dying blood cell that's been drained from its host—a host who, we find out by story's end, is the thirteenth victim of a mysterious serial killer; here, Larchmont weaves microcosm and macrocosm together so masterfully that we don't know whether the victim is the cell or the cell is the victim or whether they're both caught up in a system of violence and destruction so vast that the difference between the two is purely academic.

Needless to say, Larchmont is a curious type. We sent him a letter with the list of other attendees and a vague statement of purpose, and he was intrigued enough to show up at our doors without the slightest coaxing.

HG: What was the writing aid you provided to Larchmont?

SXS: We treated him to what all scholars want: knowledge.

HG: Meaning?

SXS: While Mr. Larchmont reclined in a very plush restraining chair, his eyes were forced open and he was fed a nonstop stream of information from around the globe on a theater screen. Stock tickers, sports highlights, pornography of every variety, Twitter feeds, mass emails, commercials for erectile dysfunction, proceedings of Congress, footage of protests in third world nations, videos of beheadings posted by militant groups in the Middle East, Instagram selfies of drunken college kids, *New York Times* book reviews, police blotters filled with domestic abuse, clips from sitcom reruns, clips from the 700 Club, clips from the nightly news: we let it all rush into him. He couldn't blink it away, couldn't avert his gaze. Media saturated, he held on for weeks without making a sound. Then he saw a news report from somewhere in California. It was about a group of youths that set dogs and cats on fire for sport, and it showed the horrific results of those actions. After seeing that report, he began to want. Truly, *want*. You could hear it— a low gurgle in the back of his throat that grew in volume and intensity until he was screaming louder than the booming screen before him. He'd finally found something to desire in that intricate matrix of suffering and banality.

HG: And what was that?

SXS: The very thing he screamed, over and over: "ENOUGH."

HG: Mr. Larchmont is now a committed psychiatric patient at Pallstown State Hospital in western Michigan. You don't believe your retreat had any influence on his mental degradation?

SXS: We didn't create the images we showed Mr. Larchmont. We wanted a serious philosophical story, but we had to pressure his mind to produce one that satisfied us. The results were more than worthwhile, wouldn't you say?

HG: "The Second Trimester of a Stillborn Universe" (Larchmont's contribution to *Desire*) is an astounding piece, yes. I wouldn't have thought omniscient second person point of view could be readable, but Larchmont pulls it off. All that aside, however, if the work made him unstable…

SXS: It's worth the sacrifice. He gave us what we wanted. The way "Second Trimester" expands upon the Platonic allegory of the cave is genius. Plato's cave as womb, the universe as a dead infant, all of us as decaying cells desperately yearning in vain to break away from the shadow world and be born into the light of Forms and Truth—every bit of the story builds a deeper darkness. Larchmont understands. The last thing he said before he left the retreat was "There's nothing outside. It's shadows of shadows and we'd be better off closing our eyes forever."

HG: Speaking of eyes, two weeks after your retreat, Larchmont gouged out his eyes with a shard of plastic from a shattered television set, didn't he? And that was why he was committed to a psychiatric facility?

SXS: I believe those were the circumstances, yes.

HG: And Bushnell and Larchmont were at the Tantalus retreat at the same time?

SXS: Yes. As were all the other contributors. All screaming together, at once. You could walk between rooms and experience the shift in tone, pitch, and intensity, and you knew that each writer was working through a distinct agonizing desire. The retreat lodge was an art installation unto itself. We should have recorded that sound, in hindsight.

HG: So Coral Kane and Ronald Case were also at the retreat with Bushnell and Larchmont? They contributed particularly notable stories to the anthology, too. Would you like to say anything about either of them or their experiences at the Tantalus retreat?

SXS: Of course. Ms. Kane is a swarm of bees masquerading as a person. Her mind scatters and returns, scatters and returns, always bringing back new and unusual pollens from its journeys. And she's also apt to mass her power and sting to death anyone who bumps up against her. Yet her talent is undeniable. She transcends genre, writing horror with as much verve as science fiction or fantasy. However, we knew that Ms. Kane's forte lies in environmental horror and the occulted aspects of the natural world, so that's what we wanted her to write.

HG: And Ms. Kane's workshop experience?

SXS: She adores nature, therefore we provided nature. We sequestered her in a five foot by five foot faux-outdoor space covered in a thick bed of rose bushes and poison ivy and granted her audience with a series of inspirational guests. First came the hissing cockroaches and the millipedes. Several thousand of each. Meeting her visitors, Ms. Kane squirmed and pounded on the glass walls. She asked to be let out but remained remarkably calm for all the legs skittering across her skin.

Next, we added a few hundred vipers drained of their venom—we're not in the business of murder, after all. Ms. Kane weathered those, too. Again, she squirmed and pounded on the walls. She screamed when the vipers struck. But she hadn't fallen into the pit of desire yet. So we let in the camel spiders and the vampire bats, the fire ants and the sewer rats. Then she descended. Then she found *want*.

The ants massed and bit. The rats gnawed and clawed. The spiders sunk fangs deep, and the bats, sensing loosed blood, dived greedily. Ms. Kane turned on them all, crushing underfoot everything that moved. She snatched up vipers and smashed them against the glass walls, squeezed spiders and rats to a pulp, and screamed not of escape or disgust, but destruction.

HG: You harmed animals?

SXS: No. We at Tantalus would never promote such deplorable behavior. What some of our writers do during their workshop time, though, is out of our hands. I will say that the violence sparked a new fire in Ms. Kane.

HG: Kane's story in the anthology, "Subkaryotes," is certainly a total inversion from her normal themes. In most of her work, nature is an ambivalent force, with both a light side and a dark side. But "Subkaryotes" presents a natural world of absolute terror.

SXS: Yes, the conceit of the story is glorious: insectoid scavengers that exist on a subatomic level in all organic matter and cause its inevitable breakdown, quark by quark. We're eaten alive by the natural world as soon as we're created within it. The scene of mass self-immolation at the end of the tale is sublime.

HG: Interestingly, Kane is one of the few authors in the anthology who hasn't stopped writing for one reason or another.

SXS: Nor should she. I believe she now has much to show us as regards the burning of the world. I look forward to her future work.

HG: So what about the grandmaster of horror, Ronald "Basket" Case?

SXS: It should be obvious why we wanted him. He's topped the *New York Times* bestseller list fourteen times, won nine Stokers, and could tile the bathroom of every house in the world with his sheer number of sycophants and imitators. The volume of his output is staggering. He writes in his sleep, some say.

Note: Case's output is, to date, twenty-four published novels, seven short-story collections, five produced screenplays, one graphic novel series, and a nonfiction book of writing advice.

HG: Case's style has been called "pure Americana" —white picket fences hiding devils, old barns haunted by ghosts, lonesome highways stricken with ancient Native American curses. It's a bit more homespun than that of the other contributors in *Desire*. Case is also close to twenty years older than most of the anthology's roster. How did he weather the retreat?

SXS: Quite well, actually. We hooked an IV drip to his arm and chained him up in what we refer to as "the white room."

The white room is precisely what its name suggests: a room painted the same uniform white color. Through special architectural flourishes it contains no edges or corners. Light constantly floods the room through the walls, which are constructed of a thin but durable plastic and backlit by halogen lamps. We've also never installed furniture in the room, so it's either quite barren or quite austere, depending on your point of view. When one is inside the white room with the door closed, it's very much like being inside a sensory deprivation chamber or a hollow egg.

In his time at the retreat, Mr. Case never left the white room, nor were any visitors allowed in to see him. He received no stimuli beyond the IV in his arm, the omnipresent light, and the whiteness of his surroundings.

At first, he used his time to call for help and struggle against his manacles. But the room works a terrible magic over the human mind. Three weeks in, Case began to talk to himself as though he were a character in a story. "Okay, Ron," he'd say. "You're surveying the room for cracks. You can break out of this prison if you just find those cracks. That's our climax, when we smash right on out of here." At five weeks, he was holding discussions with himself in various personas—none of which were Ronald Case. In the sixth week, he sang Pink Floyd's "Comfortably Numb" nonstop for twenty-one hours. By week eight, he'd stopped talking entirely. He simply hung on his wall, staring at no point in particular, and mouthed "Where are you?" over and over again.

Then he was ready to write.

HG: But only briefly. Case has officially retired from writing. In a press statement, he claimed that "I've nothing more to say about this world."

SXS: In the spaces of our white room, he discovered a silence he hadn't been in touch with in many, many decades. Fandom had been propelling his fiction for years. His true voice was drowned long ago and he finally realized that at our workshop.

HG: You don't think you drove him into retirement?

SXS: We helped him see what was left in his heart and his mind after the fame was muted. That's all. Call it what you want.

HG: I have to ask about one final contributor, and I think you know which one.

SXS: J.V. Brickley. Of course.

HG: What happened to Brickley?

SXS: At what point in his life? I'm sure I don't know all the details. And even if I did, I'm sure they'd be too sordid to share here.

HG: What happened to him at the Tantalus retreat?

SXS: Well, as you're aware, Brickley is something of an also-ran in the writing world. Before the retreat, he'd released one short story collection that garnered lukewarm reviews and edited two self-published anthologies filled with undistinguished authors. He wasn't setting the world on fire by any means. But we believed he had a spark of genius, perhaps. At very least, he had an interesting rage within him that we thought we could tap.

HG: So you realized he had anger management issues?

SXS: We surmised as much. Brickley was delighted to receive an invitation to the retreat. He told us that he truly believed he deserved the honor, that his writing was of the same stock as Bushnell and Larchmont, Kane and Case. We smiled and laughed with him and patted him on the back. We massaged his ego. Then we locked him in a pitch-black closet with speakers embedded in the walls and turned on a loop of pre-recorded—and entirely faked—messages about how terrible he was as a writer and a person. Through those speakers, he heard his wife calling him a "talentless hack" and his children—so adorable—calling him a "loser daddy." He heard Bushnell whispering that he was a "shit stain upon the ancient tapestry of art," Larchmont saying his writing was "amateurish by the standards of lower order primates," Kane explaining how she thought "Brickley's best writing is probably his weekly grocery list," and Case describing how he felt that "Brickley's first collection has a great deal of worth as kindling for your fireplace." For two months, he heard these and many other similar voice recordings nonstop.

I should also note that we didn't clean the bodily waste from his closet. We let him wade in his own filth. We wanted to immerse him in rejection, dejection, abjection.

The technique worked. Too well, perhaps. By the time we let him out, he certainly knew desire. We'd hoped it was for renewal or cleanliness, but, alas…

HG: It was for revenge. He wrote a flash fiction story for you…

SXS: A *superb* flash fiction story.

HG: …a *superb* flash fiction story, then went home and, within a day of leaving your retreat, stabbed to death his wife and two children. You don't believe there's any causation between those events?

SXS: We wanted Mr. Brickley to write an outstanding story and we helped him do so. His horrific actions beyond that authorship are his own.

HG: So you have no regrets over the retreat?

SXS: None. Look at *Desire*. Read it again. It's the essence of want. It's a remarkable achievement for all its authors.

HG: And for you?

SXS: For everyone at Tantalus Press, myself included, it's the true fulfillment of our desire.

HG: Seven people dead. More than a half dozen careers in ruins. Your desire seems to have birthed more than a book.

SXS: Perhaps. But we have no time to dwell. We're already moving forward, into our next project.

HG: You believe writers will participate in another anthology, even after *Desire*'s "curse"? Even after this interview?

SXS: Writers are already lining up to come to the next retreat. They email us every day. I don't predict that will change. Success in a world that cultivates failure is a great temptation and an even greater reward. People will kill for it. People will die for it. We hope to give some of our authors those opportunities. It's what any worthwhile publisher would do.

Note: As of this interview, Desire has received a starred review from Publisher's Weekly, maintained the number one bestseller spot in the "Horror" subgenre on Amazon (both in paperback and Kindle versions) for fifteen consecutive weeks, won a Stoker Award for Best Anthology, a Shirley Jackson Award for Edited Anthology, and is nominated for a World Fantasy Award in the Anthology category. Samuel X. Slayden and Tantalus Press are at work on their second edited collection, Sacrifice, due out next fall.

Author Biographies

Bo Balder is a freelance writer who lives and works in the ancient Dutch city of Utrecht, close to Amsterdam. When she isn't writing, you can find her madly designing knitwear, painting, and reading anything and everything from Kate Elliott to Iain M. Banks or Jared Diamond. Her short fiction has appeared in *Penumbra*, *Electric Spec* and quite a few anthologies. Her sf novel, *The Wan*, will be published summer 2015 by Pink Narcissus Press.

Lawrence Buentello has published over 80 short stories in a variety of genres, and is a Pushcart Prize nominee. His fiction has appeared in *Murky Depths*, *Cover of Darkness*, *Bete Noire*, and several other publications. He lives in San Antonio, Texas.

Roxanne Dent is the author of nine novels. Her most recent, *The Janus Demon*, is a paranormal fantasy. She writes in different genres, including short horror. Her latest, "Bug Boy," was included in the anthology, *Bugs, Creatures that Slither, Creep and Crawl*. Her short, Victorian mystery, "The Candy Cane Murders," recently appeared in *History, Mystery, Oh My*. "The Haunting of Jemima Nash," will be included in an anthology for the Whittier Museum based on a Whittier poem due out in 2015. Roxanne appeared on the Tim Coco show to read and talk about her latest Regency, "The Twelve Days of Christmas." Member of EWAG/NEHW/FWG/Sisters-in-Crime. www.TheSistersDent.com

A life-long resident of New York's haunted Hudson Valley, **JG Faherty** has been a finalist for both the Bram Stoker Award® and ITW Thriller Award, and he is the author of six novels, seven novellas, and more than 50 short stories. He writes adult and YA dark fiction/sci-fi/fantasy, and his works range from quiet suspense to over-the-top comic gruesomeness. He enjoys urban exploring, photography, classic B-movies, good wine, and pumpkin beer. As a child, his favorite playground was a 17th-century cemetery, which many people feel explains a lot. You can follow him at www.twitter.com/jgfaherty, www.facebook.com/jgfaherty, and www.jgfaherty.com.

Kurt Fawver is a writer of horror, dark fantasy, and weird fiction. He's been published in venues such as Weird Tales and Necro Publications' *Into the Darkness* anthology and has fiction forthcoming in places such as the Lovecraft eZine and Tor's *Midian Unmade* anthology. He's also published a critically well-received collection of short stories, *Forever, in Pieces*, with Villipede Publications. Kurt also holds a doctorate in literature and, in his spare time, tries to teach students why literature matters.
Website: www.kurtfawver.com

Aaron Gudmunson is the author of the novels *Snow Globe* and *Emma Tremendous* (as A.D. Goodman) and a collection of dark fiction/essays entitled *From the Dusklands*. His work has appeared in numerous publications, including *Apex*, *Dark Moon Digest*, and *Dead Harvest: 50 Terrifying Tales*.

Books in various stages of completion currently occupy Aaron's time, including a satirical post-apocalyptic sports novel, a second installment of the *Tremendous* series, and a companion piece to *Snow Globe* set in the World War II era American Midwest.

Aaron lives in the Chicagoland area but can more easily be found online at www.aarongudmunson.com.

Nancy J. Hayden is a writer, artist, and organic farmer living in northern Vermont. She is also fascinated with World War I. The story in this anthology, "No Man's Land," was inspired by a trip to the 100-year old Western Front battle fields and trenches in France and the unseen things that still linger there. Nancy had four fiction and three nonfiction pieces published or accepted in 2014 including the story "Unknown Soldier" in the dark fantasy/horror anthology, *Kneeling in the Silver Light, Stories from the Great War* (released in September, 2014, Alchemy Press). She is currently working on an historical novel and a dark fantasy short story collection set during WWI. She earned an MFA in creative writing from the Stonecoast Writer's Program at the University of Southern Maine in 2012. She also has degrees in English, studio art, ecology and environmental engineering. Her website is www.northwindarts.com with a link to her WWI Collage Blog that presents her art, research and writings related to WWI.

Tanya Jarvik has been recording her dreams since the age of twelve, and deeply respects the subconscious mind's ability to generate compelling material. Almost all of her poems and prose poems, some of which have previously appeared in *VoiceCatcher: A journal of women's voices and visions* and *The Open Face Sandwich*, began as dream fragments or were discovered in the course of stream-of-consciousness freewriting, a creative process she likens to fishing the Styx. After dispatching a B.A. and an M.A. in English, Jarvik went on to complete four-fifths of a Ph.D. in British and American Literature, and now considers herself a recovering academic – or, in other words, someone whose life is primarily about other things: building community, picking berries, getting tangled up in yarn, and writing for an actual audience. If asked to pinpoint her true calling in life, she would say it's somewhere near the intersection of stories and sex. One of her favorite gigs is writing an advice column for people in alternative relationships. She is thrilled to be featured in the same anthology as Sir Arthur Conan Doyle, whom she fondly remembers reading by flashlight under the covers as a kid, long after her parents presumed her asleep.

K. Trap Jones is an author of horror novels and short stories. With inspiration from Dante Alighieri and Edgar Allan Poe, he has a temptation towards narrative folklore, classic literary works and obscure segments within society.

His novel *The Sinner* (Blood Bound Books) won the 2010 Royal Palm Literary Award. His splatterpunk novella, *The Drunken Exorcis* has been released by Necro Publications. His narrative horror short story collection, *The Crossroads* is available from Hazardous Press.
He is also a member of the Horror Writer's Association and can be found lurking around Tampa, Florida. Website: http://ktrapjones.wordpress.com

Patrick Lacey works in the healthcare industry by day. When he's not reading about blood clots and infectious diseases, he writes about things that make the general public uncomfortable. His stories have appeared in numerous magazines and anthologies and Samhain Publishing will release his debut novella in 2015. He lives in Massachusetts with his wife, his pomeranian, and his muse, who is likely trying to kill him. Find him on Facebook or follow him on Twitter (@patlacey).

Nathaniel Lee puts words in various orders. Periodically, people give him money for this. No one knows why. His work is available in dozens of magazines and anthologies of varying physicality, most of which are available in some form online. He maintains an erratically updated microfiction blog at www.mirrorshards.org, where you can also find a full bibliography. He is also a parent and an editor, serving at both Escape Pod, the premier science fiction podcast, and the Drabblecast weird fiction podcast, which is premier only in the sense that there isn't another one like it.

Jonathan Maberry is a New York Times bestselling author, multiple Bram Stoker Award winner, and Marvel Comics writer. He's the author of many novels including *Assassin's Code, Flesh & Bone, Dead of Night, Patient Zero* and *Rot & Ruin*; and the editor of *V-Wars: A Chronicle of the Vampire Wars*. His nonfiction books on topics ranging from martial arts to zombie pop-culture. Since 1978 he has sold more than 1200 magazine feature articles, 3000 columns, two plays, greeting cards, song lyrics, poetry, and textbooks. Jonathan continues to teach the celebrated Experimental Writing for Teens class, which he created. He founded the Writers Coffeehouse and co-founded The Liars Club, and is a frequent speaker at schools and libraries, as well as a keynote speaker and guest of honor at major writers and genre conferences.

Holly Newstein's short fiction has appeared in Cemetery Dance Magazine and the anthologies *Borderlands 5, The New Dead, In Laymon's Terms, Epitaphs: The Journal of the New England Horror Writers Association*, and *Evil Jester Digest Vol. 2*. Her collaboration with Rick Hautala, "Trapper Boy"rappeared in *Dark Duets*, an anthology edited by Christopher Golden, published by Harper Voyager in January 2014. Her story "Eight Minutes" was part of *Anthology II*, published October 2013 from The Four Horsemen Press. She was the featured author in the July 2014 issue of *Lamplight Magazine* with her story "Shadows and Light," and her zombie tale "Doris and Howard" will appear in *Haunted Maine* from Haunted Maine Publishing in October 2014.

She is the coauthor of the novels *Ashes* and *The Epicure* with Ralph W. Bieber, published originally under the pen name H.R.Howland. She lives in Maine with her dogs, Keira and Remy.

"One More" owes to a disturbing dream **Gregory L. Norris** experienced about a house near the ocean harboring a dark secret within its book-lined walls. Norris has written for numerous national magazines and fiction anthologies, and has also penned episodes for TV. His first feature film, *Brutal Colors*, is scheduled for release in the first half of 2015. He is presently working on completing many of the stories in his idea catalog that howl at him in the night for their *The Ends*.

Joe Powers is a Canadian horror writer with a fondness for literary sleight-of-hand. He loves the idea of prompting a strong emotional reaction using no more than words and his slightly off-center imagination, and delights in taking the reader on journeys to previously unexplored regions. He occasionally dabbles in genres that follow safer, more conventional routes, but the path he loves most is the twisted, winding one that leads through those dark, shadowy corners of the mind where unseen things creep and slither, and nothing is ever entirely as it seems.

His work has appeared in numerous anthologies and magazines, including *Twisted Tails VII: Irreverence; Hard Luck; Twisted Tails VIII: Para-Abnormal; Fear's Accomplice: Halloween; Blight Digest;* and *Twice Upon a Time*. Dreamscapes into Darkness represents his inaugural appearance with Firbolg Publishing.

Joe hails from New Brunswick, where the harsh, cruel Atlantic Canadian winters allow for ample time at the keyboard. He is a member of ArtsLink NB, the Writers' Federation of New Brunswick, the NB Authors Portal and the Short Fiction Writers' Guild, and is active in the local arts and writing communities. You can follow Joe on Facebook, LinkedIn, Amazon and Twitter, and his website www.joepowersauthor.com.

David G. Robertson is a writer, researcher and teacher, and holds a PhD in Religious Studies from the University of Edinburgh. He is fascinated with the outer reaches of human belief and experience, and the ambiguities of our knowledge. He has always lived in Scotland, only now he has a partner and two small boys. He blogs at www.davidgrobertson.wordpress.com, and co-hosts the weekly podcast at www.religiousstudiesproject.com.

B.E. Scully lives in a haunted red house that lacks a foundation in the misty woods of Oregon with a variety of human and animal companions. Scully is the author of the critically acclaimed gothic thriller *Verland: the Transformation*, the short story collection *The Knife and the Wound It Deals*, and numerous short stories, poems, and articles. Her latest novella, *The Eye That Blinds*, is available from DarkFuse Publishing. In addition, her young adult novel *The Tower of Together* is available from Eldritch Press. Published work, interviews, and odd scribblings can be found at bescully.com.

Joe Sherry has written fiction, reviews, and screenplays. His work has been published in the anthology *So Long and Thanks for all the Brains*, and his story "Close" was featured in Hellnotes' *Horror in a Hundred* series. Recently his short film, *Giving Head*, was filmed by Kirby Productions and won first place in Tentsquare's *Zombie Bromance* competition.

Joe was recently picked to participate as one of thirteen authors to participate in David Wellington's *Fear Project* and he is currently at work revising his first novel, *Absence in Autumn*, a coming of age horror fable. Joe can be reached at http://joesherry.weebly.com

Rob Smales graduated from Salem State College in 1992 with a BA in English, but it wasn't until late 2010 that he started writing, focusing on short stories as a way to learn both the craft and the business. In 2011 he achieved publication, selling the story *Playmate Wanted* to Dark Moon Books. In 2012 his story *Photo Finish*, was nominated for a Pushcart Prize and won the Preditors & Editors "Readers Choice Award for Best Horror Short Story of 2012." Rob's first book, a collection titled *Dead of Winter*, was released in December, 2013, and won the Gothic Readers Book Club's "Readers Choice Award" the following January. Most recently Rob took a turn on the other side of the table, editing the fifth book in the *Demonic Visions* anthology series. Rob resides in Salem Massachusetts, where he thinks, writes, and, occasionally, sleeps.

Editor's Corner

Dr. Alex Scully is a historian of Irish Identity and the Victorian Era. Her research into the dusty tomes often intersects with the Gothic literature of the 1800s. There are dark secrets in the stories, poems, and novels of centuries past; secrets that have yet to be revealed to modern audiences. Yet the haunting charm and sinister fears that transcend time, so masterfully captured by the Gothic masters, live on in a new generation of writers. Our nightmares are not as far removed from the terrible undercurrents of Victorian society as we might want them to be. The past and present, side by side, are mirror images of the same ghastly face. All historians know one cannot forget the past. Nor can one ignore the present. Look them both in the eye and be afraid. Be very afraid.

www.ingramcontent.com/pod-product-compliance
Lightning Source LLC
Chambersburg PA
CBHW081149170626
46813CB00009B/3122